D0616089

Available from St. Martin's Press

The Right
Kind of
Trouble

SHILOH WALKER

St. Martin's Paperbacks

This is a work of fiction. All of the characters, organizations, and events portrayed in this novel are either products of the author's imagination or are used fictitiously.

THE RIGHT KIND OF TROUBLE

Copyright © 2016 by Shiloh Walker.

All rights reserved.

For information address St. Martin's Press, 175 Fifth Avenue, New York, NY 10010.

ISBN: 978-1-250-06796-8

Our books may be purchased in bulk for promotional, educational, or business use. Please contact your local bookseller or the Macmillan Corporate and Premium Sales Department at 1-800-221-7945, ext. 5442, or by e-mail at MacmillanSpecialMarkets@macmillan.com.

Printed in the United States of America

St. Martin's Paperbacks edition / August 2016

St. Martin's Paperbacks are published by St. Martin's Press, 175 Fifth Avenue, New York, NY 10010.

10 9 8 7 6 5 4 3 2 1

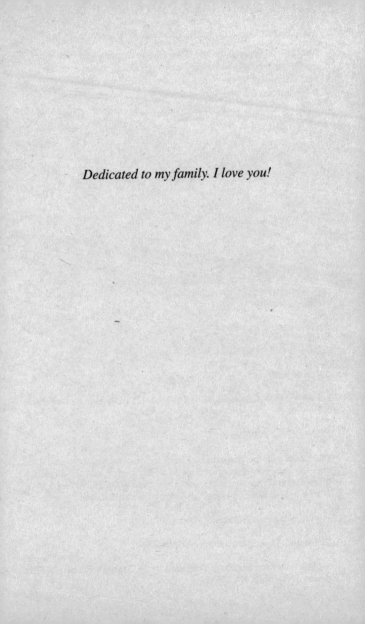

Dedicated to my family. I love you!

ACKNOWLEDGMENTS

A big thanks to my readers.
Thanks so much to the team at St. Martin's!

CHAPTER ONE

Gideon Marshall had his hands full of dirty plates and his mind full of dirty words.

He moved into the kitchen of the big, sprawling home known as McKay's Ferry, and Moira McKay, the woman he loved more than his own life, cut a wide circle around him so she wouldn't have to look at him.

"Why don't you go out there and celebrate with them?" he asked, keeping his voice devoid of emotion. "A double wedding, I'm sure they could use your organized self to talk details."

Not even an hour ago, Neve McKay, the youngest of the family, had gotten engaged. Less than sixty seconds after she'd said yes, her brother Brannon had proposed to his girlfriend Hannah. He'd been planning his proposal—Neve's fiancé hadn't known when he had popped the question.

There was plenty to celebrate.

Moira just shrugged. "This is a happy time for them. I'm just as good in here as I am out there. Nobody wants to talk plans tonight."

"You could—"

The plates in her hand smacked down sharply on the

edge of the counter, hitting with enough force he was surprised none of them broke. Moira was still staring at the plates, her jaw tight. "I could go out there and be a fifth wheel. No thanks."

Ella Sue, a genteel sort of tyrant, came bustling in and arched a brow at him before looking at Moira's stiff back. "I'm in the mood for champagne," she announced, taking up an empty space at the counter.

While she tore the foil, Gideon turned back to the sink and rinsed a few dishes off. "I used to wonder who did all of this," Gideon said. He was talking just to talk and he knew it. He didn't care for the sound of his own voice, but it was better than that terse silence. "You've got all the money in the world. You could hire people to do this stuff. Then you could hire people to hire people to do it *for* the people . . ."

Moira let out a soft, strained sigh.

He looked over at her.

Their gazes locked and held for a moment before she broke it, shifting her attention back to the pots she was putting up. "Mom and Dad wanted to make sure we understood the value of hard work. It's one of the things that has kept this family honest and successful all these years—or so they say," she said.

"I heard them tell you that, more than once." He blew out a breath, mind turning back to the man who used to watch Gideon every time he would escort Moira out the door for a date. "Sometimes I still expect to hear him, you know. Your dad, that voice of his. Big and powerful, echoed all through the place."

"I know." She glanced over at him, smiled sadly.

A few moments later they were all done.

Ella Sue pushed a glass of champagne at each of them and then disappeared—again.

"She seems more interested in flitting in and out than

anything," he said. He was under no illusions as to why, either.

"I heard you were out with Maris the other night."

Moira's voice—bright and almost too cheerful—cut through his heart like a knife.

He took a slow, deliberate sip of the champagne, the bubbles oddly flat on his tongue. It had come from the McKay cellars and chances were that the stuff cost a good grand a bottle. But it was like water to him. He still took another easy sip before he looked over at her.

He wasn't surprised Moira had heard he'd been out with Maris Cordell, one of the deputies with the county sheriff's department. What he was surprised about was the fact that she seemed to give a damn.

She tossed her champagne back like it was moonshine and she was dying for the buzz.

"We had dinner." He shrugged casually and thought to himself he wouldn't have made a bad actor.

Moira, however, never would have made it. She gave him a sharp-edged look and said, "Isn't that just *lovely*. I bet you two have a lot to talk about."

Gideon ran his tongue over his teeth. Then he shrugged and tossed back the rest of the bubbly wine. He rinsed out the glass. "I'd better head out. I've got case files to last me into the next decade, so—"

"Maybe the deputy can give you hand."

"For fuck's sake!" He spun around and glared at her.

She gave him an innocent smile as she polished off her champagne and put the flute down.

Striding back to her, he caught her arms. "What do you want, Moira? It's sure as hell not me. I spent almost twenty *years* begging for you to come back to me, but you . . ."

Tears gleamed in her eyes as she stared up at him.

An invisible fist grabbed him by the throat, by the heart. "You won't," he said bleakly. As the tears broke free and rolled down her cheeks, he brushed them away. "You won't. You're the only woman I've ever loved. Probably the only woman I'm ever going to love. But I'm tired of standing on the sidelines, of reaching out for you only to have you push me away. I'm *tired,* Moira. I'm tired of being alone and being lonely. You don't want me. I get it. But somebody else does."

"Then go to her," Moira said woodenly. She twisted out of his arms and pulled back. "I kept telling you it wasn't going to happen, that you needed to move on, Gideon."

She continued to stare at him with bruised eyes.

"Then why are you looking at me like I've broken your heart?" he asked raggedly.

"You haven't, Gideon." She managed to smile. "I'm happy for you. You're moving on. I did that ages ago."

He wanted to call her on it, wanted to say bullshit.

But she came to him and kissed him on the cheek. "I'm glad for you, baby. Now go on. Get out of here . . . you've got work to do, right?"

"Right." Dully, he nodded. Turning away, he took a couple of steps, his legs numb, his chest feeling strangely empty.

"Gideon?"

He turned, heart leaping.

But she was staring out the window into the backyard. Without even looking at him, she said quietly, "I hope this makes you happy. You really deserve to be happy."

Moira waited until he was gone before she left the kitchen.

She waited until she was up the stairs before she breathed out a low, shaking sigh.

She waited until she was in her room before letting out the next shuddering breath, because it was almost a sob.

She waited until the door was locked before she sank down on the floor and began to cry.

They were low, soundless sobs, the cries of the broken-hearted.

Then why are you looking at me like I've broken your heart?

He hadn't.

Not really.

She'd done that to herself, over and over, as she'd pushed him away.

And this time, she'd done it permanently.

It was really over.

CHAPTER TWO

"If looks could kill, you'd be dead. I'd be dead. And Moira McKay would be arrested for the double homicide of two law enforcement officers."

Gideon didn't let himself look in the mirror hanging over the bar and he didn't let himself turn his head. He'd known Moira had entered the bar because the man working behind the counter would soon be her brother-in-law and Ian Campbell had never known a stranger—he'd greeted her with a loud shout and a threat to feed her himself if she didn't sit herself down and eat.

The words had been delivered in a laughing tone, still thick with the music of Scotland. Whether or not Moira had eaten much, Gideon had no idea.

Because he wouldn't let himself look at her.

It had been six weeks.

They didn't speak outside the ongoing investigation. Somebody had set out to kill her brother Brannon. The same somebody had been stalking Hannah, the woman Brannon would soon marry.

Their most likely culprit hadn't been all that likely in the end and it wasn't like as though they could question him because the man was dead. Gideon had to give Senator Henry Roberts credit. He'd found one of the more unusual methods of suicide that Gideon had ever experienced or even heard of.

Death by anaphylactic shock—he'd been allergic to seafood and he'd requested a fish sandwich while waiting inside Gideon's jail. The officers hadn't known.

Still, it knocked the senator off the list because the problems hadn't ended with Roberts' death—they'd only gotten worse.

The one moderately bright spot in this was that he really didn't have much reason to talk to Moira. They were taking great pains to avoid each other and that had made it almost easy to pretend she wasn't the biggest part of his world.

Except for the fact that she was. At night, he felt the ghost of her presence and the memory of her hovered everywhere.

Even between him and the woman at his side, the ever-efficient and extremely beautiful Maris Cordell. Sensing that Maris was waiting for a response, he looked over at her and shrugged. "Good thing for us both that looks can't kill then, huh?"

Maris studied him for a minute and then leaned in closer, so close, he could breathe in the scent of orange blossom on her hair.

He found himself wishing it was lavender and vanilla, and he hated himself a moment later.

There were times when he could go without thinking about Moira every spare moment he had. Sometimes even most of a day would pass—most, but never all. Not yet. But even the other day, when he had lunch free, his instinct wasn't to try to hunt Moira down just to talk for a while. It had been to call Maris and see if she wanted to grab a bite.

He liked to think it was progress.

Then he had a night like last night, when he woke up at two in the morning, twisted in his sheets, the taste of Moira heavy on his tongue and the sound of her moans echoing in his ear.

"I was thinking . . ." Maris leaned closer, her breasts pressing into his arm.

"Yeah?" He smiled at her. "Why do you want to do that? I thought we were here to shut down our brains and *not* think."

"Ha, ha." She pressed her mouth to his ear.

Gideon closed his eyes. Made himself think about what she was doing, where her hand had settled on his thigh. If he thought about it—if he focused, he knew she could get him worked up.

"What do you say we take off this weekend? Just us? We could go down to Biloxi or maybe even head to New Orleans. Stay up all night, sleep in all day . . ." She sighed, and the caress of her warm breath along his nape was pleasant. "What do you think?"

He thought that it had been a while since he'd taken any personal time.

He thought that maybe it wouldn't completely suck if he took some time off.

He thought that maybe it wouldn't even be a bad idea to take some time with Maris.

Turning his head, he went to ask her a question and she stopped him with a single, slow kiss.

Content to sit back and let her control the kiss, he was breathing heavier when she pulled back and smiled at him, her hazel eyes glowing. "Is that a yes?"

A few days away from McKay's Treasure. Where he wouldn't brace himself every time he was in town, every time the phone rang, every time he left his damn house. A few days where he could focus on Maris and maybe convince himself he could be happy with her.

"Yeah." He hooked his fingers in the vee of her sweater and tugged her mouth back to his. "Maybe that's not a bad idea at all."

"Moira, that's gotta be a punch in the face."

At the sound of that low, ugly voice, Moira tensed. She did indeed fell like she'd been punched. Not in the face, but in the heart.

Slowly, she looked away from the man she was sitting with and looked over at the one who'd chosen just that moment to pause by the table where she was sitting in Treasure Island, a petty, vindictive smile on his face. "Hello, Joe," she said calmly before looking back at Charles.

Charles, her ex-husband, nowhere else.

He was the safest place *to* look, because he was the only one who wasn't surreptitiously studying her and trying to gauge her reaction to what was going on at the bar.

Okay, that wasn't true. Joe Fletcher seemed more interested in *her* reaction. And the couple at the bar was more interested in each other.

The couple at the bar.

Gideon Marshall and Maris Cordell. Maris, a pretty, confident county sheriff's deputy with *her* Gideon.

No, Moira told herself. *Not* mine. *He's not mine and hasn't been for a long time.* But in her heart, she knew she lied.

"Wonder if they'll be tying the knot soon too. A lot of that going around."

A disgusted snort came from a booth across from Moira's and the man there looked up at Joe. "Hey, Fletcher, how about you taking our order instead of gossiping?"

Joe's face went an ugly red, but his expression smoothed a moment later. "Why, absolutely, Judge Steele. I'm just trying to be friendly, that's all. The boss is always is getting on me 'bout that, ya know."

"You wouldn't know *friendly* if it bit you on the arse," Charles said, his voice chilly.

Whatever Joe's retort might have been was interrupted as Morgan, one of the co-managers at the pub, appeared, all smiles. "Everything okay over here?"

Her smile was all friendly competence. Her eyes matched. But Moira knew the other woman well enough to see the warning in her eyes when she looked Joe.

"Everything is just fine," Joe said as he turned to take the Steeles' order.

A few moments later, once Joe had disappeared into the back of the kitchen and once Moira had torn her gaze from Gideon's back, Charles reached over and brushed his fingers across her hand.

"I'm sorry."

The soft, cultured tones of Charles Hurst, her former husband, grated on her ears, but Moira looked up, a blank expression her face. "What?"

He angled his head toward the bar at the couple sitting there, heads pressed together, talking quietly. "I'm sorry. I know you . . ." He shrugged and smoothed down his tie. "Well, clearly you still have feelings for him."

She opened her mouth to lie, the words practiced and well-rehearsed. After all, it had been eighteen years. Six months. And three weeks, she thought after a quick mental calculation. Plenty long enough for her to have gotten over him.

Then she looked at Charles, the man she'd been married to. Funny. She'd actually shared a name and a bed with this guy, but she'd never hurt over him the way she hurt over Gideon.

At the time, she'd *thought* she could be content with him. They'd had a lot in common and he'd made her feel a little less . . . lonely. Not happy, exactly, but *happy* was something Moira had denied herself for a long time.

They'd been compatible, though. More, she'd hoped that maybe if he was with her, then the next time Gideon wondered back through town, he'd see her and realize she hadn't changed her mind. They were over. He'd just . . . let it go.

He would go.

And he had, for a while.

Then he'd come back.

He'd come back, and she'd divorced Charles, and still she'd had to hold herself away from him.

It had taken her no time to get over the man she'd married, but the boy she'd loved twenty years ago . . . she still wasn't over *him*.

Aware that Charles was still watching her, she managed a quick smile. "It just wasn't meant to be." She shrugged, tried to pretend it didn't matter, that it wasn't a knife in her heart to see Gideon Marshall with another woman.

Then they moved.

Like the air currents shifted and something whispered to her and she couldn't make herself *not* look—she had to look, and when she did, she saw that Gideon and Maris were leaving. Walking out of the pub, her hand in his, the two of them talking softly. Gideon's eyes, ever watchful, skimmed the crowd and for a moment, just briefly, he saw her.

Moira stiffened as their eyes connected.

He smiled impersonally and nodded.

Her heart thumped, cried pitifully.

He's mine . . .

Then they passed out of her line of sight.

"Just like *we* weren't meant to be?"

Charles' question brought her gaze back around, and she found herself staring into his soft, beautiful eyes.

"I . . ." She laughed and reached for her wine. "Charles, you and I made much better business partners than lovers. You know that."

"I know that I miss you." He covered her hand with his after she put the wine down.

Moira stilled, staring at the elegant, long-fingered hand covering hers. His touch was confident, his voice calm. He'd been a good lover. An uninventive one, but satisfying. *Definitely better than being alone*, she thought absently.

When he took her hand, she let him and brought her gaze up to study him.

"Moira—"

But whatever he was going to say was interrupted by the loud, jovial sounds of Judge "Rudy" Rutledge. "I hear we're having a wedding . . . or two!"

He dropped down into the seat next to Moira, his round face redder than normal. It got that way in the summer and when he was drinking. As it was coming up on December, Moira suspected the clear liquid in his glass wasn't water.

He leaned closer. "I always knew Trouble would turn out okay." He said it a conspiratorial tone, but it was ruined by his overly loud voice. His ability to vocalize had served him well in court up until his retirement a few years back, but he either didn't realize how loud he was or he was just way drunker than he thought. "Neve had to come in front of me a time or two, you know, Moira."

"Yes, Rudy." She sighed and looked around for his wife. "I was her guardian, if you recall."

He blinked and then smiled. "Well, I'll be. That's right." He glanced around and then lifted a hand, waggled it. "I see Brannon got it—your mama's rock. Still doing that . . . passing it down. How long has that rock been in the family?"

"That rock? You mean Hannah's ring?" She smiled coolly. "Oh, that old thing? Just a few generations, give or take."

Rudy chuckled. "A few generations. That old thing. Then there is Neve's ring." He swayed and leaned closer. "I hear there's a fortune in stuff the old captain left, and that's not even considering the treasure. How much is there . . . really?"

Moira rolled her eyes. "Rudy, can I offer some advice?"

"Sure, sure." He nodded and smiled affably.

"Find a cup of coffee, your wife, and the door."

She slid out the other end of the booth and gave Charles a tight smile. "I'm tired. I'll see you in the morning? We'll finalize plans for the barbecue we're doing this spring."

Rudy stared after her. "Hey . . . but what about the . . ." He went to get up, wobbled, then went down with a crash.

The pub went quiet.

Charles, sighing, climbed out and helped him get up. "You, old man, are stinking drunk."

Rudy Rutledge was still grumbling about Moira—who was now a mean old cow—and the treasure when one of the officers came to escort him to his brother's house. As it turned out, the reason he was hitting the bottle harder than normal was because his wife had asked him for *some space*. Reasons hadn't been given.

So Rudy was sleeping in his brother's spare bedroom and drowning his sorrows at the pub—and hassling people. As a lifetime resident of McKay's Treasure, he knew all the town's secrets, so he had a lot of material to use for hassling.

"What treasure is that stupid git nattering on about?" Ian asked Charles as the deputy's car pulled away.

Charles lifted his shoulders.

"You two haven't heard?" Griffin Parker, a member of the city's small police force, chuckled. "There were rumors that sometime before he disappeared on the mission that got him killed, ol' Patrick McKay had a great treasure. He split it up—left half of it with his wife Madeleine, then buried the other half."

"It's rubbish." Charles shrugged it off. "I've heard of it, some, but why would anybody have a treasure and bury it?"

"Well, a half-crazy Scot might." Ian grinned as he said it.

Griffin chuckled at Ian's comment. "Well, that's as good a reason as any. But it's just a story. McKay was already stinking rich, you know. He didn't need to bury his money anywhere. His wife had money and he had money and everything he touched turned to gold." He shrugged. "There were stories . . . Hannah's mom used to tell them, back . . ."

His voice trailed off, an unspoken *before* there. Before Lily Parker lost her husband, before she married an abusive bastard, before she forgot how to laugh. Before. She'd been Griffin's aunt and he still missed those times *before*.

"Anyway." Griffin shrugged. "She used to tell them. It's just part of the town's folklore. But Patrick McKay's legend was . . . well, big. Crazy big. He'd talk about his treasure and people would ask him about it and he'd laugh. I heard he killed a few men who came after him looking to find whatever he supposedly had."

"If he was a man willing to kill over it, who knows? Maybe there's some truth to it." Charles looked more speculative now.

"Or he was a man who would fight back when attacked." Ian didn't look convinced.

"Either way." Griffin tugged off his ball cap and rubbed his head. He'd been off duty when Rutledge had decided to liven up the night, and now he looked ready to get back to his free time. "Half the urban legends in this state can probably be tied to McKay or his friend Jonathan Steele or that bastard Whitehall."

"Who's Whitehall?" Ian frowned.

"He's the one who turned Patrick McKay in." Griffin gestured to the building where the police station now stood. "Went up to what served as a magistrate's office—it was there. Claimed he had proof that Patrick had gone from his mission of privateering to being a river pirate . . . and then he brought in the men he'd bribed into acting as witnesses against McKay. Within three weeks, Patrick was brought in and tried and within another week, he was dead."

Griffin shrugged and turned back to go to the pub. "Stories about some mythical treasure have gone on around here for ages. Talk to Neve or Brannon . . . I hear Neve used to go digging for it."

"Did you really dig for treasure?"

Neve looked up from the documents spread out in front of her.

Under the intense gaze of her fiancé, she could feel her face heating. And he wasn't the only one watching her, either. Shooting a look down the bar, she saw a couple of others eying her, although as soon as they saw her looking, they busied themselves doing something else . . . like studying the bottom of an empty pilsner.

"You been listening to gossip, Ian?" She studied him with an arched brow, putting her pencil down and bracing her elbows on the family tree she'd been trying to construct. Most of their history was pretty well documented, but she wanted something concrete and she wanted it printed out and she wanted information from *before* the time Patrick McKay started his own little dynasty.

"Gossip?" Ian bobbed his head back and forth like he was pondering the word. "That sounds so tawdry, love."

He bent down and placed his elbows on the bar, grinning at her. "But, aye. If it's got to do with you, then I'll listen. I'm seeing you as a darlin' little lass, running around

Ferry with a bucket in one hand and a shovel in the other, digging for gold. So . . . did you dig for treasure?"

She sniffed. "For the record, Paddy McKay didn't bury *gold* anywhere."

"Okay." Ian propped his chin on his fist and waited. "So what did ya dig for?"

"Jewels." She blew out a breath, her face heating. "Not that there's any buried there, but still. What jewels the family has are locked up. You saw Hannah's rock. Moira has her locket. There are a few things that he bought for Madeleine, and what is still in the family is kept locked up in the family vault at the bank."

"But you still went digging?"

"I didn't know about vaults and banks." She rolled her eyes and reached out, tugging lightly on his beard. "I was a kid. And the stories my family has . . ."

She shrugged. "I'll tell the same ones to our kids. And you'll see them hit the ground running when we take them out to Ferry and they'll do the same thing."

"What stories?" He caught her hand, kissed it.

Her heart hitched, her blood heated, and for a moment she couldn't breathe. Then, as he started to rub his thumb over the middle of her palm, pressing and digging into the muscles there, she forced the trapped air out and shrugged. "Just family stories. About how he came over from Scotland with hardly anything, then made it rich . . . won his first thousand gambling. Then he made even more. He met Madeleine and it was love at first sight. She was an heiress, so she had family money. They came down here and bought land. He was in love with her and with the water." She looked up, her gaze seeking out the river even though she couldn't see it. "He got into shipping, hired rough guys to work for him and they managed to stay afloat when river pirates would take others down. Got to where even the pirates wouldn't mess with Paddy McKay."

She slid him a smile. "Once they set a trap for him, planned to kill him. People would say that the river talked to him, you know that? Somehow he knew, knew where they were going to be, and he went ashore a little ways down the river, took half his men. Trapped them instead—and every one of them had a price on their heads."

"And so goes the McKay fortune . . . and the legend."

"Pretty much." She shrugged. "And he wasn't opposed to keeping whatever money and goods he found with them. Patrick was a businessman, you know."

"Absolutely." Ian leaned forward and kissed the tip of her nose. "You admire him."

"Yeah." Shrugging, she looked out the window at Main Street. "He gave his life to the river for almost twenty years. He was nearly fifty and ready to settle down, spend the rest of his life with Maddie. But the river pirates were getting worse and people from the town approached him, asked him to give them two years, help train some men to help clean things up. He agrees and ends up running into some dirty bastards who were actually *paying* the pirates. That's why he died. They were paying the pirates and he found proof. So they killed him. If he'd been willing to recant the report, say he'd been mistaken . . ." Neve shrugged. "But he wouldn't."

"That's a Scot for you. Stubborn as the day is long." He tugged on her hair. "And here's what he has to show for it. His family still thrives, generations later. You just can't wait for me to knock you up so you can tell our babes about how there's treasure buried out at Ferry, can ya?"

She grinned at him. "Well, I'm sure there are *other* reasons to have your babies, Ian."

He leaned in and pressed a hot, hungry kiss to her mouth.

CHAPTER THREE

The house seemed too big and too quiet.

Moira paced the halls, unable to sleep.

Neve was spending the night with Ian. She did that more and more, and the other day she'd mentioned they were looking to find some land, build a home.

Moira had told her they could live at the house—they *should* live at the house. Ferry needed a family in it.

But Neve hadn't wanted to hear it.

The oldest stays at Ferry, Moira.

The oldest.

She stopped in front of a mirror hanging in the hall and stared at her reflection. She might be the oldest, but she didn't need to cling to this place because of that.

Brannon already had a place, but Neve and Ian?

Why shouldn't they be here?

It wasn't like *she* was ever going to have a family here.

Not after—

She spun away from the mirror, unable to face her reflection anymore. But she could still see herself. See her face, still see the aching emptiness in her eyes.

She looked like a ghost, face pale, eyes dark and haunted.

She could just picture herself doing this very thing in ten years, twenty . . . thirty. Pacing the halls alone.

Feeling like the walls were going to swallow her, she went into her room and dressed, throwing off the white nightshirt and tugging on whatever came to hand. The longer it took, the more desperate she felt.

Suffocating. She was suffocating.

By the time she hit the kitchen, she was almost panting. Her fingers fumbled over the codes for the alarm system and when she finally had it disarmed, she stumbled outside onto the deck and still, she couldn't breathe.

Cold air flooded her lungs as she bolted down the steps to one of the paths. Landscaping lights lit up clear to the tree line.

It was dark beyond those trees and there was nobody here. Ella Sue had officially retired and her granddaughter had taken over, but neither of them had ever lived at Ferry.

Moira should go back, she knew it.

But the idea of being alone inside that house just then was more than she could handle. When she hit the tree line, she slowed. Her eyes adjusted and she could see the moonlight filtering through the trees, many of them stripped bare by winter.

The river rolled on off in the distance. She could smell it. But she didn't follow the path. She just staggered over to the bench and sat down, drawing her knees up to her chest and clutching them. Clad in a fleece hoodie and leggings, she stared into the darkness and listened to the muted silence of the winter night.

The chill sank into her bones, but she couldn't bring herself to go back inside.

To go back in there where she felt so terribly empty . . . and alone.

Tipping her head back, she stared up at the sky. "What have I done?" she asked softly.

Her breath formed foggy puffs in the night.

There was no other answer than that, but it wasn't like she needed one. She'd spent the past twenty years punishing herself—and although he didn't realize it, she'd been punishing Gideon, too. Because she'd blamed herself *and* him.

It was only in the past few months that she'd realized how stupid she was being, how *wrong* . . . but now, it was too late.

Closing her eyes, she fought against the tears that tried to rise.

She wasn't going to cry.

She was alone and it was her own damn fault, after all.

It was terribly easy to fall into a pattern, even a bad one. Maybe most *especially* a bad one.

It was midnight and again Moira was walking along the path, her breath coming out in frosty little puffs as the chill of the night air wrapped around her.

She was warmer tonight at least.

After three nights of freezing her ass off when she left the house *for just a minute,* she'd acknowledged she wasn't *leaving* simply to sit on the porch. She all but ran away from her home every night and couldn't sleep until she somehow managed to calm her thoughts.

Sometimes it took an hour or two.

Tonight, it was going on three hours and she still couldn't sleep.

Nothing stayed secret in a town the size of McKay's Treasure, and earlier in the day she'd heard the latest gossip while she sat in the chair at Bellina's Boutique and Salon. While Bellina—born Christabel Lowery—had scrubbed and massaged Moira's scalp, she'd chattered on and on about every last thing . . . including the fact that Maris Cordell had ended up renting a cabin down in Biloxi.

"The two of them are so sweet together." Bellina had sighed. "The cutest couple."

Even now, Moira could hear the shrieking in her head—shrieks of pain, denial, jealousy.

Gideon wasn't *sweet*. The idea of him being called *cute* was laughable.

Gideon Marshall was a lot of things, but cute wasn't one of them.

He was . . .

"Not mine," she reminded herself. She'd walked away. She hadn't just walked, either—she'd practically shoved him out the door and given him a few kicks in the ass for good measure.

Not mine. "Not mine." Her eyes itched with fatigue and she looked across the lawn at the house.

She thought maybe she'd sleep a little now.

Maybe.

"You're not sleeping."

"I'm fine." Moira gave Neve a distracted smile as they flipped through a bridal magazine. Neve wanted ideas on how to decorate. Hannah had told her to have at it.

They were indeed having a double wedding—and soon.

On her other side, Hannah said, "You look like you've lost weight." With one hand on the high, hard mound of her belly, she grimaced. "I think I found it for you, if you want it back."

"You're having a baby." Moira patted Hannah's belly, which was nowhere near as big as Hannah seemed to think. She was almost six months along and absolutely gorgeous. "You're *supposed* to put on some weight. What have you gained, ten pounds?"

"Twelve," Hannah said morosely.

"Oh, the horror." Neve rolled her eyes and plucked up a chocolate chip cookie.

"Watch it." Hannah mimed throwing a book at her. "Women who don't gain weight aren't allowed to comment."

"I gain weight." Neve lifted her arm and flexed it. "I'll have you know I actually put on ten pounds. But I was trying to."

Hannah cocked a brow.

Neve shrugged. "I'm tired of looking like a waif. I wanted to look healthy in my wedding pictures. I'm good now."

"The day I try to put on weight . . ." Hannah shook her head. But she understood. She'd struggled with her weight as a kid. Neve had the opposite problem—she was naturally skinny and stress made her appetite disappear. More than once, she'd been called anorexic. Neve had needed to gain the weight. But what good were girlfriends if you couldn't tease them?

Moira, though . . .

Feeling the intensity, the watchfulness of their gazes, Moira debated between addressing it and ignoring it. But Neve tackled the bull by the horns.

"You should talk to him."

She sighed and put the magazine down. "He's involved with somebody, Neve. It's too late."

But if she'd thought that would dissuade her baby sister, she was way off base. Eyes gleaming, Neve leaned forward. "So it *is* Gideon. The hot chief of police is the reason you look like hell."

"No." Shoving back from the table, she moved to the sidebar and splashed some Glenlivet into a glass. Then, because her mood was *foul,* she added some more. Tossing it back, she gave Neve a dark look over her shoulder. "*I* am the reason I look like hell. What can I say . . . you were right. I should have called him. I should have and I didn't. Now it's too late."

Hannah made a *tttttthhhpptttt* sound with her lips as she continued to peruse a catalog. "It's not like they're married, Moira. Call him."

"I can't." She clutched the glass, turning her head to stare outside. "I've . . ."

Her throat knotted around the words and she had to force them out. "I've hurt him too much. The past few weeks . . . ? I've got an idea what I've done to him and I'm done. He's found somebody he can be with. He's moved on. I'm happy for him."

"Bullshit."

The word came from Neve, low and hard.

It spiked the temper Moira had been struggling to hold on to.

Slamming the glass down, she spun around and glared at her sister. "Enough!" she shouted. "You don't get it! Okay? You just don't get it."

"Then why don't you tell me?" Neve shoved back and stormed around the table, her temper clearly up now.

Hannah leaned back, brows arched as she sat back to watch the show.

"Tell me, Moira, why you're going to settle back to be miserable, and why you think Gideon should *settle,* and why in the hell you think Maris will be happy knowing she came in second place?" Neve drew herself up to her full height, nearly six willowy feet, and glared down at her sister.

But Moira was used to be the smaller one. Thirty-eight years old and five foot four in her bare feet, she was the head of a family dynasty with a net worth in the billions.

She regularly had men tower over her in an attempt to intimidate her. It didn't work with them—it sure as hell wouldn't work with Neve. Curling her lip, she crossed her arms. "Don't loom over me, honey. I changed your diapers, remember?"

Neve propped her hands on her hips. "I'm out of diapers, Moira. And don't try to distract me."

Moira flicked her hand. "As if anybody *could*. Neve . . ." She blew out a breath. "It's *over*. He waited. For eighteen *years*, he waited. Even after I dumped him right—" She stopped, because that was one thing she'd never shared. Gideon had been about ready to propose when she pushed him away. Her twentieth birthday, him on bent knee, and she'd been eaten up with guilt for too long. She hadn't been able to handle it—the ring he'd talked about, the promises they'd made each other, all of that stretching out. But her reality was locked in McKay's Ferry, her whole world, and all of it was mired in guilt.

"I pushed him away. I never gave him a reason to . . ."

Her words trailed off and the ache inside her swelled, and in that moment she thought it might choke her.

"You wanted him to wait."

She jerked her head up and saw the knowledge in Neve's eyes.

"No." But she lied.

They both knew it.

"You didn't want him with anybody else, did you?"

Moira tipped her head back, staring up at the ceiling, fighting the tears. "I didn't . . ." The gate broke and she started to cry. Falling back against the window seat, she started to rock, burying her face in her hands. Neve's arms came around her.

"No," she whispered. "No."

A moment later, Hannah eased down to join them.

"It's not too late," Neve said. "He still loves you."

"He doesn't want me. Not anymore."

There was no moon tonight.

In the past week, Moira had taken to keeping a flashlight near her bed, near the kitchen, and even one tucked in the storage cum table out on the deck.

Snuggling deep into her light coat, she had her arms crossed over her chest and tried not to think.

Gideon wasn't around this weekend.

They had gone down to the cabin in Biloxi. Not only had Bellina been happy to dig that knife in, others had too. Okay, maybe Bellina hadn't been trying to dig a knife in. She was younger, probably didn't even know much about how Moira had thrown Gideon's love to the floor—

Stop it! She mentally shrieked.

But it did no good. She was hearing it from *everybody*. To be fair, most of them just watched her curiously, like Mrs. Mouton who'd just casually mentioned it. Or it had *seemed* casual. With Mrs. Mouton, it was hard to tell. Moira didn't think the eager old gossip had been out to cause any hurt, but there had been a questioning look in her eyes.

Moira had been getting that look a lot lately.

It was like people were asking her, *Come on . . . what are you waiting for?*

Now that half the town knew that Gideon and Maris were spending the weekend together, maybe they'd get the point. She wasn't waiting for anything.

She was done. It was over.

She kept her head up, even as she swung the flashlight around, checking to make sure she didn't trip on a root . . . again.

Her knee still ached from the fall she'd taken two nights ago. Throbbed actually, like a son of a bitch.

It was a welcome respite though, because her mind kept straying back to Gideon and nothing save pain managed to block those memories out.

So many memories. She could look at the back door and think about how often he'd come inside and sent her that slow smile. *I'm still here,* that smile seemed to say. *I'm still waiting.*

There had been so many parties over the years and she could picture him, sometimes dressed in the laid-back casual dress he considered a uniform, other times in jeans. She thought about the low, easy way he laughed . . . and the raw, demanding passion in his touch when they'd made love weeks ago. A few stolen moments. In eighteen years, the only time she'd really felt alive had been then.

Instead of grabbing onto him, instead of holding on, what had she done?

She'd gotten afraid and pushed him away, the same way she'd done so subtly ever since he'd come back to Treasure.

She came to a halt and buried her face in her hands, the metal of the flashlight cold against her face.

Misery burned inside but she kept it locked down, refusing to give into it. She'd made her damn bed, right? She'd have to lie in it. "It is what it is, right?"

She sucked in a breath, steeled herself to continue on her walk—and froze.

Eyes pricked across her skin. She could feel it. Somebody was watching her . . .

Forcing herself to move normally, she pretended to sniffle. It didn't take much. She was in such a mood anymore that crying was only a few thoughts away. She could have cried at any given time, really.

The scuffle was so quiet, she barely heard it over the sound of her own breath.

It wasn't a sound that struck her as out of place. She made it all the time, walking around in the woods. Especially at night, when the world was quiet and still, and she tried be the same quiet, not adding any extra noise to the odd peace that stole over the earth in the darkness.

But that's what was out of place.

Because she wasn't moving . . . and there was nobody else out here at Ferry.

Or least there shouldn't be.

Instinct had her turning, the flashlight lifted like a club.

She brought it down hard and felt it connect, heard it connect. There was a low, muffled grunt, followed by an angry voice, swearing. But the words were already growing fainter, because as soon as she'd hit him, she'd taken off running, still holding the flashlight.

She'd almost broken past the tree line when the weight plowed into her, taking her facedown into the hard-packed earth of winter. She screamed and swung backward with the flashlight, only to have it wrenched out of her hand.

A moment later, she froze.

The weight of the flashlight, heavy, hard, and solid, pressed menacingly against the side of her neck, shoving straight down like he intended to just crush her throat and her airway and be done with it. "Where is it?"

He let up enough for her to answer and Moira lay there, cheek pressed hard to the dirt. She struggled to breathe past the terror and the pain, struggled to *think*. "I've got . . . money . . . in the house . . ."

"I don't want money." The words were delivered calmly and in a whisper that made it impossible to tell if she knew the speaker or not. Her head was pounding and the pressure of the flashlight was brutal. It felt like it was crushing her neck and throat. She could hardly draw a breath in.

"What . . . do . . ."

"He left a treasure here. Patrick McKay. Where is it?"

Her mind went blank.

He shoved the bar of the flashlight harder, until it was

pressing painfully into her flesh and she could feel everything graying out. "It's . . ." Panic grabbed her and she
clawed at his wrist with her right hand. With her left, she
scrambled for . . . something. She needed it. What was it?

Oh. Yes. She'd put it in her pocket . . . *there*! "Please . . .
I can't . . ."

The strength drained out of her body.

Gideon's face flashed through her mind.

Is this really how it all ends . . .

He paused to check her pulse. He'd let his temper get the
better of him, had let his fury at her attack overwhelm him.
Fury at the attack, at her stubbornness—at *her,* simply for
being. For being Moira, for being a fucking McKay.

The cold bitch.

He didn't want her dead.

He wanted her to *suffer*.

But he didn't want her *dead*. Especially not without
getting the information he needed. If she was dead, she
couldn't help him.

Her pulse was steady under his fingers, though. Steady
and strong. He probably shouldn't have worried. She was
such a stubborn woman, it would take far more than his
hands wringing her fool neck to *kill* her. It might work on
other women, but Moira wouldn't be felled so easily.

"The fucking McKays," he muttered as he looked
around, frustrated. A wasted night.

This was all like looking for a needle in a haystack and
he knew it. He'd thought perhaps something would be revealed with the vaunted museum, but no. It was all about
that fool Paddy and his whore Madeleine and steamboats
and pirates.

All this time, *wasted*. He'd have to make them talk, or
he'd just keep digging around for that needle in the haystack.

Beneath him on the ground, Moira made a low sort of gasping noise as she started to come to. Then she twisted and rolled over. He crouched down next to her, watched as her lids fluttered up.

When her eyes locked on the black, blank mask that was his face, he reached out and stroked a hand down her cheek. She flinched and when she would have screamed, he placed his finger over her lips. "Please don't," he said, keeping his voice low and quiet.

Moira McKay had lovely eyes and even in the moonlight, washed of all their color, he could still see their beauty. Thick lashes fluttered and then, slowly, she nodded.

But he knew her acquiescence was only temporary.

Moira McKay might have lovely eyes—lovely everything—but she wasn't a submissive woman.

"I want to know where it's hidden, this treasure."

"There *is* no treasure," she said, her voice ragged and raw. "It's a legend."

He closed his hand around her throat, tightening it ever so slightly. "He had a treasure, Moira. We both know that."

Her eyes widened and there, in that faint flicker of her gaze, he saw it.

The truth.

"Now . . . tell me where it is?"

But in the next second, he heard a car engine. Looking up, he saw the spill of lights.

"Police," she said, her voice raspy. Then she revealed something she'd held hidden in her palm.

A key fob.

The kind one might use to unlock a car . . . or to disarm a security system. Or to activate such a system's panic feature.

He surged to his feet and took off running.

Moira remained where she was.

A moment later, he heard her voice, faint and ragged. When he dared to look back, she was waving her flashlight around like a banner.

Damn the bitch. She'd almost gotten him caught.

But, he should have expected it. Moira McKay was a fighter.

Gideon lay in the darkness, eyes wide open, while Maris lay against his side.

He'd just had what most men would probably consider a sexual fantasy come to life.

Maris Cordell was a hungry, easily satisfied woman, and she was just as willing to give as she was to receive.

And yet, while she slept on, he could think of only one thing.

The first night he'd met Moira in the pool house. The night they'd fumbled through losing their virginity together.

He still wanted her and he hated himself for it.

The quiet of the night pressed in around him and he eased out of the bed, moving to the French doors that opened out to the deck. The moonlight glinted over the rolling waters of the Gulf off in the distance.

They'd taken their weekend in Biloxi.

He still felt a nagging tug of guilt. He had unsolved cases and enough loose ends to trip an entire platoon. But he'd thought it might be a good idea to clear his head.

There was no sign of the person who'd stalked Hannah—and most likely killed Shayla and Roger Hardee. But after more than six weeks, he had come to the conclusion that until the person made another move—*if* the person made another move—they were stuck.

Kind of like me. Brooding, he stared outside. The lights of the gaily decorated Christmas tree shone behind him. He'd gone to unplug it before they went to bed and Maris had teased him, fussed about how uptight he was, said she enjoyed the lights. He hadn't cared enough to argue and that was pretty much his state of mind lately.

He just didn't care enough.

Which explained why he was in Biloxi in a rental cabin with Maris instead of back home.

Because he didn't care enough.

The one woman who might break him out of that apathy was probably tucked up snug in her bed, blocking out the world, the same way he was slowly starting to do. In a few years, he'd be the same as she was, unwilling to let anybody or anything in.

Maybe he should turn in his badge now, while he still had something in him that *could* care—at least enough to know that he was falling away from himself.

Yeah, he thought. Maybe he should just do that. Turn in his notice, empty out of his 401k, and leave. Wander until something seemed to fit.

Which meant he'd spent the rest of his miserable life bouncing around because nothing was *ever* going to fit, save for Moira. But if he was away from her, it would hurt less.

The phone rang.

His eyes cut to it.

CHAPTER FOUR

"Sorry, Chief."

Gideon stared hard through the open doorway at the pale, still form on the bed.

He couldn't even pretend it wasn't her. The deep, rich red of her hair lay in a messy tangle down to her shoulders. That would aggravate the hell out of her. Moira wasn't particularly vain, but she had a thing about her hair.

When his second-in-command, Deputy Chief Hoyt Pendleton, looked over at him, Gideon dragged his gaze away from Moira's motionless body. "What?"

"I said, I'm sorry. This is the first time you've taken personal time in two years, but . . ." Hoyt was built like a Mack truck and when he crossed his arms over his thick chest, his biceps bunched up, like they were trying to tear their way out of his shirt sleeves. A solid six foot five, the big black man stood there like a stone wall, unyielding and unbending. Sharp cheekbones made slashes against his cheeks. He had an ageless face and to somebody who didn't know him, he could have been anywhere from his mid-twenties up to the tail end of forty. Gideon knew for a fact that he and Hoyt were of the same age. They'd graduated together, had even gone off to serve in the military, although Hoyt had left a year earlier and come back two tours later.

"You said somebody was out there looking for treasure," Gideon said quietly. It made him uneasy. "Moira woke up enough to tell you that?"

Hoyt nodded and then glanced over at him. "All that's just legend, isn't it?"

"Far as I know."

But as he stood there staring at Moira's still body, he was already planning the questions he'd put to her when she was up to them. He had questions for the other two McKay siblings, and he wouldn't be waiting very long to ask those two, either.

There couldn't be much he didn't already know about the family. But he wasn't about to take a chance he was missing something.

Not when it came to Moira.

And you're getting over her . . . right?

The sly voice was one he wished he could strangle, wished he could silence, forever.

But it didn't matter if he was "getting over her" and he would argue that point unto death. Because his job was to protect the citizens of McKay's Treasure. That included Moira McKay. Whether or not he was over her, he'd sworn an oath and he'd watch over her.

Deep inside, though, in the very heart of him where he couldn't lie or be fooled by his own idiocy, Gideon knew the truth.

He might try to ignore it, but the truth wouldn't change.

If there ever came a day when he'd be able to count all the stars in the sky, or a day when he knew the answers to all the questions, maybe that would be the day he'd be over her.

But he wasn't betting on it.

* * *

Her throat hurt.

Actually, Moira thought maybe that was the understatement of the century. Her *face* hurt, from where that man had smashed her head into the ground, one palm against the side of her skull, shoving down with brute force while the other tried to push the flashlight through her larynx.

Her throat, though . . . no. It didn't hurt. *Hurt* didn't touch it. She thought maybe it would feel like this after she'd been force-fed broken glass, followed by a chaser of pure moonshine.

She'd been advised not to talk for a minimum of forty-eight hours. The IV bag dripping next to her held a cocktail of painkillers and steroids. No, that wasn't right. She'd had the painkillers pumped in. The steroids were dripping in along with the fluids.

She wouldn't be eating anything solid for a few days—she felt like she'd never want to eat anything again, *ever*—and that made swallowing pills out of the question, but they wanted her on steroids to cut down on the inflammation.

Apparently the damage to her throat had the doctors concerned.

While she was aggravated by the pain, she was more *concerned* by what in the hell had happened last night.

Brannon sat sleeping in the chair next to her bed.

Neve had finally gone home with Hannah, Ian promising to watch over both the women, and now that she had a few hours of sleep, Moira figured this was her best chance to interrogate her brother.

There was only one problem.

She couldn't speak more than a croak. She knew, because she'd tried when the nurse came in.

They'd given her a board to write things down on when she needed something, but she doubted the Spanish Inquisition had taken place via a dry erase board.

And Brannon had his head back, mouth slightly open,

slow, steady breaths escaping him as he dozed on, not a care in the world. Aggravated, Moira grabbed a pen from the bedside table and threw it at him.

It missed by a mile and she would have growled, except she knew it would hurt like hell.

"You still can't hit the broad side of a barn."

The sound of that voice made her stiffen.

Slowly she turned her head, and the sight of the man standing in the doorway made her heart flutter. For a few seconds, the pain faded away. For a few seconds, she let herself pretend she hadn't almost died, that she hadn't chased him away. That maybe, just maybe, they could have another chance.

Then the ache in her throat grew too huge and she had to swallow, and that resulted in so much pain, she had to blink back tears.

"Bad, huh?"

In response, she flung her arm over her eyes.

If life was fair, Gideon Marshall would use that excellent brain of his and realize that she just wasn't up for talking, or company—particularly his, unless he was there to tell her that he had dumped Maris, decided he couldn't live without her, and was going to make her see sense. She'd be glad to see sense now. Especially after last night.

But none of that was likely.

When the room remained silent, she slowly lowered her arm.

He was sitting down on the stool next to her bed. He'd gotten the pen she'd thrown.

Picking it up, she sighed. Then, frowning, she grabbed the dry erase board and scrawled out two words.

Go away.

Gideon cocked a brow and then held out a hand.

She rolled her eyes and turned it over. He wrote something and flipped the board around.

No.

Snatching it back, she scrawled out her response, but she wrote too large and had to start all over again. This was going to get tedious. She needed her tablet.

Once she'd finished, she shoved the board back at Gideon.

I feel lousy. I didn't sleep. My head hurts, my throat hurts, my everything hurts. I want to rest.

Gideon nodded and passed the board back over to her. "I imagine you do. But I want to find out who did this to you . . . and why."

She closed her eyes, told herself that she wasn't going to cry. Really, why should she? It was over and done. She was alive. She would get a better security system, do some upgrades. She'd thought she had a pretty decent one, but then again, how much good could it do if she was out of the house?

Maybe she should get a dog.

Yeah . . . She grabbed the cloth attached to the board and erased her last message, writing out another one.

Can you help me get a dog? For security?

Gideon lifted a brow, then after a moment, he nodded. "You want a dog, huh? I might be able to help. I know a guy who raises German Shepherds—trains them. They cost a pretty penny . . . well. In *my* book. You could buy a kennel full of them and not blink."

She made a face at him.

His gaze dropped to her mouth.

Heat exploded inside her chest as he dragged his eyes back to hers. Her heart raced.

Then he looked back at her message. Taking exaggerated care, he erased the words. "I'll get in touch with him, see if he might be able to help you out."

"I want one for Hannah."

The sound of Brannon's voice had Moira yelping. Then she shuddered as pain rolled through her. Touching a hand to her abused throat, she closed her eyes.

"Sorry, sis." Brannon brushed his hand down her hair, and she opened her eyes to meet his. He was bent over the bed now, watching her with concern written all over his face. "I didn't mean to scare you."

She managed a weak smile.

"Want me to call the nurse?"

Shaking her head, she shifted in the bed and cast a furtive look at Gideon. But he didn't look like he was in any rush to leave. In fact, as he crossed his arms over his chest and focused on Brannon, she thought just maybe he was settling in for the long haul.

Shit.

Gideon watched the cloud of sleep leave Brannon's eyes as he bounced around a few different ways to approach this. There were a few subtle ways he could try, and maybe he should. After all, Moira did look rough and she'd had a hell of a night. He could sympathize, although what he really wanted to do was grab her out of that bed and hold her, run his hands over her to make sure she was okay. He wanted to kiss the bruises, each and every one, then he wanted to yell at her—for a lot of reasons, for putting him into this shape again, for scaring him, for being *her,* for making him love her no matter what, for not wanting him enough . . . and for being hurt.

None of it was her fault, even the fact that she didn't want him enough, but he couldn't help the fact that he hurt for her, all over again.

He also wanted to hunt down the son of a bitch who had put those marks on her.

Hunt him down and kill him.

Slowly.

In order to do that, he needed to understand what was going on. He turned away and shut the door, then grabbed a chair and dragged it over to the side of Moira's bed. That done, he pulled out his notepad and braced it on his knee.

"I talked to Hoyt and he gave me the information you were able to give him," Gideon said, looking first at Moira. When she went to grab her board, he snatched it out of her reach. "I don't want to hear that you aren't up for this right now. I'll make it easy on you and recount the details he gave me—which isn't procedure—and you can nod if that's accurate and write down anything else you might have remembered. But I need to get my head around this before I can go any further."

Her eyes snapped and flashed, the elegant line of her jaw clenching as she glared at him. Then she shoved out her hand, lifting her chin imperiously. *Treasure's reigning queen,* he thought. He gave her the board.

Why are you handling this? You were supposed to be taking a few days off.

He read it with a scowl, trying to ignore the miserable sensation in the pit of his belly, one that twisted and filled him with shame and guilt. *I'm not guilty of shit.*

When he handed the board back to her, she studiously avoided his gaze.

"Too much weird shit has happened in my town, Moira.

Hoyt called me because he knew I'd want to know. I'll have a hand in this until I know it's settled, until you're safe."

Because you take your job seriously. I know that. But you don't have to put your life on hold.

"I'm . . ." *not*.

He stared at her, filled with the knowledge that there *was* no life, not without her. He'd been fooling himself, and how easily he'd left Maris was just proof of it. She'd understood. She was a cop. But while he'd feigned frustration over it, the truth of it was that he hadn't given a damn that their weekend had been interrupted. Worse, some part of him had come alive at the thought of seeing Moira again.

The word died in his throat and he stopped, looking back down at his notepad. "The job's the job, Moira. Now let's get this done." He recounted the events that Hoyt had told him, glancing up from time to time to see Moira nodding. She held up a hand near the end and scrawled out a note.

He touched me. My face. It was weird.

Brannon had gotten up to come around and stand beside Gideon, and he shot his sister a look. "The son of a bitch attacks you, half-strangles you. and the thing that strikes you as weird is how he touched your face?" he demanded.

Gideon said, "Shut up, Brannon. Weird, how?" He passed the board back to her.

She gave him an exasperated look and lifted her shoulders, irritation stamped on her features. She scrawled something else on the board and passed it back over.

Weird. It was gentle. He slams me to the ground, hurts me
and then all but pets me.

Gideon made a note, nodding, tucking it in the back of
his mind. He'd think on it later. There might be something
to it, there might not be.

"Okay. We'll go over it again when you can talk, but
for now . . ." He gestured for Brannon to sit back down,
waiting until he'd did so. Brannon slumped in the chair,
his hair rumpled, the stubble darkening his jaw. "Now, I've
got questions and one of you is going to talk." He narrowed
his eyes on Brannon. "Since Moira's sort of not able to do
that right now, I guess it will be you."

"I don't know how much I can help you out." Brannon
folded his arms over his chest and shrugged. "I'm afraid I
wasn't in the area when some piece of shit attacked my
sister. If I had been, you'd already have him . . . in the
morgue."

"Not what I need to talk about." Leaning forward,
Gideon braced his elbows on his knees, focusing completely on Brannon. "Tell me about the treasure."

CHAPTER FIVE

Moira stared at him, those words echoing in her head. If she could have laughed, she would have.

Instead, she looked over at Brannon.

He was staring at Gideon with irritation. "What treasure?"

"Don't." Gideon held up a hand, cutting off a story he'd already heard a hundred times. "There are a hundred different crazy stories spread about old Paddy McKay, and I know that as well as anybody. But all three of us know that those myths all have a kernel of truth in them."

He finally looked over at Moira, and she had the sensation that he didn't want to do that.

She thought of all the times she'd caught him staring at her, how she wished he'd stop because of all the memories it brought up. Now it was the opposite. She found herself searching the streets for a glimpse of him, had even ended up in the police station for no legitimate reason and had ended writing out a check for the local shop-with-a-cop thing they did in December, all because she'd wanted to see him.

Because it was easier, she focused on the question he'd asked instead. She just rolled her eyes and held out her hand for the board. It was closer to him and she couldn't reach it. Temper snapped in his eyes. He had a high threshold, but once the fuse was lit . . . well, she had a better of idea of just how hot that temper burned than most.

Narrowing her eyes, she snapped her fingers and then pointed at the board.

"For fuck's sake," Brannon muttered. He grabbed the board and shoved it into her hand. Then he focused on the grim face of the cop in front of them. "Gideon, man, it's a legend. The man's been dead for well over a century. Shit, it's more than a hundred fifty years now. People have crawled all over Ferry looking for a treasure. Hell, that's why Grandpa put the wall up around the perimeter. We're lucky it wasn't a mile high *stone* wall. We had so many dumbasses coming out with shovels and buckets . . ." He stopped then, laughing abruptly. "Of course, we all did the same thing."

Moira made a face and scrawled on her board.

You and Neve did it. I just laughed at you.

"Whatever." He waved it aside and focused back on Gideon. "So many people went looking for some myth-ical treasure, but you still think we're hiding some hidden cache of jewels? For what reason? In case of a rainy day?"

Gideon didn't look amused. "No, I don't think there's some pirate's chest of jewels and gold buried out at Ferry. *But* . . ." He eyed them, brow winging up. Crossing his arms over his chest, he studied each of them with cool, slow deliberation. "But I do think there's something going on . . . something else that you all know about, something that lies at the core of all these legends that might be fuel-ing a lunatic."

He braced a hand and leaned over the bed, reaching out and catching Moira's chin.

Her breath hitched and she fought her body's natural instinct to gasp. For one moment, their gazes locked and she stared at him. His gaze was magnetic. She could hardly stand to tear her eyes away, but if she was wise, that was what she'd do. That was what she needed to do, what she should do.

But then, he lifted her chin. He was gentle, but the movement still hurt and a weak protest of pain escaped her.

His free hand rested on her forearm, stroking gently. "Somebody was driven to do this to you, Moira. And whoever it was, he had been watching you enough to know that you had developed the habit of going outside at night, walking." He paused, waiting for her to argue that point. She didn't, though. It was in the report that she'd started taking walks at night—had been doing it for a few weeks, at least. "This somebody is determined and possibly obsessed." He withdrew his hands—both of them—and there were no lingering caresses, nothing she'd come to associate with Gideon.

She missed them, wanted to grab his hand and draw it back to her face.

"Now." He shoved both hands into the back pockets of his jeans and strode across the room, staring outside the window into the gray morning. "Now, the two of you want to insist there's nothing but rumors to all these legends, fine. But there's at least one person who is willing to go to desperate lengths to prove otherwise."

Moira clenched her jaw and then looked down at her board, erasing what she'd written and starting over.

For all you know, this is just some idiot who was passing through. Or he read about Patrick on Wikipedia. Aren't you overreacting?

Gideon read it. Then he held out a hand.

She glared at him and erased her message, starting over.

You can talk, jerk.

He just continued to wait, patiently. Like the Rock of Gibraltar.

Snarling at him, she threw it at him. He caught it easily and turned it around.

He took exaggerated care as he erased her message and wrote his own.

Three attacks.
Shayla.
Hannah.
You.
I refuse to believe they aren't connected.

She rolled her eyes and then passed it over to Brannon, mouthing, *He's an idiot.*

Brannon frowned, but she suspected he got the general idea. "Look, Gideon . . . I can see the attack on Shayla and Hannah being connected—and you didn't mention Roger's murder."

"That's because he's connected to Shayla." Gideon turned back to look at them. "But there's a bigger, under-lying picture here and we're just not seeing it. This attack on Moira is the first time anything has actually *pointed* at something."

"Yeah." Brannon's voice was thick with sarcasm and Moira threw up her hands, dropping back onto the pillow in defeat. "It's pointing to a dead end—*and* to my sister."

"Trust me, I'm aware." His voice was hard, tight. He shifted his attention back to Moira and asked, "You always talked about a legacy. I want to know what it is."

Brannon snorted, but when he started to talk, she rapped the board on the bedrail. He looked over at her and she shook her head. She scrawled a quick note on the board and showed it to him, then erased it before Gideon could see.

"Moira," Gideon said, his voice heavy with warning.

She wrote another note and showed it to him.

We're the legacy, Gideon. I'm pretty sure we're not buried in the dirt somewhere.

He noted that she'd underlined the *we*.

Then she threw the board down and grabbed the call light, pushing it. Turning her eyes to her brother, she beckoned for him to come closer. Ignoring the pain, she spoke this time, "Make him"—she had to pause a moment and wait for the razor blades that had lined her throat to ease up—"leave."

She was almost crying by the time she'd said those three simple words.

Brannon caught her hand and squeezed it, nodding.

Gideon heard the words, saw the pain it caused her to speak, and he blew out a breath.

Even before Brannon turned to look at him, he was making his way to the door. As pale green eyes locked on him, he lifted a hand. "I'm going," he said, voice flat. "But listen . . ."

Moira wouldn't look at him. She was staring out the window. The sight of her, looking battered and bruised, tore a hole straight through his heart. The beeps and noises of the hospital seemed terribly loud, and he was crucially aware of everything, from the way the hospital gown fell off one pale, smoothly rounded shoulder to the smudge of dirt still visible on the curve of her jaw to the way she kept kneading and twisting the sheets covering her legs. "I'm not done," he said softly. "My gut tells me I'm right. All the trouble we're looking at? It's all connected to y'all, and I know it. I feel it right to my bones. So whether you like or not, you're going to work with me and help me figure it out."

Brannon's jaw bunched tight.

Moira's eyes closed.

Neither of them made any attempt to respond.

He gave them a terse nod. "I'll be in touch about the dog."

Walking away from her caused an almost visceral pain, but then again, it always had.

He stopped once he rounded the corner and leaned back against the wall, staring hard at the vending machines a few feet in front of him. Slowly, he lifted his eyes upward, as though he could see clear through the concrete and steel and plaster, straight up into the heavens. "God, why are you doing this to me?"

He felt like he had a damn hook inside his mouth—or maybe in his heart. His soul. He'd finally done the one thing he didn't think he'd ever do. He'd pulled himself away from Moira, dragged himself out of her orbit, and had even done what he could to form a relationship with another woman. He *liked* Maris. She was attractive and fun. He had serious things in common with her and when he was with her, he was able to forget about Moira . . . for a time.

But when you're not with Maris, you don't think about her. You don't find yourself waking up hot and sweaty with your fist around your dick, about to come just because you were dreaming about her.

He couldn't say the same about Moira.

The brutal truth was that he could be sleeping in bed with Maris and wake up dreaming about Moira.

Dragging a hand up and down his face, he tossed a frustrated look down the hallway.

She was going to drive him crazy.

That's just all there was to it.

"Where is she?"

The half-panicked question came at him just as he was shoving off the wall, and he found himself face-to-face with Charles Hurst.

Cheeks ruddy, blue eyes partly hidden behind a pair of glasses, the man came to a halt, sucking air hard.

Gideon stared at Moira's ex-husband with little more than apathy.

"Morning, Chuck."

Charles drew himself up to his full height—two inches, give or take, taller than Gideon's five ten, and stared down his nose. "Don't be petty, Gideon. Where's Moira? Is she . . ." He closed his eyes for a moment. "She can't be hurt too seriously or you wouldn't be out here trying to annoy me."

"I live to annoy you, Hurst. Don't you know that?" Since Charles was trying to swing his dick, Gideon rocked back on his heels and crossed his arms over his chest. "Before you go taking off to check on your former wife, I got a few questions. Mind telling me where you were last night?"

Charles looked taken aback. His mouth flattened out and then he took a slow, controlled breath. "Is this your idea of entertainment or am I to believe you actually think *I* could have hurt her?"

"Just doing my job." Gideon shrugged. "You don't mind me doing my job, do you?"

"Yes, Chief Marshall. You do your job . . . you continue to play these petty games with me while the woman I love lies suffering in her room alone." The acid in Charles' voice, underscored by the cool, crisp tones of London, might have cut a lesser man to size.

"Nah." Gideon shrugged. "She ain't alone. You know how those McKays are. None of them are ever really alone.

Brannon's in there with her. We got a few minutes. Now . . . your whereabouts last night?"

"Two? Marshall, you're trying to kill me. You got any idea what my wife will do to me if I let *two* of our babies go?"

Gideon rolled his eyes. "Zeke . . . now correct me if I'm wrong, old man, but I'm pretty sure the reason you breed and train these dogs is so you can sell them."

On the other end of the line, Zeke made a disgusted snort. "Shit. I breed and train these dogs because I love them. I only sell them because I got no room for all of them." He sighed and then blew out a breath. "Who is it you're needing them for?"

"A couple of friends." He was proud of himself. His voice didn't hesitate at all when he called Moira a friend. He pulled his cruiser up in front of the police department and climbed out, switching the Bluetooth off as he lifted the phone to his ear. He hated the stupid gadget, but he had to set an example for the people of McKay's Treasure. If he didn't want them driving and talking on their phones, then he couldn't be doing the very thing he told them not to do. "Moira McKay was attacked—"

"Wait a minute. Did you say *McKay*? As in the fucking *McKay* family?"

Gideon came to a stop. "Is there a problem?"

There was a period of a silence so strained, Gideon thought he could hear some imaginary prickle in the air-waves between them. Then, finally, Zeke said in a terse voice, "I don't think I got two dogs to spare."

Without another word, the old man hung up.

"What the hell?"

"Chief?"

Gideon looked up from his phone and met Pendleton's eyes, found his second-in-command eying him oddly.

"You ever get the feeling that life would be easier if you just moved to a deserted island and lived by yourself?"

"Yeah." Pendleton nodded, his hangdog face pensive as though he indeed did consider that very thing on a regular basis. "But here's the problem. Where the hell am I going to get coffee, beer, and books if I'm living on a deserted island?"

"I hear you can get anything online—find somebody to ship to you." Gideon held the door open for him as they shoved into the warmer air of the station—and like a switch had been flipped, the low buzz of chatter went abruptly silence.

"Well. Nice to see business carried on as usual while I was taking some personal time," Gideon said with a wry shake of his head.

Griffin Parker cut him off. "Is Moira okay?" he demanded.

"She's . . ." He stopped and then shrugged. "She will be. She's too stubborn not to be."

Griffin opened his mouth, then stopped. Finally, he said, "Any idea what the perp wanted?" He angled his chin over at Pendleton where he sat with Detective Deatrick Outridge "Pendleton all but glued Deatrick's mouth shut, and Hoyt isn't saying anything, either."

"There's nothing to say right now." Gideon cut around the younger cop.

Destination: his office.

Goal: silence.

If he had enough of it, he thought he could maybe string together some sort of cohesive theory on what was going on, why. All of it. It was just a matter of degrees. Everything was connected. He just had to find the connection.

And two fucking dogs.

CHAPTER SIX

"You're going to make yourself go blind."

Maris came up behind him and rested one hand on his shoulder, her chin on the other.

Gideon grunted and didn't look away from the computer. Over the past few years, one of the trusts set up by the McKay Foundation—who else?—had paid for the library to digitize much of their archive, including many historical documents pertaining to their ancestry.

He'd spent every free second of the past eighteen hours going blind looking for solid data on an elusive treasure—or maybe it was illusive. It was hard to get a grip on it . . . or just it might not exist at all.

No.

There was something there.

He knew it in his gut.

There was something there and he just had to find it.

The phone rang and he snatched it up, stared at the phone number for two seconds before he tossed it down. It wasn't anybody from the department, and it wasn't Zeke. Therefore, he didn't want to waste time making nice.

"You're worked up." Maris straightened up and rubbed his neck. "What's the deal?"

He opened his mouth, a biting answer lingering there, but he stopped himself before he could let the words fly out. It wasn't her fault that he was in this state.

He couldn't even blame the woman who was tangentially responsible, and he knew it.

As long as he was around Moira . . .

He closed his eyes as the truth struck him.

He'd idly considered the idea before, but now he realized he needed to do a lot more than *consider*. It wasn't enough that he'd stopped holding out and hoping. Wasn't even enough that he'd tried to date another woman. Slowly, he straightened up, his back screaming from being hunched over the computer for hours on end.

There was a tie that ran between them, him and Moira.

What he needed to do was sever it—get the hell out of her orbit so maybe time could lessen the impact she had on him.

He needed to leave Treasure.

And fuck all that he figured it out now, when she was in danger, when everything was winding up to a fever pitch. A deserted island wasn't in his future, no. But neither was Moira McKay.

"Gideon?"

He reached up and caught Maris' hand, squeezing it gently.

Maris wasn't in it, either. And he was a miserable, selfish bastard if he kept letting her think otherwise.

He pushed back from the desk slowly, giving her time to back out of the way. She did, but instead of moving, she came around and settled in his lap. He closed his eyes, mind already whirling.

He couldn't leave *now* and he knew it. Not until he knew Moira was safe. There wasn't anybody in the department with the experience to handle what was going on. Deatrick could, in a few years. Pendleton, he might be the highest-ranking officer and he definitely had experience. He was also one quite happy in his current position. He had no desire to be in charge, a fact he'd made clear more than once. Hoyt had no desire to do it, either.

They'd have to look outside the jurisdiction, hire an outsider.

He could start looking now. Word would get out. But he wouldn't leave until this was settled. Until she was safe—all of them. They were family, in all the ways that counted. Save for Moira. She was his soul.

"Baby, what's wrong?"

He lifted his lashes and stared into Maris' eyes. She already knew, though. She was trying to pretend otherwise, but in the back of soft brown gaze, he saw the knowledge. Taking her hand, he lifted it to his lips and kissed the back of it.

"Ever wished you had control of over who and what you loved in life?"

It was almost ten, and he was just one or two more drinks from being completely shitfaced when the phone rang.

Gideon glanced at it blearily.

It wasn't Zeke. The old son of a bitch had told him off when he'd finally returned Gideon's call. *I told you, damn it. I ain't selling to no lousy McKay.*

Gideon wasn't done with him yet. But since he didn't really want to talk to anybody else, he had little interest in talking to the man on the phone.

He knew Brannon, though. The man was just as stubborn as he was.

He grabbed it in the middle of the last ring, just before it would have gone to voicemail. "You know, civilized people usually call before this."

"Well, you and me both know I'm not civilized. I need a favor."

"Too bad. I ain't in the mood to grant favors." He splashed another liberal serving of scotch into his glass and held it up, watching as the dim light from the hall reflected through the liquor.

"You will. It's about Moira."

"Again, too bad." He ignored the tug at his heart. "Find somebody else."

"Like her ex?" Brannon's voice was sly. "I bet he wouldn't mind driving her sick self home tomorrow. Sure, I'll call him."

Gideon's hand tightened on the phone, but he managed a level tone as he replied, "You do that."

He was lowering the phone when he heard Brannon's voice bark out, "*Wait!*"

He should have just hung up.

Blowing out a sigh, he brought the phone back to his ear. "What do you want, you pain in the ass?" Although he wasn't totally drunk *yet,* he was well past the point where his filter was fully engaged.

Brannon was quiet a moment. Finally, he asked, "Are you drunk?"

"Not yet." Gideon lifted his glass and took a swallow, sighing in satisfaction as it burned its way down his throat. "I'm working on it, though. So please hurry this along."

"Why are you getting drunk?"

Gideon tucked his tongue against his teeth and thought that through. "Why . . ." he murmured a moment later. "Well, let's see."

He shoved himself upright and had to pause there a moment, his head spinning around. "Let me just see . . . I broke up with Maris. She left here crying, and I wish she would have just hit me. I—don't interrupt me, McKay. I'm talking here. I spent two hours after that writing up an ad for a new chief of police—gotta run that by the city council and ain't *that* gonna be a bitch? Gonna look at putting my house on the market, figure out where to go from here . . . yeah. It's been a bitch of a day."

He wound down and stood wobbling in the middle of the room. "Yeah." Brooding into his scotch, he mumbled, "Bitch of a day."

Brannon's voice exploded in his ear. "What the fuck are you talking about?"

Gideon tossed the rest of his drink back and stared up at the ceiling. "I'm done, man. I'm just . . . done."

Then he disconnected the call and tossed the phone at the table. It missed by a mile, but he didn't care.

Stumbling back to the couch, he dropped down, face face-first. He was asleep in moments, but found no respite there.

Even in his dreams, Moira haunted him.

"I'm not kidding, if you try to leave that hospital with anybody but me, Moira, I will have your ass."

He listened for the pitiful croak that was his sister's voice, but he felt little sympathy for the obvious pain as she ground out, "It's not like I'm going to walk. Just hurry."

"I can't hurry an OB appointment." Then he disconnected and flung the phone down. The wind tore at his hair as he shot a look at Hannah. "Want the windows up?"

"No." She had her eyes closed. "I like the air."

"It's cold."

"I have a coat." Then she turned her head and looked at him. "You know he didn't mean it."

He didn't respond. There weren't many things his fiancée was wrong about, but this was one of them. He kept hearing the bitterness that underscored Gideon's voice. *I'm done . . .*

He'd heard that tone before.

In Hannah's voice.

Yeah, she'd given him another chance, but that was because he'd chased after her and realized what an idiot he was. Moira wouldn't look at Gideon and see him. Nobody could make her accept that.

"Talk to her."

Hannah brushed her fingers down his hand as he turned his over, linking their fingers as he navigated the long, winding road that led to McKay's Treasure. "You a mind reader now?"

"Well. I know you." She squeezed his hand and added, "Now that you've let me in, I'm getting to know you even better. And that look on your face? It only means one thing. You're brooding. You only brood about family."

"Gideon isn't family."

"Like hell." Her voice was wry. "He's the brother you probably never realized you wanted, but he's family all the same. You'll miss him like crazy. But that's not the point, is it?"

Brannon heaved out a sigh and glanced over at the glowing face of his bride-to-be, the mother of his child. "Why don't you tell me what the point is, smart-ass?" he asked.

"Smart-ass, huh?" She lifted her chin. In a lofty voice, she informed him, "Cracks like that will land you on the couch, pal."

"That house has got a lot of beds, sugar."

She sniffed, the perfect Southern belle acting extremely put out. Nobody could do affronted like the women of the South. Brannon would have bet money on it. "Fine. It will land you in a bed without me in it."

He brought her hand up and pressed his lips to the soft underside of her wrist, scraping his teeth along it. "I bet I could change your mind."

"I'd love to see you try."

He shot her another look, saw the gleam in her eyes.

"Might be a fun bet. Some other time. Again, what's the point . . . Hannah?"

"Moira." She said it plain and simple. "She's the point. If he leaves, she's pretty much done. She's shutting down more and more and don't tell me you don't see it. She used to go out to the pub once a week, have a drink, sit down with the girls and talk. She might come out once a month now. Once he's gone, she'll shut down even more. She's already laughing less. Living less. The two of them belong together. He knows it. Deep down, so does she. I think . . ."

When she trailed off without adding anything, he stroked his thumb across the back of her hand. "What is it?"

"Maris." Hannah cleared her throat and said, "Maris changed something in her. I'd look at Moira's face when they were out together and you could see the misery there. I think she finally realized that he was done. That he couldn't keep waiting . . . but that she didn't *want* to wait anymore. I think she was finally ready to reach out."

"*Fuck.*" Brannon tugged his hand free from hers and returned it to the wheel, staring down the ribbon of road. Not many miles remained between here and Treasure. He wanted to put the gas pedal to the floor, feel the engine come alive as he sped off, and let the controlled power of the car carry away some of the tension rising inside him. But he'd decided his need for speed was becoming an addiction of sorts and he needed to get it under control. He was going to be a daddy soon, a husband even sooner than that. So he gripped the wheel, absently twisting his hands back and forth as he stared at the road. "He's been waiting for years—like more than eighteen years in fact. My sister isn't stupid. What does she think he's been doing all this time?"

"It's not *him*," Hannah said. "It's her. She'd either convinced herself she was over him or she's a knucklehead like you. Maybe she had convinced herself that life was just easier not letting herself fall for somebody and risk losing them. Maybe it's something else entirely . . . maybe she's blaming herself over something and this was her way of atoning. I don't know. I do know she was ready to try . . . something."

"Shit."

"So . . . talk to her."

"Shit," he said again. He started to tap his fingers on the wheel as the town came into view. "Fine. I will. It ought to be you or Neve doing this, you know. I'm the guy. I don't do feelings."

"I have faith in you." She patted his shoulder and then shot him an impish grin. "Maybe I'll even make it worth your while . . . you do feelings and then I'll do . . . you."

Gideon woke up hungry, hungover, and horny. Those three things added up to make him one miserable, angry bastard.

As he brushed his teeth, trying to remove the cottony taste from his mouth, he recalled his conversation with Brannon. It had been right before he'd taken that last drink, the one that had put him over the edge and sent him into oblivion.

He'd called about Moira.

Moira.

Immediately, he groaned, because he knew why Brannon had been calling, now that he was thinking with a mostly unmuddled head.

Moira was being discharged.

But Hannah was supposed to be seeing the doctor.

Shit, shit, shit . . .

He didn't want Moira leaving that hospital and going home to an empty house.

She doesn't want your help. She doesn't want you.

He knew that—he'd gotten the original memo like eighteen years ago, and all the little reminders sent out since then. The one time he thought there had been a change in status? Back in the boathouse two months ago? Yeah. Forget that. It had been a momentary setback—that was how Moira, ever the businesswoman, would view it. The way she'd shut him cold in the weeks that followed had made him realize just how much she felt the need to keep him at a distance.

He had no doubt that she still loved him. But she didn't want to acknowledge it and she didn't want to let herself need him.

None of that mattered, though.

She was sitting at the hospital, probably waiting to be discharged and Brannon was supposed to be taking his fiancée in to get looked over. He could already hear the conversation.

We won't be long. You keep your ass there.

Moira would make that low murmur that people took for agreement and then she'd make her own plans while waiting for the doctors to discharge her.

Normally, Gideon would take that to mean there was time.

But the McKay Foundation, over the years, had pretty much bought and paid for the whole damn hospital. They didn't ask for special treatment. They got it anyway. Nobody was going to keep Moira sitting around waiting.

With the wind blowing in through his half-open window, Gideon punched in a call to the hospital and asked for Moira's nurse.

It was Kathy Rupert and he said a prayer of thanks. He'd grown up with Kathy and she was likely to be more reasonable than some. "Question . . . I'm rushing my ass to get to the hospital before Moira leaves. Am I wasting my time? You can find a way to answer that without violating patient confidentiality."

"Gideon . . ." Kathy's voice was chiding. Then she laughed. "Dr. Jacobi made the terrible mistake of going by the cafeteria for some coffee, which gave Tijuana Gilmore time to get up to the floor. You do know who is here, right . . . ?"

Gideon wracked his brain and then he groaned. "Do I need to get an officer in there?"

"Well, you're already on your way in. They saw the doctor before he could duck into Moira's room. He's cornered. You got time. Just don't stop for donuts."

He disconnected and blew out a breath. His stomach twisted something awful, and he muttered, "Like a donut would stay down."

The toast he'd eaten was sitting uneasily in his gut and it hadn't done shit to fill the empty void there, but he'd have to worry about that later.

The pale gleam of the recently renovated hospital came into view. It spoke of old-world charm, but under that façade was new-world tech. He parked as close as he could without abusing his authority—he'd done some of his training with a dirty cop, and cops who abused their authority pissed him off. Then he took off at a jog to get inside, ignoring the banging that took up within his skull at his fast clip.

Getting too old to drown my miseries, he told himself.

He was getting too old for a lot of things.

Still, he took the steps because they were closer and less busy than the bank of elevators and he knew the second he stepped through the doors, he needed to get a uniform over here. Security was already up on the third floor, the top floor of the small county hospital, and they were handling the fraying tempers with aplomb, but he had a feeling fists were about to start flying.

Pulling out his badge, he raised his voice just loud enough. "Might I remind you people that this is a hospital? You've got sick and injured people here who don't care to listen to the grievances you have with each other."

Tijuana—at least he assumed it was Tijuana—shot him a dirty look over her shoulder. Yep, it was her. Her previously black hair was now all the colors of the rainbow and her mouth was pursed in a petulant sulk. She'd been a beautiful girl . . . once. But her light brown complexion showed some scarring—of a particular sort—and he wanted to shake his head. It looked like she'd gone from drinking and marijuana to meth. The kind of scarring she had on her face was pretty commonplace for that kind of drug abuse.

Her dad was in the hospital recovering from an infection that had nearly cost him his leg, and she was most likely here to beg him for money. So she could go out and score. It was a bad cycle for her.

"You are *not* going in there and asking him for money!" Ruth Gilmore crossed her arms over her chest as she glared at Tijuana.

Gideon strode forward as Tijuana lifted a hand tipped with nails that could almost double as daggers. He caught her wrist, noting that Ruth was backing away. That woman wasn't a fool; she was fifty-five and not exactly spry, while Tijuana was whip lean. And when she was jonesing for a hit, she had a meanness to her.

As she spun around, her other fist came up. He was ready for it, shaking his head at her. "Now do you really want to add assaulting an officer to your history, T.?"

"Let me go, you son of a bitch!" She glared at him, tears of anger glittering in her eyes. There was something else, though. "I just wanna see my dad. That bitch can't keep me out. I got more of right to see him than she does."

"They're married," Gideon said gently.

"And I'm his *daughter*!" She jerked away.

He let her go, keeping his body between the two women. "You take another swing at her, you go in a cell until you cool down. Got me?"

"Kiss my skinny black ass, cop." She curled her lip at him and then shot Ruth a warning glare. "I'm going to see my dad."

Ruth opened her mouth.

"She's got a right to see him," Gideon said. "You two standing out here fighting like this isn't helping him any. He's got heart problems, right?"

Ruth's mouth thinned down into a tight line, but she nodded. "We're barely going to make it through the next few months, him being out of work for as long as he has been. If she goes asking him for money—"

"She won't." Gideon gave Tijuana a narrow look. "Tijuana, you're not going to do anything that will upset him, you hear?"

"You got no right to tell me what I can and can't say to my own dad, Marshall." She took up a rapt interest in her nails.

"No." Folding his arms over his chest, he angled his head at the doctor. Dr. Jacobi had always put him in the mind of a bald, aging mouse—beady eyes, pink face, hands that were never still. But he was sharp as a whip and he took the safety and health of his patients seriously. "That man there, though? He's your dad's doctor, as I'm sure you are aware. If he thinks you might say anything that's likely to upset him, he can decide that your visit would be detrimental to your dad's recovery. If his blood pressure goes too high . . . well." Gideon shrugged. "He's already had one heart attack."

Tijuana's eyes widened, flitting away. She licked her lips and then looked back at Ruth. "When . . . when did he have a heart attack?"

"Last Christmas. He was trying to carry in a Christmas tree and . . ." When the older woman's voice hitched, one of the nurses rested a hand on her shoulder. "It was a mild one, but that was when they discovered he'd developed some heart problems. He had to have a bypass. We tried to call, but . . ."

An awkward silence ensued, and Gideon let the younger woman process the situation. She was twitchy as hell. He'd have to have his people keep an eye on her for as long as she was in town. It could be twenty minutes. It could be ten months. Nobody ever knew with Tijuana.

When she finally stopped staring at everything and nothing, he said her name. She looked up at him. "You understand now?"

"I just want to see my dad," she said softly. Then she swallowed and bit her lip. "I . . . I'm pregnant. I wanna come home."

When Moira heard his voice, firm and commanding, she closed her eyes. Her throat was still raw and sore, but she could manage a few words today. It still *hurt,* but she could do it.

That meant when she called her brother, she could manage to tell him he was an asshole without it being pure hell.

She'd told him she'd wait.

He'd called Gideon anyway.

She shot a look down at herself, grimacing at the sight of her worn and faded T-shirt, the yoga pants. Brannon had obviously packed her clothes, going for the oldest, rattiest things he could find. Neve or Hannah would have picked out something that at least looked like it hadn't been scraped from the bottom of her drawer.

Scooting out of the bed, she disappeared into the bathroom. The one thing she could do was deal with her hair.

She had just shut the door behind her when she heard someone come in.

At least he had some sense. He didn't call out her name and expect a response. Instead he came over and knocked on the door. "Make a noise if you're in there."

She made a face at the door and flipped him off. Then she banged on the door.

"I'm here to take you home."

She didn't bother attempting a response at that. She just gathered her hair up and twisted it, smoothing it back until it was gathered into a neat chignon. Once that was done, she dug through her travel case until she found her small makeup kit. She didn't spend a lot of time, but she managed to smooth out the dark circles under her eyes and at least give the illusion of color to her cheeks.

The worst was the bruising to the left side of her face and all the discoloration to her neck.

There was nothing that could be done about that.

Sighing, she zipped up the case and slid out of the bathroom to find Gideon standing at the window, staring outside.

They were a matching set, it seemed. His shirt was as rumpled as hers. While he had on jeans instead of yoga pants, they were just as battered and wrinkled as the shirt. He looked like his night hadn't gone much better than hers. Although *he* hadn't spent it in a hospital.

Then he turned to look at her and she saw his bloodshot eyes.

He spent it in a whiskey bottle, she thought. For some reason, the idea didn't displease her. Maybe he was as miserable as she was. Did that make her terrible, to hope he that maybe he still wanted her? To hope that maybe it wasn't too late?

She opened her mouth to say something.

"Has the doctor discharged you yet?" The words came out clipped and terse.

Instead of saying anything, she just shook her head and gestured to the hall.

His mouth settled into a flat, hard line. "You heard all that."

"The dead in the morgue probably heard," she said, her voice raspy. Squeezing the words out was like shoving razor blades through her throat, but she managed to say them without crying.

For a moment, Gideon's face softened. Then his jaw went tight.

She could practically see it in his eyes. *You're not being nice anymore, Gideon.*

It made her heart hurt. But most of all, it made her furious . . . at herself, because she knew she deserved it.

"You should continue to rest your voice." He moved to the door, looking out into the hall.

It had finally quieted out there, and she hoped that meant Dr. Jacobi would be in soon. She was about two steps away from just going AMA. If Brannon was here, she could probably wheedle him into it—he didn't care about a doctor's signature any more than she did, although she'd hear the sharp side of Ella Sue's tongue if the woman heard she'd left against medical advice.

"He's heading over here." Gideon looked at her. "So you can stop planning on skipping out."

He knew her too well.

Sighing, she moved to the edge of the bed and sat down, tugging the dry erase board within easy reach.

From the time Dr. Jacobi walked in to the time the discharge nurse walked out with all her papers neatly signed, it took less than thirty minutes—probably a record for discharges. Moira was under no illusions why. The hospital staff went out of their way to treat her well, and it had nothing to do with *her* as a person and everything to do with the wing that had been named after her parents.

She wished they wouldn't do it . . . normally. But today she was happy to be out of there so quickly.

"I'm going to go bring my car to the front. They'll have somebody up to transport you in a few minutes. I should be back before then."

She didn't even look at Gideon, just nodded.

She'd already packed everything up and just wanted out of there.

When she heard footsteps a few moments later, she sighed and eased her sore, aching body up. "That was . . ." her rasping voice trailed off when it wasn't the volunteer with a wheelchair, but her brother and Hannah.

Hannah was glowing. "We heard the heartbeat again." She had her hand on her belly.

Brannon's face lightened momentarily with a smile, but then he looked at her. "You ready to go?"

She nodded, confused. "Yes, but—"

"Good, because we have to talk."

"Okay, but—"

"Stop talking," Brannon said, exasperated. "You're supposed to rest your voice, remember? Listen . . . I want to discuss this more at home, but you need to think about what I have to tell you, so . . ."

He shot a look around as he stepped closer. What, did he think the nurses had elves hiding behind the doors? Mystified, she scowled at him as he lowered his voice.

"Gideon is leaving."

"What?" she asked, shaking her head. "He just went out—"

"Rest your voice," Brannon said again, annoyed. "I told

you. He's leaving. Moving out of town. He's going to be talking to the city council about hiring a replacement as soon as everything here is settled."

Dazed, she stumbled back, half-tripping when the backs of her legs hit the bed. She sagged backward onto it and stared up at her brother. "Leaving?" she whispered.

"Rest your—"

"Shut up!" she shouted—or tried. It came out a weird, half-screeching noise that in no way resembled her normal voice. And it *hurt*. Through the tears, she stared at Brannon. "He's *leaving*?"

A sound from outside the door caught their attention before he could answer.

It was the volunteer, finally. Daisy Coulter, one of the local gossips; her eyes were wide and avid as she looked from Moira to Brannon . . . and then up to Gideon, who was standing at her side.

Gideon stared at Brannon, his gaze flat and hard.

Then he looked at Moira.

She waited for him to tell Brannon he was wrong.

But he didn't say a single word.

CHAPTER SEVEN

Gideon stood on the porch, watching as Neil Frasier and his team spread out across the McKay estate like a team of carpenter ants. They were armed with the tools of their trade—security equipment.

"Cameras on the perimeter, at the outbuildings, to start," Brannon said from behind. "We're definitely doing the dogs."

"I'm working on it." Gideon kept his voice neutral, despite the fact that he wanted to turn around and punch his friend. For a long time, Brannon had been like a kid brother and he'd grown into one of Gideon's best friends. As a friend, and as Moira's brother, one would *think* the son of a bitch would have moved with a little more tact than he had earlier.

One would think.

Except Brannon had about as much use for tact as a submarine had for screen doors. Hell, the screen doors might get more use.

The pain he'd seen in her eyes made Gideon want to hit something.

It also made him mad . . . at her.

If she cared enough that the thought of him leaving hurt her that much, than why wouldn't she . . .

Stop it. He cut the line of thought off before it could go any further. He'd spent too many years going down that road, and look where it had led him.

"I can tell you're pissed off. You might as well turn around and look at me. We can have it out here and now."

Angling his head around until he could see Brannon, he said mildly, "I'm on duty."

"That doesn't look like your uniform."

"I'm in charge. If I want to wear jeans and a T-shirt to bring the victim of an attack home, then I can wear jeans and a T-shirt." He shrugged. Then he went back to watching the security team. Most of them were out of sight now. "I want this all feeding into my station, not just the county sheriff's."

Brannon blew out a breath. "Moira won't like that."

"Too bad." Now he turned to Brannon and crossed his arms over his chest. Brannon echoed his posture and it was pretty clear that Brannon wouldn't mind going to toe to toe.

Brannon was taller and broader than him, probably had forty pounds on him too. But Gideon had done some hard time on the sands of the desert over in the Middle East and he'd spent more than a few rough years as a big-city cop before he'd come back to Treasure. Brannon McKay was a fighter, true. But Gideon was a warrior. There was a difference.

Cocking a brow, he said, "We aren't doing this. Moira's hurt. I don't know why, but she'll get over it and go on with her life. She's done it before."

"You . . ." Brannon dragged a hand down his face and then slowly, quietly, said, "You don't know *why*?"

"No." Gideon glanced up at the house, his gaze unerringly seeking out the room where she was mostly likely to be. And just as he'd expected, the curtains flickered.

There were two libraries in the house. A large, formal one on the first floor, and another upstairs. That one was Moira's place. Bright and open, with light spilling in all year long and flowers added for color—if she wasn't working or sleeping, she could be found there. "She might love me, Brannon, but she doesn't want to. She didn't say a word when I left to join the army and she didn't say a word when I came back after my discharge. She didn't say anything when she heard I was talking about accepting the job with the department in Memphis and I don't expect a big change this time either. She doesn't want what's between us. It's probably easier for her when I'm *not* here. I honestly don't even know *why* she's hurt, because she clearly doesn't want me in her life. I'm just making it easier on both of us."

He went to turn away.

Brannon grabbed his arm.

"She cried."

Muscles bunching, he fought the urge to tear away from the grip that held him in place. "You want to let me go now," he advised, ignoring what Brannon had said.

But Brannon ignored him as well.

"Every fucking day for over a month," he bit off. "After she told you it was over, she cried. After you left for the army? She cried. Every time you came home on leave? She'd do her damnedest to be in town every day, even if she had to stay up halfway through the night to catch up on school work and all the shit going on with Neve and me. All she wanted to do was see you and know you were okay. And when you *left*? She cried *every* time. That never changed."

Gideon twisted out of Brannon's grasp, clenching his jaw. He fought the urge to look up at the window again. *She cried . . .*

He thought of the look he'd seen in Moira's eyes just a couple of hours ago, wounded, betrayed. Broken.

But then he made himself stop.

He was done.

He'd finally committed to doing the one thing he'd tried to do for years. He wasn't going back down that hole again. It was too damn empty, too damn lonely down there.

"She got over it," he said, managing a careless smile. "She got married, right? She moved on. It's time for me to do the same."

He headed down the stairs, telling himself he wanted a thorough update on just what the security team was doing.

"She never once looked at him the way she still looks at you," Brannon called out.

Gideon kept walking.

"And she never once cried over him."

This time, he hesitated.

Then he shook his head and forced himself to keep going.

"Are you going to tell me what's bothering you?"

Moira gave Ella Sue a wide-eyed stare and gestured to her neck. *Gee, I wonder,* she mouthed.

"Oh, it's not that. That would make you look scared. Mad. Both." Ella Sue pursed her lips. "And you are that, I can tell. But you're also hurting, baby. On the inside."

When Ella Sue came to sit down on the window seat next to her, Moira drew her knees up to give her room. Then, because she could, she rested her head on the other woman's shoulder. "He's leaving," she whispered, staring out the window at Gideon. His dark head was bent toward Neil Fraser's bald one.

Ella Sue tensed. "Please tell me you mean Neil."

Moira shook her head.

"Oh, dear."

Ella Sue managed to pack an awful lot into those two simple words.

"Yeah."

Ella Sue's dismayed silence lasted all of ten seconds. Then she nudged Moira aside and stood up. With her back to Moira, she stared into the empty room and then turned to look outside, her dark gaze unerringly seeking out Gideon. That study was brief, but intense and Moira had no idea what the woman was thinking.

When Moira became the focus of Ella Sue's interest, she had the urge to squirm. Or remember something that suddenly needed doing. As if she could see exactly what was going on inside Moira's head, Ella Sue crossed her arms over her chest and started to tap her foot. "So. He's leaving."

"Yes." The pain in Moira's throat was nothing compared to the one in her chest, one that threatened to tear her into a hundred, bleeding pieces.

"Then I guess you had better get busy, Moira. Child, I love you, but you've been punishing the both of you way too long. It's time to stop."

Moira gaped at her. "What . . . why . . ."

"Don't." Ella Sue's eyes flashed. "I've kept quiet and I've done my best to . . . no. I *have* understood. But do you *really* think this is what your mother would have wanted? What your father would have wanted? You acted like a teenaged girl in love. You behaved like a brat, yes. That doesn't mean you deserve a lifelong sentence."

Moira flinched as if she'd been slapped.

Then, slowly, she drew her knees to her chest, hugging them as she tore her gaze from Ella Sue's. "You knew. All this time . . . ?"

"Yes." Ella Sue stroked a hand down Moira's hair, then cupped her cheek. "That crash wasn't your fault. Not yours and not his. Heavens, Moira. If your mother had wanted you home *that* badly, she would have tracked you down and brought you home."

Moira sucked in a breath, the pain in her throat almost matching the pain in her heart. *Almost.* Nothing would ever hurt that bad.

"Fix this," Ella Sue urged. "Fix this . . . fix this tear you've put between you and him, because if you don't, you'll regret it the rest of your life. And so will he."

Ella Sue left, leaving Moira alone.

TWENTY YEARS AGO

"Moira."

She looked up from the clothes she'd been digging through. She had a date with Gideon tonight and she was trying to find the best way to wow him. She didn't know what she was looking for, but she wanted . . . *something.*

"Hi, Mom."

Sandra McKay stood in the doorway, blonde and beautiful, her hair cut short, an expectant look on her face. "You almost ready?"

"Just trying to find . . ."

Neve came barging in, braids flying, a wide grin on her face. She leapt up and ended right in the middle of Moira's bed. "Neve, you brat!"

Clothes went flying, and so did the sexy little new set of underwear she'd picked up—the set she'd done her best to keep her mother from seeing.

"Don't call me a brat! Otherwise you'll have to buy *all* the tokens!"

Tokens? "Whatever." Rolling her eyes, she pushed her sister out of the way as she tried to casually gather up the bra and panty set, dumping some other clothes on top to keep it mostly out of sight. "Would you scram? Gideon is going to be here soon."

"Gideon's coming?" Neve started to bounce and squeal.

"We've got a date. It's our anniversary," Moira said loftily.

"Oh. Oh, dear . . . Moira, I asked if you had plans."

Looking over at her mother, she said, "I do. Gideon. It's our anniversary. I told you that *weeks* ago."

The look on Sandra McKay's face had Moira's stomach going tight. "Oh, don't you dare try to push Nevie off on me. Gideon and I have been planning this for *weeks*! Don't you remember me going shopping for clothes last weekend?"

Sandra passed a hand over her face. "Moira, calm down. I do . . . I must have confused the days when I asked you. Everything has been so messed up since Richard died." Her mouth tightened as she looked over at Neve. "We're trying to make . . . arrangements."

"I *have* arrangements." Crossing her arms over her chest, Moira glared at her mother.

"I don't care for that tone of voice." Sandra's eyes chilled. "Keep it up and you *won't* be going on that date with Gideon, or anywhere else for the foreseeable future."

A mutinous retort leapt to her lips, but Moira bit it back. Her mother didn't make empty threats.

"You go on your date," Sandra said, her face set in implacable lines. "But we're going to talk about your attitude tomorrow."

"Mommy . . ." Neve's voice fell into a needling whine. "I wanna go with Moira and Gideon. I wanna go on a date."

"Too bad, brat!" Moira made a face at her.

"That's enough, Moira." Sandra held out a hand to Neve. "Come on, baby. Maybe you, Daddy, and I can have a date. I need to call Ella Sue, work something else out, okay?"

"I can't believe she expected me to babysit Neve tonight," Moira said as Gideon climbed off the bike. She had a picnic basket in one hand, a flashlight in the other. "She's known I've been planning this for *weeks*."

When he stood in front of her, he bent his head and his mouth closed over hers in a deep, hot kiss that left her head swimming.

"You know . . . I don't recall us setting up a date to talk about your mom," he said when he lifted his head away.

"Ha, ha."

Gideon grinned back, taking the basket from her. They started to walk, heading around down the path that would take them down along the river. They had wanted to go to the same place where he'd first kissed her, where he'd asked her to be his.

So that's where they were going. It was only about a half mile from the house, but nobody was going to bother them there.

Besides . . . she was thinking about talking him into going to the pool house later. Her parents had indeed taken Neve out on a 'date' and Brannon was grounded, so he wasn't going swimming. Neve wasn't allowed to swim unless Dad was home and Dad wasn't going to want to swim by the time they got home, so even if they *did* end up coming back home . . .

Privacy!

"Mom just spazzes over everything. I know what the problem is. It's all because Richard died. She's like determined to find a new guardian. She's *such* a spazz," Moira said. She shot a look back at the sexy work of art that was her boyfriend and shrugged.

Gideon had been her friend first. Then he'd become her boyfriend . . . now he was her lover. He was her everything.

She wanted to feel his body pressed up against hers again.

The first time hadn't . . . well, it had hurt. It had been

awkward on top of that, but she was stubborn. And the second time? Much better. She thought maybe tonight, if she could talk him into visiting the pool house, they could have a third time and it would be even better.

"Chill out, Mac. You're lucky you got a mom who cares." Gideon's mouth tightened a little. "Shit, you got two parents who care. Toss in Brannon and Neve and you're like the picture-perfect family."

"Neve's more a picture-perfect brat," she said, laughing.

Gideon, in her mind, was about perfect. Nobody understood her like he did. Of course, he also had a mad affection for her annoying little sister, but nobody was *completely* perfect.

"She's a kid." Gideon caught her around the waist and kissed her neck. "You were a kid once too, Mac. I remember that . . . and you grew out of it. So will she."

"Humph." She elbowed him in the gut and they started walking again. "She's got a crush on you."

She saw the grin that split his face, and rolled her eyes.

"I know." He chuckled. "I'm irresistible to the McKays. What can I say?"

"Yeah, well, I think Brannon is immune."

Gideon almost choked laughing.

The chaise lounge wasn't exactly a bed of roses, but it might as well as have been as she and Gideon fumbled with each other's clothes.

They'd spent more than a few nights out here, doing this.

Their first time had been on this lounge, and she thought maybe it was her favorite piece of furniture in the whole damn world.

When he slid his mouth down to rub it against her neck, she brought her foot up and dragged it along the hard, heavy muscle of his calf. The coarse hair tickled her foot. She awkwardly lifted herself against him, and he made a low noise in his throat, driving against the hollow between her thighs. It sent a slow curl of heat through her.

When she did it again and she heard him moan, it gave her the courage she needed to slide one hand between them and rub him through his shorts.

He tensed, and when she closed her hand around him, he lifted his head, eyes glittering.

"You don't know when your folks will be home," he said gruffly.

"They aren't going to come out here this late. They never do. Dad will be too tired after working all day then going out, and Mom only swims when we make her. Come here . . ."

She slid her fingers up higher and freed the button on his shorts. His breathing went ragged. "You . . . Moira . . ."

In the dim glitter of lights that filtered in through the windows, their eyes met. She licked her lips, blood rushing to heat her cheeks as she tugged at his underwear. As his eyes went hooded, she shoved her hand down the front and closed her hand around his penis. "Again, Gideon."

She loved the feel of him. He was . . . soft. At least his skin was. Softness wrapped around the hot, heavy length of his cock, and she felt something pulse inside when he jerked in her hand.

"Again." He rubbed his mouth against hers.

They fought with their clothes, her shirt and bra ending up in a twisted tangle around her arms and shoulders, while he yanked her panties and shorts down.

He came back to her and she gasped, the feel of him passing back and forth between her thighs filling her with liquid heat.

"Make love to me, Gideon," she said, surprising herself with how easy it was to say those words.

He groaned and came inside her. "You don't have to ask me twice."

* * *

The ceaseless ringing of the doorbell woke her up.

Mom, Dad, and Neve hadn't been home when she'd gotten in—she'd checked her little sister's room. Her mood had lightened considerably and she'd thought maybe she'd see if Nevie wanted to go swimming the next day. Or maybe fishing. The kid always loved fishing, especially with Gideon.

But none of them were home and Brannon had fallen asleep playing video games. *That* was typical. It was also typical that the doorbell didn't wake him up.

What was strange was that neither Mom nor Dad beat her to the front door.

Moira rubbed the sleep from her eyes as she moved across the entryway and went to open the door. Only at the last second did she remember to disarm the system. She probably should have left it alone. She'd bet *anything* Brannon was still asleep in front of the big-screen TV in the family room. The alarm system was the one thing that did wake him up.

But responsibility bit at her, not to mention a little bit of guilt for how she'd acted earlier. She'd hoped to hear her parents come in so she could apologize to Mom, but she hadn't been able to stay awake and Moira didn't want to wake them up like *that*.

So she disarmed the system and opened the door midyawn.

Her blood froze at the sight of the police car in front of her house.

The chief of police stood in front of her, twisting his hat around and around in his hands. Two others were on the porch—no, three. Three others. Dimly, she realized Ella Sue was walking toward her. And Gideon.

Gideon was there.

And he had . . .

"Nevie?"

Neve just shoved her face against Gideon's neck and as Moira stared at her baby sister, she realized the girl was shaking. Trembling, all over. Like a leaf, she thought, feeling dazed.

I want to go inside.

Looking back at the chief, she licked her lips. She couldn't remember his name. A knot welled up in her throat, lodged there.

She wanted to go back inside. That was all she could think.

The chief said her name, but she shook her head and moved toward Gideon, intent on getting her little sister. It didn't matter that Neve already reached the middle of Moira's chest. She wanted to pick up her baby sister and go inside, shut the door and lock it.

Lock away the world, everything, everybody and wait for Mom and Dad.

"Moira, baby," Ella Sue said. She tried to catch Moira on the arm.

Moira dodged away and rushed to Gideon. "Give her to me," she demanded, reaching for Neve.

Gideon stared at her, his eyes dark, unreadable. "Mac . . . we need to—"

"No!" She screamed it.

That was when she found out something else could wake her brother up. A scream from one of his sisters.

As she tried to pry Neve's trembling form from Gideon, Brannon appeared in the doorway. "What's going on?" he asked, his voice rough with sleep, deeper than it had been even just a few months ago. He was tall, too. He might even get to be taller than Dad. *Dad,* Moira thought helplessly.

"Give her to me," she pleaded with Gideon.

"I want Brannon," Neve whispered, speaking for the first time.

Brannon approached, quiet in that way he often had, realizing something was going on.

Neve went to him and clung tight. "It's okay, monkey," Brannon said.

Neve shook her head.

Moira backed away, shaking hers. *No, no, no, no . . .*

Gideon caught her arms. "Mac."

The chief came toward her from one side, Ella Sue from the other—a silent, gentle wall.

"Moira, I'm terribly sorry . . ."

She stood there, staring at Gideon's chest as the words were said.

"Did you understand me?" the chief asked gently.

Slowly, she looked up at him and nodded.

Then she looked at Gideon. "I never got to tell her I was sorry," she said brokenly. "I never got to . . ."

The sobs tore into her then.

"I never got to tell her."

"She knew, Mac."

Wordlessly she shook her head. She wanted to tell her. She should have said it, should have done something—

She screamed then, a wordless outcry of pain and grief and guilt.

Gideon's arms tightened around as she fought to free her arms from the embrace so she could cling to him. "Don't let go," she begged, feeling like the pain was going to end her. "Don't let go."

"You don't have to ask me twice."

NOW

"You ain't gotta say that twice." Neil blew out a breath as he glanced over at Gideon.

But Gideon wasn't paying him any attention.

Moira had slid out onto the wide, sweeping deck that flowed from the house and she was watching.

She wasn't watching the work being done by the security team.

She was staring at him.

There was something in that gaze that he hadn't seen. At least, not in a long time.

Clenching his jaw, he focused back on Neil. "How is this going to affect the family? They need to have full use of the grounds, not to mention the staff and people who come in to tend the grounds."

"Not a problem. What we're going to do is have pictures of everybody who *belongs* here—the family and Miss Ella Sue."

"She *is* family," Gideon pointed out.

"True, true." Neil just nodded amicably. "Then the rest of the staff. They are the people who the system will recognize as normal. We scan them in. Then there are acceptable types. People who come and go, but it might be odd if the system picks them up here at a strange time . . . say midnight. Also, it can recognize acts of aggression. It picks up on a hundred different cues." He smiled then, a glint in his eyes. "That will send up an alert that one of us will have to check. Then there are questionable people—visitors and what not. If people show up at the front, ring the doorbell? The alert for that is different than say somebody coming up through the back, trying to skulk in."

Gideon nodded slowly, thinking this through. "That's a pretty advanced system."

"There are others that leave this in the dust." Neil shrugged. "But this one is my design and it should work for what Moira needs. It's got a weight limit on it so critters—birds, squirrels, and such—don't set it off. Body heat, too. If it sees some five hundred pound mass that's got a temperature more on par with a reptile, it's going to scan and see a gator, not an intruder."

"System like that will put you out of a job," Gideon said.

Neil made a wheezing sort of laugh. "Well, I've already got people looking to buy it. I'm going to be looking to sell soon. Retire and take my ass on down to Hawaii and live out the rest of my life, being a bum." He nodded up to the porch. "You ever going to get that woman to stop running from you?"

"No. I'm done trying. Mind your own, Neil."

"Done, huh?" Neil gave him a shrewd look, then shook his head. "My ass, you're done. She's heading this way. I'll give her a quick rundown, then I need to check on my crew and get out of here." He hesitated and then said, "Don't be a coward . . . not now. You waited all this time. What's a bit more?"

Then he glanced past Gideon, lifting his voice as he called out a greeting. "Evening, Moira. Has your brother finished planning out what he'll do once he gets his hands on the man who did that?"

Gideon bit back his instinctive response. *He'll have to beat me to it—*

He was leaving. Right?

Turning to look at Moira, he nodded at her without really meeting her eyes.

She spoke and the low, raspy whisper of her voice had him wincing in sympathy. "I plan on making him gator bait," she said.

Vicious pride twisted in him, and he shoved it down.

Then the cop in him kicked on, and he shoved a hand through his hair.

"Moira, leave that part to the cops."

"Since when did cops believe in gator bait?" She looked dead at him, something she didn't do too often. When their gazes locked, she didn't look away, either.

Drawn in by the soft, pale green of her eyes, he felt like a moth, caught by the lure of the flame. He'd danced in that warmth until it killed him. He'd been doing that for eighteen long years and it was destroying—

Neil's rusty laugh had Gideon stiffening.

Get your head out of your ass, he told himself.

"Moira, tell you what. If you catch yourself some decent . . . bait, you let me know."

"Damn it, Neil!" he snapped, pivoting and glaring down at the shorter, older man. Slapping his hands on his hips, he bent until they were nose to nose. "Can we maybe stop discussing murder in front of the chief of police? It would make my job easier."

"Murder . . ." Neil's lips thinned out. "For the love of . . ."

Two hands shoved between them, followed by a slim body.

Moira was small, but she was a force to be reckoned with.

Her father had teased that they'd named her wrong.

We should have named you Hermia . . . though she be but little, she is fierce.

It would have fit.

She wedged her body between them, knocking Neil back a step and then focused her attention on Gideon. Sparks fired from her pale green eyes, and they might have shot straight into his blood. He was on fire now. On fire and burning . . . for her. Just like always.

She jabbed him in the chest. "Why don't you yank that stick out of your ass?" she rasped.

"Stop." He caught her wrist. "I'm on duty and I'm not going to listen to your temper or your tantrums."

"My . . ." Her brows shot up almost to her hairline. "You son of a . . ."

She jerked her hand away, or tried.

"Neil." He shot him a look. "Get lost."

"Listen here, Chief." Neil coughed and shuffled his feet. "You realize Moira and I aren't really planning to cut up some miserable son of a bitch. He needs a lesson and all, but we wouldn't do that, would we, Moira?"

Moira bared her teeth up at Gideon.

"I hear you and understand, Neil." He didn't look at the other man. "Now, go deal with your crew. I appreciate them getting out here so promptly."

Moira jerked on her wrist again, and this time he let go.

She stumbled back half a pace and he reached up to steady her, but she smacked at his arms.

"What the hell is your problem?"

Her eyes, hot now, glittered up at him. "Don't touch me!"

Then she gasped and pressed a hand to her throat.

"Would you stop tearing your throat up so much?" Exasperated, he gestured to the house. "Go inside. Let Ella Sue make you a hot toddy or something. She sure as hell makes them strong enough."

Maybe it will calm you down. He thought it. He didn't say it.

But it must have shown on his face anyway.

"Maybe I don't *want* to go inside!" She shoved up onto her toes, pushing her face into his. "You don't get to tell me what to do, Gideon Marshall. Hell, you are *leaving,* remember?"

Then she spun around and flounced off.

Nobody could pull off a flounce quite like Moira McKay.

CHAPTER EIGHT

There are few certainties in life.

The sun will rise.

The sun will set.

Everybody dies.

Money speaks.

Friends will abandon you.

Family will always stand beside you.

The McKays will destroy everything that matters.

He'd grown up hearing those very truths. Even as his father lie dying, the cancer eating him from the inside out, he'd heard that truth.

They stole it all, boy. I've done what I can, but nobody listens to a sick old man. I have no voice. Money is the voice and they have it. I don't.

He knew those truths and he kept them close.

Kept them and worked hard.

Years had passed since the day his father was lowered into the earth, raining drenching him from the outside in as he stood alone by the grave.

There wasn't anybody else. It had been just his father and him.

Now it was just him.

Him and the knowledge that the McKays had taken everything from his family. Not just once, but time and time again.

He'd been nudged out of the classes he wanted over a sodding McKay—Moira McKay, the elegant, icy queen had swept into the college where he'd been holding on with a wish and a prayer. Only a day after he'd been told he would most likely be able to get into the class he needed to finish out his major a year early, he'd been notified there wasn't any room left.

And who did he discover was a late enrollee?

Moira McKay.

A few years later, he'd been working in the French Quarter in New Orleans—learning, *always* learning what he needed to accomplish his end goals—and there she'd been, this time with her younger brother in tow. On a buying trip, she'd hardly said two words to him and later, he'd walked into the pub where his girlfriend worked and discovered said girlfriend all but wrapped around Brannon McKay.

She'd all but thrown her knickers in that boy's face. He hadn't been much more than a boy, either. Hardly old enough to drink, but had that bitch cared? No. He was rich and that was all that mattered.

From that moment on, he'd hated Brannon—the kid had apologized good-naturedly after Leanna had seen him, scrambling away and tugging her dress down. Brannon had acted like he hadn't known, but the laughter had been there in his eyes. When his sister had arrived, Brannon had tossed down several bills, told the bartender drinks were on him, and had offered another apology.

He'd wanted to make the boy eat that fucking money.

Instead, he'd just left and busied himself gathering up Leanna's belongings. She'd let a fucking McKay touch her.

There had been other things since then, and as he'd worked his way closer, it had only gotten worse.

He'd prepared for that, expected it, and dealt with each problem. He had a plan and nothing would stop him.

First he had just planned to confront them—let everybody know the truth. But as he had gotten closer, he'd realized they were too stupid to understand and that his own hatred had grown.

Truth wasn't enough.

He wanted them to hurt, to suffer as he had.

Then he'd begun to dig deeper, heard more and more talk of that treasure. So much talk, so elusive, thought to be legend. But was it? Legend had basis in reality as often as not, so he'd dug deeper, read all the tales.

It had taken time, more than he'd liked, but he'd had plenty of it and nobody noticed him. He'd been there in the background for so long. Nobody ever paid him any attention. Neither of them had even recognized him when they all met up again, years later.

That moron Brannon couldn't find his prick in the dark with a roadmap, plus he was always out at his winery.

He'd long since learned how to keep Moira out of his way.

Then Neve had come home, ruined everything. She was such a nervous wreck, and *she* looked at things. She paid attention. It shouldn't have been hard to send her packing—after all, she was nothing but trouble. That's what they all called her. But planting drugs in her backpack hadn't worked to cause a split between them and she'd just further ensconced herself in her family home and now he was having to watch his back that much more closely.

But he'd get it sorted.

He was too close not to. Too close to let it all fall away.

Lying on the bed, he stroked a finger down the journal.

It wasn't the original.

That one was old, priceless. To him at least. Locked up and protected from careless handling, he'd had to use caution when he made the duplicates. Even though the copy he'd painstakingly reproduced by hand was no more than a few years old, it was already worn, the leather cover smooth in places from how often he'd handled it.

His eyes drifted closed as he thought back to what he'd done.

He'd left bruises on her.

It wasn't the first time he'd brought harm on a woman, but before it had been done simply in the name of expediency, carrying out his duty, the way he saw it. This . . . it had been different. He could feel the soft, almost delicate arch of her neck, the trembling of her body.

Her voice had shook as she answered.

As she *lied*.

"It's there."

He *knew* it was.

Everybody did.

The whole fucking *town* was named for it.

Have Ella Sue make me a hot toddy. Moira was fuming.

She grabbed a bottle of scotch and splashed it into a glass, tossing it back. It burned the whole way down, and her eyes watered. That didn't stop her from splashing more into the glass and doing it again.

When she heard a noise behind her, she slammed the bottle down and turned around, her lips peeled back in a snarl.

Seeing Gideon standing there, she narrowed her eyes to slits and pointed to the door. "Out," she said.

The scotch had done a bit to numb her throat, and she managed to speak with more volume than before.

Gideon tapped the badge clipped to his belt. "Got questions."

"Go fuck yourself, Chief Marshall. Get out."

Instead, he sauntered into the room. "Just what has you so worked up?"

She gaped at him. Clutching the crystal tumbler in her hand, she stared at him as he made a slow circle around the room. His dark head of hair was disheveled, and she found herself thinking of the times she'd run her hands through it.

Had Maris—

No. Don't go there, she told herself. She couldn't do that and still stay sane. She knew Maris and Gideon were lovers, didn't need to torment herself with imagery of it.

Maris was bigger than Moira, taller. As short as Gideon's hair was now, it was would barely be long enough to curl—

Her blood heated and jealousy burned even as the memories ripped at her heart.

He was *leaving*.

The agony just might tear her in two.

"I want you to leave," she said again.

"I've got questions, Moira." He turned and pinned her with a flat look. "Deal with it."

Her head was all full of what she *was* dealing with—the fact that he was leaving, the fact that she had really lost him, the pain in her throat, and the fear from the attack, combined with the sudden attack of dizziness. She realized she'd neglected to eat anything and that probably wasn't good since she'd bolted eighteen-year-old scotch.

Deal with it.

"Deal with it?" she said. The words shook, which just made her madder.

Since she couldn't yell, she did the only thing she could do.

She threw the tumbler at his head.

He dodged—she knew he would—it went sailing over

him to crash into the wall. It made a pretty little tinkling sound as it shattered and fell to the floor.

"What the—"

Furious and shaking, she swiped out a hand to grab for something else. *Anything* else.

Her hand closed around a small brass elephant and she let it fly.

That didn't make a pretty little sound.

Gideon swore and lunged for her.

He caught her, pinning her arms to her sides. She tried to twist away, but it wasn't happening. "Get—" Her voice splintered. It was like the dying shards of it stabbed into her throat and she gasped, the pain awful.

"What in the blue *fuck* is going on here?"

Wheeling her head around, she tried to find Brannon, but she couldn't see around Gideon. "Bran—"

She couldn't manage to finish her brother's name.

Sagging in Gideon's arms, she silently started to cry.

Above her, she heard Gideon sigh. "Brannon, do me a favor and just shut the doors. Leave us alone, okay?"

"I come in, see you grabbing her, see her crying, and you want me to leave you alone?"

Gideon jerked his head around, staring down Brannon.

"Like I'd ever hurt her," he said, voice harsh. He felt every soundless sob that shook Moira's body. He didn't know what had pushed her over the edge, but something had. Another spasm racked her body. "Brannon . . . please."

The man's mouth tightened. But he turned his back and pulled the doors shut behind him.

Scooping Moira up into his arms, Gideon carried her over to the couch and sat down.

It was agony.

It was also the sweetest ecstasy he'd known in months. Holding her like this . . . he set his jaw and tried to keep from thinking of the last time he had held her. The last time he'd touched her. Those few brief hours had given him the faintest bit of hope and then he'd gone smashing down into the darkest, ugliest pit of despair.

He'd been doing fine—

Moira shuddered again, a violent spasm that had him hugging her tighter out of instinct. She twisted out of his arms and half-fell out of his lap.

"Moira, would you—*oomph!*"

She drove her elbow into his gut and then shifted, bringing her fist upright and clipping him on the chin. It was an awkward blow, delivered with more emotion than anything else, but he ended up biting his tongue and while she stumbled onto her feet, he swallowed down the taste of his own blood.

"*Thon of a bitth!*"

She glared at him as she dashed away tears.

The sight of them was a punch in the heart.

"Moira . . ." Helpless, he lifted a hand.

She held up both of hers in a clear *stay back* gesture.

Stay back. Stay away. All she'd wanted from him since the night of her twentieth birthday.

"Fine. I get it." He swallowed down more blood, coughed, then cleared his throat. "I'll have one of the detectives take this on. You can deal with him."

He started toward the door.

A pillow hit him in the back of the head.

Blowing out a breath through his teeth, he stared at the floor.

Another throw pillow came sailing through the air and hit him in the back. He turned around just in time to catch the third as he glared at her. "Just because they are called *throw* pillows doesn't mean you can pelt me with them, sugar."

She looked around, a half-wild look on her face.

"If you throw one more thing at me, I'm going to arrest you for assault, you hear me?" He jabbed a finger at her.

Moira flipped him off and stomped over to the small secretary along the wall, just a few feet away. He swore and turned away. Something small hit him in the shoulder. He had no idea what the projectile was and he didn't care. "That's it, damn it." Spinning around, he crossed the room, pulling the cuffs off his belt.

Only to stop.

She was scrawling a message on a piece of paper.

Fine, you SOB. Go ahead. When I need you . . .

She hadn't managed to write anything else.

"What?" he asked, his voice rough.

She stood there, head bowed over her note. Her fingers were trembling. Her shoulders rose and fell as her breathing sawed out in broken, irregular stops and starts.

His cuffs hung useless in his hand. He stared at them and turned away, lifting his head to stare at the ceiling. "What are we doing to each other?" he asked softly. "What the fuck, Moira?"

The faintest scratching sound caught his ear.

He turned, but what he really wanted to do was leave before they bruised each other even more.

She was no longer by the delicate little desk.

She stood by the window, staring outside.

But the note was there.

I need you and you're leaving me.

"You don't need me, Moira," he said quietly. "Save for Brannon and Neve, you don't need anybody."

He took the piece of paper and folded it, first in half, then in fours, tucking it into his pocket.

Then he turned and walked to the door.

He turned the handle, the hinges creaking slightly. He stopped, though, pain splitting through him. There had been one time, exactly one, when he'd hurt like this and it had been the day she told him she couldn't be with him.

Now, here he was trying to pull away just to save what little remained of his soul and . . .

Slim hands came up to grip his waist.

He closed his eyes.

"Moira . . ."

Slowly, he turned, telling himself that he was going to pull away. He'd walk out the door. He'd turn this case over to his best man and keep his distance until he could get the hell out of Treasure.

But she had tears on her face and when he reached up to wipe them away, she turned her cheek into his palm.

Her breath was a soft kiss against his hand and he knew it was already over for him.

He was done, already caught back in her orbit. Damn them both.

She stared at him, the lost, hopeless look in her eyes all but ripping the heart out of his chest. He wanted to pull her up against him and take every last hurt, every last misery from her life. If only she'd let him. Her lips trembled as she averted her gaze, sagging back against one of the doors.

She was exhausted. It was written in the slump of her normally proud shoulders, in the defeated droop of her head.

"Come here," he said, keeping his voice quiet.

He didn't wait for a response, just swept her up into his arms. Using his booted foot to kick the door the rest of the way open, he carried her up the steps, taking the hall that led to the eastern wing, where her room looked over the sprawling front lawn of McKay's Ferry.

She had her head tucked against his chest, one hand clenched into a bloodless fist.

The light to her room was on, burning bright, and he sat her on the edge of the bed. "You're exhausted. You need to sleep."

Moira didn't look at him. The bruises on her neck were exposed as she lowered her head, staring at the pale silver of the carpet, the wild, silken mess of her hair framing some of the mottled bruising. Unable to stop himself, he pushed her hair aside and stared at her neck. Fury bunched and knotted inside him as he stroked a finger down her neck. She flinched.

"I hurt you. I—"

She caught his hand when he would have pulled away. Slowly, she lifted her head and met his gaze.

The pale green of hers seem to glow, something burning in those depths that would have made him half-insane, if she hadn't pushed him past that point long ago. She lifted his hand to her mouth and kissed his palm.

The feel of her lips on his skin had the immediate effect of sending his blood pooling straight down to his groin.

Then she traced her tongue over his skin, and his cock started to pulse in demand.

"Moira. This . . . don't . . ." his voice broke. "Fuck, you can't keep doing this to me."

"I . . ." A spasm of pain crossed her face, but she kept going. Her voice wasn't even a whisper, but she kept trying to force the words out.

"Don't," he said. "It's hurting you to talk, so just stop."

She jerked on his hand, mouthing something to him.

"Damn it, Moira . . ."

She lurched upright and shoved her hands into his pockets. It had him crossing his eyes, but then she stopped, sitting back down with his phone in her hands. "Moira, what the . . ."

She turned it around and displayed it.

The screen was pass-coded.

"Gimme my phone back."

She rolled her eyes and started tapping.

It wasn't his birthday.

It wasn't his mom's.

She paused and slid him a look.

Then she tried hers.

The phone unlocked.

Her heart rolled over in her chest.

He made a grumbling sound and she hurriedly found the search function, then the memo app. She fumbled through writing him a note, cursing her missing voice and the son of a bitch who'd done this. Although, she had to admit one thing: Gideon had made this decision to leave and she might not have figured things out in time to stop him if she hadn't been attacked.

Maybe being pushed down in the dirt and nearly strangled was a very extreme push, but Moira was sometimes a slow learner.

Miserable, she tapped out her message.

Miserable, she read it through. She almost erased it and started over.

But in the end, she could only tell him the truth.

Turning the phone over to him, she sat there, twisting her hands in the wedding-ring quilt that had belonged to her parents and waited.

If I begged you to give me one last chance, would you? You've already given me so many and I know I don't deserve anything else. But I've been blind

and stupid. Lonely and miserable. I love you,
Gideon. I always have. Please don't leave me.

His knuckles went white on the phone.

If she hadn't been watching so closely, she might not have noticed.

Except she always watched him.

Even when she shouldn't have.

She could have told him how many times he'd nicked his face shaving in the past month—twice—and she could have told him how many times he'd either overslept or just hadn't wanted to shave—four.

"Gid—" The pain of speaking was too much, and she couldn't even get a sound out.

He slid her a look from under his lashes before tossing the phone down. It landed with a clatter on her nightstand. Beyond that, he made no move and the room was silent for so long, Moira thought her heart, or what remained of it, was going to shatter. She'd waited too long. *Too long?* A cold voice inside her head was mocking her. *You waited eighteen years. You pushed him away and you kept pushing him away. And now you're surprised he's not interested?*

Her hands shook as she went to shove them through her hair. Upset, she forgot about the scrapes and scratches and bruises until her fingers hit them, sending tiny little shards of pain ricocheting through her skull. Groaning, she lowered them.

Gideon caught them.

Her eyes flew to meet his.

"One of these days, Moira, you'll drive me to do something desperate. Something insane." He pressed his lips to her knuckles, feathering a soft caress over the raw scrapes there.

Sensation whispered through her. Her heart fluttered. All the empty, cold places in her seemed to freeze—*waiting*.

Then he slid his hands along her forearms, up her biceps and along her shoulders, the sides of her neck. He lingered there, tracing the bruises, studying them as if memorizing them.

"Where's your locket?"

CHAPTER NINE

TWENTY-TWO YEARS AGO

Gideon thought maybe he'd been waiting for this moment his entire life.

He was nervous as hell, feeling both a little sick to his stomach and exhilarated. It was sort of like the time he'd gotten onto some cheap-ass roller coaster ride at the state fair with his friends. It had looked like it was made out of Popsicle sticks and held together by bubble gum. Sure, he might get thrown from the car and get his neck broken, but on the other hand, that wasn't likely and it looked like fun. It would probably be okay, right?

This would be okay too. Just like that ride. He thought.

But his hand shook like hell when he lifted his fist to bang on the front door of the big, beautiful mansion where the McKay family lived. It was a damn sight different from the little, rickety house where he lived with his mom, but he'd always been treated nice by the people here.

He almost froze when the door swung open to reveal Moira's father. The man's eyes veered between green and hazel and he had a wide, easy smile on his face. "Gideon, glad you came, son."

Inside, the raucous sounds of a party carried easily. The tall, powerful figure of Devon McKay stepped aside and gestured. "Moira and all her friends are out back. You're welcome to . . . are you feeling okay?"

"Yessir." Gideon went to duck past him.

Devon caught his arm and looked at him narrowly. "Your mama hasn't been taking up with that Slater idiot again, has she? He giving the two of you grief?"

"No." Gideon curled his lip, spine stiffening. Hiram Slater had hauled his fat ass off pretty fast after Gideon had gone after him with a baseball bat. The son of bitch had punched Gideon's mother in the nose. The next day, cops had showed up at the door, claiming Hiram was accusing Gideon of assault. It wasn't the first time he'd gotten in trouble with the law and maybe he would have done what he normally did—mouthed off. But the quiet defeat on his mother's face had gotten to him.

If I'd assaulted him, he'd be dead. I came in on him whaling on my mother. I hauled him off, hit him, then chased him off with a baseball bat. He ever comes out here again, I'll kill him.

"Then why does it look like you haven't been sleeping? You spend all day working out at Roy's farm or what?" Devon's face was concerned.

"No." Shoulders hunched, Gideon looked away, feeling embarrassed. He was used to the questions he got from the McKays. These people were as far from what he had at home as night was from day. He knew his mother loved him, but she barely managed to take care of herself, barely managed to drag herself to her job at the Piggly Wiggly these days, much less concern herself if Gideon looked tired.

"Boy, would you just tell me what's wrong?" Exasperated, the older man planted his hands on his hips.

"I—" Gideon stopped abruptly and then shoved his hands into the pockets of his jeans. This was pointless. It wasn't going to work. Hell, he was a Marshall. With the shit he had behind him, why did he even think he had a chance?

As Devon continued to study him, he suddenly felt pissed off.

What the hell. It wasn't his damn fault that Gideon's dad had been a miserable bastard. Wasn't his fault that the shoes on his feet were so worn out, holes were popping up in the soles. What did it matter?

He was busting his ass to save up money so he could go to college. He *wasn't* his dad. That should count for something.

Jutting his chin up, he met the eyes of Devon McKay— not only the richest man in *town,* some said he was one of the richest fucking men in the whole damn country.

"I wanted to ask Moira out after the party. I thought we could go and get some ice cream."

Devon's eyes narrowed thoughtfully. "Is that so?"

"Yes." Pride wouldn't let him look away. "I got a truck, sir." It wasn't his. It belonged to Roy, the owner of the farm where he worked upwards of fifty hours a week in the summer.

"Yes. I've seen you driving around town in it," Devon said, glancing past him to the rusting old blue Ford pickup. "Heard Roy was going to sell you his old motorcycle, too."

"Yessir. Not yet, but . . ." He stopped, knowing he was babbling. His nerves seemed to multiply as he stood there, in front of the father of the girl who seemed to occupy his thoughts more and more. When Devon didn't say anything else, Gideon hurried to fill the silence. "It's just ice cream. The party's supposed to be over at eight and we could be back by nine thirty. It will barely be dark by then and I'll drive safe and I'll open the doors and I'll treat her right—"

The booming laugh echoed around the foyer, shocking Gideon into silence.

"Hell, boy." He clapped Gideon on the shoulder. "Her mama and I were wondering if you were ever going to get around to asking her."

Staggering under the weight of that big, powerful hand, Gideon just blinked at the big man. "You . . . I . . . what?"

"Son, you've had a hook in your mouth for about . . . well, I can't even tell you when I noticed. The question is . . . how does . . ."

"Gideon! You came!"

At the sound of her voice, Gideon's heart started to race and he looked up. Moira came rushing to him, clad in white shorts and a brilliant green top that bared an inch of toned, soft flesh. She flung herself at him, and he caught her in a hug. Eyes closed, he savored the feel of her so close, letting go too soon.

She pulled back, beaming at him.

Something gold glinted from her neck and he glanced down.

Moira's cheeks flushed and she reached up, covering the necklace. "My present from Mama and Daddy. It's a locket." She cupped it in her hand and displayed it, working the delicate clasp. "It belonged to Madeleine."

As she tilted it for him to see the inside, he nodded. "Beautiful."

But it wasn't the jewelry he was talking about.

Moira's eyes skipped up to his and he swallowed. Gruffly, he repeated, "Beautiful."

She reached up to touch the locket, her cheeks going pink.

NOW

Moira reached up to touch the hollow of her throat where the locket usually rested, only to let her hand fall back to her side. She opened her mouth and then made a face at him, sticking her tongue out.

His brows went up, his gaze focusing on her mouth for a long moment before he finally met her eyes again.

Heart racing, she gestured nervously over toward her dresser. She'd taken the locket off out of habit when she'd changed out of her clothes, going through the motions of getting ready for bed. She was glad she *had* gone through the motions because if she'd been wearing it that night . . . Her breath hitched and before she realized it, her eyes were burning with tears.

Gideon cupped her chin, lifting her face to his.

She swallowed and the pull of his eyes was so intoxicating, she almost forgot to notice the pain in her throat.

"Don't cry." He moved in closer, hips angling in slightly, shoulders rounding as he drew nearer to her. She felt surrounded by him, but it wasn't enough. "Please don't cry. You gut me when you do. You know that."

Shaking her head, she reached for his waist, kneading the taut muscle there. She didn't know if she was telling him she wasn't going to cry or what. But the tears continued to burn and she wanted nothing more than to curl herself around him and cling tight.

If she clung to him tight enough, he could never leave. The scent of him started to go to her head, the rasp of his fingers sending shivers through her as he slid one hand around her neck to stroke her skin.

She caught one wrist in her hand, bringing his hand to her cheek.

Gideon had gone rigid and he didn't move at all when she pressed her mouth to his palm.

She didn't let it stop her.

She'd known he hadn't brought her up here with any intention other than to make her rest. Gideon, ever her protector.

She didn't want *protection,* though. She just wanted him. She wanted what she'd been throwing away all these years and she wanted him back for always. After she'd pressed a kiss to his palm, she nudged him back. His eyes glittered, his cheekbones standing out in stark relief against his deeply tanned skin. He was all hollows and angles and long lean lines. He'd always been able to stop her breath, and the rugged masculinity of him had become even more refined over the past few years.

She caught his face and tugged.

He resisted for a minute and she was almost certain he'd pulled away.

So she rose onto her toes and pressed her lips to his chin, slid them down. When she got to his neck, his head fell to the side—slightly. It was enough. His skin was salty and warm and she could have happily spent the next few hours doing nothing but learning the taste of him all over again. She found the rapid beat of his pulse with her tongue—then her teeth.

"*Fuck!*" Gideon's snarl was vicious and he tangled his hand in her hair.

She found herself trapped in the next moment, between his long, rangy body and the nearest column of her poster bed. Her breath stuttered out of her as he boosted her up, shoving his hips into the cradle of hers. "Don't," he said, his breath coming out in ragged pants. His eyes burned as he stared at her. "You aren't jerking me around like this again, Moira. If you don't mean this . . . if you . . ."

He stopped and looked away and she saw his jaw clenching, his Adam's apple bobbing. The emotion coming out of him battered at her and she wanted to draw him close, stroke away all the misery. But she'd caused this. She'd done this. Could she even *begin* to fix all the pain she'd brought him?

"If you're just going to walk away again, Moira . . . don't."

He put her down and started to pace. Moira wanted to go to him, but what was she supposed to do? Pantomime what she was feeling? She'd already tried to *show* him and that wasn't working.

A muttered curse caught her ears and she looked up just as he spun to face her, rage written all over his normally calm features. "You're killing me inside, okay? You're . . ."

Then he stopped, his cheeks puffing out as he blew out a slow breath. He drew in a deeper, slower one, holding it for a few seconds. She opened her mouth, but he lifted a hand.

He wasn't asking her, though. The question was directed inward.

"Look, you can't even talk," he said, turning away from her. "You can't explain what's going on and I can't see inside your head. We should do this when you *can* talk. Right now, I don't know what you want—"

She reached for the buttons on her shirt. He'd never leave without looking back at her one last time.

She didn't think.

But then again, she'd messed up something awful.

Maybe this wasn't the right way to tell him, but there were a hundred *wrong* ways to let him leave. And that was without trying again. Without reaching out, the way he'd done a hundred times.

She shrugged out of her shirt while he was still standing there. Her bra fell away next.

"When you're feeling better, we'll have to talk . . . Moira?"

She looked at him through the fringe of her hair. He'd turned around.

She found no pleasure in knowing she'd been right. She

was manipulating him and she hated herself, but if this would keep him here, with her, a little longer, until she could convince him she was tired of running, tired of pushing him away?

Then she was going for it.

When she reached for the button of her jeans, her fingers shook.

Gideon was staring at her, his chest rising and falling in a harsh rhythm. She thought maybe that if she reached out then, he might have turned and walked out. So she just pushed her jeans down her thighs, along with her panties.

Naked now, she stood there waiting. She figured this was best. If he turned around, if he rejected her while she was naked, vulnerable, maybe it would even the scales.

The old wooden boards of the floor creaked a little as he took one step, then another toward her. She licked her lips, hardly daring to breathe.

"And what about tomorrow, Mac?" he asked. "You going to push me away . . . *again*?"

She saw the answer he thought to be true in his eyes.

Slowly, she shook her head.

"Mac?"

She held out her hand.

For the longest time, he didn't move.

Then he did—toward her.

In the time it took for her to take a deep breath—whether it was to blow out in relief or to brace herself, she didn't know—Gideon had hauled her up against him and she found herself pressed against the wall.

She went to kiss his neck, but he tangled a hand in her hair and yanked, forcing her gaze to meet his. So she stood there, trembling and barely able to think past the want while he tore at the zipper of his jeans.

He let go of her hair but only so he could pick her up and brace her against the wall at her back. A moment later, he came inside her, hard and forceful, and the screams trapped inside her lungs seemed to explode throughout her entire body instead. She could *feel* that scream—it had a taste, a rhythm, a need all its own and it belonged solely to the man who held her pinned to the wall.

He withdrew, slowly, still staring into her eyes.

She was wet, but not wet enough and his cock rasped over her tissues, an excruciating lesson in sensation. He surged inside her again and she was wetter now, taking him more easily.

She went to kiss him, but he trapped her face in his hand, his palm at her neck while his thumb and index finger cradling the abused flesh with exquisite care. "I'm watching you. I want to see you come . . ." He drove in harder. "I want to see you *break* . . . and damn you to hell, Moira. If you walk away again, you might as well put a knife in me."

Tears burned her eyes and she couldn't stop them from falling, nor did she try. The tears were for him and the misery she knew she'd caused.

When he leaned in and kissed them away, she slid one hand up his shoulder, pushing her fingers into his hair. It curled—barely—around her fingers and she shook as a lifetime of memories warred with the complete and utter insanity of her need.

Again and again, he surged inside her, pushing her to one climax and then another. She tried to scream and couldn't, and the pain didn't matter because she hurt in a million other ways already. She hurt and she hungered and she thought maybe this would kill her, this pleasure, this need . . . this love.

He moved harder and faster, moving up on her body so that he rubbed against her clit with each thrust, his smooth grace falling away under the reckless desire that flooded them both.

She came again just as he crushed her mouth under a kiss so deep and intense, she thought it would consume her.

"*Gideon,*" she whispered against his lips.

Gideon . . .

The weak whisper was so quiet, he didn't know how he heard it. But he did and it struck him to his core. He stood there, the sound imprinting itself on his soul. He stood there . . . and cursed himself a hundred times over.

He didn't know if there were enough words in the English language to describe his stupidity.

It wasn't just because he'd caved when she stood there, stripping herself naked in front of him and then reaching for him.

He was a weak son of a bitch and he would have caved— *had* caved—for far less.

No, he was damning his stupidity as he lay in the bed wrapped around her because he actually believed that *she* might believe her own words this time.

The hope was there, burning bright in a place that had known only darkness for so long.

So he'd be a fool.

He'd let her *believe* he believed her and he'd know it was probably yet one more mistake in a lifetime of them.

Eyes closed, he turned his face into her hair and told himself he'd take the night and let himself be stupid. Tomorrow was soon enough to pick up the pieces.

CHAPTER TEN

Morning came softly.

Moira stirred in the bed as physical needs and stiffness from her injuries became insistent enough to rouse her from slumber. For a moment, she just lay there, facedown in her pillow as she tried to process what was different.

Things felt . . . well, not *wrong*. It was actually good. Actually, things felt all kind of right. But she wasn't used to it because *nothing* had felt so right in a long time and her brain wasn't processing it accurately.

A muscled thigh pushed between hers.

Everything inside her came alive and she jerked her head up.

It smacked against something hard.

A familiar voice filled her ears.

"Ouch!"

Tears burning her eyes, she pushed up onto her elbows and without daring to breathe, she turned her head slightly.

Gideon was no longer half-lying across her back. Weight propped on one elbow, he rubbed at his chin with his other hand. "So much for a lazy wake-up."

Twisting and squirming, she wiggled until she could sit. Staring at him, she raised a shaking hand as she went to touch his chin. Gideon sighed and settled down to sit next to her.

Last night was coming clearer in her head and she slumped down, her head falling to hit his thigh.

"Ah . . ."

It had really happened. She'd had a hundred dreams just like this, but she'd always wake up . . . alone, empty.

There was a red area on his chin and the back of her head throbbed.

But she couldn't think of the last time she'd felt this good.

He threaded his hand through her hair and said, "You do realize you're in a dangerous position, don't you?"

"I am?" It hurt to speak, more than yesterday even, and she knew she'd overused her slowly healing throat, but she didn't care. Letting herself smile, she wiggled around and wrapped a hand around his cock. His flesh jumped at her touch, and when she began to stroke him up and down, a low groan rumbled out of him.

"Dangerous," he said again.

"I might as well make the most of it." She pushed up onto her knees and nudged him flat. His gaze was unreadable but when she lowered her head, she could see the muscles in his belly flex.

She kissed him then, her lips to the head of his cock for a slow, lingering caress. When he pulsed against her mouth, she opened and licked him slowly.

Gideon muttered something unintelligible and tightened his grip on her hair.

But when she tried to take him deeper, her ravaged throat sent out a stark refusal and she pulled away, blinking back tears.

"I tried to warn you," Gideon said, his voice raw as he watched her rubbing her throat. She glared at him through her hair and he laughed, pulling her on top of him, his fingers digging into her hips. "Call me crazy," he said against her mouth. "But I don't really want to see the top of your head when I come anyway. I went too long without this and when I lose it, I want to be looking into your eyes."

The sheer, stark emotion in his voice almost undid her and she pressed her brow to his as he slowly lowered her onto his straining cock.

They were skin to skin, nothing between them. Vaguely, she realized that could be a problem, but the thought faded away as he lifted her back up, then slowly let her sink back down.

It was a wonderful, sweet friction and she curled her arms and legs around him, rolling her hips in a slow circle. He was huge inside her and her head fell back, everything inside her focused on the pulse and throb of his cock and the way they fit.

Gideon pressed his lips to her neck, gently.

The marks there didn't bother her much now, but the poignancy of the touch had a broken sigh tripping out of her.

They came together slow and lazy, sweet and gentle, a complete opposite of the past night and every bit as fulfilling.

When it ended, he lay back and she sprawled on his chest, curling her fingers in the light dusting of hair that spread across his chest. He kissed the top of her head.

"I have to go soon," he said softly.

She nodded.

Neither of them moved.

"I really have to go."

Lifting her head, she peered down at him. "So you said," she replied, her voice raspy. "But you're still here."

He pressed his thumb to her throat, frowning. "If you don't stop talking, Mac, you'll sound like a frog for the rest of your life."

She made a face at him.

He snorted and dropped his head to her shoulder.

He didn't say anything again for several long moments. When he did respond, though, it wasn't in words.

She closed her eyes as he rolled her onto her back and came inside her once more.

"We should be too old for this," she said against his mouth.

"Tell that to my cock. I've been trying to convince myself to leave for thirty minutes now. He's leading me around by my balls."

She laughed only to have the noise die away when Gideon shoved up onto his hands and thrust against her, deep and hard. The lightness had fallen from him and he looked at her with an intensity that had her shivering.

She went to twine her legs around him, but he stopped her, hooking her knees over his elbows and leaning into her harder. The position left her impossibly open and he thrust impossibly deep, stretching her until she whimpered.

His cock swelled and she tried to move.

There was no leverage and she could do nothing but lay there and take it as he rode her, ripping yet another orgasm out of her.

He came again, swearing her name and growled, head thrown back, the veins in his neck standing out, the muscles in his arms rigid.

She felt the jerk of his penis as he climaxed and she moaned, the sensation almost too much against her sensitized flesh.

He let her legs go and thrust his fingers into her hair as he kissed her.

But when she went to kiss him back, he pulled away.

Dazed, Moira watched as he moved around, gathering up his scattered clothes.

"Gideon?"

He shook his head. "I've got to go or I'll spend the rest of the damn day fucking you and making you cry out my name."

A hot jolt of lust coursed through her, her lips parting on a sigh.

"I don't have a problem with that."

But he just shook his head again. "I've got work. A meeting. I'm trying to . . ." The words trailed off and he shot her a look. "You destroy my brain half the time."

She lay in silence as he continued to dress, and when he sat on the edge of the bed to put on his shoes, she reached out a hand to touch his shoulder. He covered her hand with his, but didn't look at her.

"Will you come back tonight?"

Gideon slid her a look.

"Please."

He turned then, kissing her soft and sweet. "Have a good day, Mac. Try to rest your throat." His eyes glittered. "I want to hear you scream . . . really scream."

Clive Owings was in a fucking mess.

He'd gotten caught not only with his pants down, he might have gotten caught with his pants down while fucking a sheep for all the trouble he was in.

"Look . . ." He tried his most charming smile. It fell short even in the best of times and he knew it, but he had to try.

How the fuck was he supposed to know that shit he'd been trying to pawn had drugs inside it? He'd just *found* it, damn it. It had been right there, next to that chick who was on the phone, yelling at some dude—Tijon or Dijon, the hell if he knew. When she got up to pace, wandering farther and farther away, he'd just helped himself to the bag, adding it to the goods he'd found back in Treasure.

Should have just left the shit with that caterwauling bitch, but *nooooo* . . .

He'd been greedy. He'd seen the rings she wore and the watch. All real gold, and the diamonds on her fingers? Real too. He knew real from fake, Clive did, and since she was stupid enough to leave it . . . ? Why not benefit from her idiocy?

"Okay, see . . . this is what happened . . ." He tried his smile again as he told himself he could get out of this. He'd be fine. He always was.

The DEA agents staring at him didn't look impressed by his charming smile.

He wasn't surprised.

It had never much impressed anybody else either.

"I don't do drugs. You should call Chief Marshall back in Treasure. He'll tell you. I might find stuff and sell it, but that don't mean I'm into drugs." Actually, he couldn't stand the shit. His mom had died of a drug overdose and he'd been the one to find her. He frowned now, thinking of it. It was something he avoided doing as much as possible. "I might like my Jack Daniels a bit too much, but I hate drugs."

"I'm sure you do, Mr. Owings." The somber-faced man on the right looked like he had about as much faith in Clive as he did in the human race in general—absolutely none. Tugging out a chair, he lowered himself into it and sat down, elbows braced on the edge of the table. "Why don't you just tell us who your dealer is?"

"I ain't got a fucking dealer!" The words burst out of him in a panic. "Just get a hold of Marshall, okay? He'll tell you."

The agents shared a look, and then the blonde started

in on him. She was even more brutal than her partner, so brutal, Clive couldn't even appreciate the fact that she had one of the nicest sets of tits he'd seen in a long time and a pair of legs that looked like they'd wrap around a man and give him the ride of his life.

She could also make a man sweat, but not in a good way.

Within twenty minutes, he was ready to beg. "Please," he pleaded. "I live in McKay's Treasure. The people there, they know me. I just drove in to sell some stuff . . . I just found that bag *here*. In the city. I'll tell you where. The *only* stuff that I brought in was in the knapsack you took from me. No drugs in it, right?"

The blonde pursed her lips, and he seized on that faint pause. It was a sign, right?

"See! That's proof." He pointed a triumphant finger at nothing in particular. "No drugs on me. Just the drugs in that girl's bag."

"But there is no girl," the agent said, smiling gently. "*You* have the bag."

The two agents left the sniveling mess that was Clive Owings in the interrogation room and left, both for a breath of fresh air and some coffee. Clive was most decidedly *not* up with basic hygiene. He also didn't seem to be too big on brains, but it wouldn't be the first time somebody had played the idiot convincingly.

"There's no way this is our guy."

The woman from the park, Agent Marina Carter, pursed her lips as she studied the man through the window. She was trained to notice things. And she'd noticed him as he dropped down on the bench just down from hers. But she hadn't noticed just how closely he'd been watching her. She never would have taken him for the man they'd been trying to stake out.

But he'd taken the bag, just as they'd arranged.

She'd been working this op for seven months, closing in on one dealer after another, moving up the chain and now . . . Sighing, she looked over at the other two agents. "Can we at least check his story? I don't think it's him either, but I don't want to risk it."

"We'll call up this guy in . . ." Agent Bryan Daniels flipped out his notebook and checked the name again. He frowned and slid his partner a look. "McKay's Treasure? What the fuck kind of name is that for a town?"

"Yankee." His partner clucked her tongue. Agent Kim Wycoff folded her arms over her chest and studied the man on the other side of the glass. "I think just about everybody south of Tennessee knows about the McKays. And quite a few people north."

"Yankee." Marina grinned at her. "That's the only explanation."

"Hey." Bryan glanced up. "I've heard the name *McKay*. They own a bunch of shit."

"A bunch of shit. That sums it up. Including most of a damn town." Kim shrugged. "There's a whole story that goes back to the Civil War, or earlier. I can't remember. Anyway, this guy comes over from Scotland, the first McKay—name was Patrick McKay. I was born in Mississippi so I've heard a fair amount about him. He used to hunt river pirates, then one of his friends turned on him and he was falsely imprisoned and executed. He was a rich son of a bitch. Married, had a couple of kids. Another friend, a guy named Steele, stepped up and helped his wife out, ended up marrying her. The McKay family is practically a dynasty now. The town was named after him a few years after he died. McKay's Treasure."

Bryan rolled his eyes. "Weird."

"I've always liked the story." Marina glanced over at Kim, smiled a little. "It's . . . bittersweet, I guess."

"Yeah." Kim looked sad. "Could have lived if he would

have sacrificed his honor, but he was the kind of man who lived by his word to the bitter end. Anyway . . . I know Marshall, sort of. Had a few run-ins when he worked in Memphis. He's a solid cop. I'll shoot him a call." Kim paused and sighed. "Man, I hope he can give us a reason to push this prick. Maybe he was sent to be a go-between or something."

Bryan rubbed the back of his neck, still staring at the man on the other side of the glass. "I think I'm going to go talk to the pawn shop owner again. If he does this sort of thing often, then the guy probably knows him. If we're barking up the wrong tree, I'd rather know now."

He paused and looked down at all the stuff they'd taken off the man and shook his head, disgusted. "We need to make sure we get this all logged as evidence." He picked up a camera and hit the power button, but it was dead. The watch still ticked, and one look at the maker told him the watch was worth well over a thousand new. There was also some small electronics, including two iPods and a phone. "Tell you what, though. No way this shit was his. Asshole out there is already complaining about getting this stuff back. Think we can still track down the owners?"

"Chief?"

His assistant caught sight of him on the phone and winced. Gideon held up a hand. "Just a second—Zeke, now . . . come on, Zeke. I've taken care of two tickets for you. The least you can do is hear me out. Yeah, yeah . . . just a second, okay?"

He shot Darby a look. "Make it fast."

"I'm sorry." She nodded at the phone on his desk. "You've got a Kim Wycoff on the phone. She . . . ah, she says she's with the DEA. Calling about something regarding Clive."

"Clive Owings?" Gideon felt his eyebrows shoot straight

up into his hairline. He resisted the urge to shove a hand through his hair—and rip a fistful out. "What did . . . wait. You know what? Unless it's an emergency, Clive can wait. The asshole probably got himself in trouble again and I'm not dropping what I'm doing for him."

"And if it's an emergency?" Darby asked, looking panicked at the idea of telling a DEA agent *no*.

"Then I'll talk to her." He went to hit the mute button on the phone, but paused a moment. "Relax. I know Wycoff. She's a reasonable sort. Tell her that as long as she keeps Clive watered and he has a toilet and access to meals, he'll be happy enough. Or at least, he won't complain too much."

She nodded and he turned his attention back to Zeke.

He was on a mission, damn it, and he wasn't about to be denied.

This time, he wouldn't take no for an answer.

When he hung up the phone fifteen minutes later, all but blue in the face from talking to a wall, he had to admit defeat.

Zeke wasn't going to sell him the damn dogs.

Although, to be clear, it wasn't Gideon Zeke had a problem with.

It was the McKays.

Gideon was pretty damn sure Brannon and Zeke hadn't ever tangled. He would have heard about it. Brannon and Zeke would either get along or they'd hate each other, but one way or another, he'd know. It wasn't very likely Zeke would come into contact with Moira, and Neve had been gone.

You're fixating on this to keep from thinking about her, he told himself.

And it was nothing more than the truth.

But he was also pissed off and irritated and more than a little confused. Zeke was a businessman. Didn't make sense why he wouldn't sell some of his dogs, especially to some people who'd pay a damn pretty penny for them.

The alarm system was problematic, to say the least.

Knowing the McKays as he did—and knowing the brains behind the system, he knew he wouldn't be able to count on getting inside easily, especially not if he wanted to get in and out without anybody being the wiser.

But there were other ways to get to them. Other ways to weaken and tear at them from the inside out.

He didn't just want them *broken* after all. He wanted them to suffer.

Especially the oldest two. Moira for her arrogance, and Brannon . . . well, there were no words to describe just how many ways he wanted Brannon to suffer and no way to list how many *reasons* the man *should* suffer.

Neve . . . well, if she'd just stayed out of Treasure, he'd have left her alone. Just having her gone from here had been a chink in their armor, an invisible weak link that the other two would never acknowledge.

Pointing William Clyde at the youngest McKay after he'd "accidentally" bumped into her in New York had been a stroke of genius. He'd thought about moving on her himself, but she'd been a bit young for his taste and he'd had no desire to wait for her to mature.

He hadn't been able to do anything for the longest time. Frozen by the circumstances, and his own lack of resources, he'd had been forced to watch and wait.

When he had finally been able to take action, Neve had been the one he'd come across first and he'd considered it kismet. She'd been young, naïve, and desperate for approval—also, very, very drunk. That should have made it easy to get what he wanted from her, but when he'd pushed and prodded, she'd just giggled about how she used to dig for treasure around the estate.

Then she'd started to cry. Poor little thing—her family didn't understand her and nobody loved her. Then she'd begun to whine about a rejection from some stupid modeling agency.

If he'd had to spend a few more minutes with her, he might have put a hole in his head.

But he needed her out of the way.

She was . . . clever.

Sober, she might have been his undoing.

In between sobs and sniffles, she'd peered at him, blinking those big, green eyes. "You . . ." She'd pointed a finger at him. "Your face. It reminds me of . . . somefin . . . something. Somebody. Yeah. Somebody."

He hadn't had to wonder who.

One of the few things that hadn't been sold off or destroyed was locked away, and he had seen the resemblance himself. He wondered how she'd known, but he knew he needed her *gone*.

Later, he'd learn just how much it made them all suffer, and that was just a bonus. He'd pointed William Clyde her way, knowing the man had always loved a pretty girl and a pretty, *naïve,* and *needy* girl was even better for the miserable prick.

The stupid prat would have been drawn to Neve no matter what, but once he knew the pretty, naïve girl had a connection to a man he'd hated, William had been done for and it was just a matter of sitting back and watching them collide.

Really, he'd outdone himself there.

He hadn't expected what came later, though.

Personally, he'd found it distasteful but he knew it was

yet one more thing that would make them suffer. They *should* suffer.

He wanted them to suffer until they broke, and then he'd make his move.

The next step on his plan was subtle. Brilliant, but subtle. Brannon had provided the financing for the old goat who bought the bookstore and he was part owner—a *silent* owner, perhaps, but his name was on the deed too, and that meant only one thing.

The bookstore, and anybody associated with it, was fair game.

He'd waited until she left, watched from a window in the back as she stroked a hand down a stack of books, a smile on her creased face.

Once the old woman who ran the place had left, locking the front door and walking purposefully down the sidewalk, he went in through the window he'd unlocked when he went into the store earlier.

He'd gone in during the midday rush. McKay's Treasure was a town full of readers, and he knew just how very busy it was on a Tuesday. He'd bided his time and waited until the bathroom in the back wasn't busy and then he'd slipped in.

Nobody had noticed him move quietly to the back window, just as nobody had noticed him flipping the latch open.

Nobody had noticed him checking for cameras, either.

He'd mentally thanked the old lady who owned the store for wanting to keep the all money given for the renovations focused on the merchandise and design. She hadn't invested anything in security and Brannon, being a clueless sod, hadn't paid any attention at all to her plans.

He'd pay attention now.

Nothing burned quite like paper.

And no paper burned as well as *old* paper.

Treasure New & Old carried all the latest in bestsellers and regional and genre fiction, but they also did a bustling business in used books. Those used books filled the backroom like miniature paper columns, reaching up into the sky.

He worked in utter silence, the wind drifting in from the window he'd left partially open, bringing with it the scent of more rain.

He was good at rigging up fires.

He'd done it before, after all.

That was when they'd thrown him out of university. He disagreed on the why, of course. The fire he'd started hadn't been a big deal. They'd thrown him out because the bastards had been fools, incapable of seeing the light of reason, and they'd decided they didn't like some young upstart who was smarter than themselves.

He'd dealt with their lot before.

Actually, he'd dealt with them *after*, too. And that was the most fun.

He checked the time before looking up to study his chain, carefully constructed from old bits of cloth and paper, soaked with a light accelerant that wouldn't leave a heavy smell. It could be detected, of course, but only if they brought in an arson investigator.

The pièce de résistance . . . he pulled a pack of cigarettes out of his back pocket and lit one, puffing on it enough to make it look like it had been hurriedly smoked and then disposed of.

Everybody knew Mrs. Stafford, daughter of the original owner, was a closet smoker and everybody knew she'd been trying desperately to quit ever since her son-in-law had been diagnosed with lung cancer a few months ago.

He smashed it out and then dumped it into the trash can

before checking the setup. Everything looked good. As long as his luck held . . .

He lit the chain of fabric and paper, dropped it as it went up in a whoosh, and bolted, flying through the window he'd used as an entrance just as the room went up in a whoosh.

He took his chosen exit route and was coming down the street just as people started to notice the flames. Feigning shock, he rushed down the alley, shouting out for Mrs. Stafford, using just the right amount of fear in his voice.

He timed it perfectly.

Firefighters had to drag him outside after he'd successfully busted down the door.

"You're a fucking wreck, man." One of the firefighters handed him a bottle of water, shaking his head.

He managed what he hoped was a convincingly strained smile. "I guess I should haven't been so hasty. I just saw the store and panicked."

In the crowd gathered around him, he saw more than a few sets of admiring eyes linger on him before they slid away. Mrs. Stafford, the woman he'd supposedly been trying to save, was standing nearby and sobbing into a handkerchief.

She smelled, faintly, of cigarette smoke.

The ruse had worked.

The bookstore was ruined.

And nobody suspected him.

It was well after five—as a matter of fact, it was almost eight. If Gideon hadn't known Agent Kim Wycoff, he would have held off calling until tomorrow, but he did know her well enough to know she was going to try to peel a piece of his hide for taking so long to call back as it was. Since he was already missing a few layers of his hide, he figured it would be best to get it over with.

"About damn time," she said in lieu of greeting.

"Nice talking to you, Kim. Yeah, it has been a miserable, wet winter . . . nah, I doubt I'll do much for Christmas. What about you?"

Her laugh was soft and husky. For a few short weeks, they'd been lovers.

Kim would have been happy to make it longer, but Gideon had been reeling from Moira's marriage to Hurst and the last thing he'd wanted was a relationship. Now talking to her left him more than a little uncomfortable, just because whenever they did talk, she managed to bring up subtle hints of those few hot, torrid weeks together.

"You always were one for small talk, weren't you, lover?" she asked.

He didn't respond.

"Or maybe not." Her tone changed—a subtle shift, but Gideon could practically hear the wheels spinning in her head. "How is life, Gideon?"

"It's fine. I don't imagine that's what we've got to discuss though, is it, Agent?"

"I've always got time for old friends."

He braced himself for the barrage of questions, but to his surprise, she let it go. "I need your take on a man who says he's from down your way, Gideon. Goes by the name Clive Owings."

"I got your message earlier." Gideon rubbed the back of his neck, lifting his head to stare up at the sky. Sucking in a deep breath, he caught the acrid tinge of smoke and frowned. "Owings is a pain in the ass—a stupid one. More of a nuisance than anything else."

"Nuisance, as in small and annoying?"

Gideon snorted and sampled the air again. That smell of smoke was definitely there. Thicker now, too. Walking down the sidewalk, he looked north up Main, then south. "Kim, I've got to be honest . . . Owings doesn't possess the brain cells or the energy to be much more than small and annoying. He'd have to work to be anything more than a lazy bastard and that goes against his most deeply held beliefs."

"Well, shit." She drew the second word out into two syllables.

"Problem?"

"We picked him up at a pawn shop after the owner's new wife got suspicious about some stuff he was trying to sell. Turns out we'd been waiting for it—DEA we. It had been earmarked for possible drug trafficking, but disappeared out from under the noses of the boys on the border. Thought maybe we had a line in."

"With Clive?" Now Gideon laughed. It was a sardonic sound, but it felt good to laugh all the same. "Trust me, he couldn't think up a way to hide a pimple on his ass. No way would he think to hide something as important as drugs."

"Okay." Kim blew out a sigh, sounding disgusted. "Thanks, Marshall. We might be releasing your boy soon."

"Can't wait."

He disconnected, still doing a slow sweep of Main. An odd flicker in the bookstore caught his eye. He stared, waiting to see it again.

Then . . . *Oh, fuck*.

CHAPTER ELEVEN

It was silly the way her heart lurched when she saw him.

It was foolish the way her breath caught.

She didn't care.

Silly and foolish, she'd welcome them both, and she wouldn't even let herself feel bad as she moved into closer to Gideon through the mass of bodies gathered in clusters on the street.

One group of bodies, decidedly smaller than the rest, caught her attention and she lifted a hand in greeting. Brannon and Hannah, Neve and Ian, already here. She'd go speak to them in a minute.

Gideon hadn't seen her yet.

But before she could reach him, somebody crashed into her. She managed to hold back her instinctive sneer when she found herself looking into Joe Fletcher's gaze. His ever-present sneer was there, and she put a few more inches between them as he looked from her over toward the bookstore.

"Damn shame about your brother's place," he said.

"Yes. Excuse me, Joe."

"I mean, they just finished fixing it up. Guess it's a good thing he has insurance and all, but that poor old lady . . .

that place is her life." Joe heaved out a dramatic sigh. "Seems like everything you all touch lately is bound to get fucked up. That girl at your brother's winery dies. This place catches fire."

The edges of her temper fraying, Moira leaned in. "Joe . . . get out of my way, otherwise you're going to have *another* McKay woman put you on the ground."

His face went red but when she pushed around him, Joe didn't say anything. She made her way to Gideon without anybody else getting in her way. Once she reached him, Moira smoothed a hand down his arm and waited as he finished speaking to one of the firefighters.

Her heart ached as she gazed at the hollowed-out guts of the once-thriving bookstore. She felt Gideon's eyes skim over at her, although he didn't stop speaking in a low voice to Dirk Hutton, the fire chief.

The fireman slid her a look and on some unspoken cue, he and Gideon both stopped speaking. Dirk beat Gideon to the punch as he tipped an imaginary hat toward her. "Ma'am. We don't have much information for you or your brother just yet."

"I wasn't here to ask for any," she said mildly. Then she glanced over her shoulder at Brannon. He was with Hannah, one arm around her shoulders, while he had his other hand folded over Neve's.

Neve was crying silently, staring at the ruin of the building while tears ran unchecked down her face. One of the last places Neve had gone with their parents had been the bookstore.

Damn it all to hell.

"Brannon will be ready to push for something, though," she warned. "And soon."

At that very moment, her brother looked up and met her gaze over their sister's head. She had no doubt he was re-membering the very same night she was remembering.

"As soon as we know something." Hutton nodded at her and then turned to stride back toward the still-smoking building.

Moira reached up instinctively.

Gideon tensed.

She almost pulled away, but didn't let herself. She'd done that for too long. So long, she'd just about destroyed them both. When she wiped a smudge away from his cheek, his lids flickered. "I get the feeling you're going to be pretty tied up tonight."

"Looks like."

She smiled weakly. "I guess it would be a bad time to pout."

His gaze dropped to her mouth. "Pout away." Gideon's eyes, always watchful, slid around.

She wasn't sure why he bothered. They were standing in front of probably thirty or forty people. They had no privacy, not standing out on the street in Treasure. She didn't care, though.

"I got to admit, Mac, I half-expected you to call me and tell me something had come up."

She opened her mouth, an ache in her chest, but before she could figure out what to say to him, he looked away. "Your voice is better."

"I rested it," she said lamely. She hadn't let herself talk at all until nearly five, and she'd sipped on lemonade and tea most of the day. Her throat was still sore, but it was amazing the difference from last night to today.

Somebody called his name, and she blew out a tired sigh. "You're going to be busy for a while."

"Yeah."

"I should go then." She moved away, but he caught her hand.

She looked back at him.

His mouth was on hers in the next second.

It was a short, quick, rough kiss, one that left her panting.

When he lifted his head, he paused momentarily to murmur, "Rain check."

Then he was gone, lost in the rush of emergency personnel and other cops.

"You kissed my sister."

Gideon had been expecting Brannon to show up.

He'd even been expecting something along these lines. Since the question didn't really catch him off guard, he took his time lifting his head. He nodded slowly, pretending to think the comment through and then he said, "Well, yes. I believe I did. Quite often, in fact."

"I'm not talking about years ago." Brannon jammed his hands on his hips. "I'm talking about today."

"I was talking about today, too." Then Gideon shrugged. "Or at least last night."

Brannon's eyes narrowed. Then he squeezed them shut, lifting his face to the sky as he muttered something.

Gideon thought he might be counting.

Just annoy the bastard, he said, "Your sister knew what sex was before you knew what your penis was, Bran."

"She did not." Brannon's voice was surprisingly mild, and he finally looked back at Gideon.

To Gideon's surprise, the look in his eyes was one of sympathy. Brannon looked around the mostly empty bullpen before he slipped inside Gideon's office and sat down. "You sure you wanna go down this road, man?" Brannon asked softly.

Gideon stared at his friend. Brannon was like a brother to him. Had been for a long time. "I would have thought you'd be here to tell me to take it easy with your sister," he said levelly, slumping back in his chair.

"My sister's been carving your heart out for close to

twenty years," Brannon said, shaking his head. "I'd be blind not to see it. You almost seemed level, Gideon. You were seeing Maris. What happened?"

"I realized I was lying to myself." He shrugged and shoved upright, moving over to the window. Fire trucks were still parked out in front of the bookstore, but it had nothing to do with the blaze and everything to do with the reasons behind it. Looking for why that fire had started. "It's never been anybody but her, never will be anybody but her. I wasn't being fair to Maris. I had to end it."

"And when Moira gets scared again?" Brannon sounded uneasy.

Gideon looked back at him.

Brannon held still for a moment and then, as if the still-ness was foreign—and miserable—he all but leapt out of his seat and started to pace. "Look, I'm not saying . . . I love Moira, you know that. I want her happy, but I think she's happier being . . . miserable. Miserable and safe, so nobody can get in and hurt her."

Gideon listened, although Brannon wasn't saying any-thing he didn't know.

"So what do you do when she panics again?"

"I leave." Gideon had made up his mind during the day. He was the moth to Moira's flame and he was too weak to deny the heat of her. As long as he was here. Turning to Brannon, he told the truth. "If she turns away again, even one more time, Brannon, that's it. I'm done. I'll leave."

He made a gesture at the office, his badge. "This, Trea-sure . . . even you and Neve. I'm walking away and I doubt I'll even stop long enough to say good-bye. I can't keep living like I have been."

"Have you thought maybe it would be better to just leave now?" Brannon's voice was low.

"Yeah." Gideon dropped down behind the desk, bent over the notes he'd been making. "But I've always been a dumb-ass idiot, Bran. You know that better than most. I've got work."

There was a taut moment of silence before Brannon blew out a breath. "Okay, then. You'll let me know what you learn about the store, right?"

"Yeah." Grim, Gideon stared at his notes as Brannon left his office. He'd let him know. Shit, he could do it now.

Somebody had a big, righteous hate-on going for the McKays.

He'd heard what Mrs. Stafford had said—she'd had a quick smoke in the back. But she'd flushed it down the toilet. She always did. That didn't mean much to him. He knew it wouldn't mean much to the investigators either.

What mattered to him was every bad thing that had happened to the McKays in recent months.

Hannah's crash aside, there was the attack on Moira. Now the bookstore was destroyed.

Everybody knew the importance that bookstore had to the McKays.

Son of a bitch.

The door squeaked like a deranged mouse when Brannon let himself into the loft. He rarely slept here anymore, but he'd needed to talk to Gideon and he hadn't wanted Hannah by herself.

The son of a bitch who'd stabbed him, who had likely killed Shayla and Roger Hardee, was still out there somewhere and Brannon wasn't taking chances.

Which was why there was a big, brooding Scot on his couch.

The Scot was supposed to be awake. How he'd slept through that door opening, Brannon didn't know.

He took one step in Ian's direction, determined to club him across the head for falling asleep without setting the alarm.

"Do y'know," Ian said, his brogue thicker with sleep. "That soddin' door sounds like a mouse with rabies?"

Brannon stopped midstep. "I thought you were asleep."

"What kind of fool could sleep through that ruckus? I'm just resting m' eyes." Ian tipped a glass his way. "Had a pint while I was waiting." Then he nodded toward the spare room on the far side of the converted loft. "My beautiful bride-to-be was worn out. She's fallen asleep. I guess that means I'm sleeping over."

"I don't mind my sister bunking with me." He paused before continuing. "That doesn't mean you need to."

"Where goes the redhead, so goes I," Ian said contentedly.

Brannon flipped him off as he headed into the kitchen to pour himself some wine. He went with the scuppernong they'd bottled not too long ago and settled down on the armchair. Meeting Ian's eyes, he said, "Moira and Gideon."

"I saw." Ian shrugged. "I can't say I'm surprised."

"I sure as fuck am." Brooding, he looked into his glass. "He'll leave. She'll pull back and this time, it will be too much. He'll just be gone."

"Or . . ." Ian bobbed his head from side to side as if weighing options. "He won't leave. Because she's finally realized she's ready to let herself live."

"You're an eternal optimist, Ian. I never would have thought."

Ian shook his head. "No. What I am is a man who knows the sight of a woman when she's reached the end of her rope." He sighed, stretched massive arms over his head before he straightened up and sat so that he faced Brannon. "I've seen that look, Bran. Maybe my gran didn't have the same reasons as your sister, but desperation is desperation. Gran was looking for something to hold on to—and she had me. Then she didn't. Moira is looking for something, too. She's got something—some *body*. Gideon's always been there. She's just been fighting it. Fighting herself."

Brannon scowled into his wineglass as he thought through what Ian was saying.

"It's not the same," he said finally. "Moira didn't . . . your grandfather was an ass, Ian. I know that. It's not the same with Moira."

"No. With Moira, life is what's beating her down. And sometimes, *she* is responsible for the beatin'. Often, though, she wasn't. She loses her parents and had to raise the two of you, had to finish university, had to take over this massive empire your family has created." Ian's face contorted into a grimace. "Neve tried to explain some of the things McKay has their hands in and my eyes all but crossed. Moira was what . . . eighteen when she had to take over? And Neve . . ."

His eyes fell away.

"We fucked up there," Brannon said sourly.

"Aye." Ian wasn't one to beat around the bush, not even for his best friend. Rising to his feet, he moved halfway across the floor, his eyes on the closed door that led to where Neve slept. "I'm not going to say you're to blame. You were a kid yourself. Moira too. If Ella Sue had pushed?"

He shrugged and looked back at Brannon. "She needed a parent. Needed adults who could say no, who could make her feel safe. She didn't have that and it just made everything harder for all of you. But this isn't a case of fault. None of you had a fair shake. Moira had a man who wanted to stand with her, help her . . . but she had to play martyr."

"That's not what—" Brannon cut himself off and started to laugh. "The fuck it ain't. She wouldn't see it as playing martyr, but the hell if that isn't what she did. Gideon only wanted to be with her."

"Likely, she wanted the same. My take? She didn't think it was fair to him." Ian shrugged. "Maybe she's ready to stop being stupid, stop worrying about fair and just think about what they both need."

"If you two boys are done talking about your feelings . . ."

They both turned as one.

Brannon felt blood rushing up to his cheeks as he saw Hannah standing in the doorway of the room they shared—when they slept here. She wore one of his shirts, the hard mound of her belly making a slight curve against it. She looked insanely sexy and somehow innocent, her hair a tangle around her shoulders and her eyes sleepy.

"I'm really, really tired and unlike Neve, I don't sleep like the dead these days."

"I'm not sleeping like the dead!" A muffled voice shouted from behind a closed door. "I just like listening to them when they don't know I'm listening."

Ian's grin spread across his face while Brannon's flamed hotter.

The door to the room Neve was sharing with Ian jerked open and his little sister stood there, eyes wide. "Are you just *now* telling me that Moira and Gideon are back together?"

CHAPTER TWELVE

"Are you serious—what, no. Fine." Moira braced her hands on the desk and stared at the printouts in front of her. As a voice continued to yammer in her ear, she squeezed her eyes closed. "I said *fine*, Baxter. I'll be in there by . . ."

She looked up at the clock, gauged the time. "I need two hours."

Her admin squawked and she laughed. "I'm not killing myself to get there any sooner. I'm down at the ass end of Mississippi. Two hours is the best I can do."

"Okay . . . I . . . I guess I'll stall them or something but Moira . . . please hurry. These people aren't joking around."

"I didn't think they were. The IRS doesn't have a sense of humor."

She slammed the phone down, took a deep breath. All that did was make the phone ring again.

She wanted to shriek, and almost ignored it, but the name that flashed across the caller ID made her belly go hot.

"If you have bad news, just hang up," she said in lieu of greeting.

There was a faint pause and then Gideon Marshall said, "I guess you've been having a rough day."

"Lousy. Are you calling to make it worse?"

"Actually, I was hoping I could talk you into playing hooky for a few hours."

She wanted to say yes. Imagined calling Baxter and telling him the IRS idiots could deal with the lawyers. That's why they had them. But Baxter had told her they'd requested to meet with her . . . personally.

That was just *odd*.

It wasn't like McKay hadn't gone through audits or anything. There were probably audits she wasn't even aware of—again, that's why she had accounting and why she had lawyers.

"I can't." Regret was a knot in her chest. "I just had a call from my assistant in Jackson. The IRS wants to talk to me."

There was a pause. Gideon said slowly, "Did you say the IRS?"

"Yeah. Go figure."

"Are you in trouble?"

"I don't see how. We run a clean business, Gideon." She scowled. "Okay, we as a company are clean. But I can't speak for every single soul under me. If I find out . . ."

"Moira, take a deep breath. Find out what's going on."

She stuck her tongue out at the phone.

"Call me later, okay?"

He disconnected a moment later and she dropped the phone onto the counter, leaning forward to smack her head on the door of the nearest cabinet. It didn't help. She hit it harder.

Still no help—she was conscious.

"Try counting to a hundred."

At the sound of Ella Sue's soft voice, she glanced behind her. "It won't help."

"Why did I hear the vicious little letters . . . *I R S*?" Ella Sue looked concerned as she wandered into Moira's office.

"Because they are coming by today. They'd like to see me, ask me a few questions." Moira managed a brilliant, sharp smile. "At the main branch."

"Did that idiot boy explain that you don't *live* in Jackson?"

Moira sighed and passed a hand over her eyes. "Baxter panicked. I'll get this taken care of. It's not like I don't have records upon records to back things up. It's probably nothing major." She gave Ella Sue a distracted smile, although her mind was on Gideon.

She would have loved to play hooky.

"I need to hit the road. I'll be pushing it as it is." She gave Ella Sue a quick hug before grabbing her laptop and the backup hard drive that held the most important data.

It took less than ten minutes for her to hit the road.

By eight twenty, she was cruising down the highway, on her way into Jackson.

"Well, so much for that idea." Disgusted, Gideon tossed down his phone and then looked out the window. He'd already made plans to drive out to Zeke's and try to talk him into relenting.

The fire at the bookstore had pretty much cinched it.

Although there was no official response yet, the investigator was almost positive it *had* been arson. That meant just one more weird thing in a string of weird things that had been following the McKays around like a cloud for months.

He was going to get Moira—and Neve *and* Hannah— damn dogs if he had to wring Zeke's neck to talk him into it. He wouldn't have to, though. He'd just remind Zeke that he owed him. Zeke would balk and it would probably destroy their friendship, but it would do the job and that was what Gideon cared about at the moment.

But he'd wanted to take Moira with him.

Maybe she could help get to the bottom of why Zeke had a problem with her family.

The door to Brannon's townhouse swung open and Gideon cocked his head, watching as Neve and Ian, then Hannah and Brannon came tumbling out.

Actually . . . maybe what he needed wasn't the boss of the clan, but the charmer.

He tugged out his phone and punched in a number, watching as a couple hundred feet away, Neve pulled her phone from her pocket.

"I hear you kissed my sister."

Gideon rolled his eyes.

"I hear you've been kissing the bartender."

Neve's response was a chuckle.

"Listen, Trouble . . . I've got to do something today and I need your help. Please don't say no."

She slid a glance his way—or toward the government building that housed the police station. He didn't know if she could see him or not, but he could see her as she lowered the phone and turned her head, speaking to Ian.

A moment later, she was back on the phone. "What do you need and when?"

"Ah . . . are you sure you're not lost?" Neve looked around as Gideon pulled his truck onto the unmarked lane. They'd been driving for two hours, and they'd left Treasure and then the state of Mississippi behind entirely within the first hour of the drive.

At her question, Neve saw a grin crack Gideon's grim face for the first time that morning. "Come on now, Trouble. Since when have you ever known me to get lost?"

"Okay." She caught her bottom lip between her teeth

and tugged, releasing it slowly as she continued to study the greenery surrounding them. Kudzu was so thick, it looked like it was trying to take over the road. As a matter of fact, just about everything green was so thick. Mother Nature was fighting to take over here with a vengeance. Spanish moss fell in a heavy curtain, all but blotting out the sky, while the vines of the kudzu blocked out everything that wasn't in front of or behind them. "Maybe you're not lost. But you do know, there's a first time for everything."

He laughed. "Relax. I've been here before. Zeke just likes his privacy."

"I thought dogs needed to be around others . . . get socialized."

"They get socialized. He takes them out. He just doesn't *live* out in the middle of people."

Huffing out a breath, she crossed her arms over her chest and went to looking out the window. She'd avoided it most of the drive in, but the green wrapping around them was making her claustrophobic. "So. You and Moira in a liplock. What else?"

"I don't kiss and tell."

She slid him a narrow look and then crowed. "Hot damn! Finally!"

Gideon sighed.

"So are you two like . . . *back*?"

He shot her a look then focused on the road, coming around a turn. Finally, light showed at the end of the road—real light, not just sun filtering down through gaps in the canopy. "I don't know what we are, Neve. Not yet."

"But . . ." She stopped, frowning and shaking her head. "If you two . . ."

He chuckled. "I can't believe you're getting shy at this point."

"Oh, shut up." She stuck her tongue out at him. "I can't

girl talk with you, Gideon. Don't worry. I'll do that with Moira later."

His cheeks went red.

Cheered by the sight, Neve grinned. "Anyway. What *is* going on?"

"I'm taking it as it comes—one day at a time." Gideon eased down on the brake as the truck broke out of the trees. "All I can do, Neve."

She just stared at him.

Aware of her intense study, but not willing to look her in the eye yet, Gideon focused on the house and the sprawling grounds. "Best to take it slow, Trouble. If . . ."

When he didn't continue, Neve took over. "If she changes her mind, it will be a little easier for you if you're not head-deep."

"I've been head-deep with her since I was sixteen." Gideon didn't think anything about this was easy. But he had to protect what he could.

Neve leaned across the truck and hugged him. "It's going to work out this time, Gideon. I promise."

By mutual agreement, they climbed out of the truck.

There was a lean, grizzled man on the porch, already waiting for them.

He had to be in his sixties, but there was no spare flesh on him, and from where she stood, watching him, she could see the hard, carved lines of his face. He looked like he'd been made of leather.

He was flanked by two dogs, and both canine and human watched her.

"I take it that's Zeke." She ran her tongue across her teeth. "Okay, let me run this through from the top. You wanted to bring me out here, but didn't he say he wasn't selling a dog to no damn McKay?"

"Well . . ." Gideon drew that word out, making the single syllable into three as Neve shot him a look.

Prevaricating just wasn't Gideon's style, and when he wouldn't look at her, she narrowed her eyes. "What's up, Gideon?"

"Zeke isn't exactly expecting us." He pinned her with a direct look. "I want to see you work that infamous charm of yours. Get him to sell you a dog, Trouble. One for you, Moira *and* Hannah."

"A . . ." Her mouth fell open and she went back to staring toward the house. It was the largest of the buildings and stood in the middle of a series of fenced-in areas, while off to the back was a garage.

The fenced-in areas held a strange hodge-podge of items. It almost looked like a child's playground with its assortment of tunnels, teeter-totters, and slides. Then there were the dogs. Big, watchful dogs.

The dogs, six of them, all sat by the fence, ears pricked and eyes watchful.

"They look like they're deciding on which one of us would taste better," she said.

"Nah. I'm too old and mean and you're too skinny." Gideon reached over and tugged on her hair.

"Very funny. I'll have you know, I've put on ten pounds since I came home."

He snorted. "Only ten? With Ella Sue's cooking, it should be double that."

A cold wind whipped her hair into her eyes and she shivered, watching as the old man on the steps descended and started their way.

Lips pursed, Neve shifted her attention from Zeke to the dogs. The one on the end cocked his head, studying her.

The guy called out to the animals and one by one, they all turned away. Save for that dog on the end. He was still staring at Neve, and now he was wagging his tail.

She found herself smiling at the dog, and the tail beat harder.

The man saw it, too and gave the dog an exasperated look.

"So he doesn't want to sell to us and you want me to use my charm to . . . what exactly?"

Gideon shrugged. "Make him change his mind."

"We do business." She made a face. "Mostly Moira does business. But the McKays are in business to make money. Sometimes people's toes get stepped on, but that's life. Just how did we step on the toes of a guy who trains dogs?"

"That's why you're here." Gideon gestured toward the fenced-in areas and the man who'd moved to the fence watching them with suspicion. "See, you're the charming one, Neve. If anybody can get him to sell you the dogs, it's you. Once she realizes he's holding a grudge, Moira will shut him down. Brannon will tell him to kiss ass. You, though . . . well . . ." Gideon shrugged, that faint smile still on his face. "All you have to do is talk to him for a few minutes, Neve. You'll have him eating out of your hand."

"So you brought me here to flirt with him?" Dismayed, she glanced over at the heavy clang of metal crashing into metal.

"No." Gideon shook his head, watching as Zeke finished shutting the gate. "He wouldn't fall for that. But Neve, you just being you is enough. Trust me, I know Zeke."

"What brings you down here, Marshall?" Zeke's voice called out, preventing Neve from asking anything else.

She gave Gideon one more look and then turned, watching as Zeke came their way, along with one of the dogs. A grin burst across her face when she saw which one it was. The curious one. At her smile, the dog's tail started to wag.

The dog's ears perked, and she watched as the animal shot a hopeful look up at the man. The man blew out a hard sigh. "Torch, you're a pitiful mess, you know that? Sit down."

The dog obediently lowered his rump but started to

whine low in his throat, shifting his gaze to stare at Neve forlornly.

Going with her gut, Neve gave Zeke a hopeful smile. "Can I pet him?"

"Torch is a girl. But yeah, you can pet her. Come over here and let me introduce you." He held out a hand, sliding Gideon a shrewd glance before looking at her. "Which one are you?"

She arched her brows. "I'm sorry?"

"Which one of the McKays?"

"Ah . . ." Rocking back on her heels, she glanced between him and Gideon.

"Don't try to bullshit me, kid." He continued to stand there, waiting. "I know Gideon Marshall too well. He nagged me for three days straight and then just up and stopped calling. There's a method to his madness, always. You're the method. I shoulda expected."

Slowly, Neve put her hand in Zeke's and felt the ridges of a lifetime of callouses. "I'm Neve." Shrugging, she added, "The youngest."

Zeke just nodded. "Come on. I'll introduce you to Torch."

"But you won't sell her to me."

He shrugged. "I already made my position clear to Marshall."

"Then maybe I shouldn't get my hopes up." She tugged her hand free and gazed at the dog. Something akin to longing burned inside her. She wondered if it was possible to feel some sort of instant kinship with an animal. The dog stared at her in a way that was almost wistful when she didn't come any closer. Neve thought she heard the dog sigh and she *knew* she saw Torch look over at Zeke, her canine gaze baleful.

Zeke planted his hands on his hips, staring at the dog. "Don't you look at me like that."

"Come on, Gideon." Neve turned back to the other man who'd been silent throughout. "I'm not going to go through this, get my hopes up, only to have them crash. I've had enough of crashing in my life."

There was a snort behind her, dry and withering, and it had her turning.

Zeke watched her, his expression scornful. "Rich girl like you, what do you know about having your hopes crashed?"

"Having money doesn't guarantee you're going to be happy, Mr. . . . ?"

"Zeke'll do."

"I'm sorry." She jammed her hands into her pockets. "I tend to save first names for people I'm friendly with. No matter, though. We'll get out of your hair."

But again, before she could turn back to Gideon, Zeke grumbled under his breath.

"Spare me the stories about the poor little rich girl."

"Poor little rich girl?" Fury started to burn inside and she advanced on him. Torch looked curious now, while the dogs in the fenced-in yard started to take more interest. Neve barely noticed. "I have no idea just where to start with how wrong you are with that label."

Zeke glared at her. "Labels get used for a reason, seems like."

"Well. Let me point out how wrong you are." Neve gave him a thin smile. "I guess I should start back when I was a kid. I guess you're not from around here . . . otherwise you probably would have heard about me at some point. I'm *that* Neve . . . you know the girl who was trapped in the car with her parents when she just a little girl? I saw my mother bleed to death in front of me. I was only eight."

Zeke shot Gideon a look.

But Gideon was focused on her. He reached out to touch her shoulder. "Come on, Nevie," he said, his voice gentle.

She shrugged him off.

With a withering look, she continued, "If you haven't heard about that, I guess you didn't hear about how my father was in the car too and ended up all but beheaded—I was covered in his blood for *hours* because nobody saw the wreck. Not that I remember, though. I blocked it all out. It's been twenty years and I still don't sleep through the night well." She bared her teeth at the older man when he went to say something. "We could talk about how I got I *tired* of being poor little Neve, tired of being the screwup so I ran off and ended up with a man who *beat* me, and when I tried to run, he put me in the hospital!"

"Neve." Gideon rested a hand on her arm, but she threw him off.

She didn't know where this fury had come from.

"And even *that* wasn't enough because when the bastard got out of jail, he came after me! Again! Came after me and my sister Moira, and he'd still be trying to come after me if I hadn't killed him."

She took another step toward him.

Torch got between them and barked.

Neve jumped at the sound.

Zeke slashed a hand through the air. "Enough!"

Neve stared at him, the adrenaline that had crashed into her suddenly starting to drain out. It did it so fast, she felt more than a little sick. "Shit." She turned away, pressing a hand to her stomach. She swayed, her eyes going dim on her.

Behind her, she heard the old man mumble something.

Something cool and wet nudged at her hand and she looked down, saw the beautiful dog sitting there, nudging at her and waiting for Neve to pet her.

"Just pet the damn dog already, girl," Zeke said from behind, his voice hoarse.

Neve shot him an ugly glare before she dropped to the

ground, disregarding the cold grass. Torch half-crawled into her lap, plopping her big head on Neve's shoulder.

"A lot of my dogs end up going to some of the troops who suffer from PTSD," Zeke said. "I teach them to recognize the signs. She's . . . ah. Well. She's responding to what she perceives as your triggers, Ms. McKay."

Neve sniffed as she fisted a hand in the dog's thick fur. Torch nuzzled her neck.

After a moment the dog drew back and Neve had the impression she was being analyzed.

She must have passed because the dog dropped her head to settle on Neve's thigh.

"You should pet her. Tell her she was a good girl," Zeke advised.

"I'm not doing anything that might get me more attached." Neve curled her hands into fists before she looked up to stare at Zeke. "Not until you tell me just what in the world my family supposedly did to you."

Moira sipped the tea sweetened with honey and laced with lemon, while she reviewed the files Baxter had pulled up.

The people from the IRS were late.

It figured.

She'd busted her ass to get here and now she was killing time and twiddling her fingers while she waited. Her voice was a lot better since she'd spent most of yesterday resting it, but she had a feeling she'd end up scratchy again within a couple of hours. She'd done the tax man dance before. It never came without lots of talking, lots of looking for information, and everything else.

The door to her office opened and she lifted her head, barely keeping her look of annoyance hidden—which was good because Baxter Lindenbower was there, along with two people clad in suits—well, of a sort. One was in his mid-fifties and everything about him *screamed* IRS, from his drab navy suit and bland, blocky shoes to his wire-rimmed glasses. The other, however, was a woman whom Moira couldn't see being past twenty-five. She wore a lime green pencil skirt and a summer-weight sweater the color of strawberry ice cream. It had green accents at the neck, and her shoes—completely *adorable* shoes—had both colors. Pink heels with ankle straps of lime green.

"I want your shoes."

The words popped past Moira's lips before she even realized she was going to say them, and she clapped a hand over her mouth, closing her eyes.

The woman started laughing. "I know, right? Aren't they awesome?"

Her partner cleared his throat.

Moira opened her eyes in time to see him shooting the younger woman a narrow look.

She looked unfazed as she came toward Moira, hand outstretched. "Hello. I'm Megan Calloway, with the IRS—we're with the exemptions division."

Moira filed that away as she accepted Megan's hand. After a quick squeeze, she looked to the man, but he stood by the wall, studying some of the framed prints.

"My grandfather and great-grandfather," Moira said softly.

He nodded. "The McKay family has quite a history here in Mississippi."

"Yes."

He adjusted his glasses as he came closer. "Pardon me, Ms. McKay. I didn't introduce myself. Sam Adams." He paused and glanced down at his shoes. "I'm afraid I don't have the lovely footwear my partner has, so feel free to make a jest at the name."

"I wouldn't dream of it." Moira couldn't help smile a little. "I'm told the IRS has no sense of humor."

"Of course not. It's surgically removed the day we join

up." Sam tugged a pair of glasses from his jacket and slid them on. Then he blinked, a startled looking on his face. "Whatever happened to your neck, Ms. McKay?"

Reaching, she touched the raw skin. It didn't hurt like it had, but the wounds were still ugly, still red against her pale skin. "It's . . . complicated."

Megan's eyes lingered on her neck and she looked shaken. "It looks like—"

"Megan." Adams simply said her name.

The woman lapsed into silence.

Moira was grateful. She didn't want to beat around the bush, nor did she want to explain.

Adams nodded at the seats in front of the desk. "Might we sit down?"

"Of course. I wasn't sure what this was regarding. I have some information on hand, but as you can imagine . . ."

She trailed off as Megan bypassed the chair to place something on her desk.

"What's this?" She reached for the folder and picked it up, flipping it open.

Nobody answered, so she started to read.

Ten seconds later, she lowered it and looked up at the two IRS investigators.

"You've got to be kidding me."

Sam smoothed a hand down his tie. "No, ma'am. That's the report in its entirety as we received it."

Moira groaned. "Okay, surely you've seen the taxes filed yearly by McKay enterprises—and by me personally, as well as my siblings. You've seen the kind of figures we play with. Yet you think we're running out burying gold doubloons or something in our yard?"

The moment she said it, she sucked in a breath and her hand flew to her throat.

Blood started to roar in her ears.

Stumbling upright, she staggered over to the window. Air. She needed air.

But the windows didn't open.

"Where is it?"

Pain . . . his hand smashing into her skull, grinding her into the dirt. "I've got . . . money . . . in the house . . ."

"I don't want money."

"What . . . do . . ."

"He left a treasure here. Patrick McKay. Where is it?"

"Ms. McKay?"

She turned on shaky legs to look at the federal employees for a moment, then looked at Baxter. "Could you get me some water please?"

He looked hesitant, then smiled. "I'll get you some tea. You sound like you need that more." She smiled at him. As he slid out of the office, she sank into her chair and met the gazes of the other two. "When, exactly, did you receive this report, if I might ask?"

When they hesitated, she touched her throat. "If it helps, the answer could be relevant. I'll explain why I'm asking." She laughed, the sound shaky and desperate. "I can even have a police report sent over."

An hour later, the dynamic duo from the IRS had left with promises to follow up.

They had a copy of the report from the police department with them. Gideon wasn't back. She was more than a little thankful of that because this wasn't the sort of conversation somebody had over the phone. Now she had a few hours at least to figure out how to explain things to him. As long as nobody mentioned she'd called requesting a copy of the report.

She'd tell him once she saw him. For now, she had other things to worry about—like this bullshit report. The IRS had gotten the call two days ago, well after her attack. She commented on the speedy follow-up and Calloway sheepishly admitted that she'd been the one to take the report and it had seemed so out of the ordinary, she'd shown it to her partner.

Moira had a feeling the young woman was still in training, but Adams had let her take the lead on this. A good teacher. She had no idea how things in the IRS worked, but it seemed that something like this *should* get followed up on—even if it was proving to be a pain in her ass.

As she explained what had happened, what her attacker had said, they had looked more and more grim.

Although they didn't voice anything, she had a feeling they were smart enough to see what she saw.

They didn't even have the whole picture, either.

Somebody was looking to make trouble for her family, and it was pissing her off.

The musical ring from her phone nudged her out of her daze and she picked it up without thinking. If she had taken even a second *to* think, she might have ignored it.

She didn't want to talk to anybody.

Two seconds into the conversation, she was really, *really* wishing she hadn't answered, because she had no idea what was going on.

"Neve . . . I don't know what . . . would you start over, *please*?"

She could hear her little sister take a deep breath—and practically grit her teeth.

"Moira . . . did we . . . buy property . . . in Louisiana?" Neve asked, her voice almost falsely sweet and the pauses between words deliberate—and annoying.

"Neve . . . we buy . . . property . . . all over . . . *the fricking country.*" She rubbed her throat and got up to get the tea Baxter had brought her earlier. It had cooled off, but she didn't care. He'd laced it with whiskey—Baxter had been raised by his grandmother, a sweet lady who believed in the value of a real hot toddy for "what ails you."

Granted, Baxter hit his toddy even when he stubbed his toe, but right now, she could kiss him.

Neve made a growling sound under her throat. "Utilize those resources you were always bragging about ten years ago. Narrow it down. I need to know if we bought a piece of land—specifically a house—about an hour north of Baton Rouge . . . what was the county?"

Moira frowned as Neve called to somebody and there was a low, familiar voice that offered a response.

Moira recognized the county name. "I know where it is—who is there with you?"

"Would you just answer the question? The place is close to the state line."

"About an hour north of Baton Rouge? Close to the state line?" Annoyed, Moira put her cup down with a little more force than necessary and some of the tea splattered out, drops spraying out onto a stack of new contracts.

Grabbing a tissue, she blotted up the marks and studied it. "Neve, why don't you call the lawyers? They have better access to that info than I do. Hell, we own property in twenty-eight states, at last count. And in forty-two countries."

Neve made a disgusted noise. "Why the hell do we need so much property for anyway?"

"Because we own companies. Companies that make things. Companies need to be built on land as they haven't figured out how to do that Cloud City thing that was so cool in *The Empire Strikes Back*. Our tech departments *are* working on it, though, I promise." Her voice started to fade out near the end and she grimaced, reaching for her tea.

"Smart-ass. And you're straining your voice again."

"That's because I had an unexpected meeting—and I'm

arguing with you." She stuck her tongue out at the phone and felt a little better for it.

"We're not arguing. Has it been that long since we have that you've forgotten what we are like when we argue?" Neve almost sounded amused. "Okay, maybe this will help. The Bittner project?"

Moira paused, then resumed lifting her tea. "The Bittner project?" After taking a long, slow sip, she closed her eyes. Nothing came to mind. Finally, she turned to her open laptop and accessed the database. McKay Enterprises was the head of a huge conglomeration and they had fingers in many, many pies. She couldn't possibly keep track of all of them.

A few keys strokes had the information coming up on the screen, and it left her frowning. "Okay, I see what you're asking about. The Bittner project—home and surrounding property purchased. It's fairly local. I'm surprised I wasn't made aware of this purchase." She eyed the date, did some mental math, and suppressed a curse. She knew exactly why she wasn't more aware. The entire deal had been closed within a six-week period. The six-week period during which a certain somebody with penetrating eyes and a mouth that she could still feel against her own had been injured in the line of duty.

Mentally, she hadn't been sitting behind a desk and shuffling figures, attending board meetings, and listening to key personnel on new patents or suggestions on new product lines. Mentally, she'd been in a hospital on the other side of the world, holding onto Gideon Marshall's hand and telling him that if he died, she'd kick his ass.

He'd ended up with a medical discharge and a few months later, he was a cop in Memphis. Six months after that, she was married to Charles Hurst.

If Gideon had come home then . . .

If he'd come home, what would have happened?

She'd didn't know, but he hadn't.

A chance dinner in New York had her bumping into Charles again and when he'd asked her out, she'd all but flung herself into his arms, desperate to forget that fear, desperate to forget Gideon even.

It had been a kick in the face, in the heart for him to actually come *home* just a year later. But she'd already been married, and when he looked at her, it was with a sad sort of understanding.

They'd been over.

If he'd come home . . .

Stop, she told herself, forcing herself to focus on the details on the screen.

It wasn't a typical deal for McKay, although the notes highlighted in the file made sense in a way.

"Okay, so what about this piece of property?" Moira asked.

"I want it."

The bluntly stated words had Moira sitting up straighter. "Ah . . . Neve? It's company property." She eyed the sum paid for the said property and added, "It cost 1.2 *million* dollars."

"It wasn't supposed to be ours anyway. I want the property. I'll take the money out of my account and give it to the damn company. I want the deed, Moira."

"Well, I need more than that," she said. Her voice made a weird creaky noise halfway through and she swore. "Neve, we're not discussing this on the phone."

"Damn it, the owner promised to sell it for two hundred thousand to his neighbor. They had a contract—it was signed and the guy had even put money down. They just hadn't done anything official because the original owner wasn't going to move until he . . . shit, he was *old,* Moira. Then the old guy up and had a heart attack. His son comes along and says no dice, puts the land up for sale. Then

McKay came in, brokered this deal and bought the land, and now this man I'm here with is out fifty thousand *and* the land he'd been planning to use to expand the dog rescue operation he's got going."

At the end of her sister's rant, Moira was sitting there with her eyes covered and the bad, bad feeling that she was going to have to make some heads roll by the time she was done.

"Are you there?" Neve demanded.

"I'm here." Her voice made that weird sound warning her that it wasn't going to last much longer if she wasn't careful.

"What do we need a house for anyway?"

Good question, Moira thought. The gist of it had been in the notes in the computer, but she wasn't going into that with Neve out there and her here. "The general idea is to use it for company retreats and team-building exercises." Since nobody was around, she grabbed a pen from her desk and mimed stabbing herself in the temple. "Have you seen the contract?"

"I'm holding it right now. Most of my experience with contracts is all from my time in modeling, but it looks legit, Moira." Neve's voice was shaking. "A company retreat. This guy worked his whole life for this and our company stole it out from under him for a company retreat?"

The pure fury in Neve's voice was no surprise. Moira suspected she'd be pissed off herself before too long. Feelings, egos, and pride often ended up bruised in business, but the McKay family did business the way they'd always done it—ethically.

If somebody had ended up screwed over in a deal with the company, she was going to raise hell.

"Does it look legit?"

Neve heaved out a sigh. "I just said—"

"You majored in business, Neve. You've dealt with contracts before—you just said so. Is it for real?"

"Yes," Neve said after a moment. "It's for real. It's got a notary's signature on it. I figure somebody could find loopholes if they wanted, but that's not how we do business."

"No." Moira stared out the window in front of her. "It's not. Who is this guy?"

"His name is Zeke Sanders. I . . . well, he raises dogs. I wanted to buy one."

Something in Neve's tone had Moira's eyes narrowing, but she was already straining her voice to the limit and she couldn't deal with this if she ended up voiceless again. "Okay. Give me addresses—no, better idea. If you've got enough bars, take pictures of the contract with your phone and shoot them my way. I'll need details of what all I'm looking for, names, et cetera."

"We're going to make this right, Moira." Neve didn't wait for an answer. She just hung up.

CHAPTER THIRTEEN

Moira contacted somebody from legal to handle transfer of the house from the company to Neve, putting the price at something more fitting of what it was probably worth.

She wasn't certain just *why* this particular place had gone at over a million—it certainly wasn't worth it, not from where she was sitting. She'd pulled up the full profile on the transaction and while the property was pretty, the house itself was dated and would have to be overhauled before it could be used as any sort of retreat.

That alone would cost several hundred thousand.

And the house was just *sitting* there. Nobody was doing anything with it. From what she could tell, it hadn't been touched in the seven years since they'd acquired it.

"Sanders, why didn't you try to take us to court or something?" She rubbed at her temple. Not that she *liked* the idea of it, but this was an ugly weight in her gut and she didn't like knowing some guy had been pretty much robbed of fifty grand.

And she *still* couldn't understand why anybody would want to buy this for some so-called retreat. The location was *awful*.

It was so far away from anything, none of the staff who

would likely use it would have found it appealing after the first few hours. Moira might have just been delighted—she didn't mind roughing it when she could actually *get away*. But she knew most of her key personnel, and their idea of roughing it was getting coffee they poured themselves . . . or worse, coffee from a gas station instead of a Starbucks.

Starbucks hadn't quite penetrated that quiet little spot in Louisiana.

Neither had any store larger than a mom and pop–style grocery store or a Dollar General.

It didn't make sense.

After she'd compiled all the information she could, she put in a call to Jenny Green—the assistant for one Kevin Towers.

Kevin was the one who'd handled this project.

Kevin had been with McKay for a long time. She would give him the courtesy of trying to explain before she gave him a cardboard box and told him to clear out.

But she really, really wished she had a cardboard box in her office.

"I'm sorry, Ms. McKay . . . he's . . . excuse me one moment, ma'am. Please, Mr. Towers isn't in. One moment and I'll take a message—no, I cannot take it now." The woman came back on the phone and said, "I'm terribly sorry, ma'am. Mr. Towers isn't in. He left just a short while ago, taking the rest of the day off. He wasn't feeling well, I don't think—sir, I will be *with* you in a moment."

"Jenny. What seems to be the trouble?" Moira stared at the wall in front of her.

"Nothing I can't—"

As a male voice rose in the background, Moira pushed a button on her phone. Baxter appeared a moment later. "Baxter, Jenny Green seems to be having some trouble over in her area. Can you send security?"

Jenny's voice hesitated, then firmed. In the background,

the man's voice grew louder, a decidedly aggressive note to it.

As Baxter's jaw squared and he nodded, Moira turned her attention back to the woman on the phone. "Jenny, why don't you pass the phone over to your . . . guest?"

There was a moment of silence.

"You might want to take it, sir. Perhaps she can connect you with Mr. Towers."

A brusque, hard voice came on the phone a moment later. "Who the fuck is this?"

"Would you mind looking down at the desk in front of you?" Moira closed her eyes, brought a mental image of Jenny Green to the fore of her mind. Neat woman, tidy. Kept her desk pristine. There was a blotter on her desk, never smudged, never out of place. And the embossed *M* was hard to miss. "Do you see the blotter . . . in case you're wondering, the blotter is the big square pad—square, four sides, you know?"

"Bitch, if you don't—"

Moira continued to talk, keeping her voice low and steady. She'd learned a long time ago that the way to deal with the sort of men who *tried* to put her in her place was to just carry on about her business. More often than not, they had questions or just things they wanted to hear themselves say. Early on, there had been several men in the company who'd thought they could pull the penis card. They hadn't lasted long. Now, though, the asses she dealt were either looking to get money from her or steal business away from her, and their favorite method was laying down the testosterone.

Most of them learned pretty quickly, though. They all wanted something and they'd be quicker to figure out how to get it if they listened to what she was saying.

This idiot was no different.

After a few seconds, he realized she hadn't shut up and

he lapsed into silence. She shifted the call to her Bluetooth seamlessly and started to walk. She thought she'd timed it right.

"So you see the blotter? There's an *M* on it. That's short for *McKay*. As in *McKay Enterprises*. That name sound familiar?"

"Seeing as how that's the damn building I'm in, it should."

"Good. Then let me introduce myself." She rounded the corner and pushed through a pair of frosted glass doors—the doors that led from *her* executive offices to the rest of them.

A big, bulky man with a shaved head stood holding a phone to his ear. Jenny sat at her desk. Two security guards came through the door only seconds after Moira.

"The *bitch* you're talking to would be Moira McKay." She turned off her Bluetooth and waited for him to notice that he could still hear her. "As in . . . *the CEO* of McKay Enterprises."

He turned slowly and stared at her.

She gave him a polite smile. "Now, sir, let me ask . . . *who the fuck are you*?"

Moira rubbed her temple as the head of security updated her.

He'd been the one to take the thug down.

Grizzled and graying, Hank Sheffield didn't look like much at first, but under that professional veneer, the man was like a rattlesnake. It wasn't wise to cross him.

"His name, according the city cops, is Landon Hayes. Got a record. A local leg-breaker for a small-time bookie."

Pressing her fingers to her eyes, she said softly, "Please don't tell me that Kevin had a gambling problem."

When Hank said nothing, she looked up at him.

He shrugged. "You asked me not to tell you." He leaned

forward and peered through the window. "They're loading the big moron now. Stupid as he is, he might not make it through the first night in the joint. What was he thinking, coming in here like that?"

"Well, he does work for a small-time bookie," Moira said, going for a little levity. "If he was any good, he'd have moved up to the big leagues."

Hank shot her a grin that made the creases in his face deepen. "Good point, Ms. McKay."

She rubbed at her neck and fought the urge to slump in her chair. Too many people were manufacturing excuses to come by her office. She wasn't about to be seen looking like she wanted to collapse.

Of course, Hank was there, but Hank was . . . different. He was a friend.

He'd come on board a few years before her father died, and he'd been one of the people who'd guided her through when she was fumbling to find her way.

"Maybe that's why he pulled this shit with the house."

"Ma'am?"

She looked over at Hank and shook her head. "Nothing. I've just got a mess on my hands and Towers was involved. I'll have to talk to him." She didn't know if she wanted to wait until Monday, either.

Especially not if he had some leg-breaker—she shuddered at the image—trying to hunt him down here at his place of employment.

"Why don't you go on home, Miss Moira?" Hank said, falling back on the name he'd used for her when they first started working together. "You're not going to fix anything right now."

She should argue.

She knew she should.

But he was right.

She needed to step back and think, get her head cleared so she could look at all of this with a fresh outlook.

So she nodded. Maybe Hank looked a little surprised and that made her smile.

Impulsively, she moved over and hugged him. "Thank you," she said. "For always being there."

The older man was blushing when she pulled away. He awkwardly patted her shoulder and jerked a thumb to the door. "Go on now."

The drive back home was too damn long.

Moira could think of only one thing that would make anything about this day remotely salvageable. That would be to just *undo* it. If she could figure out a way to rewind and just erase it all, that might work.

She didn't even want a *re*do, because how could she make any of it turn out any better?

That being the case, she thought maybe the next best solution would be to find a bottle of Macallan down in the basement. On rare occasions, sitting down with a bottle of fine scotch was really just the only answer. It was only for *rare* occasions, but she didn't often have a day like this.

If she didn't have any down in the basement, then damn it, she was going over to Brannon's to raid his supply. He stockpiled liquor the way a miser hoarded gold.

She'd bring a bottle to Ferry and get good and wasted. It wouldn't change anything that had happened, but it would buy her some oblivion and when she sat down to think about this again—after her hangover cleared up—she would have a new perspective on everything.

Granted, she didn't know how a new perspective would help.

The IRS agents were giving her and her family the benefit of the doubt, it seemed, although they did want to come over and take a look at her property, inspect what they had at the family vault and all that jazz. They wouldn't find anything.

Somebody was trying to cause grief for them on that front, claiming treasure was buried on their land.

Uneasy, she rubbed her throat.

Then there was the weird deal with that house that Neve had told her about.

A house they didn't *need*.

One they'd overpaid for and was somehow connected to a man who had a bookie out looking for him. Yeah, this was all kinds of bad news.

She'd tried to call Towers several times on the drive back home with no luck. She would get in touch with him somehow. The man's job was history. Her executives were expected to uphold a high moral standard, and he'd gotten himself in enough trouble that he had a bookie coming to *her* company. Jenny could have gotten hurt. Anybody in the building could have gotten hurt.

And it wasn't even the first time that scumbucket had come around. A few of the others had recognized him. One of the junior execs had even sheepishly admitting to lending Kevin a few thousand dollars to "buy some breathing room."

As she swung the car up the drive and waited for the gates to open, told herself to stop thinking. She needed to get inside Ferry, get her some damn scotch and just shut her brain down. Completely.

The late winter sun shone down, the rays hitting the multitude of windows and shattering into a thousand dazzling beams. Normally the sight brought at least a small smile to her face, but not today.

She was so twisted with anger and confusion, she didn't think anything could make her smile.

A few moments later, though, after parking her car in the garage, she had to admit, she was wrong.

Even after more than twenty years, Gideon Marshall could still make her smile and he could still surprise her.

Of course, she had always known he could make her smile. But she wouldn't have thought he could manage it today.

Not even Gideon should have been able to pierce her gloom.

But how could she possibly resist the sight of a beautiful man stroking his hands down the lush, gleaming coat of a beautiful dog?

Moira stopped, gazing at the tableau in front of her.

The shepherd turned his head and stared at her.

He didn't have the typical coloring.

No, he was *white*.

She'd seen white shepherds before, but never this close.

"Wow." She blinked and shifted her attention to Gideon. He continued to rub his hand up and down the dog's back. "You've got a new friend. He's gorgeous."

"*She's* gorgeous. Frost is a lady, Mac," he said easily. "And technically, I brought her out here thinking she'd be *your* new friend, but I think I'm in love with her, Moira. She likes me, too. You don't mind, do you?"

Moira cocked a brow and stared at the dog. "I think I can take her."

To her surprise, the dog gave a slow wag of her tail. Like she'd understood.

Abruptly, Gideon's meaning penetrated. "What did you mean you brought her here to be *my* dog?"

"You said you wanted a dog. I got you a dog. Like I said, her name is Frost." He slanted a look at her from under his lashes before he went back to stroking the dog. "Well, you have to pay for her. Zeke isn't letting them go cheap."

"Zeke . . ." She said the name slowly and then looked over as Neve came running around the house.

With a dog.

Another one.

Again, a shepherd, although she had more traditional coloring.

The dog stopped when she saw Moira and sat on her heels, waiting.

"Family, Torch. That's Moira," Neve said. She had a wide grin on her face when she looked at her sister. "Moira, this is Torch. Torch, Moira."

"Am I supposed to shake?"

Both dogs lifted their paws.

It was a wonderful thing to realize after an absolutely *shitty* day that she could laugh.

A glass of wine was placed in front of her.

Moira leaned back, studying the wine with pursed lips for a moment before looking up to see Gideon as he settled down in the seat next to hers.

Frost politely nosed at his thigh and he scooted over obligingly. The big dog stretched out, pausing only to look up at Moira as if to say, *Is this okay?* Moira reached out and stroked a hand down Frost's silky coat. "She's so pretty."

The dog rolled her eyes up to look at Moira, and damned if the thing didn't look smugly pleased.

"I think she's also vain," Gideon said. He nudged the wine closer to Moira.

"I've been working up the energy to go raid the cellar." She sighed and reached out, picking up the glass. "You foiled my plans."

"If you want to do that . . . ?" He shrugged and made to reach for the glass.

"No." Protectively, she turned away, using her body as a shield.

He canted a grin at her. "Greedy."

"Damn straight. Also, lazy." She took a sip and let her eyes drift closed. "It's been a hell of a day."

"Shut your brain off a while, Mac. Relax."

"I can't." She took another sip of wine before putting the glass down and leaning forward, staring at the notes she'd made. She'd had a heavy class load in college, but it had served well, majoring in business along with accounting and finance. She was a McKay to the core and had never thought about anything else but following right along in her father's footsteps.

That accounting degree was what made it easier—*easier* but not precisely *easy*—to notice the irregularities in Kevin Tower's expenditures. Gideon leaned over and eyed her notes. He came in so close, she caught the heady smell of him and it distracted her. Slipping a look, she said, "Do you mind?"

"Not at all." His gaze slid to her mouth, then back up to meet hers. "Do you?"

Heat started to twist through her. "This is . . . kinda important."

"So important it can't wait until Monday?" He went to tug the pencil out of her hand.

Moira sighed. "I don't know." She relinquished her hold on the pencil and was rewarded when he curved a hand over the back of her neck, setting strong fingers to work on the knots he found there. "I just . . . hell, Gideon. I feel like I'm being punked—business edition, hosted by some sleazeball business icon. Donald Trump, maybe."

"Why don't you tell me what's going on? I won't follow half of it, but you'll feel better."

She snorted. "I don't know about that." But it couldn't hurt.

Yet when she opened her mouth to talk, Gideon brushed his thumb over her mouth. "Not here."

Puzzled, she watched as he rose and held out a hand.

"Take a walk with me, Mac."

She glanced over at the paperwork.

"If it can't wait, then bring it with you." Gideon's smile was wry. "I know you. Until you solve the puzzle, you won't let it go anyway."

CHAPTER FOURTEEN

Something was eating at her and it had put darker shadows under her eyes.

Gideon didn't think she'd slept well since her attack.

Her attack—fuck, they had nothing on it.

Not a fucking thing.

Nothing else had been attempted.

Well, unless you counted the fire at the bookstore.

That had to count.

All of these things, he thought . . . everything done to Neve, to Hannah, the fire at the bookstore . . . all of it had a specific purpose—targeted strikes at the McKays.

Eyes on Moira's downcast face, he felt a smile tugging at his lips when he realized she had been eying him from under her lashes. The expression in those beautiful green eyes set his blood to a low boil, but he kept his focus and shifted his attention to her neck.

The bruises.

Another strike.

Against her, yes.

But more specifically . . . his man had been looking for something.

The treasure.

Where is it? He'd been specific, demanded to know where the treasure was, wouldn't listen when she was it was just legend. She'd told Gideon the same thing, had tried to brush him off.

Where is it?

That was what she said the man had said.

Where is it?

"So where are we going?" Moira asked, folding her hand around his.

He hitched the bag she'd crammed all of her work into higher up on his shoulder and shrugged. "One of my favorite places. Haven't been there in forever."

Moira's brows arched, but she said nothing.

She looked mildly intrigued when he didn't stop at his car and even more intrigued when they bypassed the garage, heading up the long, cobblestone path.

She stopped in her tracks when she realized where they were going.

Gideon did as well, since she'd taken his hand and he had no desire to break any connection with her, ever. She was maybe six inches in front of him, their linked hands stretching between them and he could see the rush of heat spreading up to turn her cheeks pink.

"Your favorite place?" she said, her voice husky.

"Yeah. Pretty much." He shrugged. "Back when I was in the hospital after . . ." He almost said something stupid, like *after I about bled to death,* but her face had paled, so he just let it trail off. "Anyway, they were always coming in and doing therapy and shit. There was this one therapist—pint-sized, I swear. Even smaller than you. And she'd do these exercises. I kid you not, I think she came from the very bowels of hell. I'd lay there, sweating like a pig and trying not to cry and she would be chirping out . . . *Just go to your happy place, soldier. It'll be over in no time.* The only happy place I could think of was here."

She turned her head back and looked at him.

"You never called me," she said, her voice rough.

He stared right back. "I called you every single day." Then he shrugged. "But I hung up before the phone would even start to ring. You told me we were over, that you didn't want to be with me and that I had to move on. I couldn't do that, but I'd be damned if I called you when I was flat on my back halfway across the world."

Moira tore her hand from his and strode away from him.

She took maybe five steps before she stopped and he watched as she stared at the pool house.

He'd made love to her here for the first time.

He'd made love to her here for the last time.

In his dreams, he'd made love to her here a thousand times.

And now he planned on doing it again. Moving up behind her, he ran his knuckles up her spine.

She shivered. It was faint, so slight, somebody standing a few feet away wouldn't have even noticed it.

But Gideon noticed everything about Moira.

Including the fact that she was trying not to cry.

Curving his arm around her waist, he pressed his mouth to her neck. "Mac . . ."

"What?" In a truculent tone, she tried to shrug him away, but he wasn't going anywhere. Not until she forced him out.

"I'm planning on taking you inside there . . . and then just taking you. It's going to interfere with my plans if you start to cry." He kept his tone light, borderline playful.

The quick, erratic break in her breathing goaded him into sliding his hand up until he could cup a small breast in his hand. "Can we start moving again?"

She broke away, turning around. Her gaze was solemn, her mouth unsmiling. Her eyes gleamed wet.

And she was still so beautiful, it made his heart hurt.

She bit her lip, tugging it inside her mouth and releasing it slowly. The gesture made him want to do the same damn thing, but he held himself still, tried to seem as relaxed and calm as he pretended to be.

Finally, she nodded. Lips pursed, she said, "I still have to figure out what's going on, Gideon."

"It almost sounds like you're putting me on a timetable, Mac." He scratched his chin as he took a few steps toward her, closing the distance between them. "That's fine. I always did just fine under pressure."

Did he ever.

Moira shuddered as he came to his feet and caught her knees in one smooth motion. She ended up penned between him and the wall, her slim-fitting pencil skirt pushed up over her hips while her panties lay on the ground. She'd been hopeful when she got dressed that morning and had put on stockings, and although she'd almost regretted it as the day remained chilly, she was glad that streak of hope had burned so bright.

He'd discovered the thigh-highs when he went to his knees to work her skirt up and the soft kisses he'd pressed to her thighs had progressed to kisses against her panties and then more intimate kisses after he'd stripped her panties away.

"I want your mouth, Mac," he said.

She lifted her face and groaned as his tongue swept inside. He was salty, tasting of her now just as much as he tasted of Gideon. He moved closer and she would have moaned if he hadn't had been making excellent use of his mouth—and hers—at the moment. The head of his cock passed over her, once, twice . . .

Then he stopped, cursing.

"I need a fucking rubber. I . . . just wait, okay?"

But when he went to pull away, she caught his wrist.

"No."

Gideon stared at her and she felt like he was peeling away all the layers until he saw down to the very core.

"It's only been you and . . ." She trailed off, not daring to stay Charles' name, but it wasn't necessary. He knew. "Nobody since . . . him. There were the nights with you and that's it. It's always been you, Gideon."

He caught her face in his hand and pressed his brow to hers. "We already messed up not using one last night and . . . hell. We can't keep doing this. There are things besides whether or not we're healthy."

"I know."

His chest rose and fell. "You're on the pill?"

She almost lied.

But she couldn't do that.

Staring him dead in the eye, she rested her head against the door and gave him the truth. "I'm not. I don't want anything between us, Gideon. Not anymore."

His long, lean body shuddered. He hauled her up against him, his mouth sealing over hers in a kiss so deep, she thought it might forge them together for all time.

Except that had already been done . . . decades ago.

Dying for want of him, she curled her arms around his neck and rose up on her toes. She couldn't get close enough, couldn't hold him tight enough.

Gideon swept her back up and in seconds, she could feel him nudging against her, the broad head of his cock slowly forging inside her. He tore his mouth away and when she would have closed her eyes, tried to gather up the scattered pieces of herself, he tangled a hand in her hair. "Look at me, Mac. Look at me."

The words were a ragged growl.

She felt caught, lost in him.

"Gideon."

He started to drive into her, hard, short digs of his hips

that had her back sliding up and down the wall. She clung to him, nails digging into his arms.

"Tell me you're mine," he demanded, his fist tightening in her hair. "Tell me, Mac."

"You know I'm yours, Gideon."

She wanted to tell him something else—something important.

But he changed the angle of his body and it had him riding her clit, and thought dissolved away on a wave of bliss. The orgasm grabbed her, swallowed her whole.

"Sex is very refreshing." Moira sipped from the glass of tea that Gideon had come up with from somewhere. She eyed the plate he slid down in front of her and paused long enough to take a good long look around the pool house. It had a small area that was fitted out like a living room, complete with a TV and a kitchenette, along with a small bedroom off to the side. Not that they'd used it . . . recently.

They'd let guests use the pool house when visiting for a few days, but it had been a while since Moira had anybody who had come over for that long. Probably a year . . . no, longer. She'd had a couple of girlfriends from college that she still kept in touch with come by a few months after her divorce and two of them had decided to crash out here.

That had been years ago. She scowled, realizing just how much she'd shut herself down, but instead of brooding, she focused on the man across from her.

"You know . . . I'm pretty sure we don't keep the fridge out here stocked."

"Is that a fact?" Gideon cocked a brow. "Well, I've gotten good at planning things."

"So you planned this." She rested her chin on her fist and eyed the plate of cheese and crackers. It had Ella Sue written all over it. "I guess you contacted my Ella Sue and told her to plan for a seduction?"

"Like I'd dare." Gideon gave her a rakish grin. "I just told her I was going to steal you away for a few hours—if I could—and could she help me out with something for you to munch on while I cook."

She had been in the process of popping a piece of cheddar into her mouth. Now she sat there, hand frozen in the air. "You cook?"

"I do quite a few things for myself, Mac." He gestured to the plate. "Eat something. Get your work done. Food will take a while."

She blew out a breath before popping the cheese into her mouth.

A man who cooked for her.

Mind-blowing sex.

The day from hell didn't seem so bad all of a sudden.

At least that was what she thought until she plunged back into her paperwork.

Twenty minutes later, she had to push everything to the side. She was almost positive she had figured out as much as she could without talking to Towers. And she *would* be doing that, as soon as he returned her calls.

Slipping Gideon a look, she reached for her phone and punched in a number she'd already memorized.

It rang. Once. Twice. Three times.

"Bored already?"

She disconnected as Gideon settled down next to her, placing a glass of red wine in front of her.

His eyes skimmed along the pages she'd spread out before he slanted a look at her.

"No." She made a face and shoved her hands through her hair. The headache was making a comeback. She stared again at the phone, practically willing Towers to call her back.

The stubborn phone refused to ring, though. Either that, or her powers of mind control never had manifested.

Sighing, she looked back down at the papers just in time to see Gideon pluck a sheet from table.

"Hey."

"Hey, back." He picked up her glass of wine and took a sip, his eyes moving back and forth over the information.

Would he see it—

"Somebody's skimming."

Impressed, she leaned back in her chair and stared at him appraisingly. "You can tell that in under five seconds? I think I need to hire you."

He shrugged. "No. You don't want to hire me. I'd get fired for sexually harassing the boss." He winked at her and then put the paper down, nudging it over to her. "You know I was always good with numbers. These dates . . . every week on a Tuesday. He goes to the same place—a restaurant."

Moira frowned. She hadn't noticed anything about a restaurant . . .

Gideon walked her through it and she swore hotly once she realized what he was getting at. "I'm going to have to contact the restaurant. The credit card companies. Who knows . . ."

"You won't have to do it. You've got handy, dandy investigator types who can do it for you."

With a withering look, she made another note. "None of this makes any sense. I pay him a hell of a lot more than he's stealing."

"That you know of—he could have hidden a lot more. You need to get an outside company to look at your books and uncover his tracks." He threaded his fingers through her hair, tugging lightly, and then started to massage her scalp. "What made you start looking at him?"

She made a face. "If you want *that* story, you need to stop stealing my wine and pour your own. I've got to catch you up on some other stuff anyway."

* * *

Gideon managed, barely, to bite back the insane fury that punched through him when Moira explained her role in confronting what turned out be a rather well-known petty thug.

He was going to put an unofficial be-on-the-look-out for the man. Landon Hayes might be in jail at the moment, but sadly, petty thugs and scumbags who really just needed to be in prison were often the ones the sharks got out the easiest.

He hadn't had any personal run-ins with Hayes, but Gideon knew he'd seen the man's name on a couple of hot sheets and there had been more than a few *official* BOLOs, too.

He didn't entirely manage to stay so serene when she told him about her visit from the IRS—yet one more strike from the McKays still faceless enemy.

It was all cold, calculated, planned, small, focused digs on various fronts. It made him think that somebody had decided to wage a war of sorts, a silent one. The most deadly sort, because how could they fight back without knowing who their enemy was?

"So. That's one of the reasons I'm going over everything Kevin had his hands on . . . or what I could dig up in a short amount of time." Moira gave him a tired smile. "The other reason . . ."

When her words trailed off, Gideon finished. He'd already pieced it together. There had been references in her notes about the Bittner project, so he hadn't needed to think too hard. "Zeke."

Her full lips compressed to a tight line. "He handled the whole deal. I want to know *why*. He overpaid for it, using company funds for a place we're not even *using,* and he screwed some guy over in the process."

She went to pick up the phone again.

Gideon caught her wrist. "Is he the one you keep calling?"

"Yes."

When she tugged against his grip, he just lifted her hand to his lips and nibbled on her knuckles. "If I make a deal with you, will you agree to let this go for a while?"

"That would depend on the deal," she said, her eyes dark with suspicion.

That was his Mac, all right.

"I've got some friends in the department in Jackson. I'll make some calls, see if they can swing by your man's place, just to check on him." He cocked a brow. "They can't compel him to call, but I get the feeling you're not just pissed. You're getting worried."

Moira sniffed. "He had a leg-breaker in my place of business. Nothing to stop somebody from showing up at his house. And I'd rather know what's going on before he ends up with his leg—or neck—broken."

"Yeah, yeah." He flicked his tongue at the sensitive area between her fingers, watched her lashes flutter. "And . . . after dinner . . . I'll drive you up to the house. The one that started all this mess. After all, you own it."

"And why would I want to go there?" A shiver raced through her and he had to remind himself that dinner was going to be done in ten minutes. If he started doing what he really wanted to do—and that involved stripping her naked and pulling her into his lap—then the food would burn.

"Because you want to know what the deal was." He shrugged, crooking a grin at her. "I know you, Mac. There's a part of you that is just eaten up with wanting to know the *why*."

A faint smile curled her lips. "Deal."

"Will you let me know what happens with the IRS thing?"

"Yeah." She huffed out a breath, rubbing at her neck as her eyes drifted away.

He didn't think she was looking at anything in particular. Just . . . staring, thinking.

Because he wanted her thoughts on him, he leaned in and kissed her.

Later was soon enough for them both to go back to brooding on their unknown enemy—and it was *their* enemy. The man had fucked with the McKays—had fucked with *Moira*.

That meant he'd made an enemy of Gideon Marshall.

When she called again, Kevin had to fight the urge to answer.

He'd always sort of liked Moira McKay, had wished he had the balls to ask her out, but she was sort of . . . icy. Elegant, but icy. Remote. He thought maybe that was the very thing he had liked about her. Of course, she was a fair boss and she'd treated him well.

That didn't mean he'd been opposed to screwing with her, when the plan was put before him, especially once he understood *why*.

But that had been back before all the crazy shit started to happen. It seemed to Kevin that the son of a bitch thought Kevin was stupid enough to believe it was all coincidence.

"Coincidence, my ass." His voice echoed in the big, old log cabin. It was a pretty old house, one that desperately needed updating, but he still didn't understand why he'd risked his job to secure this place. Kevin had also spent the past few years burying the paperwork and hoping nobody would connect it to him.

Everything was coming back to bite him, and he had only one person to thank for it—that crazy cousin of his.

He hadn't believed him at first—hadn't believed any of

the shit the man had told him. But he'd sounded so . . . logical. He'd had proof.

Everything they have . . . it should have been ours. Yours, mine.

The man had found Kevin when he'd been at his absolute worst, nearly a hundred thousand in debt to a loan shark and the idea that he had money coming—

The phone rang *again* and Kevin grabbed it with the intention of hurling against the wall. If she kept calling—

But it wasn't Moira McKay.

It was him.

Kevin's cousin. Reluctantly, he answered, knowing it wasn't wise to delay talking to the man.

"There was some excitement at your place of employ today, Kevin."

The cool voice came through as clearly as if he'd been standing in the room with Kevin and out of nervous habit, Kevin tossed a look back over his shoulder.

But he was alone.

In the distance he could hear a dog barking, and he shuddered. All those dogs . . .

He hated dogs, had had a passionate fear of them ever since he'd been attacked by a stray when he was a boy. Still, the occasional bark was enough to tell him everything was calm, everything was quiet.

"Was there?" Kevin managed to keep his reply level. "I'm afraid I had to leave early. Had some bad sushi at lunch, I think. Food poisoning . . . it's the worst."

"I wouldn't know." The line was silent a moment. "Somebody showed up looking for you. A Mr. Hayes . . . ?"

Kevin passed a hand over his sweaty forehead. Yeah, he knew. The calls left on his voicemail . . . they hadn't all been from Moira McKay.

"Well, too bad you weren't there, but I suspect you can find out what the problem was when you return to work on Monday. You'll have a nice, long weekend to rest up—a bit of a bank holiday, yes?"

Kevin licked his lips. "Ah . . . well. I suppose. Although I'm not sure if I'll have much of a job left after I go in Monday, man. Moira—I mean, Ms. McKay wants to speak with me. I think . . . I think she knows what I've been doing."

"Really. What a terrible shame."

But Kevin didn't think he was telling his cousin anything the man didn't already know.

The sweat beading on his brow, dripping down his nape, began to go cold. "Yes, well . . . I'm sort of thinking . . . I dunno, but it might be a good idea to lay low for a few days. Just stay out of sight. See, if Hayes is looking for me, he'll just keep looking. If I'm gone a while and then show back up . . . well, you know what a softie Moira is under all that bitch exterior. I'll come up with something, make her think I had to hide a while."

"Perhaps. Hmm. Yes, perhaps you should."

The call ended a few minutes later.

Kevin didn't waste any time punching in Moira McKay's cell phone number.

After she'd called him so many times tonight, he had it memorized.

But before it rang the first time, he disconnected.

CHAPTER FIFTEEN

"You're sure this is . . . never mind."

When she spoke, Frost lifted her head and poked her nose between the seats from the back of the cab. This time, Moira managed not to jump in surprise.

The dog was so big, but so quiet.

She reached up and buried her fingers in the thick ruff of fur at the dog's neck before looking at the house she could just now make out through the thinning trees. As Frost leaned into her ministrations, Moira managed a casual look down at her phone.

No new messages.

Two hours and twenty minutes ago, Kevin Towers had texted her.

He'd told her he wanted to speak to her.

She'd asked why, keeping an eye on Gideon out of the corner of her eye as he went about cleaning up. She'd argued and told him she would, but he told her that would be her last chance to deal with paperwork, since it was dark in the car and she owed him the rest of the night.

"This is the place," Gideon said easily, eying the shadowy outline of a house. "Somebody left the lights on."

"Security measure?"

He grunted as he threw the truck into park.

She felt bad not telling him about the few texts Kevin had sent, but she knew her cop. He wouldn't want to come out here if he knew Kevin was here. He'd be worried Kevin was up to something. But while she was pissed off at Kevin's embezzlement, she knew the man well enough to know he didn't have a violent bone in his body.

He was, in fact, a chicken shit coward.

He'd known Landon Hayes would be looking for him, he'd admitted in the text. He'd been sleeping in hotels the past week, dodging him, and Hayes had gotten impatient.

Kevin had seen him lingering around the parking lot when he came in so he'd decided to leave.

Leaving everybody else there to deal with the mess.

Moira wanted to punch him.

But she'd do it after she had answers.

"Moira . . ."

The low, rough sound of Gideon's voice made her shiver, and she turned her head.

He leaned toward her.

Instinctively, she echoed his movements.

And then she squawked and shoved at him, trying to grab back the phone he'd just swiped out of her hand.

"Give me that."

"Sure. In a minute." Gideon's quick, nimble fingers held her at a distance as he tapped at the screen. Thanks to the glow, she knew exactly when he found the messages.

She should have deleted them.

His eyes narrowed and came up, meeting her over the phone.

"He's here?" he asked, voice silky.

"Yes."

"And you were just going to merrily walk in there . . . and let me walk in there. Without telling me."

"No." Huffing out a breath, she crossed her arms over

her chest and stared out the window. "I planned to tell you as soon as we got out of the truck, Gideon."

"And why should I believe you, Mac?"

Stung, she jerked her head, but he was gazing toward the house, his face unreadable. "Because I don't lie to you."

He made a derisive snort. "You've lied to me for the past eighteen years. Maybe not in words, but in deeds, in actions."

"That's different." Huskily, she murmured, "I can't apologize enough so I'm not going to try. I would undo if I could, but since I can't . . ."

Gideon heaved out a harsh sigh.

In the dark cab, their gazes locked.

"I have to talk to him," she said, her voice pleading.

"He's a criminal. He could be dangerous."

"Oh, please. Ms. Mouton is more dangerous than this guy. I *know* him, Gideon."

"Then why didn't you realize he was embezzling?" Eyes sharp, he waited for an answer.

She flicked a hand through the air. "That's not the kind of thing I'm talking about. This guy is a coward. Chances are if you showed him your gun, he'd pass out. I saw him almost puke when somebody cut their finger in the break room."

Gideon's lips twitched, but he shook his head. "That doesn't mean much. He's scared. People do weird things when cornered."

"Then don't corner him." She jerked open the door a split second before he realized what she was going to do. Hopping out of the truck, she whistled softly to Frost.

Gideon swore.

She stared in at him, the faint glow from the dome light highlighting the irritation in his eyes. After a moment, she shut the door. The dome light came on again almost immediately as he opened his door and climbed out. She heard the solid thuds of his boots on the ground as he came around and stopped in front of her.

"You and I are going to talk about this," he said, voice taut.

"Okay."

He leaned in and curved a hand around her neck, tugging her in closer. "You and I are going to talk about a lot of things."

"Oh . . . okay." She licked her lips. He went to lower his hand, but she caught his wrist. "You're not . . . Gideon, please tell me you haven't decided you're going to leave anyway. We can make this work, I know we can."

"I spent a long time fooling myself, Moira. I'm done with it."

With an ache in her chest that threatened to split her open, she whispered, "What does that mean?"

"It means just that. If you want me, then this is it. You know how I feel. I can't make it any plainer, but I can't let you rip my heart out anymore." He turned away and she watched, oddly numb as he reached inside his leather coat and pulled out . . .

"Shit. Is that a *gun*?" She gaped.

"I am a cop, remember?" He checked it with a quick competency she found oddly compelling.

"You had that on you this whole time? But . . . you're off duty."

"I'm a cop."

Apparently that was his answer.

She lunged after him when he took a step toward the house. "You might be a cop, but I'm a McKay. I came here for answers. He's screwing with my company, pal. That doesn't mean I want you waving your weapon around like some . . . some . . . some phallic symbol."

"Phallic symbol?" Brow winging up, he looked down at her, expression a mix of amusement and aggravation.

"It's not a symbol. It's a weapon. Again, I'm a cop. He's a criminal. You might insist he's nonviolent, but he wouldn't be the first nonviolent person to snap. I'm not taking chances."

Then, to her surprise, the irritation faded and he reached up, cupping her face in his hand. "I sure as hell won't take chances with *you*."

His lips brushed over hers. "You're mine, Moira. Nobody is going to hurt what's mine—not if I can stop it."

A sigh shimmered out of her as he let her arm go and they broke apart. "Fine," she whispered, her voice thick. "So. Let's . . . um . . . go."

She turned away and started up the path. Moira made it precisely two steps before a hand in the back of her jeans caught her and brought her to a halt. "Not so fast."

Then he whistled under his teeth.

Frost came padding up.

As she turned to scowl at him, Gideon knelt down in front of the dog, spoke in a low voice.

Front gave a low yip, too quiet to really be called a bark.

Then she took off into the night, her white coat making her stand out like an eerie shadow.

"What are you doing?" she demanded.

"Making sure we're not walking into a place that's been set to blow up around us, for one." He glanced over at her. "I've done that once—I'd just as soon avoid it."

"I'm telling you—Kevin Towers is too chicken shit to hurt me." Miffed, she folded her arms over her chest and stared into the darkness, trying to see her dog. *Her* dog. The dog Gideon had found her, because she'd asked him.

"Yeah? Then what about the guy he's working with?"

Moira whipped her head and stared at him. "What are you talking about?"

"I'm talking about the guy pulling the strings, Mac. And

somebody is pulling the strings—it's just a bigger stage than I thought."

"Again . . . what are you talking . . ."

But Frost came running back up to them. She gave another short, quick bark.

"Did Timmy fall down a well?" Moira asked, unable to stop herself.

Gideon cocked a brow. "If he did, you're going after him. No, that just means she didn't smell anything that concerns her." He studied the dog's ears, which were still alert, studied the way she stood. "But she's . . . edgy."

He didn't speak dog—that was Zeke's specialty, but he'd been around canines enough to know when one was on skittish. Frost wasn't scared. The dog was about as calm and steady as they came, the perfect match for Moira in a million ways.

But something had her alert.

"You stay behind me," Gideon said, firing a look at Moira. "And if I tell you to *run*, you do it. Otherwise, I'll have Frost take you down."

Moira started to laugh, but the sound faded away into the night.

"No," Gideon said grimly. "I'm not joking. She's big enough to do it and she's trained. You wanna test me?"

"Ah . . . no. No, I don't." She tucked her hands into her back pockets and rocked onto her heels, shifting her gaze from him to the dog.

Gideon watched as she withdrew one hand from her pocket and snapped her fingers.

Frost trotted happily over to her and Moira started scratching her ears. "You wouldn't take me down, would you?"

Gideon blew out a breath and focused on the house. The dog would respond to a *protect* command, but he was kind of torn on who would out-stubborn the other . . . Moira or Frost.

Keep her safe, he thought in a silent prayer. He didn't do much of that these days, hadn't ever since he'd driven away from McKay's Treasure, the day after Moira told him it was over.

But special circumstances sometimes warranted it.

"We'll keep to the tree line." He took point, using the light of the moon as he made his way toward the house, taking care to be quiet. Of course, he wasn't sure it mattered. Moira trampled on every leaf, every branch. Once, he stopped and looked back at her. "Are you trying to announce that we're here?"

She smiled at him sweetly. "I'm so sorry, sweetheart. I was kind of not around the day they taught you how to walk like a damn ghost."

He had to bite back a snort and slowed his steps a little, giving her more time to pick where she put her feet.

It helped. A little.

Still, there was no sign anybody heard them.

But somebody *was* in there.

Gideon had seen a shadow in the window two or three times now and he was torn between sending Moira back to the truck or just making her wait here in the darkness with Frost.

A familiar, buzzing sort of noise filled the air, and he glanced back.

The glow lit the night like a miniature star and he shot out a hand, grabbing Moira's phone.

"He—"

He clamped a hand over her mouth and hauled her deeper into the trees. Not far, just a few feet, but he stood there, waiting until she got the point before he let go.

"What is *wrong* with you?" Moira glared at him.

"Again, are you trying to announce we're here?"

"Oh, for fuck's sake." Moira planted her hands on his hips. "I'll humor you—lets say he does have nefarious plans. We don't even know he's *here*!"

"Somebody is." Gideon tugged her closer and pointed toward the house. "Watch the window, second from the left."

As she did that, he pulled up her messages and read the one she'd just gotten.

I thought you were coming. If you're not, tell me because I can't wait forever. I'm sorry, Moira, but there are some problems I've got to deal with.

Disgusted, Gideon just shook his head. He almost passed the phone back to her, but then, as an idea formed, he started to smile. He tapped back a response.

Moira saw what he was doing and she craned her head, trying to read the message.

"Now you're the one announcing we're here," she said, rolling her eyes.

"No, I'm telling him you're almost here. I want to see what he does. Now put that in your pocket and don't touch it again until this is done." He could all but hear her gritting her teeth over that comment, but she didn't argue. One thing he'd always adored about Moira McKay was her brain. She was smart. Once he'd pointed out the potential danger, even if she didn't want to believe him, she'd been willing to let him do what he did best.

As he waited, his eyes skimmed the house, every sense alert.

His gaze swept back to the house just as the door opened and he held his breath, hand resting on the butt of his weapon as he strained to see past the darkness.

Just one man.

Too far off to make out much of anything else about him.

As he descended the stairs, the light from the house provided some illumination but it only allowed Gideon to see the man's profile—and his hair.

"That's him," Moira whispered.

"It's dark," he muttered.

"The hair."

Narrowing his eyes, Gideon focused on the Mohawk.

"It was a fundraiser for cancer. Him and about twenty others did it. A local boy . . ."

"Okay, okay. Hush."

Hell, taking Moira out on a stakeout would never happen.

She rested a hand on his side and leaned in as she peered around him. The soft weight of her body pressed to his and he clenched his jaw, reminding himself they had problems. He needed to focus on the problems they had to deal with before he and Moira could work this out once and for all. And tonight, at least, they needed to deal with this—with Kevin—before he could drive her back to Ferry and get her flat on her back again.

So . . . focus.

By his feet, the dog whined. It wasn't one of those anxious ones, it was almost as if the dog was trying to get him to do something.

As the man out in front of the house swung back around and headed inside, Gideon eased out of the shadows of the trees and took her hand. "Come on. Let's figure this out."

He watched the remote feed streaming across his computer.

It pissed him off that he was here instead of out at the cabin, but he understood priorities.

His house wasn't particularly a home.

He'd avoided making anything a home, because he had no place to make one. Everything that should have been his had been stolen from him and that was just the way of it.

But that didn't mean it had to *stay* the way.

He could get back what was his.

He was close.

So close.

"What are you *doing*?" he muttered to himself as Kevin Towers paced back and forth across the living room. The carpet was ratty and old and needed to be replaced, but that was a task that would wait for later. Much later.

This place, it too was rightfully his and one thing Kevin had done right was secure it for him. It had cost a pretty penny, far more than it was worth, but he had money. He had, after all, a generous employer, and few expenses.

He smirked, amused with himself.

But the smile faded as Kevin stopped in front of the table.

Finally.

They didn't much look like they were family, but the relationship was distant and watered down. Towers was very much from the idiot side of the family branch, truly. The stupid hair, for one.

Eyes narrowed, he waited for his long-lost cousin to reach out and take the bottle.

Please don't go helping yourself to my food and drink. Buy your own. He'd told Kevin that as he shoved the food he'd bought just for this occasion into the cabinets, including something he'd noticed the man had a fondness for.

The chocolate almonds were a specialty item. Nothing like them in stores. Then there was the whiskey. One of the two would get him. Kevin had a weakness for sweets and for the bottle.

Rubbing his fingers together, he leaned closer, waited.

And Kevin spun away, yanking his phone from his pocket.

"No, no, no, you stupid . . ." He blew out a breath and lifted his face to the sky.

If the fool didn't make it easy for him, he'd just have to take Kevin out up close and personal. He didn't want to do that.

So caught up in his aggravation, he missed Kevin's action until it was almost too late.

He was . . . texting?

A knot settled in the gut of the man on the chair.

In a hotel room from nearly an hour away, he reached out and adjusted the control that would let him hear.

But Kevin said nothing.

He just started to pace, his agitation growing.

When Kevin Towers burst out of the house without touching any of the poisoned sweets or the doctored alcohol, his long-lost cousin started to cuss in long, ugly streams.

It took far longer for him to calm down than normal and when he finally did, so much time had passed that Kevin was back in the house, back to pacing even.

And Kevin was no longer alone.

Through the speakers came Kevin's voice, almost *relieved*, as he said, "Fuck, you scared me to death."

CHAPTER SIXTEEN

"You realize I want to *beat* you to death?" Moira demanded, glaring at Kevin.

He flinched, his face pale. Kevin was a big guy and he looked even bigger with that ridiculous Mohawk. If he'd learn to find some balls, he'd probably cut an impressive figure, tall and broad-shouldered, a green-eyed blond with a dimpled smile.

But he had no spine.

That wasn't a particularly attractive trait, Moira supposed.

"I . . ."

She narrowed her eyes. "I don't want excuses or lies. I want answers."

She was surprised when he turned his head and stared out the window. "I know," Kevin said quietly.

He shot a quick look at Gideon. "Guess you brought him to arrest me."

The man was an idiot, Moira decided. How had she not seen that? Gideon wouldn't be able to arrest him—Kevin *would* be arrested, unless he magically had all that money stuffed away somewhere and could return it and even then, she didn't plan on letting him off with a smack on the hand.

But the crimes he'd committed had been in Jackson, far outside of Gideon's jurisdiction. Not to mention that they were in Louisiana now, not Mississippi. She might not work in law enforcement, but once you crossed state lines, things got dicey.

But maybe Kevin wasn't thinking straight. He'd seen Gideon, recognized him, and assumed. She wasn't surprised Kevin had recognized Gideon. Most of the people who worked at headquarters came to Ferry at least once a year if not twice—for the annual Christmas party and for a Memorial Day barbecue. And Gideon was always there.

Has always been . . .

Gideon shifted his weight, and she could practically *hear* his low, steady voice, pointing out that practical things like Kevin's crimes had been committed outside his jurisdiction. Before he could say anything, she placed a hand on his arm.

She wanted Kevin freaked out, not relaxing. "Whether or not I have you arrested is all going to depend on what you do in the next few minutes, Kevin. I suggest you start talking."

All he did was nod.

When he moved deeper into the house, Gideon shot out a hand and caught her arm, eyes narrowed. She gave him a look.

It said, *Trust me.*

But Gideon chose not to acknowledge it.

She found Kevin sitting in what had to be the living room with his elbows on his knees and a pensive look on his face as he studied a bottle of liquor. Moira felt her jaw literally *dropping* when she saw recognized the bottle.

Kevin Towers might make good money working for her, but if he was having the kind of money issues she suspected he was having, then why did he have a bottle of

Macallan 25 sitting in front of him? There was a glass beside it, like he'd been about ready to have a drink when they showed up.

"Interrupting something?" She gave him a sharp-edged smile. "Is that what you're doing with the money you've been stealing from me? Buying booze?"

Kevin gave a short, ugly laugh. "No. This was . . ." He shrugged then, as if it didn't matter. "You've been a good boss, Moira. I learned a lot at McKay. I shouldn't have— hell, it's too late for that now. Too late for a lot of things."

Scowling, she shoved her hands into her pockets. "I don't want—"

Gideon's hand came down on her shoulder and he squeezed. There was enough pressure there that she lapsed into silence. As he stepped past her, she caught sight of the look on his face. All cop.

He wasn't even pretending otherwise now.

"Why don't you talk to us, Towers? Seems to me you're in trouble."

Kevin's gaze flicked to him, then away.

Moira saw the man swallow, the skin around his eyes going tight. Now that she was really looking at him, she couldn't help but notice that Kevin looked like he had aged a good five years over the past few months. Why hadn't she seen it?

You haven't been looking.

"I don't think 'trouble' touches what I got going on." Eyes dull, Kevin reached out and picked up the bottle. He slid Moira a look. "You want to join me? I've never had any of this before. Heard it's damn good."

Moira's belly revolted a little but she managed a smile. "Sure. It's beyond good, though. Like silk and fire, all at once."

"Heard Brannon has some of the Macallan 42. He probably uses it to rinse out after brushing his teeth." He snorted as he got up, heading into the kitchen. He glanced over his shoulder at Gideon. "You on duty?"

Gideon shrugged. "But you two . . . feel free."

A few moments later, Moira closed her hands around the glass and clutched it on her lap while Kevin lifted the whiskey to his nose and swirled it around, sniffing in the aroma slowly. "Man, that's amazing," he said.

"Tastes even better."

He nodded, but didn't drink. "I guess you heard about my gambling problem. Drinking . . . hell, I could go a month without drinking and never miss it. Never did like to smoke. But you could ask me if I thought it would rain, and I'd strike a bet on the answer. It was just . . . my weakness."

"We all have them."

He nodded, shifting his attention back to the Macallan.

Moira no longer wanted hers, though.

Still, out of courtesy, she held on to it.

"I was in trouble. Owed almost fifty grand to this guy. It was his asshole that came to the office, looking for me, I think. I actually got square with him once, but then there'd be a fight or somebody would ask me if I wanted in on the big poker game . . . I got in over my head. Again and again. And then . . ." He stopped abruptly, his knuckles going white against his skin as his fist tightened around the glass.

He surged upward and started to pace. The whiskey splashed around to splatter on his hand, but Kevin didn't even seem to notice. His eyes were overbright and when he swung around, he looked a little wild. "I didn't have any family, you know. Not after my dad died. Mom died when I was little. Suicide. Everybody acted like she got sick, but what she did was pop some pills and then went to sleep and never woke up. Dad soldiered on and he did a good job, but still . . . it was just us. I never had a family. I had my work. I had a few friends. And I was good with cards and shit. Then this guy comes along . . ." Kevin started to laugh.

Something about that jagged noise was like knives digging into Moira's ears and she wanted to clap her hands over them to make it stop. He went to take a drink, but stopped, staring down into the scotch like it had suddenly turned into cat piss on him. Revolted, he slammed it down and came striding over toward Moira.

Gideon cut between them.

"Ease up there, Towers," he said, his voice still calm and easy.

Moira wondered if he had any idea how ready Gideon was for him to do *anything*. Anything at all. He had one hand up in a calming gesture, the other hooked in his pocket. Moira had seen how quickly that same stance could go to gun raised. She'd seen it. Only once, thank God, but she'd seen it.

"Don't worry." Kevin apparently spoke cop. He backed up, his own hands up. "I'm not going to hurt her. I just . . ." His gaze swung to Moira, or what he could see of her.

She shifted out from behind Gideon, not completely, but enough that Gideon could see her face.

A weak smile quirked his lips. "I used to have a thing for you, you know? I imagined asking you out about once a week. Then you got married and I figured there went my chance." He skimmed a hand back over his hair.

Moira's smile froze.

Kevin's eyes slid back to her. "Don't worry. That's over. You'd slice off my balls and feed them to me. And everything now . . . it's all shit. It's all messed up."

"You've mentioned that." Gideon shifted so that he stood where he could keep Moira in his sight, but close enough that he could still catch Kevin.

He was wasting his time.

She wasn't in any danger. Not from Kevin, at least.

He looked down at his hands and frowned. Gideon seemed to breathe a little easier when the other man turned away and found his drink. Slowly, he sank down on the couch to stare at nothing. "He comes up to me and I couldn't believe it when he tells me that we were cousins. He starts showing me everything, how he found me . . . the family tree."

A cold chill broke out down her spine at the absent, sort of lost tone in his voice.

Kevin shook his head as if he realized what was going on and he lifted the glass to his lips. He took a small sip, then sighed in appreciation. He took another one, draining half the glass that time. "That's some good shit." He smacked his lips and tossed back the rest before he refilled his glass. As he did so, he looked over at Moira. "It's all about you, you know. You and your brother, your sister. He fucking hates you, Moira. I didn't realize it. I mean . . . it didn't make sense. If I'd known that, I woulda stayed clear. You never did nothing to me. But I didn't see it. The man *hates* you. He hates you and he wants you to suffer."

"Who?"

Kevin's mouth twisted in a sneer. "That's the funny thing." Bottle in hand, he came back over to the couch and sat down. He drained another half glass, staring at her with overbright eyes. "One thing about him—he might be fuck-all crazy, but the bastard has excellent taste in liquor."

Brooding, he stared down into the glass, but he wasn't seeing it. Moira had no idea what he saw.

Uneasy, she edged a little closer.

"Crazy bastard. You should have heard him rant, Moira. About the museum . . . or when you would go on a buying trip or Brannon was going up to some no-name winery in the middle of no-name Ohio. He'd rant and rave—throwing things and cussing everybody from you to that Whitehall guy to . . . you."

His voice slurred and he reached up, rubbing at one eye while Moira stared at him. "White . . . Kevin, what in the hell are you talking about?"

"That's what 'm trying to 'splain here, Moira," he said, talking in a voice that was too loud and too slow—and still his words were jumbled together.

His hand shook as he refilled his glass, splashing more than a little of the pricy scotch on the table.

"Okay." Moira approached, the fumes from the spilled scotch rising in the air. "I think you've had enough. Give me the bottle."

Kevin closed his hand protectively over it.

She snapped her fingers and said, "*Now.*"

"Fine." He shoved it toward her but turned his body away as he said, "But I'm keepin' this."

To demonstrate, he took another quick swig from the glass.

"Fine, you lush." Moira glanced down at the bottle of Macallan and then sat it down, moving to closer to Kevin. "Gideon, could you get a glass of water?"

Kevin's eyes were blurry.

Behind her, Gideon said, "I don't know about . . ."

"Oh, for crying out loud. He's already half-piss faced. I'll get it."

She shoved upright and moved into the kitchen, opening cabinets at random until she found a glass. She filled it with tap water and moved back into the living room, the dim light making it seem gloomier, darker than it really was. Kevin was curled up the corner of the couch, staring at nothing.

"Here."

He looked at the water and shook his head.

"Take it," she ordered. "You should drink it."

"What? Oh. Yeah. I got a drink. Fan . . . thanks." He blinked as if having trouble focusing. At the same time, he took another drink. Half of it spilled, but he managed to get the rest of it down his throat.

In the next moment, the glass fell from his hand.

She tried to catch it and couldn't.

Kevin blinked, three times. And each time, his lashes lingered down a little bit longer.

When he slumped forward, she tried to catch him.

Gideon knocked her aside just in time.

Moira jumped as she bumped into the glass of scotch Kevin had given her. It hit the hardwood floors and shattered, shards of glass and droplets of Macallan 25 spraying across the floor.

Gideon caught Kevin, eased him down.

By the time Gideon had the younger man on the floor, Kevin's face had gone slack.

But his eyes were still open.

Open and staring straight ahead.

"Shit," Moira whispered, staring at his lax face. "Is he . . ."

"No." Gideon pressed two fingers to his neck, then tore at his collar. "Get to the car, Moira. Now."

"But—"

"*Now!*" Gideon whipped his head around and shouted at her. "We need to get him to a hospital."

It was somewhat problematic.

Studying the feed streaming live to his computer, he stared at Moira's face. He poured the Macallan from the decanter into a crystal highball and toasted the screen.

"Run, run as fast as you can," he taunted the screen as Gideon Marshall hefted Kevin Towers' inert body into a fireman's hold.

It was a pity, but Kevin had proven to be a hindrance. That meant he had to go.

He'd be dead soon.

That was what happened when people talked.

They could try to get to the hospital all they wanted, but he'd perfected this particular little blend and he knew almost to the milligram how much time Kevin had.

Judging by how quickly he'd been tossing back the scotch, it was probably under ten minutes. The nearest hospital was a good twenty minutes away and it was a miserable little county affair. Not the nicely outfitted one all fixed up with McKay money, but a broke little place, scraping by on what the government could spare and what little people sent their way.

Marshall would never get him there in time.

Assuming by some chance he did, by the time the local idiots even have a chance to look him over? Well, Kevin would be dead.

It was a pity, but a necessity, too.

Kevin knew too much. When people knew too much, they became a liability.

The man watching the monitor stood.

He'd get over there. Clean up. Dump the rest of the tainted scotch.

But the door swung back open and Moira came striding back in, pausing to look back over her shoulder. She made a face and nodded.

Her unseen audience began to swear as she paused and tugged something on. Gloves. Marshall had given her a pair of gloves.

The son of a bitch knew.

She hurried into the kitchen, throwing cabinets open, and he almost grabbed the monitor and ripped it out of the wall when she pulled a jar out. One of those stupid mason jars—the previous owner had kept them all over the place.

She poured the liquor into it. Every last drop.

Then she grabbed something he hadn't seen.

A box.

He recognized it now.

It was the box Kevin had used the last time he brought Chinese food out to the place. She put the bottle and the mason jar and the glass Towers had used inside it.

Then she headed for the door.

"What the fuck is . . ."

There was a dog.

When had she gotten a dog? He leaned forward until his nose was almost touching the screen, eying the big, pale dog. He punched a control on the computer, zooming in.

And the dog's pale head swung around, its eyes zeroing in exactly on where the camera was hidden.

"Fuck me."

It was like that dog was staring straight at him.

CHAPTER SEVENTEEN

"You realize this looks really bad."

Gideon thought if the man wearing the county sheriff's badge pointed that out one more time, he just might rip off the badge and use it to gag him.

"Yes, sheriff. I realize it looks really bad," he said, parroting the words back. Maybe saying exactly what the other man was saying would make the guy get the point.

Gideon was a fucking cop. This looked bad—yeah, he got the point.

"You say you were just coming out here to look around and your girlfriend knew he was here, but she didn't tell you?"

Gideon pinched the bridge of his nose.

He'd gone through this three times already. Logically, he knew what the law enforcement officer was doing. Repetition was everything. There was no telling how many times a suspect had slipped up over the stupidest little detail. Those details got lost in the telling—hard to keep your story straight when you made it up and pulled it out of your ass.

But Gideon was a cop and he knew how all of this went

down. On top of that, he was tired *and* fed up with all of this bullshit.

Spreading his hands out wide, he said, "I'm going to go through this again."

So he did.

The sheriff nodded slowly and took notes.

Gideon didn't think the man learned anything new.

Gideon told the story over anyway.

And all the while, Moira sat huddled on a chair, staring outside while Frost curled around her in a big, canine hug. Every now and then, the dog would nudge her and Moira would respond by stroking a hand down the dog's back. Then the woman would go back to staring outside. Frost would patiently wait. Then after about ten or twenty minutes, Frost would nudge her again.

The dog shouldn't be in here. So far though, nobody had pointed that out.

"And you're thinking the alcohol was poisoned?"

Gideon shifted his attention back to Sheriff Herron. "I'm not thinking anything. I'm just offering it up as a possibility. Towers acted like the bottle wasn't his—said something about how this cousin of his had excellent taste in scotch. It's expensive—a brand called Macallan." He paused, red flushing up the back of his neck as he tried to figure out the right way to say this. "I'm familiar with the brand. A friend drinks it. It comes sealed. Most alcohol does these days. But it wasn't sealed when I saw it. I don't know if it was a gift or what. I'm just speculating."

Dutifully, the sheriff nodded and made notes. "Okay, Chief Marshall. I think that will do it. I might have to call, touch base." He paused and then looked over at Moira. "I'll give her a day or two before I do any more follow-ups. She looks a bit shaken."

"Thanks." Gideon nodded, appreciating the courtesy.

The sheriff had kept his questions for Moira short and sweet, so despite Gideon's irritation, he owed the county sheriff a debt for his kindness to Moira.

Gideon went back to look at Moira, his gut clenching at the thought of her holding the glass in her hand. If he was right about the scotch being poisoned, then he had been *that* close to losing her.

That close.

It had been so hard all this time never really having her, but for her to be gone—

Abruptly, he spun around and strode down the hall, away from the lounge. He kept right on going until he was in the parking lot of the small hospital, right next to the emergency room.

The sheriff's car was parked there, along with another deputy's car.

The sheriff had told him he had a couple of people out at the house, processing the scene.

That was all well and good.

Gideon didn't know if they'd find shit.

Somebody had been fucking around with Moira—with all of them—for weeks. *Months.*

It's all about you . . .

He hates you.

That's what Kevin had been saying. He'd known who it was.

"White," Gideon muttered. "What did he mean by that?"

"Whitehall."

At the sound of Moira's soft voice, he stiffened.

He wasn't certain if it was wise to be around her right now. All he wanted to do was grab her, hold her, never let go. But they weren't exactly in the right place for him to touch her, kiss her, reassure himself of all the things he needed to be reassured of.

He was so on edge, and the thought of just how close he'd come to losing her . . .

Gravel crunched under her feet as she drew closer, and he also heard the *click-click-click* of the dog's claws on the ground. He focused on the dog and turned, looking at Frost as the big dog observed their surroundings, her eyes alert, head cocked.

"Whitehall," Gideon prodded when Moira didn't elaborate. *Focus on the job. Don't think about what could have happened. Not here. Not yet.*

"He was . . . well, George Whitehall."

Gideon shot a look at her. She had folded her arms over her belly and was staring at nothing. "What are you talking about?"

"He's the man who turned Patrick McKay in—"

"Shit, I know who he *was*," Gideon said, cutting a hand through the air. "He's also been dead . . . what a hundred years now?"

"I don't know. Neve could tell you—to the day. She's been following the family histories online." Moira's smile was cynical. "I do know he married, had one legitimate son, possibly several illegitimate ones, and his wife died not long after he went back to England."

The smile on her mouth, cynical or not, struck him in the heart and he reached up, cupped her cheek. "If that scotch was poisoned . . ."

"I'm fine," she said, closing her hand around his wrist and squeezing. "I was too nervous, too pissed to drink anything anyway."

He went to tug her in close. "Never thought I'd be grateful for your . . ." He stopped mid-sentence as something she'd said finally connected. "Whitehall had illegitimate children?"

She pursed her lips. "That's what you're thankful for?"

"Moira . . ."

She rolled her eyes at him. Rising up on her toes, she pressed a quick kiss to his lips. "Yeah. That's the rumor at least." She rolled her eyes and reached down to scratch Frost's ears as the dog sat by her feet.

Kevin had mentioned a cousin.

Eyes locked on the pocked, pitted mess of the parking lot, he asked, "Any chance Kevin might be a descendant of one of them?"

The kid had died under his hands as Moira powered the truck down the county road toward the hospital. She'd done an admirable job of driving and talking to the local dispatch. Halfway there, emergency medical personnel had met them and she'd practically collapsed into a boneless pile of female flesh as he helped her out of the cab, but she'd rallied once he told her they had to get to the hospital.

She hadn't known Kevin was already gone.

He hadn't known how to tell her.

They'd still been doing CPR when they rolled him away.

But they had stopped en route.

Moira had found out at the hospital.

Her fingers stroked Frost's neck in a soothing rhythm, and Gideon found his eyes following them as he played back her words.

Cousins.

Illegitimate children.

The McKays.

It was all about them.

He'd thought that for a while.

Nothing had seemed like it was flowing in a way that made sense.

"Gideon?"

He shook his head, feeling like he'd come out of a daze and looked up at her, realizing he'd been just standing there, staring at her for some time.

Frost's mouth gaped open in a doggy smile, and Gideon scowled at her.

"We need to go back to Treasure," he said, looking back at her. He had to start digging around and he thought it might take some time. He only had to go back, oh, say . . . a hundred fifty, a hundred sixty years. Somehow, he didn't think those records were going to be quite so easily accessed.

"It's gotta be nice, using that badge to make things happen," Moira said, striving to keep her voice light as they barreled down the road in Gideon's truck.

She didn't think she was fooling Gideon, though. He shot her a narrow look that lasted less than a second.

He'd also put his lights on—the lights, no siren, thankfully. She wasn't sure her aching head could take the noise. Her gut was in knots. Her throat felt like she'd swallowed a boulder.

She kept seeing Kevin . . .

Stop it, Mac. Just stop.

Pasting a smile on her face, she swung her head around and concentrated on Gideon's hard profile. "The badge, the lights. I mean, you were there when somebody . . ."

Her voice cracked.

"Moira . . ." Gideon reached over and cupped the back of her neck.

"No!" *Damn it.* She smacked at his hand, but he wouldn't budge. "I'm fine."

From the backseat, Frost poked at her with a wet nose. That only made it harder to keep steady, but Moira kept trying. She didn't need to break down.

She didn't need to break down.

She didn't need to—

"Oh, *fuck*!" She clamped a hand to her mouth and tried

to swallow the sob. It wouldn't be stopped, though. It tore out of her like it had claws, followed by another and another.

She didn't even notice Gideon pulling the truck off the narrow, two-lane highway. Didn't notice him turning off the flashing lights or hitting the emergency blinkers on the dash. But when he pulled her into his arms, she noticed that.

"It's okay, Mac," he whispered against her temple. "You don't have to be so tough around me. Just get it out."

She shuddered and curled her arms around him, half-choking on the sob.

The sight of Kevin swaying, then collapsing, the look on his face.

And Gideon, when he'd told her that Kevin was dead, that the EMTs hadn't been able to save him.

It's about you . . .

"Who is *doing* this to us, Gideon?" she choked out between sobs.

"I don't know." He rubbed his lips against her cheek, kissed away a tear, then another. "But I'll find out. I'll figure this out, Mac."

She turned her face to his, intent on asking him something. How, maybe. How did he plan to figure it out.

But he was so close.

And his mouth was right there.

The terror and frustration inside her gave way to something else—need was better than fear, wasn't it?

But when she leaned into kiss him, he angled his head back. "Not now, Moira. I'm on edge."

"Gideon . . ."

"No!" He shoved a hand into her hair and tangled it, holding her still when she would have kissed him again. "If I touch you now, I'll bruise you. You don't know what it did to me inside once I figured out what had happened—you had that glass in your hand, Moira. One sip and it might have been *you* I was trying to save."

His voice cracked. "It might have been you."

The hand in her hair loosened slightly.

She leaned in. "I want your hands on me right now. I need them on me, Gideon. Please. Make the shadows go away. Make the last eighteen years go away."

Make the last eighteen years go away . . .

He could hear the threads of his control snapping—only these weren't threads. They were tension wires, holding back the weight of his need and hunger, one that had been building for years.

He'd been holding back all this time, afraid to really give into it for fear of what little might be left of him if—*when*—she changed her mind again. For him, it wasn't even a question.

He'd stopped believing in her.

In them.

But she'd just destroyed his final attempts at self-preservation and he damned them both.

He yanked her against him, cursing them both.

Behind them, Frost made a low noise in her throat. He barely had the presence of mind to give her the command to stay before he closed his mouth over Moira's.

The steering wheel pinned them and he couldn't get his hands on her the way he needed. Swearing, he fumbled them both out of the truck while she scraped her teeth down his neck. In one final, clear-headed moment, he grabbed his keys and shoved them into his pocket and then instinct took over.

He hauled her into the trees along the side of the road, just out of sight.

If he'd had the sense, he would have backed the truck

up more to give them some cover, but he hadn't just lost control of his senses—he'd lost his fucking mind.

Moira sank her teeth into his lip and he felt the nerve endings start to sizzle, then explode, one by one. Spinning her around, he fumbled with her jeans, shoving them down to just below her hips. "Gideon," she whimpered, trying to turn back to him.

"Too cold," he muttered. He wanted her naked, but the chill in the air sort of removed that possibility from the equation.

There was nothing cold about her, though.

After a quick fumble with his own jeans, he had freed himself and without waiting another moment, Gideon lifted her up. She strained to spread her thighs more and he caught her hands, guiding them upward one at a time, leading them to a sturdy limb just above her. "Hold on," he muttered against her ear. With her weight partially supporting by the tree branch overhead, he lifted her, angling her hips so he could slide in. The wet glove of her sex closed around him as he lowered her back down, anchoring her rump against him with one arm around her waist.

He drove up into her, bracing his other hand against the rough bark of the tree.

Moira cried out, shuddering on his cock as he impaled her over and over.

She squeezed down on him and he thought he just might die from the pleasure.

"Gideon . . ."

His name was a broken moan, but it wasn't enough. Grabbing her face in his palm, he pulled her head around until she was looking up at him. She let go of the branch and gasped as it drove her more firmly down on him. Her hands gripped his forearm, nails biting into his skin.

"Tell me you love me," he whispered against her cheek.

"I love you. Please . . ." She strained against him, but there was no leverage.

He lifted her up, slowly let her come back down.

The desperate hunger in her voice was like a drug, sending him into a fevered frenzy. "Say it again."

"I love . . ." Her body arched back against his, locking. "Gideon . . . please!"

"Say it!" He caught her earlobe between his teeth and bit her.

This time she moaned it, and it reverberated down his spine as though she'd dragged a silken glove along his skin. He staggered forward a step, using his arms to cushion her as he leaned against the tree, and proceed to thrust against her, up into her wet, waiting depths. The need to come, the need to mark her, claim her . . . whatever it took to *keep* her was overwhelming.

He clenched his teeth, fighting back his orgasm as he felt hers moving in closer.

It wasn't until she started to climax that he loosened the reins of his control.

After she whimpered his name one more time, he fisted his hand in her hair, slanted his mouth over hers. Just before the climax ripped out of him, he rasped, "I love you, Mac."

CHAPTER EIGHTEEN

Morning dawned gloomy and gray.

Moira lay on her side staring out Gideon's window, the scent of coffee heavy in the air.

There were also lesser, but still important scents—like bacon. Eggs, maybe.

"Morning, sleepyhead."

She closed her eyes and smiled. "How do you know I'm awake?"

"Sixth sense."

As the bed gave under his weight, she rolled onto her back and looked up at him. "I should call home. They'll worry."

"I already did." He sipped from a cup of coffee, staring down at her. "I assume by *they*, you mostly mean Ella Sue. So I sent her a text when we got in. Then I sent one to Brannon, mostly to wake him up and piss him off. Also sent one to Neve. I'm sure it woke her up, too, but she'll be too giddy to be pissed."

Moira rolled her eyes before focusing them on the coffee. "Here I was hoping that was for me."

"Oh, it is. So is the tray I left on the dresser. You can have it when you sit up."

Moira pursed her lips. "I'm sort of naked."

"I sort of noticed." He lowered his gaze to stare at her. "I'm waiting."

"You're still seventeen somewhere under that cop exterior, aren't you?" She eased upright, keeping the sheet tucked up against her naked breasts.

"Aren't all men?" Eyes on hers, he reached out, caught the sheet, and gave it a gentle tug.

But she resisted. Something was bothering her. *Tell me you love me* . . . He'd wanted her to say it almost every time he touched her. He'd waited until she was practically lost to sensation and need before he'd admitted it, though.

Maybe it was the most she deserved.

"Do you still love me?" She stared at him, feeling exposed. It had nothing to do with being naked under the sheet, either.

Gideon's eyes fell away. Under the simple black cotton of his shirt, his shoulders rose and fell. "I've loved you since you were fifteen years old, Moira. Why do you think that's gone and changed now?"

"Maybe a better question would be do you still *want* to love me." She managed a small shrug, even a smile. "You don't seem to want to look at me. We . . . hell. This is hard. We don't talk like we used to. I can't . . . I'm trying to fix things and it's like I'm reaching across a chasm sometimes just to touch you."

His gaze came to hers and in a voice that sounded painfully grim he said, "I love you, Moira. You know that."

"But . . . ?" Her throat tightened as he came toward her. There were things in his eyes, words he wasn't going to speak just yet. She could see it.

"No buts. I love you. First, last, always. Everything else? Maybe that's the 'but.'" He caught her face in his hands and kissed her. "We've got a mess around us and we need to deal with it. You—*all* of you are in trouble and I can't get distracted from that. Take the coffee. Eat."

He brought the tray closer and left her alone in the bedroom.

He hadn't even tried to talk her out of the sheet.

That feeling that something was wrong hadn't gone away.

If anything, it had spread.

"Moira, I don't have time to . . . look, I get that you say it's important, but my fucking bookstore burned . . . what do you mean do I have insurance? What—no. Son of a bitch."

Brannon lowered the phone back to the cradle and stood there staring at it.

Hannah came out of the bedroom, wearing a pair of cargos and a bra. The bra was a soft, icy shade of blue. Brannon had picked it out for her, along with a matching pair of panties. Seemed a shame she was going to cover it with her uniform. But he didn't figure a paramedic needed to run around in a pair of pants and a bra.

She could cause heart attacks, especially lately. Her breasts were bigger now, fuller. He had entire fantasies spun around her breasts and now that she was pregnant . . . well. Brannon had no problem admitting he was something of a pig when it came to her body.

"Sounds like you and Moira are getting along lovely, just like always." She paused by him to kiss his cheek.

Before he could turn his head and catch her to deepen the kiss, she was already moving away.

"It's something to do with McKay Enterprises." Irritated, he crossed his arms over his chest. "She can figure it out. That's what she does. I think it had something to do with a buyer. Moira is talking to cops and all now."

"Hey, stop the train." Hannah held up her hands. "Just why is Moira talking to the cops?"

Brannon groaned and rubbed his temple. "There was a dead body."

"*What?*"

"Well, I'm not entirely sure. She said she'd give me more information when I got to the house." Broodingly, he stared at the floor. It looked like he'd have to if he wanted answers. "Hell, if it wasn't for the body, she couldn't even make me go. I don't deal with buyers of any sort. That's all business. Business makes my head hurt. Moira *loves* it. She doesn't need my help on any of this."

"She *asked* for your help, though."

Opening his mouth, then closing it, he sighed and looked away.

Well, shit. Hannah had a point.

Moira didn't ask for much, which meant when she did, he kind of felt like he had to help. He glanced across the street, his gaze lingering on the bookstore—or rather, the burnt out husk that had *been* the bookstore. "I'll call you," he said when Hannah came back into the room a few minutes later, all dressed and ready to go.

She was neat and tidy in her uniform, hair pulled into a ponytail, her belly a high, hard mound. He wanted to go to her and muss her all up, but he stayed where he was. "When it's close to end of shift, I'll call you. If I'm not home, I'll have you come to me . . . or something."

Hannah rolled her eyes.

"That's not necessary," she started to say.

He shook his head.

"It is."

There was a fire at the bookstore he owned.

Moira had to talk to cops about a body.

Idly, he wondered if his baby sister had been having any kind of fun today.

* * *

Neve hitched up her shoulder when Ian started nuzzling her neck. "Stop it. I swear, I'm going to start checking to see if you're popping blue pills or something—we just about broke our necks in the shower and you're ready to go again?"

"Neve, I'm a man and you're laying on the bed in my shirt," he pointed out. "That's way better than any blue pill."

She snorted, nudging him in the gut when he leaned in closer.

He sighed and settled down next to her, staring at the screen of her laptop. "You spend an awful lot of bloody time on that site."

She slid him a look. "It's interesting. Haven't you ever wondered where you come from?"

"Of course." He shrugged. "But not so much that I'd go blind on a genealogy site. Half those people are probably doing it wrong."

"Probably." Neve grinned. "But it's still fun. And I'm *not* doing it wrong. We've got our family tree all the way back to Patrick's great-grandparents tucked away in this big family bible. Madeleine's, too. We're about as Scottish as they come on his side."

"Who would have guessed, with the name *McKay*." Deadpan, he shook his head. "What 'bout her, Madeleine?"

"English. Through and through. Her mother's family came over late seventeen hundreds. Madeleine's mother went back when she was eighteen for a visit and met the guy she'd marry. They came back here and that's all she wrote."

"When did McKay come over? The Clearances chased a lot of people out, especially up in the Highlands."

Neve sighed. She'd read so much about the Jacobite rebellion and the Clearances—how the face of Scotland had forever been changed. "Most of the McKays did leave. Patrick's father stayed, because *his* father had lost a leg, didn't think he'd survive the journey and his mother wouldn't leave without him. He met a girl, fell in love . . . had Patrick. But . . . well, hell. You know more about the history than I do. Life sucked there for a lot of people for a long time. Patrick was sixteen when he decided he wanted more and he left."

She clicked on one of the little leaves, then made a face, deleting it. "Some of these stories people come up with."

"What are these for?" Ian flicked at the leaf twitching on her screen.

"Hints." She arched a brow. "Haven't you seen those commercials?"

"I'm not much for commercials. I want the action."

"I never noticed." Rolling her eyes, she clicked on the icon and showed him. "Different things. Might be a story or a public record, that kind of thing. Who knows? I've found a couple of people who are probably legit distant cousins, but some of the stuff I've already known or it's just crap. It's probably more fun when you go in not knowing as much."

"I should do me sometime." Ian slid her a wicked grin. "Unless you'd rather. Do me, that is."

"You are hopeless." She shook her head and tapped the leaf connected to the icon with Moira's picture just as the phone rang. Sighing, she closed her laptop without reading the information that had just popped up.

A few minutes later, she climbed over Ian's sprawled body. "I've got to go to Moira's. It's about that house I was telling you about."

Ian craned his head up and looked at her. "She find out who it was that fucked things up?"

"Yeah." She pulled out a bra and put it on before she

turned to face Ian. His gaze dipped to her breasts. "He's dead."

Pale eyes went as cold as winter frost as Ian's gaze slanted up to lock on her face. "What the bloody fuck?"

"You heard me. He's dead."

Ian kicked his legs out of bed. "Well, it's a good thing I've been taking Saturdays off. I think I'll just ride along with ya, my beautiful Neve."

"Well. Nobody told me there was a party today."

Ella Sue stood in the doorway of the large living room. Although she had indeed retired, as they'd all expected, Ella Sue still spent almost as much time as McKay's Ferry as she did at her own home.

She usually took Saturdays off, but Thanksgiving and Christmas were drawing close and that turned her into something of a fright—the decorating kind.

Cornucopias had been unpacked and lovingly placed while gourds and pumpkins were set with bunches of fall-colored flowers.

The Friday after Thanksgiving, Ella Sue would be back, like clockwork, and all the Christmas decorations would be up by evening. If she had her way, she'd draft all of the McKays into helping.

Moira wasn't entirely certain she was ready to think about the holidays, not with dead people and burning buildings and threats seeming to haunt her every waking thought.

"It's not a party." Gideon flashed a bright smile at Ella Sue. "It's a . . . discussion."

"Discussions go better with food. What would ya'll like?"

Moira glanced at Brannon, then her sister. This involved them, so it involved Ella Sue, too. "Ella Sue, you should be in here."

Ella Sue came inside, her gaze sliding from one face to another. As she took her seat, Moira started to talk.

"I think . . ." Brannon said after a few moments of silence. He pushed back his chair and stood, keeping his hands braced on the table. "I think that you need to take a step back and look at this again."

Moira stared at him.

The others were quiet.

"You think I need to step back and look at this again." Moira started to tap her fingers on the arm of the chair. "How do you suggest I look at it? Should I reevaluate how I was attacked? Reexamine how the bookstore was burned? Review what all took place right before Gideon and I watched a man drink something that was apparently poisoned?"

"Exactly." Brannon made an annoyed gesture with his hand. "*Apparently* is the key word here. They haven't determined cause of death or whatever it is, have they? Look . . . we know we've got some nutjob there who's trying to cause trouble—he tried to gut me, remember? But that doesn't mean there's a vendetta against the whole family."

"Actually . . ." Gideon put his phone down and flicked it, set it to spinning like a top. "I just had a message from the cops over in Louisiana. Coroner found poison."

His eyes slid to Moira's. "It was in the scotch," he said quietly. "There was also poison in a box of candied nuts—some specialty deal, too. Can't be bought in your typical Walmart or down at the Pig."

Moira's head started to spin and she thought she might be sick, right there on the pretty, pale green carpet. "Okay . . . okay. I"—she shoved upright and took a step, then another one—"I need air."

Gideon was there when she started to sway. "You need

to sit," he said softly. But he steadied her as she stood there, her fingers kneading his biceps restlessly. As he held her, he looked over at the only male McKay, his eyes grim. "She had a glass of that scotch sitting in front of her, Bran. She didn't drink any, but if she had?"

Brannon's lids flickered and he turned away. He said something under his breath, something low and ugly.

Moira didn't need to hear it to understand the meaning.

"It's about *us*," she said, easing away from Gideon. She looked at her brother, then at Neve. "Kevin admitted as much. Now, granted . . . I can't say I'd put much stock in what he had to say, but I'm not seeing much reason for him to lie."

"Deflect attention from himself." Ian had been quiet up until now, and when people looked at him, he shrugged. "Hey, I've read a book or two. It could be the case."

"There were cameras—several of them, and the feed was intermittently coming on until somebody started trying to track it, so there is at least *one* other individual likely tied into this." Gideon managed a faint smile. "The county boys are keeping me apprised of what's going on. I've . . . advised them that whatever happened to his man might be connected to some matters we've got going on here, so we're sharing information. I'm not going to totally rule out the possibility that he was looking to deflect attention— I've read a few of those books, too. But the thing is . . . he was being recorded. It looks like we were as well. The techs found them during the search. They're activated by motion and sound, but can be deactivated remotely. The sheriff ended up calling in for assistance from the state once the scotch came back showing up traces of a rather complicated poison."

"Complicated how?" Brannon demanded.

"Complicated as in there's not just *one* poison—the small county hospital actually has access to a medical

examiner who spent about twenty years working up in
Baltimore until he decided to come home due to family
illness—needless to say, he has some serious expertise
under his belt and he got to work on Towers' case as soon
as he found out there was something with meat to it."
Gideon shrugged. "So far, he believes GHB was used, in
conjunction with at least one other compound—possibly
a heavy dose of digitalis."

"Foxglove," Ella Sue said quietly.

Brannon paused by Ella Sue and rubbed her thin
shoulder. "For those of us who don't know everything?"
he asked, focusing his eyes on Gideon.

"Too bad Hannah isn't here." Gideon gave him a thin
smile. "She could break it down in laymen's terms. Digitalis is a cardiac medicine—slows down the heart, makes
it pump more efficiently."

Ella Sue covered Brannon's hand with hers. "Digitalis
is also what the flowers are called—the scientific mumbo
jumbo." She smiled a little. "It was used in natural reme-
dies for centuries."

"So somebody dosed this guy with something that will
slow down his heart *and* they roofied him." Neve sat on
the edge of the couch, staring at nothing in particular.

"Basically."

Moira tried to push away the remaining vestiges of nau-
sea and focused on everything else Gideon had said.
Kevin was gone. He'd done something terrible and stupid
and he'd been sad and pathetic. But in the end, it was like
he'd been discarded, like he'd been nothing. Now all she
could feel was some vague sort of pity for him—and a lot
of rage at the nebulous coward behind all of this.

Cameras. She seized onto that and locked gazes with
Gideon. "You said there was a signal—they tried to trace
it. *Can* they?"

A smile tugged up the corners of his mouth. "I love a

smart woman." He shrugged. "I've no idea. The geek speak is a little out of my league, but the state's got some amazing electronics and computer people on hand. It's going to be a question of who is better—them or the man behind those cameras."

"How good can he be?" Ian shrugged. Though he looked laid back and relaxed, there was a world of tension vibrating in that big body of his and his pale eyes were frosted ice in his face. "The nutter went and kept trying to see what was going down even after he likely knew his man was dead. Should have called it a loss and let it go, but he had to see, now didn't he? So he's either stupid or obsessed. Probably both. But if he was *really* good, he'd know to cut his losses and run. He didn't."

"Why *did* he set up cameras?" Neve asked. "I mean . . . what's the deal with the house? What's the deal with all of us? It doesn't make a lot of sense."

"Sure it does." Gideon's eyes held hers. "We just have to find the connecting thread."

"You didn't tell them what he said about him being cousins with somebody." Leaning against his truck, Gideon studied Moira's downcast face.

He had to go into the office for a while. Saturdays might technically be his day off, but he had a report on the dead guy back in Louisiana and the sheriff's department had been kind enough to send a preliminary on the sweep the techs had done, too.

Moira's pale-green eyes met his. "No. I want more concrete answers first."

Shoving off the truck, he moved around until he could cage her up between him and the vehicle's grill. "Don't go playing Nancy Drew. Your brother finally seemed to get it and I think Ian pretty much connected the dots. I know Neve did. Until I find out more about what's going on—and stop this fucker—you keep your pretty ass out of trouble."

"I wasn't planning on whipping out a magnifying glass and argyle socks." She pursed her lips. "I think she wore argyle socks. I never much paid attention to those books."

Gideon skimmed a thumb under the hem of her shirt and stroked it across her skin. "You can wear whatever you want—or don't want. But keep out of this, Moira."

She rolled her eyes and pushed up onto her toes. "I saw enough last night to convince me that investigating isn't my forte, pal."

"Good." He cupped her head and rubbed his lips against hers, slowly, lazily deepening the kiss until their breath fused and it seemed their very hearts were beating in time. "Moira . . ."

She hummed a little in her throat and curled her arms around him, straining to be closer although the only thing that separated them was their clothing.

Gideon caught her wrists. "I need to go. I've got things to follow up on."

"Okay." She studied his mouth for a moment and then looked back up at him. "You coming back here tonight?"

"Do you want me to?"

For an answer, she tugged his mouth back to hers for one last, hard kiss.

CHAPTER NINETEEN

"I'm afraid there's not much I can tell ya, Marshall."

Tired after yet another two-hour drive to Louisiana, Gideon walked along with Zeke and one of his dogs as they circled the perimeter of the Bittner house.

In a few weeks, the McKays would be transferring the property over to Zeke.

It had only been a few short days since Kevin Towers had been killed inside those walls. It had been a concoction of Rohypnol and GHB, laced with heavy amounts of digitalis, enough to take down an elephant.

Their presence hadn't made much of a difference.

The medical examiner, a stern-faced, middle-aged man with an already naked scalp, had told Gideon it wouldn't have mattered if they'd been talking to Towers in an apartment two blocks away from the hospital.

He had been dead from the moment he took that first drink.

They had a murder on their hands and Gideon wanted to know why. It wasn't in his jurisdiction, but it *was* about his woman. It was about his family—and that's what Brannon and Neve were. No matter what happened, the McKay family was the only one he really had and he was going to figure this out even if it killed him.

His phone buzzed and he tugged it off his belt, glanced at it. It was a message from Wycoff, the DEA agent he'd shared a bed with once upon a time. Grimacing, he shoved the phone back into place. It was Sunday, for fuck's sake.

"I don't know how you put up with that damn thing," Zeke said companionably.

He no longer seemed so pissed off at Gideon. He'd never been one to hold a grudge and once he'd come to realize there was something weird going on with the house, he'd loosened up around the McKays, too. It had taken Gideon all but threatening to knock his head off before he'd been willing to talk to Moira, but once he'd done that, he'd taken what he'd called a *walk . . . to think things through.*

He'd seen something in Moira that he recognized, Gideon figured. The kind of person who just didn't bullshit.

"In my job, it's sort of a necessity," Gideon replied. They paused at the tree line, looking up at the old Bittner house. The police tape was still up, a grim reminder as to what had happened. "How much of the history do you know about the place?"

"About as much as anybody." Zeke paused. "Well, maybe a bit more. Abe Bittner liked to talk, you know. He might have lived another twenty years if he hadn't liked the drink so much. Guess maybe what I should say is that it's a miracle he lived as long as he did. Went through a fifth of whiskey about as fast some people go through a bottle of pop, you know that?"

Gideon knew when a person was talking just to talk and he nodded.

"He was a good man, though. Couldn't stand a wife beater, an animal abuser or a cheat. That adds up to a decent man in my book. He tried to raise his kids right, and that boy of his . . ." Zeke turned his head and spit into the dirt. "Shit."

"Seems like that boy of his is a piece of work."

"You ain't lying. Already run through that money. Don't be surprised if he tries to come sniffing around the Mc-Kays for more once he finds out about this."

Gideon turned his head, frowning at Zeke. "How you figure that?"

"He buys into all that shit, that's all I'm saying. Abe never did. But his boy, Clint? He was like his grandpa. Now that man? I remember him. Even though I was just a boy when he died, I remember him. Stingiest, greediest piece of shit you ever did see. He thought everybody owed him everything but damn if he was willing to pay up what *he* owed." The dog at Zeke's side nosed him, and Zeke nodded at him. "Go on. Take care of your business, Solo."

"How's Chewy doing?"

Zeke shook his head. "Not good. Her hips are getting to her. I don't think I can put her through another winter after this one. I think it will break Solo's heart, but I'm going to have put her down before another year goes through."

"I'm sorry, man."

Zeke just nodded. There wasn't much left to say. He watched as the dog sniffed around through the woods before finding a tree and taking care of business. Solo—short for Han Solo—and his girl Chewy had been two of his first dogs and they were still his favorites. He loved them more than he probably loved anybody, save for his wife. "Anyway, about old Bittner. He always talked about changing his name. That's what she'd done, see." Zeke squinted.

Gideon recognized the look. It was the look of somebody trying to recall details, and he knew the etiquette. He was, after all, somebody who'd grown up in a small,

southern town. There was no *straight* answer. There were
just roundabouts and side trips.

But fuck if he didn't want to shout *Get to it already!*

"It was probably two or three generations back. See, the
first one was a bastard and nobody likes that word. Even
now, leastways in towns like around here. He'd promised
he'd marry her. Marry her and take her back to England
with him and when he didn't . . . it almost broke her."

"Who?" Gideon growled out.

Zeke looked over at him. "This piece of land used to
belong to the Whitehalls. That's what the story was. Of
course, she wasn't really a Whitehall, but that wasn't figured out until years later. She was dead by then. The house
went to her daughter . . ."

Gideon listened, torn between astonishment and dread
as Zeke relayed the history of the house. "Anyways, by that
time nobody could have taken that land away from old
Bittner. Not for anything. He always saw himself as a
Whitehall and grew up on tales about how his granddaddy
was the real hero of the McKay legend. It was all a cover-
up, see. Ol' George knew what McKay was really like and
the men he'd convinced to help bring him to justice ended
up so scared for their lives after they'd punished the son
of a bitch, they sent George back off to England so the
Steeles—you know about Steele, right?"

Gideon grimaced. "Hell, I'm *from* Treasure, Zeke. I
grew up hearing all of this stuff. And for the record, Whitehall was no damn hero. If anybody was scared of anything, they were scared that Jonathan Steele was going to
hunt them all down and skin the hair off their balls, then
just break their necks."

"This is kinda far away from Treasure, son." Zeke
shrugged, unperturbed. "And you gotta admit, it's weird
the way that family, hell, half the town still memorializes
the old man all this time."

"It's called having pride in your roots." Gideon wasn't going to get distracted by any of this, though. "So Bittner . . . the one you were friends with, he was what. . . ." Gideon barely recognized the growl that was his own voice.

Zeke lifted a brow. "See, that's why I didn't think there was much to it, them wanting this land. Ol' George had fucked them all over, the whole damn family doing what he done."

"That was a long time ago!" Gideon half-shouted.

"Yeah. But look at what Moira's doing. That museum . . . seems to me they all still hold Paddy McKay pretty near and dear."

"They wouldn't—"

"Shit." Zeke clicked for Solo, and as the dog came running at him he looked over at Gideon. "I know that. I figured that out fast enough. Still, if they weren't after the place with it once being Whitehall's . . . what?"

Where is it?

Moira's recap of her attack leapt to life in the back of Gideon's head. Somebody whispering to her as he pressed a knife to her throat. *Where is it?*

Somebody thought there was a treasure.

We're *the legacy, Gideon.*

"I got to go, Zeke. You want me to run you back home?"

"Everything okay?" Zeke's thick brows arched over his eyes. "You look like a ghost just bit you on the ass, Marshall."

With a hard, grim smile, Gideon said, "One might have just kicked me there. I'm good, Zeke. You need that ride or not?"

"Hell no." The older man cut him a sideways grin. "I been running these woods half my life. Longer. I can probably get home before you even reach the road."

Gideon held out a hand. Zeke gave him a quick shake

and they split ways. Before Zeke had even lost himself in the woods, Gideon had forgotten about him.

Where is it?

Gideon had an even bigger question.

What *was it* . . . and who.

Gideon waited until he was far enough back into civilization that he knew he'd keep his connection for more than a few minutes. He'd made enough trips out to visit Zeke over the years that he knew how quickly the calls could drop.

Gideon had met Zeke when they had been serving together in in the army. Zeke had been on his way out and Gideon on his way in, two southern boys stuck in that armpit, miserable desert. They'd struck an easy friendship, Zeke looking out for Gideon until he found his feet and then Gideon reading to Zeke in the days after the man took the injury that had ended his career.

Years later, Gideon would sustain a similar injury.

They had a solid bond, the two of them.

Too fucking bad Gideon hadn't ever talked to him about the property he'd once mentioned wanting to buy. He just might have figured out the connection a lot sooner.

Whitehall.

Shoving all of that out of his head, he settled down and turned on the Bluetooth to initiate a call to the department.

As soon as his assistant Darby came on the line, she said, "Chief, you've had three calls from that DEA woman. And Clive is hanging out here being a pain in my behind."

She said it like *bee*-hind, and the way she raised her voice at the end made Gideon think Clive was probably right under her nose. "Tell that idiot if he needs to talk to a cop, he can talk to any damn cop. Otherwise, he's loitering and he can either leave or get arrested. Now, listen, I need . . ."

He stopped talking when he realized Darby was parroting his words back to Clive. Tapping his fingers on the steering wheel, he checked the time. It was going to take way too long to get back to Treasure. He needed to get to the library. He had to go through records that might not even be digitized yet.

Son of a bitch.

"Okay, Chief. About this DEA lady—"

"Darby, I ain't got time—"

"Is Marshall already talking to her?" Clive demanded, his voice so loud Gideon heard it clear through the Bluetooth.

"Clive, I am *busy,*" Darby said.

Gideon just barely resisted the urge to drive his fist into the steering wheel. "Darby!" he shouted.

He said it with enough force that even Clive must have heard it.

Silence fell, followed by a timid, "Yes, Chief?"

"Put me on speaker."

A second later, he heard the odd echo that let him know she'd followed his order. "Which of my officers is there right now?"

"I'm here, Chief," he heard Griffin say.

"Parker, get that idiot Clive and arrest him for loitering. He was told to discuss whatever matter with an officer and he refused. Put him in a cell."

"That's fucking *bullshit!*" Clive bellowed.

"Darby, take the phone off speaker." As the flurry of activity and shouts rose in the background, Gideon took a deep breath. He briefly considered pulling over and getting out of the car so he could kick a tire or hit a tree, something, *anything* to relieve the anger that was burning like a fire in his gut.

But he had to get back to Treasure.

Darby's voice was soft, hesitant as she came on the line. "Clive's taken care of, Chief. What did you need?"

"I need you to start tracking down some information for me. Do you have plans for the night?"

"Plans, sir?"

Rolling his eyes, he said it again, "Yes, Darby, plans. As in . . . *are you doing anything?*"

"No, sir. Other than dinner and watching TV."

"Order in. Get something from the pub and have them put it on my account, order me some fish and chips. I'm an hour out. Just have it ready when I get there. You always want some overtime, so if you're up for it, I need you."

"Well, I could use the Christmas money," she said slowly. "What's going on, Chief?"

"Getting to that part." He explained what he wanted her to start researching, and when he finished, Darby was quiet. He could hear her pen scratching on the notebook she used.

When it stopped, he waited for her to ask if there was anything else, but instead, she cleared her throat and then, voice still tentative, she said, "Sir, are you . . . it's just . . . what's this all about?"

He didn't have the patience—or the temper—to get into that just then.

"Just start looking, Darby. I've got other calls I need to make. I'll explain what I can when I can. Keep quiet on this, you hear me?"

He disconnected the middle of her murmured, "Of course."

Without letting himself brood over the decision, he punched in Moira's number.

* * *

"She's rather lovely, Moira." Charles knelt in front of Frost.

The dog deigned to allow him to pet her after Moira had given her the okay.

"So she's trained?"

"Yes." Distracted, Moira continued to search through the files she'd had sent from the main offices. In comparison to her office in Birmingham, the one in the museum was small and the boxes took up almost half the northern wall. The western wall was made entirely of glass, allowing her to look out over the river, but today, she'd pulled the curtains. She needed to focus.

Not that she was having much luck with that with Charles here.

They'd already gone over the schedule of events for the opening.

Two weeks away.

Just two weeks.

"What sort of training does she have?" Charles asked.

She glanced up to see him still stroking the dog. Frost had her eyes half-closed.

"Security, protection of her owner. That sort of thing. The guy who raised her sells a lot of his dogs to former military, so he also teaches them to recognize triggers for PTSD attacks."

"Hmm." After a final stroke of the shepherd's head, he rose and settled in the chair across from hers. Frost padded around and settled in what she had already decided was *her* space—right next to Moira's chair, on her left-hand side. "I imagine you feel safer having her with you at night."

"Yeah." She smiled a little, and the smile grew as she thought of the other reason she'd been feeling safer. Gideon had spent the last two nights with her and, after they'd exhausted themselves, he'd fallen asleep behind her, with his arm wrapped securely around her waist.

Charles sniffed across from her, and she glanced up to see that his eyes were red.

"Well, this is annoying," he murmured, pulling a handkerchief from his pocket. Ever the gentleman, Charles.

"What's wrong?"

He grimaced, glancing around for the dog. "I used to have a dog when I was young. Mum had to give him away. Turned out I was allergic. I always hoped I'd outgrow it. Doesn't look like I will. No worries, though. I'll just go pop an antihistamine and I'll be fine."

"Okay." His nose was looking pretty red there.

He sniffed again as he rose but instead of heading out, he paused by her desk. "What is it you're doing here? You've got enough paperwork to make you blind, darling."

"Tell me about it." She sighed and gestured toward the boxes. "One of my employees was embezzling money. There's this house—" She stopped and glanced up at him. "You don't want to listen to this, not when Frost is making you all . . ." Waving a hand at him, she finished lamely with, "You know."

"I've always got time for you, Moira." He smiled gently at her and rested a hip on the edge of her desk. Holding out a hand, he asked, "May I?"

She shrugged and offered him one of the spreadsheets. He'd minored in finance and while she hadn't seen anything pop out other than what Gideon and she had discovered, it wouldn't hurt to have a fresh set of eyes on it.

Charles just grimaced. "He was rather free with McKay money, wasn't he?"

She'd noticed that, too. Some of the business expenses

should have been flagged. She wasn't sure why anybody needed to spend four hundred dollars of company funds at a mini-golf and entertainment park.

"What exactly is it you're looking for?" he asked after dabbing at his nose again.

"I'm not sure yet, other than discrepancies. I've got an appointment later this week with a man from a group that specializes in this sort of thing—finding paperwork trails, discrepancies, all that. Towers is dead and . . . what?"

Charles was gaping at her. "Towers is what? Kevin, you mean?"

"You knew him?"

"The sod had a thing for you, darling. Yes, I knew him. How did he die?"

"He . . ." Blood rushed to her face and she looked away. Gideon had seen it, Charles had seen it. She felt foolish for not really realizing it, not that she ever would have done anything about it. Kevin hadn't been her type and now, knowing what *type* he had been, he was even *less* her type. "It's complicated, Charles. There's an investigation going on. I'm sure you'll hear more about it soon. Anyway, I'm having some people look into it. It's just a mess."

Leaning back, she rubbed at her eyes for a moment while her head pounded. "He bought a damn house, you know that?" She looked back at her ex-husband, glad that they'd been able to stay friends, glad he was such a good listener. "He used the company as a front—that's all it was. A front. The house is useless to McKay. What I can't figure out is why . . ."

She trailed off as the phone rang.

It was her personal phone and she reached for it, smiling as she saw who it was.

Charles pushed off the desk. "I'll be going. Need to get that medication."

"Yeah. Yeah." But her mind was already on the other man.

The one who'd owned her heart for so long.

There was no guessing as to who'd been calling Moira.

Charles leaned back against the wall for a moment, recalling the smile that had lit her face.

He wondered if he would have married her had he realized just how desperately she still loved Gideon Marshall.

Of course, he hadn't known about Gideon when he proposed. Well, he'd known vaguely, but she'd said the relationship had ended some time earlier and he'd taken her at her word.

She'd never smiled at him like that.

She'd never cried over him either.

There had been a few times, even during their brief marriage, when she had cried over Marshall.

It had been a blow to understand that the woman he'd asked to be his wife wasn't *his*.

It was awful, but he was rather aggravated to realize that she just might find whatever it was she'd been looking for with *that* arrogant prick.

There was no reason he couldn't have made her happy when they were together.

Her voice drifted to him and he sighed quietly.

What a pity.

Other than the fact that she hadn't wanted to be happy.

Some people, it seemed, didn't know how to be happy.

"Wait, Gideon . . . I'm confused." Palm pressed to her head, Moira closed her eyes. Frost made a low, whining sound and nosed her thigh. Absently, Moira stroked the dog's head and murmured, "I'm okay, girl."

But she wasn't. Her head had already been pounding from the numbers. Eying the door Charles had left open, she walked over and closed it. Frost got up and watched her closely. The dog seemed to think the floor or the door might attack her.

"Explain this thing to me . . . Whitehall had kids over here? Everybody knows he had a couple of illegitimate kids—there was some girl across the river that he kept on the side . . ."

"I know. Did your side ever keep track of what happened to her?"

"Hell, no. Gideon, you're talking about Southerners and Scots—two groups that hold a grudge like nothing you've ever seen. I've seen people spit on the ground when you even mention Whitehall." She couldn't stop from wrinkling her nose as she said it.

"Your face pinches up like I shoved a lemon in your mouth."

Moira couldn't stop from laughing. He had her there. "True. But that's the whole point—we didn't give a damn about anything that had to do with Whitehall. Why should we? He'd killed Paddy. If it wasn't for Jonathan Steele, he might have forced Madeleine into marriage. What's this about?"

"That house," Gideon said, his voice low and intent. "It's built right in the middle of the property that Whitehall *owned*. And that girl he had on the side? She somehow came up with a phony marriage certificate that looked real enough to fool people into thinking she was his wife and she took over that house, lived there. She called herself Tilly Whitehall. Her granddaughter married herself a man by the name Elias Bittner."

Moira froze. "Bittner. Son of a bitch."

"Yeah." His voice was low and angry. "I know you say that Towers didn't have a mean bone in him—lazy and greedy, but not mean. Are you sure he couldn't have been more deeply involved in this?"

"I'm almost positive, baby," she said. "I'm bringing in an independent party to go over the records, but I'd just about swear that he had to have . . . Wait. The cousin."

Gideon was quiet a moment. "We have to figure out who the cousin was."

"That's not going to be easy," she muttered. "He's kind of not here to ask."

"We'll get it figured out. I'm meeting Darby at the station and we're going to start digging around. I'll let you know if we find anything."

"I'm going to meet you there."

"There's not much you can do, Moira. Why don't you—"

"I'm meeting you *there*," she said. "I'll call Neve and Brannon, too. If we're looking for a needle in a haystack, we might as well get as many eyes on that stack as we can."

"Mac—"

"I gotta go. Need to finish going through this. I love you."

She hung up the phone and slumped in her chair, staring at the spreadsheets so hard, the numbers blurred.

Whitehall.

How could this go back to Whitehall?

CHAPTER TWENTY

The crowning jewel of the McKay empire was, without a doubt, the sprawling house and the beautiful grounds that had been dubbed McKay's Ferry. Once, the entire town had been named that.

He could remember the first time he'd seen it, his father holding his hand as they stood just outside their car.

"See that, boy? It was meant to be ours."

"What do you mean?"

"It was going to belong to one of your many times— great grandfathers, son. But they stole what he'd worked for, put him on a boat and forced him to return to England a laughing stock. He took ill, never did recover. Over time, our family lost everything. But we'll find a way to get it back, won't we?"

He tried to understand what his father could mean, but he didn't find an answer soon enough. A brutal hand closed around his neck and yanked him forward, squeezing with awful strength. "You heard me, right? Answer me, boy!"

"We'll find a way." It never once occurred to him to say anything else.

"Good boy. That's a good boy. Right, then. Come

along. We need to be getting on. Have to get ready for that meeting. If I get this teaching job, then things will get better. You'll see. You'll see."

He followed along in his father's footsteps, rubbing absently at his neck where strong, big fingers had curled in.

In the back of his mind, he heard his father's voice as he murmured, We'll find a way . . .

Now, decades after that chilly day in January, he stood staring again at the house McKay built. It was a picture this time, a large painting done by a regional artist of some renown. Apparently, the artist had had a good relationship with the deceased Mr. and Mrs. McKay and the former McKays as well. He'd died recently, but this painting had been a Christmas gift to the family some years back.

Now it was the focal point of the lobby of the McKay Regional Riverboat Museum.

He curled his lip, reached up to stroke a hand down the painting, feeling the texture under his palm, the wooden surface of the frame.

He'd thought he'd found his way, but decided over the past few years that he'd rather do *more* than what his father had previously planned. He didn't give a shite about that sprawling monolith of a house. He wanted to get back the flat he kept in London. He'd made a right nice life for himself and he missed it, wanted to get back to it.

But until he was finished here, it wasn't an option.

His father hadn't raised a quitter.

As he had grown, so had the power of the McKays— the fucking McKays—especially thanks to the financial genius of Devon and the brilliant mind of Sandra Lewis McKay. She'd help pioneer any number of new medical instruments and taken research and development in the medical field in entirely new directions. The money from those patents was still rolling in—he had no doubt of that.

As that power had grown, his father's rage had exploded.

As his father had lain dying in his bed, his lungs eaten up by a virulent strain of cancer, he'd grabbed his son's hand.

"Make them . . . suffer," he'd said. *"You hear me? It's their . . . fault. Their fault."*

He'd just nodded.

They'd tried to get him in on a trial for a new cancer therapy, one that might have saved him, or at least given him more time, but he'd been rejected.

The company sponsoring the drug tests was in partnership with McKay Enterprises. They knew it then, both father and son.

The rejection had happened because he was a descendant of George Whitehall—there was no other reason they could fathom.

It wouldn't have occurred to either of them that the McKay family had no direct contact with the day-to-day runnings of the numerous companies they had connections to, that they couldn't keep track of everybody who came in contact with those companies—that number would run into the millions.

But a mind fueled by rage and hate sees little beyond that rage and hate.

As the old man grew sicker, he blamed the McKays more and more each day. *They know about us, boy. You got to hide yourself. Don't . . . don't let them know. And you . . . make . . . them . . .*

He'd started to cough.

A few minutes later, he'd lost consciousness.

He'd never woken back up.

There are few certainties in life.

The sun will rise.

The sun will set.

Everybody dies.

Money speaks.

Friends will abandon you.

Family will always stand beside you.

The McKays will destroy everything that matters.

He'd told himself that at the grave as his father was lowered into the dirt, and he told himself those very words now.

In his hand, he held a gas can, filled with a special accelerant, the kind that just couldn't be found at the local *Pump N Go*. He splashed some on the floor in front of the display where the painting was and then left a trail all the way up to Moira's office, all over the papers she was reviewing. It wouldn't solve anything, burning them. She would have digital copies of the data, but this would slow her down and more . . . it would piss her off. He took care to hit other areas of the office, her chair, her desk, and then the large painting hanging on the wall. It was the last one ever done of her with her siblings and her parents. On a whim, he drew the boxcutter from his back pocket and slashed an ugly *X* through the canvas. His gloves were a strange, surreal blue, making his hands look almost inhuman.

He moved on throughout the museum, leaving accelerant behind him. Almost like the trail of breadcrumbs in the forest, he mused. But so much more effective.

He only had so much time and he made quick use of it, hitting the areas that would cause the most damage possible before going out the backdoor and leaving it open. There, he withdrew a device from his pocket and knelt, taking care to put it in place before rising and strolling away. He kept his head down and averted from the cameras. Although he had his mask on, he didn't want anybody to take notice of him until he was well out of view.

Once he was, he pulled out his phone.

He'd heard the idea of *dialing it in* on a movie once. Some of his best ideas came from movies.

He hadn't taken the idea seriously at the time, but with the changes in technology, he realized it really was possible. All with the right tools and a bit of research . . .

He hit send.

A moment later, the building went up in a rush of flames.

He was already halfway through town and talking, sans mask, to Mrs. Mouton.

He feigned surprise when she shrieked and he caught her arm. "Are you all right?" he demanded.

"Oh, mercy. Oh, dear heavens . . ." She lifted a hand and pointed. "The . . . *oh, my!* Look!"

He turned his head and stared.

With everybody around him, he didn't dare let himself smile.

Mrs. Mouton started to struggle. "What if Moira is in there . . . or any of the others? We have to get help!"

As they all swarmed closer, he did the same.

Absently, Moira popped a fry into her mouth before pulling one of the wrapped sandwiches out of the bag.

Ian had met her on the sidewalk, his arms laden with a box full of food and he'd winked at her, asked if he could join her.

Assuming he'd gotten Neve's call, she grinned at him.

Now, as they unpacked the food, Gideon shot her a disgruntled look over the top edge of his computer. His assistant Darby was digging into the food Ian had brought over.

"This two-person team has grown significantly," Gideon said as the door opened.

Neve, Brannon, and Hannah came inside, Hannah noticeably less energetic and still wearing her uniform.

"You look tired, Hannah." Gideon gave Brannon a pointed look. "Take her home."

"Not happening, Chief," she said easily. "I'm tired, not fragile. I can look at records or research stuff as well as anybody else."

"True, but this is a police investigation."

"As of yet, seems to be a wild goose chase," Ian said. "You're just digging up old family records or trying to. How is that a police investigation?"

"Gideon?" Moira set his food down in front of him and bent to kiss him. "You're arguing with a rock wall trying to dissuade all of us, and you know it. Why bother?"

He grunted out something unintelligible and sighed. Then he took a pointed look around. "Just where is your canine companion, Moira?"

"I took her home. I didn't know if she was allowed in the station."

The look he gave her could have frozen the flames of hell. "*I* get to decide who and what is allowed in my department, Moira. You aren't supposed to be going places alone."

"Well . . . you can always drive me home." She winked at him, then stole one of his fries.

He caught her wrist before she could grab another. "You're interfering in a police investigation, Mac. Don't make it worse by stealing a cop's fries on top of it."

She laughed as he bit into the fry she held before letting her go.

A few minutes later, as they all spread out, he reviewed the information he had and pointed them toward the best databases.

Neve pulled out her laptop, and Ian cocked up a brow as he saw the now-familiar website pop up. Leaning over, he whispered softly, "Now that's not very nice. You're slacking."

"No, I'm not." She slanted a look at him from the corner of her eye. "Watch."

She went to the advanced search and typed in *George Whitehall*, filling in his country of birth and estimating about when he would have been born, plugging in a few more details.

"Viola."

"Cheater." He grunted and used the laptop he'd brought from the pub to go to the government website Gideon had suggested.

After a few minutes of what felt like fruitless searching, he glanced around, then decided to follow Neve's lead.

Of course, that required he set up a bleeding account.

Neve snickered to herself when she saw what he was doing, but she didn't blame him.

The ancestry website was mostly for fun as far as she was concerned, but it accessed *huge* databases, including the ones Gideon had pointed them do, searching through them so they didn't have to. This seemed like an awfully far-fetched idea, but she'd definitely heard of weirder ones, so she wasn't going to toss it out altogether.

One of the leaf hints popped up and she clicked on it, but it was a dead end from what she could tell.

Blowing out a breath, she rubbed at her head and refreshed her window. It was easy to get lost in all the searches. There were so many hints up in the box now, she didn't know which way to go.

A noise from outside caught her attention just as somebody out in the station shouted.

Gideon's phone rang.

Too much noise . . . Distracted, she moved the laptop from her lap to the table. Absently, she flicked a finger down the touchscreen watching as a list popped up, full of those little leaves. One name caught her attention and she sneered out of habit, flicking at it.

Her *flick* really meant *go away*. But her computer didn't get that.

It opened the hint, and a picture started to download.

She groaned.

Outside, the noise from the street started to grow louder.

Somebody burst into the room with a suddenness that had Neve leaping out of her chair, her heart racing. She liked to think she was over what had happened. She liked to think it . . . even she knew she was lying to herself.

Moira had gone pale, her hand pressed to her chest.

Gideon had answered his phone, rising to turn away, communicating in a series of monosyllabic grunts.

But now, Beau Shaw practically tumbling to the floor as he came to a halt, Gideon turned around. "Officer, please step outside," Gideon said, striding toward him.

But Beau's eyes were wide, locked on Moira. "Thank God. Shit, Moira. Everybody was . . ."

She looked around. Neve felt a curl of dread settle in her gut.

Slowly, she reached out to close her laptop, not bothering to close the picture.

"What's wrong?" Moira asked.

"The museum," Beau said.

"Officer!" Gideon half-shouted his name now.

Beau tensed, then shook himself, clearly coming out of whatever shocked state he'd been in. "Yes, sir!"

"What's going on?" Moira demanded, her voice low and angry.

Gideon blew out a breath. Then he moved to Moira. "I don't know just yet, but I just had a call. The museum, Moira . . . it's on fire."

CHAPTER TWENTY-ONE

"Are you okay, Mac?"

Dully, she lifted her head and saw Gideon kneeling in front of her. He was sooty, rivulets of sweat leaving somewhat cleaner trails on his face. His eyes were almost brilliantly blue against the dirt as they stared at her with concern.

"Okay," she echoed, trying the word on her tongue.

Behind him, the walls of the museum rose up like skeletal arms. So much of it was gone. The fire department had been on the scene almost immediately and they'd acted as fast as they could, but Moira was a realist. It looked like a third of it—at least—was destroyed. She'd imagine much of what was left wasn't going to be salvageable.

"Who is doing this?" she asked quietly.

Gideon sighed and reached out to take her hands. "I don't know. But I will find out."

"Do that." The fury struggling to break free under the numbness rose a little closer to the surface, and she felt like she was going to snap. "Do that because I'm ready to rip his guts out."

Wisely, he just nodded.

Then, reaching out to cradle her head, he drew her in

close. His lips brushed her brow. "I'm so damn sorry, Mac."

"Don't. Not here. Not now." Tears burned her eyes and she whispered, "Please don't. I'm about ready to break as it is."

"The good Lord knows you can't let the world see you're human." He said with a faint smile, but nodded and let go. "I've got to get back to work. Why don't you go hang out at Ian's place with him and Neve?"

"No. I can't . . . No."

"Then wait for me."

She managed a wobbly smile as he walked away. She turned her attention back to the devastated ruin of the museum. She'd put the past five years of her life into this place. More, really. She'd been thinking about creating something like this for more than ten years and it had actually been an idea her parents had talked about. They'd never been able to make it happen, so she'd decided to make it happen for them. Now it was ruined.

She rose and took a few steps, turning from the sight of the museum and all those ruined dreams. It was too much to look at just then.

A man's face, the familiar sneer, caught her eye and she turned away before Joe Fletcher could draw near. "Fucking leech," she muttered. He always seemed to be around whenever her misery was at its all time highest.

She bumped into somebody and this time it was a familiar voice that reached out to her. "Moira."

"Charles," she said, feeling deflated. The strength drained out of her and she sat once more, right in the middle of the sidewalk. Charles looked around and then shrugged, sitting with a smile next to her. Nobody gave them another look.

She wished she had the energy to put on a brave front, but she was so tired and all she could do was nod at him.

"This is . . . awful."

"Yeah." She nodded in agreement. There really wasn't anything to say.

"Do they have any idea what happened?" Charles stared out over the museum, the same as she.

She didn't answer, staring at the fireman who'd just emerged. He had something in his hand. Frowning, she tried to see it and then, as he held it up, she thought she might be sick.

"Is that a . . ."

She lurched upward and stumbled off to the side.

There was no *thinking* about it now.

She wretched, the small bit of her dinner boiling up out of her throat to splatter onto the pavement.

A gas can. One of those old-fashioned, metal gas cans. Somebody had actually done this on purpose.

A gentle hand smoothed her hair back from her face.

Charles. She was so tired, she almost leaned against him.

But then she pulled herself together and staggered upright, somehow.

"Let me take you home," he said quietly. "You being here, this isn't helping. It isn't good for you."

The sight of that dick Hurst hovering around Moira made Gideon wanted to hit something.

Actually, it was like that in the best of times.

Right now, when she was fragile and looking bruised, it made it about ten times worse and *something* wouldn't suffice. What Gideon really wanted to hit was Hurst. He wanted to hit him hard and fast over and over.

"If looks could kill," Dirk Hutton said to Gideon, "that man would be dead and you would be in jail."

Gideon looked away without responding. If looks could kill, Hurst would have been dead long ago and Gideon would have been rotting away in a cell all this time.

Focusing on the men in their fire gear as they swarmed around behind Hutton, he asked, "You got anything for me?"

Hutton gestured to the can his men were carefully packing away. "You already saw that. Pretty damn clear this was no accident. Unless of course that old can was on the display and they just forgot to drain the accelerant in it."

"Accelerant?" Gideon narrowed his eyes.

"Yeah. Not going to speculate on what just yet, but I can tell you that it wasn't gasoline. Place went up to fast, burned too hot and too long. We'll get it figured, though."

Pulling out his notepad, Gideon made a couple of notes. "Anything else?"

From the corner of his eye he could see Charles murmuring to Moira as he stroked her hair. Gideon wanted to take that hand and break it, break every last finger.

"Need a minute?" Hutton asked, clearly amused.

"No, I don't need a minute." He glared at the fire chief. "Would you just do your damn job?"

Ignoring the demand, Hutton reached up and rubbed at his jaw. It smeared the soot and muck on his face. "Yeah, I see how fine you are, dumbass. You look like you want to go bag yourself an uptight prick. Why don't you just get it over with, beat on your chest and tell him to keep his hands off your woman?"

Gideon gaped at him.

The man had to be out of . . .

Then he caught the sly humor glinting in his eyes.

Only an idiot or somebody looking for hurt would say *your woman* in Moira's hearing.

"Somebody needs to take her home," Hutton said, the amusement leaving his face, replaced by grim lines.

"Yeah, well, in case it's escaped your attention, this is a crime scene." He gestured around with his hand, then tapped his badge. "I'm a bit of a stickler for being around on these things, especially one of this magnitude."

"I didn't mean you specifically." Hutton shrugged, lifting one shoulder. "Although you've got good men in your department. Have one of them take over while you run her home. She needs some rest, man. Hell, for that matter Ian's apartment is right over there. Find Ian and Neve, explain the situation, and have them invite her to stay. She'll probably say yes. She'll want to be around until she has answers, I'm thinking."

"How about you stop telling me how to do my job?" he suggested. *And maybe you stop thinking about telling me how to take care of my woman?*

Just then, Charles emerged from the throng of people. Voice cool, he said, "Chief Marshall." He didn't even spare the other man a look. "Moira is exhausted and upset. I'm going to take her home. She's had quite enough of this today."

Gideon had to give the fire marshal some credit. He turned his laugh into a very believable cough as Gideon crossed his arms over his chest and met Charles' gaze dead-on. "No. She's can't leave yet. I'll have quite a few questions when we're done. I need her close."

Charles's eyes flashed. But his voice was just as calm when he responded. "I believe she would appreciate the comfort of her home around her. Perhaps Ian and Neve could join her there."

"Sorry, Hurst. That isn't going to work." He turned away as he pulled out his phone and sent a text to Ian and Brannon, quickly summing up the situation. "She needs to be in town where I can talk to her. Again, I'm going to have questions and I don't want her thirty minutes out."

"There is this strange contraption called the telephone." Charles lowered his eyes to stare at Gideon's. "I believe you're familiar with the concept."

"This old thing?" He held it up, then shrugged. "Sure. But this matter is rather urgent and I'd prefer her to remain close by."

"And you've a valid reason none of this can wait?" Charles demanded. "The poor woman is exhausted. She's upset. This has traumatized her."

Guilt rose up in Gideon's gut, but he wasn't about to allow Charles to intervene or come between them again.

"Tell me something, Chuck." He took a couple of steps until he stood almost nose to nose with the other man. "How would you like to spend the night in jail? Interfering with a police investigation isn't much fun when it comes with consequences."

"Excuse me?" His expression turned wintry and he took one single step toward Gideon.

"Are we ready to go?" Moira soft voice came to Gideons as if over a distance and he managed to restrain himself, although it took a lot of mental fortitude to keep from grabbing the English schmuck and throwing him on the ground.

Charles smoothed out his features before he looked over at her, and Gideon had to give him credit because none of the temper he had displayed showed in his voice. "No, love. Your . . . friend says he would rather you stay in town for a bit yet."

Gideon set his jaw before looking over at Maura. "You need to spend the night here. I'd rather you not be out at Ferry alone."

"I can't stay here." Her voice shook with the intensity of her emotions. "I want to go home."

With a smug look on his face, Charles moved to take her arm.

"I'm not kidding, Moira. You are not going to be out there alone tonight. This has gone too far. You're either staying with Neve and Ian or Brannon and Hannah."

Moira bared her teeth at him, temper flaring in her pale green eyes. "Fine. You don't want me alone? I'll have them come out and stay with me. I'm sure Ian and Neve won't mind having a slumber party at Ferry."

"Not good enough." He loved this beautiful stubborn woman more than he could ever say—and if she thought he'd let her go *anywhere* alone, she was probably as crazy as she was stubborn. "Not good enough by far, Mac. Neve and Ian won't give a damn if you stay the night. Hell, Neve would probably feel better if you did. But you're not making that drive out to Ferry without me. Not tonight."

She took a step toward him, lifting her chin.

He wasn't surprised by the flare of anger. He was actually almost relieved by it. Better her anger than that broken look on her face.

"Yeah?" She curled her lip at him. "And if I decide to get into my car and drive out there? What are you going to do about it, Chief?"

"Don't push me, Moira."

She jabbed him in the chest with a nail slicked the color of cherries. "I'm pretty sure that's exactly what I'm doing."

Ian and Neve arrived at that very moment. Gideon managed not to blow out a sigh of relief. "Ian. Neve. Can Moira spend the night at your place?"

"I was kinda hoping you would." Neve's smile wobbled a little before it firmed as she went to hug her sister.

A frustrated little scream emerged from Moira's throat as she shoved her hands into her hair. "Stop it!" She spun away, shoulders bowing forward as she stared at the ground. "I don't want to stay in town. I don't want to stay with Ian and Neve. I want to go to my home, stay in my bed and I want a bottle of wine from my cellar and I want my tub and I want to curl up in my chair and cry! Is that so hard to understand?"

Neve looked to Gideon, rolling her lips in. *Ah, you better do something,* she seemed to say.

He was tempted to shake Moira. He wondered if that was what Neve meant.

Before he could even figure out the first thing to say that might calm things down, Moira spun back around, jerking a thumb at her chest. "I'm an adult, got it? I'm older than *both* of you." She glared at Ian and Neve and, when Ian looked like he was smothering a laugh, she gave him a look that was so withering, it almost shriveled Gideon's balls. Ian's face sobered as he hung his head, rubbing at his neck.

He was tempted to smack Ian across the head. He'd wanted these two to talk her *down,* not make it worse.

"I don't need babysitters." She raked the crowd with a look, and the sight of everybody suddenly finding something else to look at only made her more disgusted. "And I don't need to give the town anything else to talk about. I've had *enough* today, Gideon. Enough."

She had. He knew that.

But he wasn't going to let her make that drive.

"Wait for me," he said, his voice low and intense. "I'll finish as fast as I can and take you home. If you're going to be that damn stubborn—"

"I'm not being stubborn!" she shouted. "I just want to go *home* and I want to go now!"

Fed up, Gideon shoved his face into hers. "No." Taking care to enunciate each word, he said, "No, Mac, you are not. You are staying in town. Now if I have to, I can force the issue." He paused, watching as her porcelain complexion slowly turned a blushing shade of pink as her anger began to skyrocket. This was going to get ugly. He should have asked her go inside the pub or something. But fuck it all—he was on duty and he needed to be talking with the fire chief, trying to find witnesses, not fighting over this.

Moira sucked in a breath, but before she could say anything, he continued. "I really don't want to force the issue, though. Please don't make me. But if you insist on trying to drive thirty minutes to a house that is now empty, then I'm going to have one of my officers take you into custody for your own safety. You will spend the night in a cell."

Her jaw fell open.

"Don't make me do that, Mac."

For maybe ten seconds, all she could do was gape at him. Then she exploded. Shoving her hands against his chest, she shouted, "Are you kidding me? Threatening to arrest me all because I want to go home? Why kind of bastard are you?" Her voice broke.

"Surely you can't be serious about this," Hurst said from the side. His voice was low and thick with disgust, but Gideon heard it loud and clear. "Are you that much of an ass?"

Whipping his head around, Gideon glared at the man. He'd put up with plenty from Moira. But from this dick? No. "You want to back off, Hurst. And you want to do it now. Otherwise, I'll throw *you* in a cell for the sheer pleasure of it."

Hurst must have seen something in Gideon's face because he backed up a step, although he didn't leave. He murmured quietly to Moira, stroking a hand down her back.

Gideon wanted to break his fingers, starting at the knuckles. He'd work his way up from there.

"Why are you doing this?" Moira demanded, her voice shaking. "What is going on with you?"

"With *me*?" She had to be blind. Either that or the shock

was affecting her thinking. Closing the distance between them, he caught her arm. When she tried to pull away, he simply moved with her, stepping aside so that nothing obstructed her view of the museum. "What's wrong with *you*? Don't you see it, Mac?"

The smoking remains were a stark, haunting image against the night sky, backlit by the streetlights from the parking lot. A murky haze lingered in the air. The smell of smoke would take days to fade.

"Because of *that*. Because of the bookstore. Because Kevin Towers is dead and he was talking about somebody who hated you."

Lowering his voice, he turned to her and grasped her arms, pulling her closer.

People around them had fallen back, as if recognizing the raw, painful intimacy of the moment. Raggedly, he pressed his brow to hers. "Somebody wants to hurt you, Mac. They want to hurt you, Brannon, and Neve. So if you want to hate me because I want you safe, then hate me. I can live with you hating me as long I know I took care of you."

She wrenched away, her voice shaking. "I can take of myself. I've got a dog. I've got an alarm system. Brannon's got more guns than the damn Pentagon by now!"

"Don't bet on it." Tired now, Gideon stared at her. "And you're still not getting that you are thirty minutes from Ferry. It's a thirty-minute drive and you're not taking it alone."

She went to argue.

Frustrated, he caught her arm and half-dragged her over into the yawning doorway that led to the burnt-out husk of the bookstore. Two of his officers seemed to understand why and they followed, using their bodies as a barrier to keep people a good ten feet away.

"Don't you get it, Mac?"

She tried to look away, and he shoved his hands into her hair, forcing her to meet his eyes. "Whoever this is, Moira . . . you *know* him. He knows you, your brother, your sister. This kind of obsessive hate doesn't come without somebody *knowing* you. You might have known him all of your life. You probably trust him . . . hell, it could be a *her.* We don't know."

"That's . . ." She licked her lips. "Gideon, that's insane."

"Is it? How did they get inside the museum? The alarm system didn't go off. It's Saturday, so the museum wasn't even being worked on. That system is keyed into the department. I would have known. You would have known. How did they get in?"

Her eyes went blank.

"There's an explanation—" She started. She took a deep breath and blew it out. Some of the anger had faded, and he watched as the fear began to leech its way into her eyes. He hated to see it but he'd rather she be aware now. If she was aware, then she'd be more careful.

"Then what is it?"

Her gaze fell away.

A moment passed and she shoved past him.

"Don't make me stick a cop on your ass, Mac," he warned her.

"Fuck off, Chief."

"Moira, damn it, would you just listen—"

She spun back around, her eyes wild once more. "I am! You wanted me scared, fine. I am. I'm terrified and now I feel like somebody ripped something out of me too. Maybe you figure I got it coming."

"What . . ." He sputtered and shook his head. "Look, just . . . you need to get some rest. You're exhausted and . . ."

"Stop telling me what to do!" Her voice cracked as the words came out. "Go do your fucking job so I can go back to my house, Gideon! You hear me? Do your job and find this son of a bitch. If you were any good at being a cop, you should have already found him anyway!"

Gideon stiffened.

All around, people sucked in collective gasps as her words rang out across the gathered crowd.

She blinked, shoulders rising and falling. Then, abruptly, she spun on her heel.

And crashed straight into Brannon's chest.

"Hold up, sis," he said, looking over her shoulder to meet Gideon's gaze. Brannon gave a single, short nod.

Gideon read an entire conversation in that look.

I'll take care of her.

She won't be alone.

She didn't mean it.

Yeah. He knew all of that.

Still, he had a hollow heart as he turned away and focused on the smoldering remains of the museum.

He needed to do his fucking job.

And she wasn't wrong. If he was any good, he would have figured this out already.

CHAPTER TWENTY-TWO

Moira stood at the window staring out at the small town where she had lived all of her life. She loved it.

McKay's Treasure was, in a way, every bit as much her home as McKay's Ferry was. It was her home and the people were her family.

Granted, she didn't always like all of them.

But she knew them. Well, she *thought* she knew them and she felt like she could trust most of them to an extent.

Don't you get it, Mac?

Gideon's voice was a haunting whisper in her ear and although he hadn't said it to be cruel or callous, she felt like curling in on herself and hiding.

This kind of obsessive hate doesn't come without somebody knowing you.

Swallowing, she leaned forward and pressed her forehead to the smooth pane of glass, her hands spread wide on the smooth wood of the window frame. Slowly, she drew in a breath, holding it a moment before she let it out.

You might have known him all of your life.

She wished she could hate him for what he'd said, wished she hadn't felt each word like a knife strike. But now, with her mind cleared, she couldn't do anything *but* think.

Moira had been blessed—or maybe she'd been cursed—with an overabundance of logic. Some people might look toward the end goal. Others might look at the things on the journey. Moira had always been able to see those things on the journey as well as the roadblocks *and* what lay at the end. It was that *end* that had finally helped her to make the agonizing—and now she understood—*wrong* decision to push Gideon away all those years ago.

One day, she'd have to explain.

One day soon.

She'd been so angry with herself, an anger she'd buried down deep, deep inside, but every day it had grown.

The misery that had settled inside her that night when she'd answered the door to find the chief of police, along with Gideon, Ella Sue, and her baby sister, had festered and spread, blooming into a deadly, poisonous thing that had infected her every waking moment—and almost all of her sleeping ones as well.

She'd never been able to show it, either.

Not Moira McKay, the head of the fine, upstanding McKay family—what a fucking joke.

The three of them—Moira and her siblings— had almost been the downfall—no.

"*I* was almost the downfall." It had started and almost ended with her. All because she had been too proud, too arrogant to see how much help she'd needed. And too pathetically spoiled that day her parents had died. They'd wanted to arrange for Ella Sue to have guardianship of them but Moira had insisted on having her date.

It had taken years, but she'd finally forgiven herself.

Forgiven Gideon too—though she never should have blamed him to begin with. It had taken her even longer to understand that she shouldn't have blamed herself, either.

Tears burning her eyes, she closed them. Those tears fell like acid down her cheeks as memories of the days, weeks, months, and years that followed beat at her.

If she'd just called Gideon and told him they needed to change up their plans, maybe Mom and Dad would have been alive, maybe not. She didn't know.

That was the reason she'd hated herself for all those years and why she'd pushed him away—she didn't deserve to be happy. That was what she'd believed, why she'd pushed him away.

Some selfish part of her had thought maybe he'd realized the ugliness that was festering in her and that he would come to hate her, and she hadn't wanted that. Another part of her had wanted *him* to be happy even if she'd never allow it for herself. But no matter which way she'd looked at it, eighteen years ago she'd seen no happy ending for them. Not together.

So she'd pushed him away.

It had only been in the past couple of years that she realized how stupid she had been and only in the past few months that she had taken the next few vital steps—forgiving herself.

Forgiving him . . . well, that had been the first—and easiest—thing to do, something she'd done years ago without even consciously realizing it. He'd done nothing wrong.

It was her own lack of guilt that had taken all this time to accept.

She'd mentioned the stubbornness of Scots and Southerners to Gideon just days ago—had it even been a *full* day? She wasn't sure, but while she was possessed of that annoying logic, her own stubbornness had blinded her to so many things until recently.

Now, though, with the blinders ripped away, that frustrating and nagging logic was pointing out small little details from the past few months.

Neve's arrival in town.

The trouble she'd had.

Shayla's odd death.

Hannah's accident.

They'd attributed all of Neve's troubles to Clyde, save for the drugs. Brannon had hired an investigator that had turned up proof that William hadn't even hit the state yet when that happened.

Somebody else had done that—somebody who *didn't* know Neve intimately.

You could have known him all your life.

"No," she murmured. "He would have known that."

Neve's fear of needles was legendary. It was one thing that had been joked about often enough that it had even reached Moira's ears when her little sister had still been in high school—*At least they don't have to worry about her doing those kind of drugs you shoot up. She'd pass out before she even touched the damn thing.*

It had alternately embarrassed and enraged her, the way they'd talk about Neve, but then Moira would go home and Neve would be in trouble again, or money would missing from yet *another* store in town—or some other thing that had always been tied in with her baby sister.

Tucking the drugs into the back of her mind, she swung her focus to another element—another piece of the puzzle.

Hannah. She didn't know exactly where things stood with that. Brannon had pushed for information and Gideon had shared *some* of what he had. Some, not all.

Whoever had attacked Brannon, whoever had chased Hannah that night in the winery, might as well have been a ghost. Senator Henry Roberts was connected to some of Hannah's troubles—*some*—not all. He sure as hell hadn't been the one chasing them through the winery. He'd been very busy being dead and all.

William couldn't have killed Shayla.

Neve's head spun as she ticked off one detail after another, pushing each one off to the side once she'd decided it wasn't pertinent to what was going on *now*.

She had facts, she had information—Brannon had pushed for some, Gideon had given what he'd felt he could. The man and his badge, she had to give him credit, he stood by that badge and the oaths he'd taken. But she had access to other information, thanks to her hardheaded brother. He had quietly used the investigators McKay Enterprises had access to, copying her and Neve on all reports.

"Take William out of the picture," she muttered, turning away from the window and pressing the tips of her fingers to her eyes.

If they only pinned Neve's attack, and the mess with Ian's bike, on William . . . then everything else . . .

Everything else.

Don't you get it, Mac?

Somebody she knew, and knew well, just as Gideon had said. But he was wrong on one front. He—or she—hadn't known her, or her siblings—their *whole* lives, or if he had, he hadn't known them well. A distant connection. Somebody fairly local.

"It could be anybody."

Swearing under her breath, she rubbed at the back of her neck and lifted her eyes to the ceiling as a headache pulsed behind her eyes. How many people did she *know*? How many people had a reason to hate the McKay family or McKay Enterprises and its various business arms?

If she looked at it from a personal standpoint . . . well, they had a list of people who didn't much care for them and a list of people who outright hated them—on a personal level. On a business level, those lists got even longer.

"Kevin," she whispered. "Kevin works—*worked*—for McKay." Maybe that was where she needed to focus. If somebody had approached Kevin, it was more than likely it had happened through McKay Enterprises. Screw all this bullshit about familial connections—she'd heard Kevin talking about having no family. She knew what it was like to *miss* something. She had her brother and sister, yes, but she'd spent the past twenty years missing her parents, just wishing they were there to tell her which step to take, which decision was the right one. All somebody would have had to do, she suspected, was talk to the guy for twenty minutes and they'd know he was lonely, that he wanted to . . . belong. Maybe he'd just been an easy way in.

But everything seemed so ugly. So personal.

Don't you get it, Mac?

She closed her eyes and made herself think back—again—over everything that had happened. The bullshit report to the museum, the attacks on Hannah and Brannon, the drugs planted on Neve, the fires in the bookstore and the museum. All ugly, cruel things. Some small and petty, others big and dangerous. But all of them designed to strike at them, designed to hurt.

"We know him," she whispered.

"It's somebody I know," she whispered. "He knows *us*."

Just like Gideon had said. Right before she yelled at him and told him to do his job.

A headache pounded behind her eyes and she rubbed at the back of her neck. Her thoughts just wouldn't shut down and she couldn't get away from *any* of them.

It was why she hadn't wanted to be here. If she'd gone home, she could have hidden from this reality, but here at Brannon's she could still smell the stink of smoke and see the movement from the firefighters down at the blockade they'd erected at the end of Main. The one thing she couldn't do was shut down her thoughts.

A faint noise from behind her set her heart to racing, and she spun around, her hand pressed to her chest.

When she saw Hannah standing in the door to the room she shared with Brannon, Moira practically collapsed against the wall in relief. "Damn it, it's you."

"I'm sorry." Hannah gave her a sheepish smile. "I didn't mean to startle you."

"It's okay." Moira said. "Jumpy."

"At this point, if you weren't jumpy, I'd been questioning your mental status." Moving deeper into the room, Hannah rubbed at her swollen belly. "I'm getting the munchies all the time these days. Can't wait for this baby to come."

Moira calculated the time and managed a smile—a real one. "It's just a couple of months now." She grimaced as she realized how close the holidays were—Hannah was due in late February and there was a wedding to squeeze in between Christmas and Hannah's due date. Both the brides-to-be had agreed they didn't want a Christmas wedding, and Branon was adamant that he marry Hannah *before* the baby came, while Neve demanded she have time to plan a *real* wedding. So . . . January.

"Want to join me for a snack?" Hannah asked hopefully.

Although she wasn't hungry, Moira appreciated the distraction and went to join Hannah in the kitchen area. When Brannon had taken over this building, he'd all but demolished the top level and had the entire loft done to his specifications. The top floor was his "in town" home. Now, instead of small, dusty rooms, he had a wide, open area that served as both living room and kitchen and dining area, with several bedrooms as well as the master. Moira was using one of the guest bedrooms. In addition, there was a small gym, a laundry, and two bathrooms.

Brannon didn't do small scale.

Hannah rubbed at her belly and groaned as she stared into the kitchen. "This baby wants to be a linebacker, I swear."

"Just a few more months," Moira said again, distracted by the pieces of the puzzle still running through her mind.

Instead of feeling reassured, Hannah snorted. "Don't remind me. I'm going to be the size of a houseboat by the time she gets here. She's already using my bladder as a trampoline."

Moira would've thought it would be impossible to laugh but Hannah startled one out of her. "What an image. So I guess she's moving around a lot."

"Yeah." A soft smile curled Hannah's lips despite her wry tone. "It's tickling Brannon to pieces, but he's not the one who has a ping-pong game going on his belly." Hannah opened the refrigerator and stared inside but then closed it, her face dark. "I want pizza. Why don't we have an all-night pizza place here?"

Moira pursed her lips. "The demographic in Treasure doesn't really call for that. I think it's just pregnant women."

"The way I'm going, I can keep an entire chain afloat for years." Hannah rubbed a hand over her belly as she opened the freezer. She pulled out a box of individual frozen pizzas and gave them a look of distaste.

"Grumble too much, you're gonna wake Brannon up." Moira glanced over her shoulder, half-expecting to see her brother there, pulling on his shirt and shoes to go on a pizza hunt. "He'll go dig up some pizza from somewhere."

"Normally that idea would guilt me into stopping." Hannah shrugged as she ripped the box open. "But he's not going to go anywhere with you here, and I'm not leaving the house. He'll actually just heat up the pizza here or just help me make some. I'll head it off and eat this stuff."

Moira pursed her lips as she tried to picture Brannon dragging his lazy ass out of bed to make pizza in the middle of the night. Go *buy* it, sure—that required little brainpower. But making it?

"You hungry?" Hannah asked, interrupting her mental reverie. As she tore open one of the pizzas, she gave Moira a hopeful look. "Please don't make me eat this alone."

Moira wasn't really hungry, but she smiled at Hannah. She hadn't had dinner and she suspected she wouldn't want to eat much in the morning either. "I can eat."

"Good," Hannah said, sighing happily. "I hate to be a glutton alone."

A few minutes later with microwave pizza, water for Hannah and wine that cost three hundred dollars a bottle for Moira, they sat down at the table. Hannah took one bite, chewed, and swallowed before looking over at Moira. "So how do you plan on making up with Gideon?"

"You know, Hannah?" Moira had lifted her glass to her lips, but now she lowered it, focusing on the glossy wood surface of the table. The wine warmed her belly and she had a feeling it was going to go straight to her head. Save for those few fries she'd stolen—and then puked up—she hadn't had anything since breakfast the day before. Although it hadn't quite been twenty-four hours, it felt like an entire lifetime ago. "This is one of the things I love about you. Some people would hesitate to ask such a personal question, but you just jump in, feetfirst."

"Not enough time in life to beat around the bush." Hannah took another bite of pizza. "And you didn't answer."

"That is because I was trying to dodge it." Moira grabbed a bit of uneaten crust and tossed it at Hannah. To her surprise, Hannah swayed to the side and caught the small piece in her mouth, right out of midair. Yet again, she startled a laugh out of Moira.

"I know you are trying to dodge me." Hannah shrugged. "But I'm not that easy to dodge. After all, I'm hooked up with Brannon, and he is master of the dodge."

"Point taken." Brooding, she picked up her wine and took a healthy swallow. Before she answered, she forced herself to take a bite of the pizza, although it was bland and tasteless, the dough more like tomato smeared cardboard. "I don't know what I'm gonna do. I messed up. And after how often I have messed up with him? I'm almost afraid to even look at him, Hannah."

The sensation in her belly got worse, and she pushed the pizza away. "I knew I was overreacting. I knew I was being stupid. But I couldn't stop myself. Now . . ." She closed her eyes, dropping her face into her hands. Heels to the sockets of her eyes, she said, "Now I've got to talk to him and find a way to fix this."

"Is that why you're up? Waiting for him to walk by on his way home?"

Moira frowned. "No. I just . . . hell, I can't sleep. All of this is whirling around in my head. And some of the things he was saying . . ." But her eyes strayed to the window once more. Had she been looking for him? She didn't know.

"Give yourself some time." Hannah reached over, covering Moira's hand with hers. "Try to rest and wait until tomorrow. You're exhausted and you're hurting. Get some rest and talk to him tomorrow."

"Yeah." She feigned a smile and got up, carrying the dishes over to the sink as Hannah finished up the last bit of her pizza.

"I still can't sleep." Hannah yawned and looked over toward the TV. "Want to find something stupid to watch?"

"Wow. What an invitation."

"Aw, c'mon. Sometimes, when I couldn't sleep at home, Mom and I would watch TV. The stupider the better." Hannah grinned at her. "You'd be surprised at how much easier it can be to sleep with something really brainless on the tube if you've got a friend there. Company can make all the difference."

A few minutes later, they curled up on the couch, each with a blanket and pillow scavenged from the guest bedrooms. The stupid movie of choice was a zombie flick that had them laughing and cringing within ten minutes.

They were asleep within thirty.

Like a few hundred people in town, he'd had a front-row seat, or close enough, to the spectacle that had happened last night.

Actually, *two* spectacles had happened.

That incompetent cop had lost his temper with Moira McKay, and she'd left practically in tears.

Poor Moira.

If she had gone back to McKay's Ferry . . .

He'd had hopes.

She *had* wanted to leave. Half the town had seen that much—had heard it, too.

He'd been watching, waiting, listening . . .

But in the end, she'd listened to her brother, and he had to assume she'd gone with that moron back to the apartment he had in town.

Brannon lived close to Neve.

For a few moments, he'd entertained the idea of another fire, one severe enough to set a few buildings ablaze. But he feared he'd be pushing his luck. He couldn't risk Moira dying, after all. He needed information from her and he didn't really see any reason either her or Neve had to die unless they had to.

Now, Brannon . . . well, that bastard, he did want him to die. If he had a way to kill two people—Brannon and Gideon—he'd try to make that happen, but in the end, if they *suffered*, that would suffice. Mostly because they were arrogant pieces of shite and he detested Gideon for that alone.

But the McKays—his war was with the McKays in

particular, so his personal vendettas would have to come later, and that meant focusing on the information he needed from Moira, and making sure he kept the promise he'd made to his father.

Making them pay.

If one of them died, it would hurt them, yes, and he liked the idea of that. But if they *all* died, what was the point?

Death was easy.

Death ended everything.

He didn't want them *dead* . . . he wanted them *miserable*.

It wasn't just that he *hated* the McKays. He hated everything they all stood for. Hated everything they were and everything they'd built and the hypocrites they were. They acted like such martyrs. But they were just greedy liars like anybody else.

Thieves and fools, all of them. They'd stolen everything from his family.

Picking up his phone, he checked the time and then surveyed the room. He'd spent the past few hours finalizing everything. He hadn't bought this place solely to fuck with Moira. That had been fun, true. But it should have belonged to him—to the Whitehalls all along. He had to give that whore Tilly credit. If she hadn't lied and claimed this house as hers through marriage to George, then it would have been lost and he wouldn't have had a chance to reclaim it.

And he wouldn't have a chance to do this now.

Stroking a hand down the carved back of the chair, he turned and looked around. Everything else was done.

All he had to do now was bring Moira here . . . bring her home.

Company did help. Moira didn't remember falling asleep.

She came awake almost instantly and knew by the colors bleeding through the sheer curtains that it was early yet. The sun was starting to rise.

Hannah was still asleep on the couch.

She wondered what had happened with that hot guy who had been trying to rally the survivors in the zombie flick.

Careful not to wake Hannah, she slid off of the couch and into the guest bathroom just off the side of the large, open living room. She took a quick shower, wrapping up in the robe Hannah had given her last night. There were plenty of toiletries. Brandon hadn't forgotten the lessons Ella Sue had drilled into them on etiquette.

Sadly, Moira had no clothes and while she could put on the ones she'd been wearing yesterday, her stomach started to churn when she picked them up.

They stank of smoke, and just the thought of smelling that on her skin all day left her feeling nauseated.

Wrapped in the robe, she left the bathroom in search of her phone. She'd call Ella Sue. A lifetime of experience told her that the lady would already be up. Their former housekeeper rarely slept past six and it was already showing past that.

Sure enough, Ella Sue answered on the second ring, her voice already clear and awake. "Honey, please tell me you're not sleeping at the house."

Moira made a face at the telephone. Childish, certainly, but it made her feel a little better. "I'm not sleeping at the house. Apparently everybody has decided I'm just not capable of taking care of myself."

"Girl," Ellis Sue said. "You are more capable than just about anybody I have ever met. It doesn't mean you need to be tangling with somebody who likes to play with fire. Chances are he's well aware of just how capable you are."

Moira swallowed.

As the silence stretched out, Ella Sue said softly, "You've never been an idiot, Moira. Don't you start now."

That no-nonsense tone got through in a way nobody else had been able to.

Resigned, Mira said, "I just don't like feeling out of control. I've been out of control since all of this started. Now I can't even sleep in my own bed."

"I imagine if Gideon hadn't had his hands full last night, he would've been more than happy to come back to Ferry with you."

"I know that." Moira's voice thickened as a knot settled inside her throat. It was a punch in the gut, those simply stated words. Gideon would have done just about anything to make yesterday easier on her and she had no doubt he was busting his ass to figure out things out now. What had she done?

Quit it. Guilting yourself to death isn't going to undo or fix things.

She needed to focus and she needed to fix things.

She couldn't do much of anything just yet. She needed clothes, first and foremost. "Look, Gideon has me here on lockdown. He doesn't want me going anywhere without having somebody with me. I'm at Brannon's and I need clothes. If I have to wear what I had on last night . . . "

"Say no more, honey." Ellis Sue spoke briskly. "You just need clothes or do you need personal items too?"

"Just clothes. No, wait . . . on second thought, Brannon always has extra here, but I might not be staying here tonight. Bring my toiletry case."

"Not a problem." Ellis Sue paused, then gently, she asked, "How are you doing, baby?"

The obvious concern in her voice was almost enough to shatter the wall that Moira had built up during the night. "At some point, I think I'll get past the shock. Once I get past the shock, I'm gonna find my mad. I'm waiting on that."

She disconnected then and left to busy herself with finding some clothes she could throw on until Ella Sue showed up.

Some years back, the McKay children had decided Ella Sue needed a porch built onto the back of her house. So they had one built for her. As the sun slowly rose up over the horizon, Ella Sue sat in her favorite rocker on that porch and stared out over her gardens. She wasn't out there for the view. It was winter and the colors were muted, but she still found peace there.

At least she did most days.

Now though, she simply rocked and thought about her children.

That was how she thought of the McKay kids.

Sandra and Devon might be the parents, but they'd died so long ago.

The night they'd died, they'd actually had plans to speak with her. The person who'd originally been the chosen guardian for the kids had died of a heart attack and they'd asked if maybe Ella Sue would take over the task. Ella Sue had needed to consider it, and she'd called them, asked if they could meet that night.

She would have told them yes.

It hadn't worked out.

But it didn't change the simple fact that she saw them as hers.

And somebody was threatening her beloved children. She loved them as much as loved her own girls, and the rage she had inside her over what was happening was gut wrenching.

Even before the fire, she'd been afraid and mad.

But now . . .

"You're finding your mad, aren't you, Moira?" she murmured as she placed the phone in her lap.

It would be a good thing if Moira did just that.

Ella Sue wasn't above of a bit of gossip; she liked to know what was going on with who and when. She didn't fancy mean talk and rather despised those who enjoyed carrying on with backstabbing and cruelty. That sort of spite, she liked to think, ended up showing in a person's life, whether it was on their face or in their general happiness . . . or lack of.

She found the best kind of gossip on Facebook. True enough, she also found the worst kind of trash. Just a week ago, she'd seen a man in town tell his wife he wanted a divorce—*on Facebook*. They'd been married for twenty years. Such a coward.

She'd been on Facebook last night when she read about the fire. The fear that had filled her had all but drained the strength out of her. She hadn't been able to move for a full thirty seconds. One of her granddaughters had sent her a message and it had been that little sound, like a bubble bursting, that had snapped her out of the shock.

When she'd finally been able to think, she'd started scrolling through the posts, reading about the fire, searching for news.

Then she'd seen pictures of the McKays, Moira first, then Neve and Brannon, along with pictures of the two who'd soon join the family, Hannah and Ian.

Gideon was there, as he always was. Where Moira was, Gideon would be somewhere close.

For the first time, she'd been conflicted. She'd wanted to rush to their side, but she hadn't been able to tear herself away. She had a schedule and her kids knew it. If they needed her, they'd try to call her at her house, not here.

And they *would* need her.

So she waited, sitting right there with a front-row seat of all the updates.

Including one that was recapped by a good twenty different people from Treasure, with commentary from double that. Pictures from so many people. Snide commentary from a few, including the good-for-nothing Joe Fletcher and Mrs. Mouton. Bless her heart, the sweet old lady just might have run into the museum if she hadn't been stopped. She was a gossip, true, but her heart was a good one.

The altercation between Moira and Gideon had been mostly one-sided and a lot of people had chimed in to talk about what a cow she was being, how she was acting like the spoiled rich bitch everybody knew she was.

Some of the people that Ella Sue thought to be levelheaded chimed in, and she read their comments over and over.

She gets attacked. She saw a man die in front of her. Her museum gets burned down. Not that long ago, her brother was stabbed and Hannah was nearly killed in that wreck before that. And don't forget what Moira and Neve went through. What's the matter with all of you?

That had come from Mrs. Mouton, and Ella Sue wanted to kiss her for it.

After skimming the comments, Ella Sue had a decent idea of what had happened.

The fire at the museum was the straw that broke the camel's back—*Moira's* back, in particular.

Now Gideon, well, Ella Sue knew him to be a levelheaded, patient man and she didn't think he'd take the things Moira had said to heart. But he'd taken some hard things from Moira for far too long.

She hoped this wouldn't be another one of those straws.

Gritty-eyed and tired, Gideon stood on the deck and stared out over the Mississippi. He could still smell the smoke on himself, despite the fact that he'd taken a shower that had used up every last bit of hot water he had in the tank.

He was tempted to climb back in there and try again. His muscles were aching and tired. Every last bit of him was aching and tired to be honest. He felt like he'd spent a month climbing uphill and had just been told he'd have to do it again.

Some five hours ago, after that shower, he'd collapsed in his bed and lost himself for a few hours—just over four, to be exact. He'd surfaced thirty minutes ago, and he needed to get his ass moving, but he just didn't have the energy.

If you were any good . . .

"Stop it," he muttered.

He drained the rest of his coffee and shoved off the wall.

It was Saturday. Officially, he was supposed to be off duty.

But that was before some sick fuck had set the museum on fire. Curling his hand into a fist, he wondered what he was going to do when he found the son of a bitch. He would find him. No doubt. He would find him.

He needed to find him before anything else happened. If he had to see that misery in Moira's green eyes again, he thought he'd go insane.

If you were any good . . .

Those words had come from a place of anger and fear and frustration and he knew it, but fuck if they weren't digging a hole into him.

CHAPTER TWENTY-THREE

Moira found some clothes.

The good thing about yoga pants was that they stretched.

The even better thing was that they came in a variety of lengths.

In the laundry room, she found a clean pile of clothes and poked through them until she found a pair of Hannah's yoga pants—she assumed they were Hannah's, although the idea of Brannon in yoga pants was sort of amusing.

She took those and grabbed a T-shirt of Brannon's that he must have grabbed from the pub. There was a hoodie hanging in there too, so she grabbed it.

There wasn't any help for it, so she had to put on her underwear and bra from yesterday, but it was only for a little while and the smoke wasn't as bad once she put them through the steam cycle on the dryer.

"Technology is a beautiful thing," she said softly.

Said technology also produced a quick, quiet cup of coffee.

The apartment was all but silent and she didn't want to wake anybody up, so she took her coffee and phone and slid out the backdoor and headed down the steps into the small garden.

The sight of it made her heart sigh. "Wow," she murmured, settling into one of the Adirondack chairs by the little gurgling brook. It hadn't been there before. She knew Brannon wasn't planning on staying here much longer, but he certainly believed in making his place comfortable.

The air was still cool and she shivered, snuggling deeper into the hoodie.

"Good morning."

At the familiar voice, she looked up. Out of habit, she smiled. "Hey."

"Couldn't sleep?"

Neve shivered as Ian came up behind her and slid his lips down the arch of her neck. "Hmmm. No. I didn't wake you up, did I?"

"Well, yes. See, I'm used to having this Neve-shaped beauty next to me in my bed and when she wasn't there, my body realized something was amiss and it told me to wake up. So I did."

"Neve-shaped beauty?" She giggled as he rubbed his beard against her neck. He pulled her onto his lap and settled his chin on her shoulder.

"There you go, stealing me things again." He sighed as he tapped at the edge of the computer screen. "Look at this. First my heart, then half my shirts, now my computer."

"I left mine at the station."

Ian nodded. "Trying to bore yourself into sleep"

"Ha, ha." She drove her elbow into his gut. "I think Gideon is on the right track. We just didn't have time to get much done yesterday before . . ." Her voice trailed off and she glanced toward the window. She couldn't see much of anything from here, but in her mind's eye, she saw the museum. The hungry flames hadn't quite gotten to finish their job before the firemen stanched the worst of it, but the damage had been done.

Ian stroked a hand down her side. "The three of you, you're strong. You're going to get through this."

"Brannon and I didn't put our hearts and souls into that place, Ian. Moira did. Without Gideon, this just might break her."

"But she's got him, yeah?"

Neve turned her face into his neck, thinking of the fight Gideon and Moira had had last night, although fight wasn't really accurate. What they had had was a one-sided argument where her sister had done all the arguing and Gideon had simply stood there, taking it.

Proving once again that he was a mind reader, Ian said, "Neve, she was hurt." He hugged her back against him. "Marshall knows that. He's a smart man. She's had to handle too much lately and last night . . . Well, anybody with a brain had to understand what that was doing to her. Marshall has brains enough for two people. It's going to be okay. Now . . . why don't you and I . . ."

Neve gasped as he slid his hands up her torso and cupped her breasts through the old soccer shirt she'd stolen from him. He'd insisted he'd have to have it back, peeling it off of her and leaving her naked the morning she'd walked out of the bedroom wearing it. Then he'd made love to her on the kitchen table—again. Later, he'd said she could keep it. "Manchester United has never looked so good, sweet Neve."

He unerringly found her nipples and worked them into taut points, and she squirmed, struggling to get closer. His cock pressed against her butt. "Why are you wearing clothes?" she demanded.

"Why are you?"

She snorted out a laugh, half-turning to face him, forgetting about the computer.

It hit the floor with a crash.

Ian laughed and eased her off his lap. "You need to take better care of my toys if you're going to use them."

He picked up the laptop and eyed all the windows she had open. "Neve, sweetheart. You've got eleventy bajillion windows open."

"I do not." Flushing, she grabbed the computer.

He let her and settled back against the couch, stroking a path up and down her thigh.

She shivered and started closing the windows of all the hints she'd been looking at last night. "I'm just trying to get a handle on the Whitehall family line."

"And you're doing that with eleventy bajillion windows?"

She rolled her eyes. "No." She paused on one of the tabs.

Ian's fingers skimmed the sensitive flesh of her inner thigh, and her breath hitched.

"Then . . . we can maybe let this wait?"

She closed two more tabs. "Yes, I just . . ."

He took the computer and leaned forward to put it on the table.

Neve couldn't even argue.

The muscles in his back flexed and arched as she bent over and pressed her lips to his smooth skin.

It dawned on her then that he'd gone tense.

"Neve."

That tension wasn't just in his body.

As he sat back on the couch, still holding the laptop, she felt something cold settle in the pit of her stomach. "What?"

Instinctively, she looked at the laptop.

She couldn't see it. He'd angled the screen away.

"Take a deep breath, love. This . . ." He blew out a breath. "Look, it might not be anything, okay? Really."

* * *

By now, it was no surprise to wake up feeling like a boulder had settled on her bladder, but that didn't mean Hannah enjoyed having to practically run to the bathroom.

After she'd washed her hands, she went ahead and stripped off her pajamas and climbed into the shower. Sleeping on the couch hadn't been the best of ideas. Moira was the smart one. After the movie ended, she had obviously decided to go into her bedroom. Now Hannah, fat and pregnant, had even more of a reason for her back to hurt.

Couches were murder on the spine.

The multiple sprays from the shower helped loosen the kinks, but she was still half-slumped against the wall when the door opened and Brannon came through the billows of steam. "I'm not up for water sports, gorgeous," she said groggily.

"I'm just looking to conserve water." He wrapped his arms around her. "Back?"

She nodded.

He nudged her around.

It didn't take anything else to convince her and a moment later, hands slicked from soap, Brannon went about working the knots from her back. He had her limp as putty before she even knew it.

When he cupped her swollen breasts in his hands, she braced her hands on the wall.

"Still not up for water sports?"

"Would you just shut up and fuck me already?"

Brannon laughed and nudged her upper torso forward before grasping her hips.

He came inside her, deep and slow, and Hannah closed her eyes, already aching for more.

"Zeke Sanders called about bringing a dog out for us."

Hannah opened one eye. Brannon was all sexy, awake

and alert . . . and apparently dealing with life and phone calls and all.

She was sleepy and sated and just wanted to go back to bed.

The man who'd sold the dogs to Moira and Neve was being a bit more cautious with her and Brannon. Once Gideon had mentioned she was pregnant, Zeke had said he'd be introducing them to a few dogs before they all decided which one seemed to be a fit.

So far, they'd met two. Hannah had loved one of them, but neither of the dogs had much liked Brannon. He hadn't been amused by it, but she had.

"Fine," she mumbled, trying to shift around in the bed. "I feel like a beached whale. You gonna make us some breakfast?"

"Us?" Brannon grinned at her, amused. He covered her belly with his hand. "I guess I can cook for my beautiful wife to be and my baby."

"I meant me and your sister."

For a moment, Brannon looked blank. Then he blinked. "Shit. I forgot. Moira's been so quiet. She's got to be exhausted. She's still sleeping. I didn't see her out there . . ."

Somebody pounded on the door, the knock so loud, it had Hannah jolting on the bed.

"Brannon. Moira. Open up! It's Gideon."

Brannon rolled his eyes. "Like I don't know that voice by now." He kissed Hannah quickly and stood up. "Dumbass."

Hannah grinned at his back and snuggled deeper into the blankets. "I want bacon. Tell Gideon it better be life or death if he's trying to come between me and breakfast."

On his way to the door, he shouted for his sister, although he imagined she was already awake after that knock.

There came another one, and Brannon shouted, "For crying out loud, give me a minute."

He opened the door a few seconds later and glared at Gideon. When he saw Neve and Ian behind the cop, he frowned. "What's up?"

Gideon didn't respond, just pushed his way past Brannon. "I need to see Moira."

Brannon looked over his shoulder at her still-closed door.

"If she's still asleep, wake her," Gideon snapped.

"She was up pretty late," Hannah said from the doorway, wrapped in a blanket. She knuckled at her eyes, scowling at Gideon. "Neither of us slept very well last night, Chief."

Gideon didn't even blink. "Sorry, Hannah. It's urgent."

"What's going on?" Brannon demanded.

"I need to talk to Moira, first."

Brannon blew out a breath and turned toward Moira's door. He knocked, but when there wasn't an answer, he turned the doorknob, easing it open slowly. Then he shoved it open wide, because the bed was the first thing he saw when looking in this room. And the bed was empty.

Neatly made, and empty.

"What the hell . . ."

Gideon heard him and came storming over, shouldering Brannon aside.

Brannon looked over at Neve. "What's going on?" he said again.

She opened her mouth, but Gideon cut her off. "Did she leave?"

"What? No." Brannon shook his head. "She might be out in the garden." He headed over to the back of the loft, moving quickly through the mudroom and jogging down the steps that led into the private garden.

Moira wasn't there.

However, she had been.

There was a cup of coffee, still fairly warm, sitting on the little table by one of the Adirondack chairs.

And on the stone path that led out of the garden, half-buried in the flowers, Neve saw something else.

Moira's phone.

Gideon saw it and immediately turned away, grabbing his radio from his belt and speaking into it with that low, clipped voice Brannon had come to call his "cop voice." He communicated in a series of orders and codes, and most of it was practically a foreign language. But there were a few things that Brannon recognized . . . like his sister's name, the color and make of a car . . . and his eyes narrowed when he heard another name.

He practically lunged for Gideon then, but Ian caught him.

"Ease up, mate. I'll explain, yeah? Just . . . just let him finish. We got to focus on Moira now, right? She's what matters."

"Brannon?"

At the soft sound of Ella Sue's voice, he looked up.

She stood at the top of the stairs, holding a small suit-case as she looked around. "Where's Moira? I've got the clothes she asked me to bring."

Brannon closed his eyes.

Gideon stopped talking for a moment, staring up at Ella Sue.

"What's going on?" she asked softly, voicing the exact same question that Brannon had asked.

But this time, Gideon answered. In a flat, hard voice, he said, "I think Charles Hurst has her."

CHAPTER TWENTY-FOUR

Moira continue to feign sleep. It had been pure dumb luck that Charles had stopped the car and gotten out now when she came to awareness. He hadn't stopped for long—whether he was grabbing coffee, filling the tank, or just enjoying the damn sunrise, she didn't know. And she didn't dare crack more than an eyelid either because she was too busy trying to remember, to understand.

She'd come awake, her instincts screaming and that alone might have been her saving grace.

Unable to move, her head foggy, she'd panicked and almost screamed, but then one memory leapt into clarity.

Charles had clamped an arm around her neck right before he jabbed something into her arm.

"I remember putting these bruises on you, Moira . . . I didn't enjoy doing it. Don't make me do it again."

Bruises . . .

Her mostly healed throat now ached again, and it was because of him.

All of this was because of him.

She'd been calm when he got back in and continued to act as though she was trapped in the grasp of whatever drugs he had given her. Acting as though she was still asleep, she lay still, frozen as he leaned over and brushed her hair aside.

"Are you awake there?" He'd tapped her cheek.

It had taken everything she had not to bite his hand off at the wrist. Sitting there still had been an act of supreme willpower. Now as they continued to drive through the countryside, he hummed endlessly under his breath.

She thought she'd scream if she had to listen to that much longer. She sat awkwardly, half-twisted in the seat with her head resting on the passenger side door. Earlier, she'd started to shiver. It hadn't been from cold, but from shock, a reaction she hadn't been able to control. Charles hadn't known the difference though and he'd tossed a blanket over her.

Such a considerate kidnapper.

She didn't know how much longer she would be able to pull off the sleeping bit, but her ex-husband seemed to recall how hard drugs had always hit her. If her internal clock was right, it had been maybe five minutes since he'd tapped her on the cheek once more and then muttered to himself, "That might have been too strong a dose."

That's right, you son of a bitch. Keep thinking that.

Whatever he'd given her had left her thoughts muggy, and she'd had to piece the events of the morning together bit by bit. But she was thinking clearly now. After some grunting and shifting around, she'd managed a furtive look at the clock.

It was nearly eleven.

It had been just after seven when she'd slipped outside. She doubted she'd been out there more than ten or fifteen minutes before he'd shown up.

People back home would know she was missing by now.

She'd dropped her phone. Had he seen it?

She didn't have her shoes.

She didn't have her purse.

She didn't have her keys.

Ella Sue had been bringing her clothes, and if she knew anything about that woman, when Moira wasn't there to get the clothes she'd called about, Ella Sue would be raising hell.

Or at least, raising Gideon.

People would know.

Gideon would know.

The miserable ache in her back forced her to shift again. She didn't want to, but if she didn't, she worried she wouldn't be able to move—or run—when the chance came.

This time, though, she wasn't able to do it without Charles taking notice.

"Are you waking up over there, are you, Moira?"

Better not make him suspicious. She made a low noise in her throat and shifted again.

He sighed. "About bloody time. Of course, it's too bad, really. You'll have to nap again before too long. Can't have you spoiling the fun, now can I?"

Mentally, Moira counted to twenty, then shifted again and made another noise and tried to stretch. When she couldn't, she muttered and shifted again.

Then, hoping like hell she could pull this off with some of Neve's flair for drama, she jerked upright and looked around. "What the . . ."

"Hello, love."

Charles gave her a serene smile.

She blinked and let herself relax a little, as if calmed by a familiar face. She yawned, moving as if to lift her hands.

The lap belt stopped her.

Charles had trapped them under the belt when he snapped it into place, leaving her pinned and mostly helpless. She'd been able to twist and work her wrists to some extent, loosening the ropes bit by bit. But she still couldn't move them enough.

He laughed.

"What's going on?"

"Oh, we're taking a bit of a drive, love. You used to enjoy them, remember?" He gave her the slow, sardonic smile she remembered from when they had first started to date.

"A drive?" She blinked, shaking her head as if to clear it, trying once more to move her hands. This time, when she couldn't, she began to struggle. Harder this time, putting more effort into it and managing to get more slack in the seat belt—and in the ropes around her wrists.

The rough weave of the blanket snagged on the seat belt, hiding the movement when she managed to pull her hands out from under the lap restraint.

Charles, eyes on the road, didn't seem to notice. He reached over and rubbed the back of her neck. "Yes, darling. We're taking a drive. I've things to show you."

She jerked again, limiting her motions and hoping he'd think it was the seat belt.

He chuckled. She wanted to slam her fists into his larynx.

For some odd reason, she found herself thinking about a self-defense course Gideon had given. She'd gone with a couple of friends from Treasure, thinking it would be taught by one of the officers—that had been the plan, Gideon had later explained. But the officer down to teach the class had an accident while out hunting—one that involved falling asleep in a tree. Gideon had taken over.

I heard that you can get out of zip ties, Shayla Hardee had said, flirting with him. *Is that true? Could you demonstrate? You can tie me up . . . or I'll tie you up.*

Gideon had taken the question at face value, ignoring her innuendo. *Given the time and opportunity, it's possible to escape such a restraint.*

He'd also talk about what to do if somebody was ever abducted.

Wait for the ideal moment. You might only get one chance.

That advice in mind, she evaluated her situation. She was tied up, restrained by a seat belt that had locked in place just a little loose and he was speeding down a country highway. If this was her ideal moment, she was screwed.

As much as she wanted to make him choke on his laughter, she'd rather do it at a time when she had a better chance of survival.

So she waited.

At the same time, she tried again to right herself and pull her hands free. The blanket fell away this time and she lifted her hands, twisting them a bit so he couldn't see how much slack there was in the rope.

Distraction—that was key. She had to keep him distracted.

She sucked in a breath.

"What in the hell is this?" There was a tremor in her voice, and as much as she wished she could've kept it from showing, she hadn't been able to.

Charles *smiled* at her. The bastard *smiled*. "The meaning? I would think that was obvious. I'm kidnapping you."

Her mouth fell open—and that had nothing to do with her trying to convince him of anything. As she stared into his eyes, Moira saw something she had never before seen. Charles Hurst, her ex-husband, her former lover, the man she would've called friend even just that morning, was crazier than a bag of cats.

Neve paced back and forth in front of the large plate-glass window. On the other side, Gideon was talking to Sheriff Tank Grainger.

Tank was listening, but Neve had no idea how to read him.

Tank was . . . well . . . like a tank. His birth name was Tarrell but he'd been called Tank since high school, she'd been told, when he'd mowed down the opposing team on the football field on a regular basis, leading the football team of McKay's Treasure to its first state championship.

He was as hard to read as a piece of metal, and about as unstoppable from everything she'd heard. When she was sixteen, somebody had T-boned Tank's car—intentionally.

Tank had walked away from the accident.

Ella Sue had mentioned off the cuff that he had just had a bout with cancer—of the male variety—and had beaten it, but then, everybody knew you couldn't stop Tank. Definitely not something as trifling as cancer—that was how Ella Sue had phrased it, her eyes glinting with dark humor.

That was his slogan come election time, too.

Nothing can stop Tank.

Every few minutes or so, he'd look at her with a reassuring smile.

She wanted to hope that smile meant something, but just then, there were only a few people she counted on. Most of them were in the room with her. Hannah, Brannon, Ella Sue, and Ian were as upset and stressed-out as she was.

Gideon looked as stone-faced and unreadable as Tank, but she knew him.

Unlike Tank, she could read Gideon. The taut muscle that kept jumping in his jaw, the eyes that kept flicking from Neve and Brannon to the big white board his men had finished setting up some twenty minutes earlier.

Gideon was worried.

And if Gideon was worried . . .

She swallowed.

That meant she should be terrified.

A hand brushed her shoulder and she jumped, a startled shriek rising in her throat.

"It's just me, darling Neve," Ian murmured, moving in to hug her.

"Damn it," she whispered. "I'm sorry."

"No. Don't be sorry. I'm worried, too." He held her tighter, and for a moment she let herself lean against him.

"Why didn't we see it sooner?" she asked raggedly, damning herself to hell.

"Don't do this." Ian kissed her temple. "This isn't your fault. It isn't mine. It's not Moira's or Gideon's. It's on that fucking piece of shite's head. And I swear to you, Neve, if I'm the one who finds him, I'll rip his skull off and we'll both take turns pissing on it the rest of our days."

The vivid and disgusting image startled a laugh out of her.

"That's gross." She turned in his arms and pressed her face into his neck. "That's really, really gross."

"I'll rip his balls off too, straight out through his nose."

She cringed. "How . . . macho of you."

"Moira will be fine." Ian pressed his lips to her ear. "She's a canny woman, that one. Even on a good day she can terrify me, and I'm a smart man."

"I don't think Charles has the sanity to be afraid of her," she whispered.

"And that's where he'll mess up." Ian cupped the back of her neck. "I've seen her slice off a man's balls with a simple look. That bampot doesn't likely have that much sense."

She sniffed, not certain if that comforted her or not.

"She'll be alright," Ian whispered again.

She squeezed her eyes shut tight and chose to believe he was right.

* * *

"If you keep this up, you're going to pace a hole right through that floor and then you and me are both going to crash right through and you'll be freaking out because you'll have to rush me to the emergency department and deal with handling me *and* what's going on with Moira."

At the sound of Hannah's calm, steady tone, Brannon stopped his pacing and turned to stare at her. He'd *heard* the words and the tone, but none of the words had made sense.

Except "emergency."

"Huh? What?" As those words made a deeper impact on his consciousness, he crossed the floor to her and closed his hands around her arms. "Damn it, Hannah, are you okay? Is it the baby? Is it the—"

She rose onto her toes and pressed her mouth to his. "Stop it," she said after a few seconds. Then, because Brannon was a big believer in tactile persuasion, she took his hand and guided it to her belly. "She is *fine.* See?"

As if to back her up, the little baby proceeded to do a series of flops and flips, kicking up against Brannon's hand.

He blew out a breath and pressed his brow against hers. "Then why are you talking about going to the hospital?"

"Never mind." Hannah cupped his face in her hands. "You need to calm down."

"I can't—"

When he would have pulled away, she simply tightened her grip and pressed her lips to his once more. "You can."

He sighed against her mouth. "Hannah . . ."

"Calm down. You know this guy, Brannon. You don't like him, but you know him. You know people, period. Now calm down . . . think. Stop panicking and think. Moira is smart. She knows him better than anybody and she can buy herself some time, but you need to help her there. *Think.*"

When Brannon lifted his head and met her eyes, she stared back levelly.

"Since when were paramedics crisis-management types?" He focused on the dark, steady strength he saw in her eyes.

"Seriously?" She laughed up at him as she curled her arms around his neck. "Half the time, all we *do* is manage crises. It's either somebody convinced their gas pains are heart attacks—or ten somebodies who wrote off their heart attacks as gas pains. You'd be amazed at how cool I am under pressure. Now . . . are you ready to think there, big guy?"

"Yeah." He nodded. Thinking wasn't exactly what he *wanted* to do. What he wanted to do involved a lot of blood and pain. But thinking was what would help Moira now.

The blood and pain could come later.

The door opened and Brannon looked away from Hannah's eyes to see Gideon filling the doorframe. "I'm going to give you an update on what we have so far."

His eyes lingered on Brannon's for a moment, then moved to Neve's.

The look on his face was enough to tell Brannon two things.

Gideon didn't know where Moira was. And Gideon wanted to kill somebody possibly more than Brannon did.

A few minutes later, Brannon found himself standing in front of a huge whiteboard. In the top middle of the board was a kids' group photo. If Brannon hadn't already seen it, he might have been pissed off, but he had. The image had two of the students circled. One of them was Charles—a much younger Charles. His image was circled in red. Off to the side and down a few rows was another youth's face, circled in purple.

That was Samuel William Clyde.

Brannon had a feeling the bastard had ended up a pawn

in whatever game Hurst was playing. And there was a game, Brannon had no doubt. Somehow, that shithead Charles maneuvered Clyde into Neve's orbit.

"Okay, officers"—Gideon paused to add—"and citizens with a vested interest. Let's talk about what we know."

I'm kidnapping you.

His words were still ringing in her ears, her brain still struggling to process them when Charles casually swung out a hand and smacked it into her mouth.

Blood exploded over her tongue and her eyes began to water.

"Nothing to say there, darling?" he asked. "Did you not understand? I am kidnapping you."

Moira let a breath shudder in, then out of her lungs.

She wasn't going to answer him right now. She didn't dare. Blood pooled in her mouth and she swallowed it before she gave into the urge to spit it into his face.

Had she had her hands free, she would have lunged for him, wrapping them around his neck and damn the fact that he was speeding down the twisting country highway.

It might have been a blessing that she hadn't quite managed to work her hands loose of the rope just yet.

She could remember telling Ella Sue that she'd find her mad soon.

Charles wasn't going to be overly thrilled that he'd been the one to trigger that discovery.

Through her disheveled hair, she stared at him.

He cast another glance her way and chuckled. "You look brassed-off, love. I suppose I can understand. Don't fret, though. You'll understand what this is all about here in a bit."

She almost snapped at him, told him she had already connected those dots—not all the way, maybe, but they'd been looking for a connection and now with her ex-husband merrily announcing he was kidnapping her . . . well . . . Moira wasn't exactly an idiot.

So she bit her tongue. *Don't give him any advantage. Keep him in the dark.*

She had to buy time. Her family, Gideon, all of them— they had to know she was missing.

Charles might've thought he'd have an hour or two, that there would be some confusion, but he wouldn't have had more than thirty minutes at the most before Ella Sue would sound the alarm.

The efficient older woman had likely already been half- way to town by the time Charles had Moira in the car.

When Moira wasn't found at Brannon's, they wouldn't waste time calling Gideon.

Her heart wrenched at the thought of that. She should have called him first thing.

She should have sent him a text, told him she was sorry, instead of brooding and trying to think of the *right* way to say it. There was only ever one way.

Now she had to wait for them to find her . . . or wait for her chance to escape.

They'd piece it together. She had no doubt of that.

When they didn't find her at the loft, Charles would be one of the first people they checked with. And when he wasn't found, he'd jump right to the top of the list.

You probably trust him . . . Gideon's voice haunted her.

He'd been right. She had trusted him.

Charles had been right there when Gideon threw those words at her, all but begging her to listen, demanding that she understand.

Well, she did now.

"How could we have missed this?" Brannon's voice ex- ploded through the station.

Gideon blocked it out, relying on Hannah to keep

Brannon under control. She did, speaking to him in a no-nonsense tone that would cut through his rage far better than any soothing murmur ever could.

Gideon tuned them both out.

Neve sat with her laptop open, her face stark. He wanted to take it away, because he already knew what she was doing. Now that they had a name, she was finding all the connections, all those little pieces that connected Charles Hurst to the Whitehall family. His father's mother had been a Whitehall and all of them, it seemed, had been twisted by that ugly hate, a seed that was passed down for generations.

"They look alike," Neve whispered. "This picture . . . I've *seen* it." She pointed at something on the screen.

Ian looked and then leaned over and closed the computer. "Let's focus on your sister, Nevie. We'll deal with him later."

As she turned into him, Gideon looked away.

Tank Grainger was already in the station, as were the deputies he'd called in to help.

"I don't understand exactly what we are doing here," Deputy Paul Lewis said, his ruddy face twisted in a scowl. Lewis had been on call this weekend and most people knew he spent his weekend on the river fishing. Granted, Lewis's idea of fishing involved a lot of beer and very little bait—or fish. He didn't particularly care to have it interrupted for much of anything. "Ms. McKay hasn't been gone for twelve hours, much less the mandatory forty-eight. And you believe she is with her ex-husband. All we know, they might be . . . reconnecting."

To Gideon's surprise, it was Maris who gave Lewis a withering look and cut the idiot down to size with the impact of that glare alone. "First of all, a woman doesn't go disappearing anywhere without taking her purse." When Lewis went to argue, Maris took a step toward him and continued in a flinty voice. "Chief Marshall has already told us that she left without her purse, without her shoes, without her phone. She did it without telling anybody she was going anywhere. Moira McKay is a smart woman and she's already been attacked once, threatened, with her throat almost crushed."

Lewis reached up and rubbed at his neck, glancing around the room as if searching for support.

Nobody seemed too keen on meeting his gaze.

Maris wasn't done. "There's a fire at the bookstore her brother helped renovate. The museum was targeted. Then a few days ago, a man she worked with is murdered in front of her." Maris went back to perching on the empty desk of an off-duty patrol officer. "I don't know about you, but I'm not so big on believing in coincidences."

"Who said anything about coincidences?" Lewis puffed out his chest, jabbing a finger toward himself. "I'm just looking at this all logical-like. This McKay chick is important—"

"McKay chick?" Maris narrowed her eyes.

"Excuse me, Ms. PC Police." Lewis pronounced it *PO*-lice, rolling his eyes for effect. Again, he looked around, a smirking grin on his lips, but it faded when nobody seemed to share in his amusement.

"Lewis, son. You know what? Maybe you should just take yourself back on down to the river." The sheriff gave himself a slow shake of his head.

Confused, Lewis stared at the sheriff. "Excuse me?"

"You heard me, deputy." Tank looked over at the board. It held stills of Moira, Charles, and, although he was dead, Samuel William Clyde.

There weren't many details posted as of yet, but Gideon did have information. Thanks to some calls Ian and Neve had made once they had discovered that picture online—what a fucking stroke of luck—Gideon actually had a fairly substantial amount of information, but he wasn't certain just how much of it would be admissible. None of that was his number one concern—Moira was—but he didn't want Charles Hurst skating out from under the justice that he had coming his way, either.

Ian knew some cops—bobbies or whatever they were called—over in Glasgow. Neve had called her friend back in Carrbridge, the one she'd described as a big teddy bear. He'd saved her from William once, and his name was Angus Reid. Reid was a security specialist and he'd provided more information than Gideon could have hoped for.

Each piece of it had made Gideon's gut grow a little more cold.

Charles Hurst was a great deal smarter than anybody had known.

Gideon had known the man was smart—Moira had married him and she'd never been one to tolerate fools or idiots. Even if she'd just married him because he had a pretty face and she'd been looking for . . . something, she'd hired him to help with the museum and that museum had been her baby.

She wouldn't let anybody without a sharp mind near her baby.

But Charles was more than just a sharp curator. He was well above genius level. He'd started university at the age of sixteen, had graduated at twenty and continued on another year, pursuing an advanced degree of some sort and had also helped out with several teachers.

During a summer camp, he'd met William. Although there had been an age difference between them, they'd connected.

That was the information Reid had collected so far.

Gideon wasn't surprised they'd somehow become friends. Like attracted like, and both of them seemed to be evil sons of bitches, and crazy to boot.

Whether they'd stayed tight had yet to be discovered, but Reid was trying to find out if the two of them had connected at some point in New York. Gideon suspected the answer would be yes. He had a feeling Charles had pointed William in Neve's direction.

But that was low on the priority scale.

One thing he did have confirmed was that Charles Hurst was a direct descendent of George Whitehall, possibly the last direct one in the line. His grandmother had been Elisabeth Whitehall Hurst. She'd raised her son—that would be Charles' father—alone after her husband had died—cause of death had been listed as suicide.

Her son had been named Charles George Whitehall Hurst.

He'd been ten when his father died.

The father who'd committed suicide had left behind massive amounts of debt. Those debts had cost Elisabeth a house that had been in the Whitehall family for generations.

She'd died less than ten years later.

It seemed that bad luck plagued the Whitehalls.

Behind him, Deputy Lewis continued to delay leaving. "Look, I ain't trying to cause no trouble, Sheriff. It's just . . . well. Everybody knows the chief has a thing for Ms. McKay. On top of that, it ain't like that family isn't treated as royalty 'round here. I know they done some important things, but is it right that we circumvent procedure?"

"Are we circumventing procedure? Here I was thinking we were taking the necessary measures when it's deemed that a citizen of this town is in all likely in danger." Tank's level voice was a sharp contrast to his sudden movement. He'd placed his body between his deputy and Gideon.

As explosive as his temper could get, it wasn't Brannon who might need to be held back if this shit kept up. Gideon sucked in a breath through his teeth and tried to clear the red fog from his brain. Tank's hand was the size of a dinner plate and it was braced against his chest in a silent, physical warning—*think*.

Out loud, Tank addressed his officer. "Deputy, I'd like to ask you to turn your attention to the board over there. You see the picture dead center on the top? That would be Moira McKay as I'm sure you are aware. Please take note of the bruises on her throat. That's from the attack that Deputy Cordell mentioned earlier. We call that assault in our line of work."

"Sheriff, I ain't saying there might not be cause for alarm." Lewis set his jaw, face going red. "But it's awful early to be saying there *is* anything wrong—"

"That's enough." Gideon shoved past Tank. The sheriff gave him a warning look, but Gideon ignored him. He had his temper under control now. He wasn't gonna do anything stupid. Doing something stupid would keep him from finding Moira. Nothing was more important than that. "We have probable cause and a good reason to suspect Charles first. Maybe you have forgotten the basics of law enforcement, but I assure you that I haven't. That man that Cordell told you about being murdered? He gave us a confirmation that the McKays were being targeted.

"Now maybe you've forgotten something else—but when a woman is a target of violence, more often than not, it's an intimate partner, an ex-husband . . ." Gideon let a sneer fill his voice. "Does that ring a bell? If not, maybe you ought to consider whether or not you should be carrying that badge. Regardless, I want your ass out of my station. Now."

Tank shot him a fulminating look, but Gideon didn't give a damn.

Lewis turned on his heel and stormed out, muttering under his breath.

Once he was gone, Gideon swung around to stare at the board.

Without looking at any of the men and women in the room, Gideon said, "Anybody else want to imply that my emotions are going to interfere with my job?"

"I think we all know that you have a little more than the typical interest in Moira McKay, but that's been the case for a long time. During all that time, you've never had a problem doing your job. I don't see that changing now." Maris cocked a brow at him. "As to Hurst? Well, I can't say I ever liked that prick. I see the cause for concern."

Tank caught Gideon's eyes. "How about we get to that debriefing?"

CHAPTER TWENTY-FIVE

The stupidest thing Charles could have done—aside from kidnapping her—had been casually mentioning that he planned to drug her again. Granted, he'd thought she was still under the grip of whatever shit he'd pumped into her system, but that wasn't a good enough excuse to talk about his plans, was it?

When he casually reached into the side pocket on the driver side door, she was ready.

He had turned onto a side road not too long ago, and she recognized where they were.

The sight of the trees wrapping around the car like a tunnel made a mad hope flare inside her. Gideon would think to look here—or having somebody look.

Had it really only been a few days since she'd been here with Gideon? Since she'd talked to Kevin right before he'd taken that sip of scotch that had ended his life?

It felt like a lifetime.

The car slowed as they crept over the pitted and narrowed road and she started to breathe in shallow, short breaths. This wasn't good. Not at all. Something ugly and hot climbed up her throat and it only got worse when he slowed the car to a crawl.

The seat belt should have held her snugly in the seat, but she'd been slowly inching her way forward, trying to give herself room to move and when he slammed on the brakes, the locking mechanism clicked in with several inches to spare. The rough edge of the belt's material rubbed against Moira's already abused throat and she fought not to gasp.

With her feet braced on the floor, she shoved herself back as quickly as she could, turning to face Charles as he looked over at her.

She had the blanket.

A pitiful weapon, but it was all she had.

When he sprang into motion, she jerked up the blanket between them. Something wet trickled through and she just shoved harder.

Charles growled, and she sensed more than felt his hand withdrawing.

Then he shoved with a force that had her head smacking against the window.

Dazed, her reaction time was slowed, and she cried out in shock as he jabbed the syringe's needle into her thigh, straight through the material of the pants she'd swiped from Hannah.

"Stupid bitch," Charles swore, his voice ragged.

She lifted her wrists and balled them up, swinging at him. The drugs hadn't hit her system, but her arms felt heavy and the blow glanced over his chin without making much of an impact.

Still, it infuriated him and he grabbed her bound wrists. She gasped, hoping he wouldn't noticed the loosened ropes. He didn't seem to, hauling her up against him. "Listen, *pet* . . . I've been tolerant with you, but try to hit me again and you'll be sorry for it."

"Tolerant . . ." She said it slowly. "Sure, Charles. I'll be tolerant. You can get right out of this car and go fuck a gator and I won't judge you at all. How is that?"

For a moment, the pretty blue of his eyes went diamond hard.

Then, to her annoyance, he bent his head and pressed his lips to her brow. "Moira my love . . . you always did enjoy trying to push your luck. But you won't get out of this one with words, my pet."

She thought she said something else, thought maybe he even answered.

But his words were . . . far away and she couldn't really focus on his face now either.

The howling of his dogs wasn't precisely what Zeke would call an unusual noise but he couldn't exactly call it commonplace, either.

Zeke rose from the table where he and his wife Ida had been enjoying a cup of coffee. Behind him, Ida continued to pore over the blueprints they had set aside years ago.

Just a few days ago, Ida had been the one to pull them back out.

He had no idea where she'd put them, just knew that she'd put them away and told him they had to let it go, had to move on. *We can't keep letting this eat at us, all this anger, all this hate. It's not good for us, honey. If it's meant to happen, it will. I'll pray about it. If it's meant to be, God will find a way. But this isn't good for us, baby,* she'd whispered to him.

When he'd told her that she was wasting her time with prayer, she had simply kissed him and said, *That's what you think . . . but I prayed for you every night you were gone. Every time you had to go on tour, I prayed. And every time you came back.*

She was always tripping him up.

She'd even managed to trip him into going to church.

He'd told her that if she wanted to pray, she could pray. If they ever ended up with getting their land, he'd even start going to church with her, every Sunday for the rest of his life.

He had already made good on the promise too.

He'd been more than happy to sit with his wife in the third row of the county Christian church where they had been married almost forty years earlier. He hadn't minded a bit when people came up and shook his hand and chatted with him either, keeping him and Ida there for almost an hour after the service.

Granted, it had kept him away from his dogs.

Zeke had never much cared to be kept away from his dogs for longer than he had to be, but on occasion it was nice to talk with something who actually spoke instead of wagged a tail.

It was more annoying when he had to listen to the comments like, *I do hope it's not so long before we see you again. Most times, it's a wedding or funeral that brings you out.*

But those comments wouldn't keep him from coming back the following Sunday. After all, he had made his wife a promise, and Zeke was a man of his word.

Just as he was a man who listened to his instincts.

Right now, as he sat there with the howls rising in the cool, midmorning air, his instincts were screaming. There was more to the caterwauling of his dogs than whatever the canines had perceived as an invasion on their territory. He'd trained them better than that.

They didn't bark because they smelled a rabbit or even a stray dog.

They only raised hell when they sensed a threat.

"Gracious, Zeke." Ida frowned, concern lighting her pretty, pale eyes. "They certainly are all worked up today, aren't they?"

"Yeah." Without elaborating, he moved over to the radio on he kept on the long, skinny counter Ida had long since dubbed his "junk station." It was organized to a fault and every spare inch of space was utilized. There were harnesses to repair, lists of potential owners for his dogs, lists of potential breeders. None of that held his attention, though.

He went straight to the radio.

He kept it on at all times.

Most of the time, the voices on it were white noise, talking about how the world had gone straight to shit and on occasion there would be argument about who was to blame and why and which politician had fucked it up the worst.

The few times it wasn't white noise, it was because something in the region was going on. It didn't matter if it was a storm or a missing child or somebody's Auntie Bess had taken a walk and hadn't come home. Usually Auntie Bess was going senile and would be found some miles from home. Once, a call had gone out for a little boy's lost dog.

Zeke turned up the radio and listened, head cocked as he focused on that noise instead of his dogs.

"... *a BOLO out of Treasure over in Mississippi. Got us a pretty redhead gone missing. They think her ex-husband has her. Name's Myra McKay.*"

Zeke's eyes narrowed.

"*You got the name wrong there, Bobcat. It's Moira. We got eyes up in Dechamp?*"

Zeke hit the button and went to respond as Ida came closer. "Swamprat here. I got eyes. Me and my dogs will be watching."

"*Hey there, Rat.*" Bobcat's voice came out tinny and thin through the radio. "*I'm hearing they think this Hurst guy might head your way if he's in the area. Stay sharp.*"

In the center of his workstation was a sink. Over it was a rifle. It was the first one he'd ever owned and while it wasn't the most accurate, the Remington 700 BDL Varmint was still his favorite. He'd spent many days out in the woods with that weapon, listening as his dad taught him all about how to hunt, how he'd once helped his own father hunt and trap for food.

Closing his hand over the Remington, the wood worn and smooth and familiar, he looked over at Ida.

She didn't say anything, just turned back to the table.

He gently turned down the radio until it receded to little more than white noise.

Zeke had been trained as a sharpshooter in the military.

It wouldn't much bother him if he had to raise his weapon now. Whatever had his dogs so worked up certainly wasn't because some poor soul had up and found themselves lost on the way to Grandma's house, that was certain.

"You won't go doing anything foolish, I hope," Ida said as he took down a harness from the series of hooks on the wall.

"You know me, Miss Ida."

"Again . . . you won't do anything foolish, I hope."

He gave her a smile as he slid out the door.

The dogs saw him and fell silent.

He called to Solo, and his best dog moved to the front, tail wagging, eyes locked on the harness. "It's time to go to work, boy."

Charles hefted Moira's slim body out of the car, grunting as he was forced to settle her over his shoulder.

One thing he hadn't prepared for all the way was the awkwardness of carrying her.

Logically, he knew that dead weight was just that. Dead weight. She might only weigh roughly one hundred twenty pounds, but that weight seemed magnified when she hung limp over his shoulder.

He didn't have time to spare either.

He suspected half the dose he'd given her had been wasted, and he couldn't risk giving her more. Not with her small frame and her tendency to react badly with medication anyway.

The single dose he'd given her earlier should have only put her under for an hour, but she'd been unconscious for nearly three. He'd needed her to sleep longer this time and had prepped a dose that he would have thought would suffice, but after how long she'd stayed asleep, he'd modified it slightly, squeezing half a milliliter out.

Then she'd gone and fucked things up good and proper, jamming that blanket into him as he'd gone to inject her, as if she'd known.

She slept now, but he didn't have the time he'd hoped for to prepare her.

They had to hurry.

Off to the northeast, he could hear dogs barking.

That stubborn old git who'd caused trouble early on.

Charles hated those miserable dogs. He wished they'd just turn on their master.

It had been nearly ten minutes since he'd started down a path he knew like the back of his hand. The barking had stopped maybe five minutes earlier and he breathed a sigh of relief when he caught sight of the small boat, powered by a quiet little trolling motor.

He dumped Moira into the boat and then slid in as well, sitting down. The motor purred to life. A cold breeze blew off the Mississippi but he had worn a coat, prepared for the chill. Moira shivered by his feet. He ignored it. She didn't need to be comfortable now, did she?

The low-lying branches bent over the river, forming a tunnel of sorts. This was one of the few places he actually enjoyed here. If he couldn't be at Edgeworth House, then this place was one of the few he wanted to be. Edgeworth

House . . . the house his father had been forced out of when he'd only been a boy, recently orphaned.

Of course, he'd take the place that *should* be his.

McKay's Treasure.

Here, people hailed that worthless sod Patrick McKay as a hero, but they didn't know what Charles knew. Patrick had been a vile, violent man. The men he'd taken onto that boat he piloted up and down the river had been former pirates, yet he had the nerve to act outraged when others looked to the river for a profit themselves.

He'd just wanted it all for himself.

As he cut through the water, Charles heard his father's voice, reading the stories from the journal to him. That journal and a few other trinkets, a locket that had belonged to Elizabeth . . . all that was left of the Whitehall family.

Do you think it's still there? Charles imagined he was asking his father the question again.

George would suck on his pipe and ponder the night sky. *Who is to say, boy? McKay was like any Scot—crazy and paranoid. Sly, though. Very sly. He went aground once, just before he would have been ambushed, they say. Old Whitehall wrote in his journal that people said the water would talk to him. Maybe it did, because no pirate alive ever got his hands on McKay. McKay, though, he got his hands on many a pirate and he stole the treasure from many a pirate. And Whitehall says he buried some of it in the very cove where the pirates tried to end him.*

Do you think it really happened?

There's no telling, boy. Then he'd smile at Charles, his teeth a bit crooked and yellow from the smoke. He looked rakish, Charles had always thought. Like a pirate himself.

Charles had spent a great deal of his life hunting down artifacts and treasures for others all for one simple purpose. The better he became at it, the more he would learn about the art of *finding* things.

Because there was an art to it.

Coming here all those years ago had been a strategic move and it had allowed him the time to begin his own search.

Moira might insist no such treasure existed, but she was wrong.

The town whispered of it.

Entire legends were based on it.

And every legend began somewhere . . . many even had a thread of truth.

Charles was willing to lay odds that this was one of them.

At his feet, Moira moaned.

He smiled down at her and stroked her hair.

"Soon," he murmured. "Soon."

Zeke had seen weirder things for certain.

However, he couldn't recall if there had ever been a time when he'd seen a man dressed like he might be a banker out on a business lunch sitting in a jon boat trolling down the lazy waters of the Mississippi. It was a chilly day and the idiot did have the presence of mind to put on a coat, but he didn't have on a hat or gloves and he definitely didn't look like the kind to be out fishing.

He also looked like he was talking.

While Zeke didn't see anybody else, he had a strange feeling the man wasn't just *talking* . . . he seemed to be listening too.

A crazy man on my river. Shaking his head in disgust, he almost turned away, but then he paused, watching as the man looked down at something in the bottom of the boat. Whatever it was, Zeke couldn't see it. But the man bent, touched it.

Was it an *it*?

Solo whimpered, his ears pricking up.

He was staring at the boat, too.

Zeke settled back behind a tree and gave the dog a low command. "Quiet, Solo. Quiet."

It was a simple command and the dog obeyed, going to the ground with his head resting on his paws, but he continued to watch the boat. Zeke knew his dog well enough to know one thing.

It wasn't the man that held his interest.

Solo had been trained as a rescue dog and he'd always shown an interest—a soft spot, almost—for people in distress and needing help. He was displaying some of those signs now.

Making a decision, he tugged out the sat phone he'd grabbed on his way out the door and punched in a number.

Nobody answered.

A quick search yielded the information he needed and he shot another look down the river. They were getting farther away. "Come, boy. Watch." He pointed at the boat, signifying that they were going to keep an eye on the boat. If he gave another command, *follow,* they'd be moving in much closer, and he didn't want to do that yet.

Solo crept along close to the ground while Zeke followed, ever vigilant, watching for any sign that the man might have heard them. He was so far down the river, it wasn't likely, and Zeke was worried they'd fall too far behind.

"I need to speak with Chief Marshall," he said when a woman's harried voice finally came on the line.

"I'm afraid he's unavailable."

"Make him available. I think I might have a line on the man he's got a BOLO out on." He hesitated before adding, "Tell him it's Zeke Sanders—and FYI, *he* owes *me* now."

It didn't take thirty seconds before his call was connected to Gideon's. There was some interference and he could tell that Gideon wasn't in the station, but that didn't matter. "I hear you're wanting to find yourself a man. He about your age, Marshall?"

Gideon wasn't one to mince words and he didn't waste time with chatter. "Yes. Where are you?"

"Out by my place. Along the river. Dark hair, looks pretty neat? Like a banker?"

"Well . . . yeah, I guess that suits him. Build, eye color?"

"Wasn't able to discern that much. He's in a jon boat, Gideon. Heading north up the Mississippi. I got eyes on him but I can't chat and keep watch, too."

"He got a woman with him?"

The tension in the chief's voice had Zeke biting back something ugly. "I can't say yes or no to that. I think he might have somebody with him. He was . . ."

"He was what, Zeke?" Gideon snapped.

"Talking to somebody. Down in the floorboard of the boat. At least it looked like he was."

Wait for the ideal moment. You might only get one chance.

Moira kept the words at the forefront of her brain as Charles climbed nimbly out of the boat.

She'd sort of been planning on taking *that* chance, because the man she'd married had been an absolute nightmare in nature. Or so he'd always seemed to be. They'd gone camping once—Charles' idea of camping. It involved luxury tents and catered meals. He'd decided then and there that he loathed the outdoors and never wanted to go anywhere that didn't come with air conditioning and hot tubs. He'd been uneasy under the wide-open skies and he'd fumbled when their guide had shown him how to pilot the pontoon out on the glittering blue waters of the lake.

That man had disappeared, replaced by somebody who

handled the jon boat capably, tying it off at the small dock as though he'd done it every day since he'd been a boy.

Through her lashes, she watched him, her hair providing additional coverage, but she suspected he was getting suspicious. He hadn't given her as much medicine and the lulling rhythm of the boat ride had made it hard for her to tell how long it had been since they'd gotten out of the car.

She didn't know how long she'd been unconscious, either.

Something nudged her shoulder.

She shrugged it away and grunted.

It came again and she swore, batting at it with her hand before lifting her head.

She wasn't going to be able sell this one as good and when she saw Charles standing on the dock, looking competent and comfortable, she wanted to scream. The idea to grab at his legs and just jerk them out from under him came over her, but she didn't think it would do any good.

"Get out." He eyed her expressionlessly.

"Kiss my ass." She shoved her tangled hair back and shivered, the cool air seeping through the hoodie she'd swiped from Brannon's.

Charles hunkered down on his heels, a placid smile on his face. "You can fight this all you want, love. But in the end, you will do what I say."

"Yeah?" She jutted her chin up. "Or what?"

He lifted his right hand.

A cold, hard knot settled in her throat at the sight of the matte-black gun he held.

Moira hated guns.

Brannon had a keen, crazy love for them, but she didn't like them. She didn't have some driving urge to see them regulated, though, and the fact that her brother enjoyed his indoor firing range with what she considered a boyish zeal really didn't bother her.

But Moira hated guns.

That was the beginning and end of her knowledge.

However, she had a feeling that the weapon Charles held aimed at her was more than enough to do whatever damage her ex-husband had in mind. "Wow," she said, keeping her tone steady through sheer will alone. "So this is the treatment I get for *not* taking your shares away from you when you cheated. Maybe I should have gone for the balls in the settlements."

"Your jokes aren't going to do you much good here. But if you want to pretend they will . . ." Charles shrugged. "Don't make me say it again, Moira. Get out of the boat."

Curling her lip, she shifted around until she had her balance and then went to brace her hands on the dock. She'd never been quite the river rat her sister had been, but she knew her way around a boat well enough. Her legs were stiff though and the drugs were making her head woozy. She groaned a bit as her vision tried to do a tilt-a-whirl on her. Instinctively, she lifted a hand and pressed the heel of it to her eye—or she tried to. The boat wobbled and she gasped, immediately scrabbling at the dock to steady herself.

Charles swore and bent down, grabbing at the back of her sweatshirt, hauling her upward.

Wait for the ideal moment. You might only get one chance.

One chance.

He was off-balance.

So was she, but she didn't have her head pointed down with her butt sticking up in the air.

Taking a deep breath, she lunged for his belt and pulled.

Charles howled and she flung herself into the floor of the boat as he tried to grab her. He missed, barely, toppling into the murky waters of the Mississippi. No sooner had she heard the splash than she was hauling herself up onto the dock. Her bare feet slapped against the boards of the dock as she hurled herself farther and farther away from Charles.

Get away.

That was her one goal.

Get away.

CHAPTER TWENTY-SIX

Zeke had hung up the phone with one final order for Gideon, *Bring her damn dog, you jackass.*

Frost was riding shotgun with him, ears pricked, eyes watchful.

He was muttering to himself and every so often, her head would swing his way, like she was listening to him. "You know, you could nod or wag your tail. Something to make me feel like I'm on the right track," he said.

Frost went back to staring out the window.

"Not much for false reassurances, I see." She was the perfect dog for Moira.

Images of what might be going on flashed through his mind, but he refused to give into them.

Four cars sped along behind him while in front of him, a state trooper from Louisiana was speeding with lights and sirens as they hurtled ever closer to the house where Kevin Towers had taken that fateful shot of scotch just a few days earlier.

Gideon heard from the sheriff who was in charge of handling Towers' case. Apparently, the computer geeks from the state had been able to give him good news—and bad news.

They'd traced the feed from the cameras that had been recording everything going on inside that house.

It came from a hotel.

It had been paid for a month in advance . . . under Kevin's name.

But the clerk said the man who came and went from the room wasn't Kevin. *Tall, hot. British.*

Gideon hadn't bothered to tell her that the tall *hot* British guy a likely a criminal, quite possibly a murderer and a kidnapper.

Charles Hurst.

The son of a bitch had been planning this, playing them all for years.

Now he had Moira—

His phone rang.

He didn't bother fucking with the Bluetooth. He grabbed it and hit the talk button when he saw Zeke's name pop up. "Go," he said shortly, falling back on long ago protocol.

"It's her."

Those two words from Zeke made a harsh sigh burst out of Gideon's lungs, a breath of air he didn't even know he'd been holding. "You see them?"

"Not her. Not now. But I did see her, I'm pretty sure. Short, skinny redhead, runs like a demon. I can see him though. She dunked him the river. He's wetter than a drowned fish and madder than hell. She took off. He's looking for her. Marshall, we've got a problem."

A moment later, Gideon dropped the phone. He blew out two slow breaths and told himself that he had to stay focused to help her.

He had to.

Then he reached for the radio.

"We need to put on a bit more speed."

* * *

"Damn." Zeke breathed out a sigh of admiration as the red-haired woman scrambled up the steep embankment. The admiration didn't last long, though.

He doubted she realized where she was. The asshole who had her—what was his name . . . Hurst, yeah—that Hurst guy had kept her down in the bottom of the boat and she wouldn't have been able to see shit. But she didn't have much of anywhere to run.

Moira McKay was trapped.

He'd taken her to an island, and it wasn't one of the bigger ones either.

Zeke knew that island.

There wasn't much about the miles around his property that he didn't know. Even the acres that belonged to Abe—the land that would soon be his—were familiar to him. Abe hadn't minded at all if Zeke used the Bittner property to train his dogs, and more than once Zeke had used the river and the islands.

That island there, though, he avoided.

If anybody called him superstitious, he would have laughed at him, but the truth was, just being on that island gave him a bad, bad feel. His skin crawled and the hair on the back of his neck stood on end even passing by it.

Bad things had happened on some of these islands in the country's earlier days and Zeke suspected that one had a bloody past. But that wasn't the problem.

It was small, it was treacherous, and there were only so many places to hide. *That* was the problem.

It had only been a few seconds since she'd toppled Hurst into the water. The surface rippled, then exploded as he came surging up like a Leviathan, arms clawing and tearing as if going after an attacker.

The one glimpse Zeke had of his profile was of a face locked in a sheer, utter rage.

Crouched in the tall grass, struggling to catch his breath,

he flicked a look up just in time to see Moira disappear into the dense greenery.

Hurst was struggling to pull himself up onto the dock.

Zeke breathed out a bit of a sigh.

Then, after stroking Solo's head and giving him the command to stay, he lifted his rifle and settled the Remington into place.

He couldn't exactly shoot the man, he knew.

But he could lay down some fire and let him know he wasn't alone out here with that woman.

Smiling a little, he took a few seconds to take in the wind as he focused on his target.

Mouth open, he squeezed on the trigger.

He was on his belly and crawling to a new spot before Hurst had even figured out what had happened.

Moira darted between several trees, searching for a path or anything that might lead *away* from Charles. She was certain she was heading east—she had her back to the river and the Louisiana side of the Mississippi, so she should be on . . .

Water glinted just ahead.

She stumbled to a halt just as she burst into the open, right before she would have taken a header over the steep bank that sloped almost ninety degrees down—right back into the slow-rolling waters of the Mississippi.

She stared briefly at the far banks of what had to be her home state. Freedom and safety had never looked so far away. She briefly entertained the idea of diving in and swimming, but the idea was brief. Very brief.

It wasn't precisely freezing out. The temperature in Mississippi, especially this far south, never really got *cold*, but it would only take a minute or two in the water for it to affect her, and she knew it. She was a good swimmer but not a great one, and while she was in decent physical condition, *decent* wasn't going to be good enough to get her across the Mississippi in water that was likely fifty degrees or so.

In the few seconds it took her to process this, several things happened.

There was a loud, echoing *crack*.

Somebody bellowed.

And she heard the familiar noise of an engine—a barge.

Her heart leapt in hope even as panic flooded her.

That crack.

A gun. Shit. Charles had a gun and she was standing there, right in the open.

She spun around and fled to the north, down a sloped, faint path that led deeper into the thick, enveloping growth of the island.

Dimly, she heard somebody shouting and her mind took in the words, but it wasn't until she stopped, back pressed to the trunk of a tree, that she realized what those words meant.

"Who the bloody fuck is out there?"

That was Charles.

What did he . . .

She sucked in a breath.

That hadn't been him firing.

Charles yelled again, and Moira focused on the sound of it. Although she knew that the river could distort or amplify noise, she thought he sounded farther away.

She eased herself along the path, keeping to the line of the river and moving north, opposite of the direction she thought Charles had taken.

Her goal was to circle around and draw nearer to the Louisiana side of the river again. She almost wished whoever had fired that shot would do it again, although that could be a dangerous wish. What if it was just some local

yahoo out having fun and being stupid? The world was full
of dangerous, stupid yahoos after all.

It could be an even-worse scenario, and her mind con-
jured up a dozen of them.

Another crack ripped the air just then and a scream
bubbled its way up out of her throat. She barely managed
to clap her hands over her mouth before it escaped.

Charles, however, apparently didn't see the need to be
quiet. His bellow of rage erupted, echoing in the air almost
as loudly as the gunshot had.

The echo of even that died and she lowered her hands,
easing to the edge of the path and placing her back to a
tree as she forced herself to blank her mind and think.

Have to think . . . You can do this, she told herself.
Breathe, just breathe.

Her heart rate slowed and her mind slowly cleared. She
wouldn't call herself calm, but at least she was able to
function somewhat past her terror.

As if it had been waiting, the anger that had been bub-
bling just below the surface surged up and took control,
banishing the shaking hands and the panic, burying it all
under a layer of icy calm.

Moira welcomed it.

Under that cold blanket of false calm, she was able to
listen as Charles' mostly disjointed rambling came to a
stop and he began to speak in a clear, furious tone.

"Who do you think you are, shooting at me? Do you
have any *bloody* idea how fucking *stupid* you are, you
idiot? I'll find you and take that gun from you, shove it up
your ass, and pull the damn trigger."

To Moira's somewhat surprised amusement, there was
actually a response this time. It came from the Louisiana
bank, a low, raspy voice that held a thick layer of scornful
disdain. "Let me share something with you, son. What I'm

shooting here isn't a *gun*. This here is a Remington 700, and I can put lead between your eyes from where I'm sitting without breaking a sweat. How about you get back in that jon boat of yours and leave the girl alone?"

Moira's heart leapt.

He knew.

Whoever that guy was . . . he knew she was there.

She lunged forward, determined to get to the bank. The sun beat down on her back, warming her, and she panted, putting on a burst of speed.

The low hiss was the only warning, and Moira instinctively froze, her eyes rolling to the right.

The reptilian gaze locked on her, dead and flat . . . and enormous.

It normally took Gideon two hours to make it from Treasure from to Zeke's place, maybe ten miles south of Lake Providence. Thanks to Trooper Bradley White from Louisiana, they made it in roughly ninety-five minutes. They probably could have made it a little faster if it wasn't for the rutted, crooked mess that served as the drive for the properties belonging to Abraham Bittner and Zeke.

Well, both pieces of land were Zeke's—or they would be soon enough.

The dirt road was the sort that would tear up anything short of a tank or a vehicle specifically meant for off-road driving unless the driver kept it to a slow, steady crawl.

The squad cards held up damn well as long as they watched their speed. Gideon might have been tempted to fuck caution—after all, he'd brought his truck and it could handle a rough drive, but White was in front and he was forced to keep his speed down.

Just ahead and off to the right, the road veered a bit. Zeke had told them to ignore the fork in the road and come straight to his place. He'd been on the old Bittner property when he called, but he'd made it clear that it would be faster to cut across his land.

It was another few minutes before they finally reached Zeke's place. His wife Ida was out there waiting. She had a harness in her hand and smiled when she saw Frost jump out of the truck at Gideon's command. Frost wagged her tail when she saw Ida, but the dog didn't run to her. "Good girl," Ida said approvingly before shifting her attention to Gideon. "I wasn't sure if you would have thought to grab her harness or not. I have one you can take."

She held it out and Gideon accepted, awkwardly trying to fumble it into place.

"Here," Ida said, moving to take over after thirty or forty seconds passed. "If you don't mind?"

"Not at all." Gideon called to the men as Ida gave Frost the command to sit.

A few of the men gave the big white shepherd a side-long look but most of them were focused on Gideon and the trooper. White folded his arms over his chest, muscles bulging under the short sleeves, his dark eyes flinty. Bradley White was a big man, nearly six feet five with a broad chest, wide shoulders, and a voice like a booming cannon. He'd gone to college on a full scholarship, playing football. Everybody had assumed he'd tried to go pro. He'd already been planning on a career in law enforcement though and as soon as he'd graduated, he'd returned to Louisiana and his home parish, applying for a job with the state police.

He and Gideon had met during an inter-agency investigation when Gideon had still been working in Memphis.

He was a good cop, and right then he wasn't overly happy.

But he was a friend and he knew Gideon—Gideon's gut was screaming and he knew it wasn't just because it was

Moira. Nor was it because he hated Charles Hurst with a passion.

"You're sure she's out there," White said, his dark face set in a hard mask.

"I had eyes on her, Brad."

White narrowed his eyes and looked around, blowing out a hard breath. "Okay. My sergeant's been talking to me and he says I'm to stay with you. We go back a ways, Marshall. You're a good cop. Don't do something stupid and fuck things up . . . for either of us."

Eyes on the woman stroking the dog, White cocked his head. After a moment, he glanced at Gideon. "This Sander's place?"

"Yes."

White gave a thoughtful nod. "He the man who had eyes on your vic?"

My vic . . . Gideon's gut rolled. He hadn't let himself think of Moira that way, not even once, and he wouldn't do it now either. She was his heart. His world. His everything. But he nodded tersely. "He had a radio on. Somebody heard the BOLO and his dogs were raising a ruckus about something. He headed out for a walk, looking around."

"Okay, then. We'll do the same."

Most of the law enforcement around here knew of Zeke. He did a lot of work with cops. Zeke and Ida had joined in on volunteer searches with Solo and Chewy more than once. They weren't search-and-rescue dogs, but they were good at it nonetheless.

Zeke was also a hardass.

Sometimes, hardasses got into trouble.

Ida approached them and Gideon accepted the lead. "If you tell her to find Zeke, she will. Remember how he'd play hide and seek?"

At those words, Frost's body tensed.

Gideon glanced down at her, watched as her tail thumped the ground hard and fast. Just once, but everything about her changed. Her eyes were brighter, her ears perked.

He nodded.

Ida was smiling a little.

"Okay, then. I'll get out of the way."

She turned and started back toward the house.

The dog's excitement seemed to vibrate up the lead and transfer to him as he turned to speak with his men. "Okay, people. Listen up."

By the time he was done, Frost was all but quivering, her entire body practically straining, although she hadn't moved a muscle.

He knelt down in front of her.

"You want to play?" he asked softly, rubbing her behind the ears.

Frost whined low in her throat and started to wag her tail.

"Yeah, I bet you do." It took a lot of control to keep his voice easy, but he did. This was all a game to her and he had to make sure he didn't communicate any of the worry or fear he had. Slowly, he unclipped her lead. "Quiet, though. Frost. Understand? Quiet."

She stopped whining.

"Find Zeke!"

She lunged and he took off after her.

The one saving grace was that white coat of hers. She stood out like a ghost in the dull browns that had taken over as winter settled in. He took off after her, running at a quick clip.

Most of the others fell behind pretty fast.

But his officer Beau Shaw, Deputy Maris Cordell, and . . . unsurprisingly, Trooper Bradley White all kept pace with him.

It was Maris who spotted the dog after they first lost sight of her.

Frost came running back to them the second, wagging her tail in delight at the fun of her game.

Beau saw her the next time.

The next—and final—time, all of them saw her, because she was rolling around in delight at the feet of her former master and he was scratching her belly. She still wasn't making any noise and when Zeke looked up at them, he pressed a finger to his lips and then lowered his hand to the ground.

Instinctively, Gideon dropped.

After a moment, so did the others although they weren't quite as good at the belly crawl. Gideon figured you could take the soldier out of the army, but he's still going to be a soldier.

They were quiet, though. Gideon would give them that. But they weren't going to fool anybody who was combat trained. Good thing Charles wasn't combat trained.

He might possibly be crazy or he could just be an evil son of a bitch. Gideon didn't know or care. All he cared about was getting Moira before she was hurt.

Please. Please, God. Don't let him hurt her.

Crawling through the dirt wasn't as easy now as it had been back when he'd been in the army, but he didn't think it took that long. It just felt like it. From a logical standpoint, he understood that it did not—*could* not—take hours to crawl those few yards to where Zeke lay hidden in the tall grass at the river's edge.

When he reached Zeke, the other man gave him a nod, never once taking his eyes from the island. Gideon studied it. It was a decent-sized one, situated about halfway between the Mississippi and Louisiana sides of the river.

It was an ugly spot, too.

Most of the islands on the river were beautiful, overrun

with virgin trees, looking like they hadn't ever seen the touch of man. This one, though, looked like a pocket straight out of hell.

Some of the tree roots that spilled out over the edge made him think of the claws of giant monsters, lying in wait to grab some unsuspecting passerby heading downstream.

Something shifted in the grass. Gideon's lip curled.

Charles' black hair was plastered to his skull. "Looks like he took a dip in the river," Gideon muttered.

"Yep." He flicked a look back at the others. "Ya'll are going to want to be quiet and stay low. He's got himself a weapon. Can't shoot worth shit, but if he's aiming at you, it's possible he'll shoot the person next to you on accident."

Gideon huffed out a disgusted sigh. "Any idea what he's got?"

"A semiautomatic, a forty-four, I think." He paused, then added, "He's inching his way back into the cover. I'm trying to keep him from doing that, but it's just me."

"It's not just you now." He nodded at the others, jerking his head to indicate he needed them closer. "You got any suggestions on how to get over there without him noticing?"

"I got a friend upriver. He's about a half mile down with his boat." A smirk came and went. "I don't think your boy will expect anybody to hop on that thing willingly, but we'll need to get our asses out of here to meet up with him before he heads this way. Think we can do that without him seeing us?"

Gideon almost laughed at the idea, but then he had to stop and think it through. Charles Hurst had deceived them all. A couple months ago, the idea of that uptight prick dragging Moira out in a jon boat onto a little island in the middle of the Mississippi would have been laughable.

Not so much now.

But he went with his gut.

"It's not likely," he said, shaking his head. The man had spent a long time building up this fake life he'd sold to Moira—to the whole town and they'd all bought it.

"Hold up," Zeke said when Gideon would have said something else. The old soldier lifted his rifle, steadied. "Idiot thinks he's going to slip by me. Who does he think he is? Oughta just put one in his balls and end this shit."

"Sorry, Judge. My finger slipped," Gideon said soberly.

Mouth parted, Zeke breathed slow and steady and then squeezed.

A blast shuddered through the air, followed by a torrent of curses.

"Think we should let him know we're here?" Beau said softly.

"Not us." Gideon shook his head. If Charles realized he was here, he would know his time was up. Slanting a look at White, he arched a brow. The big black man nodded and cupped his hands around his mouth.

"Mr. Hurst. This is Trooper Bradley White with the Louisiana State Police. I have reason to believe you have a woman with you who might not be there willingly. I need to speak to her."

The response wasn't probably the best one—at least not for Charles.

He fired and Gideon had a quick glimpse of the firearm—black as death and it looked too big in his hand. Desert Eagle. Dumb-ass.

White pressed his back to the tree, calmly pulling his radio from his collar and speaking into it. "We've got a situation," he said to his sergeant.

Gideon met Zeke's eyes and nodded. "Frost," Gideon said in a quiet voice. But Zeke shook his head. *Not yet,* he mouthed.

Gideon blew out a breath and then pointed to the ground. "Stay."

Frost's ears drooped a bit, but she planted her butt in the dirt and stayed. Her eyes wandered to the island, though. He wondered if she could smell Moira.

As they were crawling off into the grass, White whispered his name.

"Don't do anything stupid, Marshall,' the trooper said.

Gideon gave a short nod.

Of course, his interpretation of stupid and White's interpretation might be two very, very different things.

"Are you there . . . what was it, Trooper White?" Charles called out, his voice mocking. "Did you catch my answer there?"

"Oh, I caught it all right. Loud and clear. Sir, I'm going to ask you to put your weapon down and lift your hands."

Gideon didn't look back.

As he crawled away, he heard another round of fire.

It was followed by an answering roar—this time from their side of the river.

Stay safe, Mac. I'm coming.

CHAPTER TWENTY-SEVEN

Staring into the dull eyes of the alligator, Moira felt her heart stutter to a stop. It wasn't a big one, as far as gators went. If she had to guess, it was maybe ten feet. To Moira, though, that was massive.

It was certainly large enough to kill her in a blink.

Her breath squeezed out of her in a rush and she gingerly side-stepped away, scanning the area as best as she could with her peripheral vision while trying to keep an eye on the alligator.

Sometimes, not always, but sometimes, these things *did* come in groups.

Water lapped against the banks, but other than that Moira couldn't hear anything save for the sound of her own ragged breathing.

The alligator continued to stare at her with flat, alien eyes.

It was the stare of a predator, the kind that could and would kill if it decided you were a threat.

Right now, Moira suspected she was being sized up.

It might be winter, but that didn't mean that alligators weren't active. Most people who lived in alligator country knew how things worked. The big creatures did not hibernate. They went torpid and as long as their environment stayed cool, they pretty much slept.

But have a day where the sun was shining down and the microclimate around a gator's chosen den warmed enough to bring the alligator out of its torpid state, and the big creatures started stirring.

Instinctively, Mora moved into the shadows thrown by the trees towering over much of the island.

The alligator hissed again at her movements, and she jumped.

The gator didn't like that.

Too bad. Moira didn't like the gator. In fact, she didn't like anything about this place.

There was another gunshot and she swallowed a gasp, easing farther back into the cooler, dark shadows of the trees. Something scuttled around near the big reptile, and Moira's belly roiled, fear becoming an acrid taste in the back her throat as she saw what she'd missed earlier.

There were babies.

None of them were longer than a couple of feet, but now this wasn't just a gator. She was a mama gator, and Moira had inadvertently stumbled too close to the place this mother had claimed as her own for her and her young.

Mama alligators were fierce creatures. *Okay . . . okay . . .* She backed away another step, wishing she could tell the protective mama that she wasn't there to hurt her babies.

But the alligator wouldn't care.

It was that whole *lizard* brain thing, she supposed.

She eased deeper into the trees, shivering as she lost the warmth of the sun, but thankful, because the colder *she* was, the colder mama gator would be and the harder it would be for her to try to eat her.

Stay in the trees, she told herself. *Keep moving.*

She wasn't entirely sure which one would be the worst to deal with.

As she started to slip in what she hoped was a north-western direction, she heard something.

A boat.

Relief began to flood her but there was no time to enjoy it.

There was another crack from a weapon, but this one didn't come from the Louisiana side or the Mississippi side.

It came from Charles and he laughingly called out, "See, boys? You're not the only one who knows his toys."

Charles.

He was also a lot closer than he had been not even five minutes ago.

Once they reached the spot Zeke had wanted, he gave a harsh whistle, one that Gideon wasn't prepared for.

Nor was he prepared for the furry white bullet that all but bolted out of the grass a few short moments later. Frost butted him in the leg and he rubbed her head.

"Good girl," he said when he saw her tail wagging, keeping his voice low.

"That's how we race," Zeke said, his eyes on the water. They'd moved maybe a quarter of a mile down the river. He could still see the island but the natural curves and twists of the river kept him from seeing the bank where Charles had been.

A low grumbling noise came to his ears and Gideon turned his head, blinking hard and fast as a wide, flat-bottomed boat came into view.

Zeke waved an arm once before moving back into the cover provided by Mother Nature.

"Is that . . ." Gideon stopped, blowing out a breath. Small mountains placed in precise areas around the pontoon had him rubbing at the back of his neck. It wasn't summer so he couldn't catch any scent on the air, but if it had been in the eighties or nineties, he suspected he might have gotten a lungful of something nasty.

"A garbage boat." He looked over at Zeke. The long, flat boat came to a gentle stop a few feet from the outcropping of rocks, and Zeke was the first one to ease out, his Remington 700 held up as he studied the island.

Although he couldn't see him, Gideon heard the smile in Zeke's voice. "We needed something quick and unobtrusive, Marshall. Marvin here travels up and down this stretch of river two or three times a week, rain or shine. It's his own personal contribution to mankind, cleaning up our beautiful river here. Nobody thinks twice of seeing him around these parts."

Gideon blew out a careful, controlled breath and then nodded.

"All right." But he couldn't keep from shaking his head a little as he eased himself out onto the outcropping of rocks. He was going to save Moira by hitching a ride on what look like a do-it-yourself garbage boat.

When the boat's owner caught sight of his face, a grin split his wizened face. His skin was a dark, leathery brown, his hair like thinning snow on his scalp. He cackled a little when he held out a hand to steady Gideon as he came aboard.

"Look at yourself, cop. Think you never did see a boat as pretty as mine afore," the man said.

"I'm sure I haven't," Gideon said wryly. He nodded. "Pretty or not, I appreciate the help, sir."

He paused, uncertain how to proceed. He wasn't about to put a civilian in danger. "We need to be on that island, but the man is armed. It would be best if you stayed behind."

"No, sir. It wouldn't." Marvin nodded easily and gestured to the piles of trash. "You might find it easier to hide back over there. Nobody will think twice if they see me. But cop, you stand out."

Zeke knelt at the side of the boat, speaking softly to Frost. Her ears flicked, but her tail wagging was a little less pronounced now and she looked more reserved. She jumped onto the boat, her tail clattering on the slick surface, and she slipped a little. Zeke steadied her with a hand on her harness.

"That's a good girl, Frost," he said. "Good girl."

She poked him with her nose and then moved to Gideon. Zeke studied her and then shook his head. "I'll be damned. I think I've been replaced."

Frost sat at alert, staring down the river.

Gideon didn't like the intent expression that had settled over her face. "Let's get moving." He shot one last look at Marvin. "Sir, are you sure you won't stay behind? I can strip out of my uniform shirt, put on Zeke's ball cap. It's not perfect, but it's better than nothing."

"And you'll be going over there without your vest on. I don't think so." Marvin shook his head. "I'm just doing my job, cop. Cleaning up the river. I ain't even getting off my boat."

He grinned as he said it.

Gideon blew out a harsh breath between his teeth before nodding.

A few moments later, the pontoon moved away with a slow, easy purr as Gideon shot Zeke a narrow look. "You really think we'll get anywhere near that island without being noticed? On this?"

"Hell, yeah. Seems to me that Hurst fellow knew exactly where he was going. That means he's been out here before. So he's seen Marvin. Chances are, Marvin's just invisible to him."

Gideon set his jaw and fisted a hand in Frost's thick fur. *Please . . . please . . .*

Infuriated and freezing, Charles followed one of the footpaths, looking for some sign of Moira.

It was hard to tell if anybody had been on it recently and he could have kicked his own bloody arse for not having a pair of shoes for her. Shoes left more-obvious tracks. He could look back and see where he'd walked just now easily enough.

Bare feet, though . . . not quite so easy.

A noise caught his ears and he swore, rushing east and following the trail up the hill until it crested. It was that crazy old garbage collector. The sight of him made Charles curl his lip, but he couldn't just ignore the old goat this time. He had to make sure Moira wasn't anywhere along the Louisiana side of the island. Easing his way down, he kept his gaze on the old black man, watching as he puttered around on the boat.

When he shouted out, Charles jerked as if he'd been jabbed with a hot poker.

"Hey up there!"

Charles looked around.

It took a moment to realize the miserable old duffer was talking to him. After a moment, he lifted a hand in greeting then retreated deeper in to the shadows. There was a quicker way across the middle of the island. He trotted back up the incline and cut through the woods until he found the path. The overgrowth was heavier for much of the way, but once he reached the top, it was rather clear and he could see down. He glanced over, trying to see the boat, but the trees along the northern edge blocked his line of sight.

Swearing, he continued along the path.

Another shot rang out.

The man on the boat yelped, his high-pitched scream almost exactly like a woman's. "What the sweet hell is that . . . did you hear that?"

Charles ignored him as he crouched on the ground. Would have been nice if a stray bullet had caught the man, saved him the trouble of worrying about him. Although . . . frowning, he shot a look toward the Louisiana banks. Hadn't they seen the garbage boat? Why were they still firing?

The old man was still swearing and raising hell—enough noise to draw Moira to him, too.

He didn't have time to worry about the old goat. "Barmy old codger." He reached inside his wet coat and pulled out the Desert Eagle he'd bought. He'd already ejected the cartridge and put in another. Water had gushed out and he'd taken a practice shot across the river to make sure it would still fire.

While it wasn't as accurate a shot as he'd like, mostly all he needed to do was keep the buffoons across the river off his arse—and then maybe use the weapon on one or two others, after he'd taken care of things with Moira.

She was stubborn, his lovely ex-wife.

But she was also intelligent.

She wouldn't chose death over some misguided loyalty to a dead man and it wasn't like she didn't have enough money without Paddy McKay's fucking treasure. She wouldn't choose death over protecting *that*.

Movement off to the side caught his attention and he looked to the south, following the sound.

A flash of something tan and dull caught his eye.

It was over almost as quick as it had appeared, but in that space there everything else was shades of green or the dead of winter brown . . . and still.

Moira had been wearing a tan hoodie from her brother's idiotic pub and he'd seen that bit of tan inching away before it disappeared behind a tree.

With a smile curling his lips, he rose and started toward the stand of trees.

There was another shot, this one tearing into the dirt not even ten feet from him.

"You need to get on that island."

Gideon bit back the sarcastic response that practically leapt to his lips.

Really?

Instead, he said calmly to White, "We're doing that."

"Cordell is laying down fire, Marshall, but your vic is less than twenty feet from the perp. Again, you need to get on that island. Both were last seen on the southern side."

"Fuck." Gideon dragged a hand down his face while the tension in his gut twisted higher and higher.

Frost sat at the edge of the boat, growling low in her throat.

"Coming up on the dock, boys. Get ready to disembark." There was little humor in Marvin's voice now.

"Can you get us closer to the southern side?" Gideon demanded.

"No can do." The old man turned his head. "And you better be careful—and fast. There's a mama gator down near that end. This time of day, her little spot gets some sun, too."

Gideon felt his belly clench as he lifted his head and focused on the southern spot.

"Son of a *bitch*." He narrowed his eyes on the old man. "Are you positive?"

"Yep. She got pissed at me just a few months ago. You can see the parting gift she gave me on the back of the boat if you wanna take a look-see." Marvin's face was grim.

"Aw, hell," he whispered.

"No doubt." Marvin nodded as another shot shattered the silence of the air. It came from high and to the south, maybe twenty yards down. Marvin gave an ear-piercing scream, but his face was neutral.

The man was one hell of an actor.

"If he's where he can see me, I can't give you any cover," Marvin said, shaking his head. "But I don't think you can wait."

The radio chirped and White's voice crackled out. "There's a hill on the island. He's running south along it. I think he's seen your vic again, but we lost sight of her. Your best chance. Move."

They moved. Frost leapt after them, a low growl rumbling in her throat as she burst ahead of them.

Her lungs burned as she burst between a couple of trees standing close together. She'd seen them some yards back, thought there might be some place to hide.

But the moment she shoved past their odd growth, she'd realized her mistake.

Coming to a halt, she stood, oddly frozen.

She was in the middle of what looked like a . . . well, a circle.

Only it had been crafted by nature. By God. No man's hand had done this. The trees rose all around her, creating a living barrier to everything outside this strange little area, their branches stretching so far overhead that little light penetrated.

Little, yes. But not none.

Still, nothing grew in that circle. No grass. No leaves. No young saplings with thin branches straining overhead to seek the sun.

Nothing.

Something cracked behind her and she whirled.

Her heart leapt into her throat and she wanted to scream when she saw Charles emerge from the trees. "Ah . . . I should have known you would find it without me. After all, I had no trouble discovering it for myself. I think it calls to us, Moira."

Idiot. Fool. She barely heard his words, too busy yelling at herself for not running.

Charles paced a little closer, but instead coming to her, he began to circle around her.

"Do you know where we are?" Charles came to a stop in front of her, less than five feet away.

In his right hand, he held the gun, but it was lowered to his side, the muzzle pointing straight to the earth.

Moira dared to let herself breathe a little easier at the sight.

"My version of hell on earth?" she suggested. "It wasn't so bad being trapped on an island with you when the island was Fiji, but I think this is a little much."

He clicked his tongue. "You want to be nice to me right now, Moira." Waving his hand around, he said, "After all, you *are* trapped on an island with me and I have this."

Now he lifted the gun, pointing it at her.

The sight of the massive handgun would have been laughable if he hadn't had it pointed directly at her face. Just went to show that she knew more than she thought she did about weapons—she knew that gun. It was a Desert Eagle and thanks to Brannon's love for weapons, she knew a thing or two about it. It was one of the most sought after weapons *and* plenty of people who got one bought it without knowing much about it. It was too big for Charles' one-handed grip and she knew it would kick when he fired.

Yes, it might have been laughable, except for how close he was. Whether he could fire at a target twenty yards away didn't matter when she was just a few *feet* away.

Still, she kept her voice relatively calmly as she said,

"The next time you want a weapon, have Brannon take you out shopping. That thing won't kill what you point it at—it will *pulverize* it. There won't be enough to put into a body bag at this range. So if you're trying to terrify me into silence"—she let fear bleed into her voice—"go ahead, keep swinging it. But if you actually have some bragging or questions that you want to address, you might want to get that done first."

To her surprise, Charles cocked his head to the side and then nodded. He lowered the gun but he didn't put it away.

"You didn't answer me, love." He waggled his left finger in her face. "Do you know where we are?"

"I did. It's my version of hell. A small island . . . alone. With you."

A tic pulsed in his cheek and his eyes flashed. Moira didn't let herself jump when he took a step toward her. She knew Charles. Maybe she didn't know him as well as she thought, because clearly she hadn't seen the crazy in him, but she knew him well enough to understand what was going on. He might try to kill her—and while that thought was enough to loosen her bowels—he wasn't going to do it yet.

He wanted to brag about something. One of the things she'd come to hate about him was how he loved to lord his intelligence over others. And he had that glint in his eye again.

"No, my darling," he said, keeping his voice soft. "This is Paddy's Point, Moira."

She stared at him.

"What . . . don't you know about Paddy's Point?"

When she didn't respond, Charles took another step toward her, lifting his weapon hand and using the muzzle of the mammoth handgun to nudge her tangled hair back. "It was here where he waited, along with George Whitehall, Jonathan Steele, and some of his own men.

The pirates had to go through a gauntlet and they didn't even know. Half of the men were on this side, half on the riverbank, just a little farther south so they wouldn't get hit by friendly fire. Your sainted ancestor was quite the strategist. They slaughtered the pirates, boarded the ships, and made off with gold and jewels and goods."

"You don't know this is the place," Moira said, withdrawing from the cold, matte surface of the gun he stroked down her cheek.

"But I do. See, Paddy kept journals, didn't he? So did George."

His eyes were all but blind now, blind and fervent.

"George."

"Yes." He lowered his head, whispered softly. "He kept journals . . . he drew pictures. The geography of the river hasn't changed *that* much, my love."

"You . . ." The feel of his lips against her ear made her want to retch, but she didn't want to jerk or tense away when he had the gun so close to her. No, she was almost positive he wouldn't kill her yet, but she wasn't going to be stupid and push her luck. "Do you have journals that belong to Whitehall? How did you get your hands on those?"

"Hmmm . . ." He turned his face into her hair.

She tried not to shudder.

He pulled back and smiled down at her. "Pet . . . don't play dumb. I was watching the feed, you know. I'm certain by now that the bobbies, inept as they are, have found them and let your precious Gideon know about them. You all were closing in, I had to do something."

He shoved a hand into her hair and fisted it, jerking her head back so hard, it brought tears to her eyes.

Moira bit her lip to keep from crying out, glaring up at him.

"Tell me, Moira . . . how much do you know?"

Trying to breathe past the pain in her scalp, she smiled up at him. "Well, a bit of this. A bit . . . of that. Starting with the fact that you're a crazy-ass bastard. Should I go on?"

He let go so suddenly, she swayed caught off-balance.

A moment later, she was on the ground breathless while Charles stood over her. He calmly holstered his gun before squatting down in front of her. "Moira, my dear. We really do need to talk. Acting like that is not going to help your situation at all."

CHAPTER TWENTY-EIGHT

"Bad angle," Zeke breathed out, his words barely a whisper. "Can't get past him at all. Got to move . . . or make him move."

Gideon expelled his breath and rose.

Zeke grabbed his arm. "Boy . . ."

"You're the one who said we gotta make him move."

He emerged from the trees. It wasn't until he'd done it that he realized his mistake. Frost was right at his knee. He hadn't told her to stay. She was whining low in her throat now and when Charles whirled around, hefting Moira up with an arm around her waist, those whines turned into outright growls.

They were deep, low in her chest, and tension rolled off the dog in waves.

Gideon could only see one eye peering at him over Moira's shoulder. Charles had both arms wrapped around her struggling torso now, making her a very effective body shield.

Frost slunk low to the ground, ears flattening to her skull.

Her tail wasn't wagging now.

This was no longer a game.

She saw Moira and the fear on her face, the terror . . .

Gideon stared at her.

She stared back.

For a long moment, neither of them spoke.

Charles was the one who shattered the silence.

"I should have known you'd hunt us down. It's like she's a bitch in heat and you can't stay away. Even after I spent three years shagging her, you still can't stay away."

Rage was a hot, greedy monster in Gideon and all he wanted to do was grab, rip, rend, tear.

But Gideon smiled. "Hey, maybe if you'd been any good at it, she wouldn't have wanted me."

Charles just laughed. "I'm not going to trade insults with you, you stupid Yank. You're not as thick as you might let on so don't bother with me. I know you, probably better than you know me."

"Is that a fact?" Gideon nodded slowly. "Okay. Tell me something, since we're being honest here. When you changed your name a few years back, was it because you were just keeping your cards close to your chest or because you were ashamed of being a Whitehall?"

The single eye Gideon could see narrowed, and the skin around it went a dull, ugly red. He went to straighten, but abruptly, he froze. "Good one . . . like I said, you're not so thick. But I'm not about to stand up and make myself a target for whatever fool cop you have hiding in the trees over there. How did you get onto my island, Marshall? Was . . . wait. The old man. You had him bring you. Didn't you?"

"You're not so thick yourself, Georgie." Gideon smiled at Moira, keeping it smooth and calm. "He was named after his dad, you know. Charles George Whitehall Hurst. Changed it when he was twenty. I guess you could say he's been planning this little get-together for a while."

"All my life." Charles' voice was silky and smooth. He slid one hand up Moira's throat and started to squeeze. "What did you think when you saw the bruises on her, Marshall? Were you angry? Did you want to kill? Do you want to kill now?"

Her breath released out of her in a burst while Gideon fought now to lunge for him.

Next to him Frost was quivering and snarling.

He gripped her harness but she was started to tug and jerk.

"Better shut that soddin' dog up or I will."

"Might be hard," Moira said, her voice rough. "Your hands are full."

"Be . . ."

A shot rang out.

Blood spurted and Charles howled.

Moira screamed.

Gideon swore.

Charles stumbled back a few feet, but didn't let her go. He'd straightened only a brief second, too brief to really make a good shot. What was Zeke . . .

Make him move or I gotta move . . .

He lowered his eyes to Charles' empty hands.

He had a weapon, yeah. But right now, he wasn't carrying it. One reason why a cop should never work a case involving somebody he loved. They got stupid.

Gideon let go of the dog.

Frost darted forward and sank her teeth into Charles' wrist.

His bellow echoed throughout the noontime sky and he let go of Moira, unable to hold on with the huge shepherd clamping down on him. He tried to shake her off, but it wasn't happening.

Gideon saw him going for his weapon, the action slow

and awkward because Frost had gone after his right hand. "Don't go for that gun, Charles, I'll shoot you right here, so help me God."

He heard movement behind him, but he didn't dare look.

"I'll keep him covered if you want to get her off so you can cuff the son of a bitch."

Gideon took a step forward, uncertain about how to do that. Oh, he'd seen handlers pull their dogs off people before, but he wasn't a handler and this dog wasn't K-9 trained. She was trained to protect and that was what she'd done.

He hesitated and that fraction of a second cost him.

Charles swung out with his left fist, brutal, hard and fast, punching Frost in the throat.

She made pained noise but didn't let go.

Not the first time.

But the second time . . .

"Stop!" Zeke bellowed.

Charles was like a man possessed though and he smashed his fist into the dog's skull. Frost went limp. Moira screamed like a demented banshee and lunged between Gideon, Zeke—and their weapons—to get her dog.

She came nose to muzzle with the gun Charles had pulled from an ankle holster.

"Not so thick indeed, Marshall, eh?" He gestured to Moira. "Up you go, pet. We're going for a walk. After all, I'm not done with you. We've talking yet to do. I'm here for a reason, you see. You're going to help me find what was taken from Whitehall."

She stayed by the dog.

"I'd rather you just shoot me," she said flatly. "I can't help you find something that doesn't exist."

"Then I'll shoot him." Charles knew her well enough to know she wasn't going to bluff—after all, he couldn't force her to do anything if he followed through with his threat, and she was too smart not to think about the fact that if he shot her, Gideon and the old man with the rifle would take him down in the next blink.

Charles' mouth twisted in a smug smile and she knew he'd already thought of all that through as well.

He had the gun aimed at Gideon's head.

Not at his chest, protected by his vest, but at his head.

Moira slid a look at Gideon. Slowly, she stood.

"Don't even think about it," Gideon growled.

Her mind spun at a million miles an hour. "I can't let him shoot you, Gideon. You know that." She reached up to touch his cheek. Behind her, Charles got to his feet. There was a grunt of pain and she saw the older man's eyes narrow.

"Point it elsewhere, you old git, or I'll shoot her in the back, here and now."

"Knew you for a coward the second I saw you." The old man spat on the ground.

"Truly, my feelings are shattered. Moira."

"Don't," Gideon said again, grabbing for her.

She backed away. "Gideon, I'd much rather see him gator bait . . ." She slid her eyes to the side, wondering if he'd understand. "But you know I can't let him hurt you."

Gideon's eyes flickered.

Did he know?

"Damn it, Mac!"

She backed away another step and turned, walking swiftly to the south.

"Ah, she's in a hurry, my darling wife."

"*Ex*-wife," Gideon snarled.

"Lower that weapon, Chief. See? I'm turning around. You want to shoot a man in the back?"

* * *

Gideon swore as Charles did just that and then sprinted across the small clearing just as Moira disappeared behind a tree.

He heard her startled cry, followed by a furious yell.

Snarling a low command into his radio, he met Zeke's eyes.

"Think she knows about that gator Marvin mentioned?" Zeke said, his voice low.

"I don't know." Gideon nodded at the dog. "Take care of her."

"Marshall . . . you know why we have dogs . . ."

"I know Moira will be heartbroken if something happens to her dog. She's a pet, not property. That's what Moira will think."

"They are my family," Zeke muttered. "But—"

"No buts. Take care of the dog. Hurst isn't going to shoot Moira yet. He wants something from her first."

And he wanted it enough to die for it.

He slid through the trees, falling back on the stealth tactics he'd learned so long ago, using the shadows of the trees and the natural camouflage of rocks and fallen limbs as he made his way down the hill, not moving in a straight path. He'd silenced his radio, not wanting to risk any noise distracting him—or alerting Hurst.

He could see them now, Charles' tall frame and Moira's disheveled red hair.

She stumbled once.

When she braced a hand on a tree, Hurst smacked on the back of her head with his hand—the weapon hand since his other one was all but useless, dripping blood and hanging limp at his side.

Gideon began to cut through the trees, moving at a diagonal line, placing each foot deliberately and rolling it down heel to toe, his department-issued weapon held in a loose two-handed grip as he kept his eyes on the people he could only see intermittently. Charles kept shooting looks up the hill. *Smart boy . . . you know I'm coming after you,* Gideon thought.

But Charles didn't realize how precarious a position he'd placed himself in, and it had nothing to do with a gator that Gideon wasn't entirely sure was down there.

Moira was a Mississippi girl, born and bred, and she knew all about living in gator country. Charles . . . well, he might have lived in Treasure for a few years, but it wasn't like they often had them coming up out of the bayous. It happened, but it wasn't a regular occurrence and they sure as hell weren't seen around winter.

While he was almost positive Charles didn't know that Moira might be leading him right in the jaws of a potentially pissed-off mama gator, he wasn't going to risk that he and Zeke were inferring more into her comment than what was there.

And that was *Moira*.

He wasn't going to let *her* near a fucking gator either.

Especially a mama with young.

Charles, though . . . well. Moira had mentioned him being gator bait.

Breathing slow and steady, Gideon continued his deliberate trek through the heavy growth, never once taking his eyes from Moira and Charles.

Each time Charles stumbled, Gideon weighed his options.

Each time, the son of a bitch steadied himself before Gideon had the chance to decide if he could safely get in a shot.

Keep her safe. This time, he wasn't praying. He was demanding. He knew it didn't work that way, but he didn't care.

* * *

Moira's head bobbed and swayed and the red seemed to blur in and out of focus, but Charles kept his eyes focused on the one that seemed most . . . well, real.

Every once in a while, there would be three of her and wasn't that a pisser.

One Moira McKay was quite enough, thank you.

The shock had long since faded and Charles thought briefly of making her stop and do something to tie off his arm. He was losing blood and quite a bit of it, but it was no longer pulsing from him in a steady flow, so there was no arterial damage. He remembered that much from university, back before the stupid fucks had decided he wasn't quite up to snuff.

Not that he'd wanted to be a bloody doctor anyway, but it would have been useful. Had proven useful anyway in the long run, hadn't it?

He could make it to the jon boat and once he did, he'd figure out what to do with his arm.

Bugger, but it hurt.

That dog.

He should have killed it when he had the chance.

Moira stumbled ahead of him and he snarled. "Fuck me, Moira. You're all cack-handed. Can't you stay off your bloody arse?"

She turned her head as she rose to her feet, giving him a chilly smile.

Perhaps that smile should have warned him.

But he'd seen that icy smile before.

It was the one she wore when she was brassed off and he hadn't expected anything less from her. He truly *hoped* she'd be angry. Because it would be that much more enjoyable to crush her to nothing.

She caught a tree when her foot slid on something and she gasped.

Swearing, he shouldered past her. "Stop your bloody whinging."

"You're not the one stomping around in the winter barefoot, you dumbass," she said from behind him.

"There's my dear wife. So eloquent and elegant." He said it mockingly as he squinted into the bright sunlight. The tree line had ended some yards back but they were just now breaking free of the shade. He squinted into the light as he turned to look at Moira. "Come along, love. We've got so much to discuss. You cannot possibly understand how long I've waited for this."

"Sure." Moira took one slow step toward him, her eyes flicking past him. "Ah . . . Charles? You might want to be careful."

He gestured at her. "Enough with the games, pet. Come *on*."

She took one more small step forward, her eyes still on the ground. "Know what I said I'd do to the man who put these marks on my neck? I told Gideon I'd turn him into gator bait."

"Yes, I'm sure you did." He dipped his head and gestured toward the riverbank—and his boat. "Let's *go*."

He took one step.

There was a strange hissing sound.

"Charles . . . did you know that alligators don't hibernate in the winter? They go torpid, but if it warms up enough . . ."

Moira's eyes were narrowed and she was no longer looking at the ground. She was staring at him with cold practical calculation. Slowly, Charles lowered his gaze.

His breath froze.

His very blood froze.

The knobby eyes protruding from the top of the skull looked up at him with nothing more than pure, predatory intent. There were smaller ones around the big one and dimly, Charles had some vague memory of his father talking about his mum—it would have been Charles' gran. He'd never met her. But his father had talked of her often . . . *She was something, Charlie. Would have fought the devil for me. Would have taken on ol' Paddy McKay himself too.*

The alligator hissed. Charles threw himself toward Moira, grabbing her. "Not so fast, you little cunt," he snarled. She drove her elbow into his gut. A shot rang out. It hit the dirt near his feet.

"Try it again and I'll throw her to that fucking monster over there!" he roared.

Moira sank her teeth into his hand, fighting like a wild beast. She kicked at his shins and swung back with her head.

"I'll fucking do it," Charles said, wheeling around to look for the alligator.

It was back in its spot, staring at them as they struggled. He hauled Moira farther into the trees. It took them closer toward where the gunfire had come from, but he had a feeling the shooters would easier to rationalize with than a prehistoric eating machine.

The alligator slowly lowered her head.

The adrenaline flooding him started to ebb.

Another shot came tearing out of the woods and he swore, wheeling around. But it hadn't come from the hill.

Eyes wide, he looked up.

Gideon stepped out from behind a tree, weapon steady.

The one Charles held was anything but, and his vision was graying around the edges too. He grabbed Moira's throat, struggling to think. That dog. Stupid, miserable dog.

"I should get that dog, feed it to the alligator," he said against her ear as he stared at Gideon.

She called him a coward, and he squeezed her throat until the noise cut off.

"Let her go, Charles. You got nowhere to run and you know it."

As if to reiterate that, the white dog emerged from Charles' left, followed closely by Zeke. Charles started to edge through the heavy growth toward the west. There was no path there, but they could all see the river—

A line of fire was laid down.

Gideon smiled at him, his eyes cold and flat.

Those eyes made him think of the alligator's. Full of nothing but predatory interest. "Maybe I'll just take her with me," he said, surprised at how level his voice was.

"We'll kill you before you have the chance, boy," the old man near the dog said. "Although I'm thinking I'll just shoot you in the fucking kneecaps and let the gator eat you. They don't get as much to eat in the winter. And they ain't picky. They'll eat any old piece of shit."

He eased up on the pressure on Moira's throat as he thought through his options. They were getting decidedly slim.

However, he wouldn't die on this island. Not here. Not where everything had started. Patrick McKay had started it all here. He'd taken the money that would have been his—*George's,* he told himself. But it would have come to him. He would have had his own fucking dynasty, just like the McKays.

He squeezed Moira's throat one final time, hard, brutal, fast.

Then he flung her toward Gideon. "Here. Take your slag, Marshall."

He darted behind the fallen tree near him, ignoring the voices shouting after him to get on the ground. Like that would bloody happen. Another shot rang out, close—too close. He crashed into a rotting stump when he instinctively ducked, his right arm smacking into it. The scream that tore out of him sounded like nothing human.

Sensing the men drawing closer to him, he lurched out of the trees, focusing on nothing but the glint of sunlight on water.

He didn't see the wriggling little body until he'd already stepped on it, nor would he have cared.

Mama gator cared, though.

There was a shout. If he heard the panic, it didn't quite penetrate.

It wasn't until something grabbed his leg that the urgency in those shouts actually penetrated the pain fogging his head, and then the pain got worse.

So much worse.

He went down.

Instinctively, he kicked out, but part of him thought . . . *well, mate, that's it then . . .*

A boom echoed in his ears.

Somebody shouted.

A face appeared in his line of vision and then hands grabbed him, dragged him away. He found himself looking up into Moira's face.

She really was rather lovely.

She glared at him. "Don't say that, you son of a bitch."

"I di . . ." He frowned. Had he said that outloud? And why couldn't he . . .

He was cold.

Reaching up, he went to rub at his eyes.

Seemed darker than it should be. Something smacked him in the face and he blinked, confused.

The locket.

Moira's locket. Everything felt slow and stiff as he grabbed at it, held on.

"Where's the treasure, love?" he asked, his tongue so thick it was hard to form the words.

"There isn't . . ." She sighed. "Let me have my locket, Charles. I'll show you how to find it."

"That's right, love." He blinked hard, trying to clear his eyes, then he swore as pain tried to eat up his leg.

Voices clamored all around, like gnats buzzing in his ears. "Fucking noise. Sod it. Where's the treasure, Moira? Told my father I'd find it. Promised."

"I imagine you did." She held something up and he looked.

"I don't . . ." He blinked and tried to catch the swaying, shining . . .

Moira guided his hand, steadied it as she guided the locket closer.

His gaze swam in and out of focus.

From a distance that seemed like miles, he thought he heard Marshall barking orders. "Keep him talking, Moira . . . *fuck.*"

"Tell that prick to . . ." Charles blinked, then his voice trailed off as the words on the locket finally swam into focus. "No. No, that can't be . . ."

"It is. It was there all the time, Charles."

CHAPTER TWENTY-NINE

"He didn't make it."

Moira rubbed the locket with a soft rag somebody had given her. She didn't know who. She'd been cleaning unseen blood from the surface for what seemed like hours.

They'd sat in the small, rundown county hospital for nearly two hours while doctors tried to save Charles Hurst, the man she'd tried to convince herself she loved.

Gideon sat across from her.

"Mac?"

Slowly, she lifted her eyes and met his, a knot in her throat bigger than the entire damn state. "Am I a killer now?" she asked, her voice raw.

"No . . ." Gideon came to her, his voice raw. "Baby, no."

"I knew that alligator was there. I knew she had her young with her and I knew Charles probably didn't know much about them." Tears blurred her eyes. Pressing her face against his neck, she tried to hold back the sobs, but she couldn't. They ripped out of her and for the next few minutes, it was a chore just to breathe with all the pain that came tearing out of her.

Gideon rocked her, stroking a hand up and down her spine, his cheek resting on her hair.

When the door burst open, he wasn't surprised to see Brannon and Neve, followed closely by Ella Sue and her husband, along with Ian and Hannah. Hannah was moving a little slower and Ian stayed with her, allowing the siblings to get to Moira first.

Family, he thought absently. It was a family bearing down on them.

But they came up short when they saw Gideon holding Moira cradled against his chest.

Neve went to lunge for them, but Ella Sue caught her arm, giving Gideon a questioning look. He lifted his head just a fraction and shook it in response to that silent question.

Not yet.

So they retreated.

Because that was family . . . sometimes pain cut too deep to share all at once.

Long moments passed before the storm of misery eased. Gideon didn't think Moira had even realized the others were there. From time to time, he saw them pacing just beyond the narrow slit windows, their frustration palpable. But his concern was Moira. As it always was.

She sniffed against his neck.

"How mad are you?" she asked, her voice raspy.

He didn't pretend not to understand.

"At you walking off with a man who had a loaded gun? Oh, I don't think mad covers it. I'm thinking about spanking you."

She gave a watery laugh, then snuggled in closer. "Okay."

"It's no fun for me if you're okay with the idea. Well, yeah it is. But you could pretend some reluctance." He rubbed his cheek against her hair.

"I don't have the energy for that." Another sigh shuddered out of her, a wet sound that was too much like a sob for his comfort. "I keep seeing the way he looked when he went down."

"He could have lowered that weapon at any time, Moira. He could have walked away. He made his choices. You told him that she was active—he's seen enough gators moving around in the summer to know what that means, baby."

He's . . . Mentally, he corrected himself. Charles *had* seen. He'd never see another.

The mother alligator had sank her teeth into his lower leg and torn at him, ripping at his leg and severing it right at the knee.

Logically, Gideon could say she'd been doing what any decent mother would do—protecting her babies. Charles had stepped on one of them when he'd been stomping off after Moira had already warned him about the alligator.

If he hadn't already had some blood loss, Gideon and Zeke might have been able to do more for him, but by the time EMTs, quickly followed by paramedics, had arrived, Charles had already been hovering right at death's door.

Gideon didn't mourn the bastard.

But he mourned for Moira.

Sinking his fist into her hair, he tugged until she lifted her head and then he rubbed his lips across hers. "You are not a killer. You were fighting for your life . . . for mine. He's been targeting all of you for years. You were fighting for all of you. You're a fighter, Mac.

A sigh escaped her and this time, it was steadier.

It parted her lips, and he let himself kiss her.

A quick kiss, he told himself. Just one.

But as she opened for him and sank into his arms, he had hot, ugly flashes of the day slam into him. One right after the other. Neve showing up at his house, showing him the information she'd found. Himself, showing up at Brannon's only to find Moira missing. Charles' house, empty.

The call from Zeke.

Seeing that son of a bitch holding her, one hand at her throat.

Moira whimpered against his lips and strained closer. He shifted her around in his lap and shoved both hands into her hair, craning her head farther back as he hauled her closer.

Need punched into him hard and brutal.

She was alive.

She was safe.

She was alive.

Part of him still didn't believe it, not yet, but each stroke of her tongue across his and each delicious bite of her fingernails into his arms made him more and more aware.

If it hadn't been for the gentle clearing of a throat, Gideon later realized, he might have done something that would have embarrassed them both.

Tearing his mouth away from Moira's, he looked up, dazed and a little surprised to see the plain, utilitarian white walls of the surgical waiting room around him.

Hospital.

Damn.

Hell.

"Shit."

Ella Sue cocked a brow at him.

She stood inside the door. She was the only one *inside,* but several other faces were all but smashed against the glass. Neve wagged her eyebrows. Brannon scowled at him, while Hannah and Ian looked like they wanted to bust out laughing.

Moira stiffened in his arms, her breathing slowly returning to normal. "Why do I get the odd feeling that Ella Sue is staring at me?" she asked, looking at his throat.

"Well." Gideon flicked a look from Ella Sue to Moira. "You called them."

"I did."

Moira dropped her head onto his shoulder. "That's . . . well, that's good. I guess they've been worried."

He slid a hand up her back. "Yeah. Look at it this way. I think you've scarred your brother for life. Your day has one bright spot, right?"

She snorted out a laugh. It had that odd, half-sob sound. She went to hug him, and her locket smacked into his cheek. "Beating me with jewelry won't help, Mac."

He tugged it from her hand as she looked over her shoulder at Ella Sue. "They can come in," she said softly.

Ella Sue stepped aside. Brannon was the first one in.

"Say one thing, kid, and I'll tell you all about the time I walked in on Mom and Dad having sex," Moira warned.

Brannon stopped dead in his tracks.

Hannah sniggered.

Gideon smiled a little but was staring at her locket. She'd shown this to Charles as he lay there, bleeding to death. She squirmed off Gideon's lap, glancing down at him before she turned to face her siblings and Ella Sue.

While they wrapped her up in hugs, Gideon flipped open the locket.

There was a tiny, hand-painted miniature that he knew was of Madeleine, Patrick McKay's wife. On the opposite side of the locket was an inscription.

Gideon frowned as he read it through once, then a second time.

My Greatest Treasure

Moira eased down into the seat next to him. Everybody was firing questions at her, but when they saw the look on her face, oddly enough, silence fell.

Moira took the locket from him gently. "He was looking for a treasure. The past hundred fifty, hundred sixty years people talked about some mythical treasure that

Paddy had buried somewhere, all because of a few words he wrote in a journal that disappeared. He'd talk about it, too, I know, when he was drunk, which was probably more often than he needed to be. But they never seemed to get it."

She lowered the locket and Gideon watched as she pressed on something with the edge of her thumb.

"Madeleine was pregnant when he had that commissioned," Neve said.

Gideon looked up, saw the smile on the youngest McKay's face. She leaned against Ian, her head on his chest. Although Brannon didn't say anything, he reached over and rubbed at Hannah's swollen belly.

Understanding dawned even before Moira put the locket into his hand.

There was another inscription, hidden under the miniature.

Lies Here

"My greatest treasure lies here," Gideon murmured. "It was his family. His legacy . . . that's what you were talking about in the hospital."

"Yeah." Moira shrugged a little sheepishly. "He gave her the locket after the baby was born. The baby—Patrick's son—he was the one who really started to build his father's empire, helped clear his father's name. He was thirteen when it all went down, and by the time he was twenty it was all he could think about. He asked his stepfather Jonathan to help him, and so that was what they did. They hunted down the men who'd set Patrick up—all save for one."

"George Whitehall."

Gideon looked up at Brannon.

Brannon shrugged. "Hey, I might not have all the stories memorized and I didn't go treasure hunting in the backyard up until I was ten"—he shot Neve a smirk—"but

I know my history. Whitehall was back in England, but
most of the men who dealt with him . . . well, they were
more afraid of Jonathan than anything else, especially considering Jonathan's connections. One by one, they con-
fessed. It started that day when Paddy was supposed to
be ambushed but he was actually the one who did the
ambushing. Why Whitehall went along, nobody knew.
Maybe he didn't realize how big a party Paddy was bringing and he thought he'd have a chance to kill him and then
still make everything work out. The pirates had a haul
worth nearly a hundred thousand—back *then*."

Gideon whistled under his breath. "A lot of money."

"Yeah. And Patrick had promised a fair split for those
who helped him handle those who were dirtying up his
stretch of the river." Brannon smiled thinly. "That didn't
go over well with Whitehall. Patrick's interference was
going to mess up everything."

"It came full circle," Moira murmured. She went to put
her locket on, but Gideon stopped her, taking it from her
hand and settling it into place himself. "Charles . . ." She
sighed. "You'll have to tell them. I can't. Not right now.
But I think it started with Whitehall. He passed the hate
down like an infection. Maybe Charles didn't even stand
a chance."

"I don't believe that." Brannon's voice was thick with
derision. "When I get my hands on him . . ."

"You won't." Gideon covered Moira's shoulder with his
hand. "He's dead, Brannon." Then, warningly, he added,
"And you aren't going to say anything else on it."

Gideon doubted it was his words that convinced Brannon, rather it was how Moira lowered her head.

Am I a killer now . . . ?

She leaned against him.

There was no hesitation at all either.

He closed his eyes as he wrapped his arms around her.

CHAPTER THIRTY

January, cold and gloomy, was winding down. Almost two months had passed. The holidays were little more than a memory and all of them were longing for spring.

Moira had arranged for Charles' body to be flown back to England and she'd taken care of a small funeral.

It wasn't widely attended.

She was there, along with her brother and sister. She was surprised Brannon came, but she also knew it had to do with supporting her more than anything else.

He'd said something to her two nights after Charles had kidnapped her—and died only hours later.

I can't believe that he was fucked up from the get-go. But maybe you do. Maybe you saw something else in him. Either way, I'm sorry for what you had to see and what you had to do.

That meant something to her. It meant a lot.

Gideon, Ian, and Hannah came too.

Nobody else did.

During the months since Charles' death, Gideon had been . . . well, busy. A video camera that Clive Owings had apparently gotten his hands on was one that had belonged to Shayla Hardee, and they finally had the answer to that mystery—Charles had killed her as well. Gideon theorized that she'd hidden it in a tree to record a meeting she'd set up with Charles. News of her blackmailing had already been trickling around town. Shayla must have seen something or known something that Charles hadn't wanted spread around.

Although there was no hard evidence to place him at the scene, Gideon had told Moira he suspected Charles had also been behind the death of Roger Hardee as well. Some digging around had turned up witnesses who had seen Charles and Roger having lunch together not long before his death, and as things started to come to light, somebody else had shown up to talk to about Charles.

Dr. Ellison Shaw.

Apparently Ellison and Charles had been sleeping together off and on for some time. With her marriage to one of the cops on the force somewhat rocky, Dr. Shaw had moved out of Treasure, taking a job in Baton Rouge while they tried to work things out.

Moira had been going over some of the renovation plans with her brother. They were rebuilding. She was determined to have her museum. Many pieces had been destroyed, but some had been salvageable. She'd buy other pieces and she'd already received offers of donations and loans from both museums and private collections. Both she and Brannon had been surprised when Ellison Shaw had pulled into the parking lot and when Ellison asked to speak to Moira alone, Moira had gotten a bad feeling.

She hadn't ever really talked to Ellison much. Once Ellison had started to explain why she was there, Moira tried to make the other woman go to Gideon, but Ellison had been looking for forgiveness as much as anything else. Moira suspected Ellison needed to forgive herself and she had no anger inside her for the sad woman so she had listened. Then she'd insisted Ellison call Gideon. Whether or not the vague memories she had of Charles questioning her about Hannah would be worth much, Moira didn't know, but maybe a few more threads would help with the big picture.

The big picture.

She'd been married to a half-crazed, obsessed murderer. *That* was the big picture and he'd died because of those obsessions. A rather sad end to a sad life.

My greatest treasure lies here. Moira rubbed a finger over her locket and thought back to her brief marriage.

She had cared about him, or at least the man he'd pretended to be. Maybe she'd married him for the wrong reasons—Gideon had just been hurt, she was looking for something to hold on to . . . sometimes she didn't know why she'd said yes, but she *had* cared about him and sometimes, she'd *almost* been happy with him. Especially in the beginning.

Had he even had that? A fleeting glimpse of happiness?

She doubted it.

A knock at the door of the pool house had her turning around.

Gideon stood there, his hands on his hips and the dog at his leg.

Frost thumped her tail when she saw Moira.

Frost hadn't been hurt too much by Charles. She'd moved sluggishly for a day or so, and the vet who'd looked at her told Moira to keep an eye on her, but he said she had a good strong dog and Frost should be fine.

"You realize I don't have time in the middle of the day to come rushing . . ."

He stopped in the middle of the sentence, looking around the room with its candlelight and the meal on the table.

It was pizza.

That had been their first date.

"I talked to Hoyt. He said he could handle things for a while." She twisted her hands around and around as she stared at Gideon. "There was . . ."

Licking her lips, she took a nervous step toward him.

"You said this was urgent." Gideon's eyes strayed toward the pizza, then the candles, before coming back to rest on her face. "Mac, as much as I'm enjoying the symbolism, a candlelit lunch isn't an emergency."

"My sister and my brother are getting married in two days." She blurted the words out, uncertain why she was leading with that.

Gideon's eyes softened. "I know. You're not allowed to get cold feet, baby. That's Neve's job—and she won't have cold feet. She's about ready to drag Ian down the aisle. As if she'd have to. And Hannah won't have cold feet."

"Hannah can't *see* her feet," Moira said.

"That's not nice." Gideon looked like he was biting the inside of his cheek. He smoothed his hands up and down her arms. "Okay, look . . . let's sit down . . ."

She caught his hand. "I'm doing this backward, but I can't think of the words. It should be me. It should have been me—*you* and me—eighteen years ago. Fifteen, even five. But I was stupid. And I don't want to wait any longer."

Gideon's eyes narrowed as she lowered her head and focused on his hand.

"Mac . . ."

She wouldn't look at him.

Gideon really wished she would.

But her hands were shaking and he had a feeling she might be crying a little bit too.

She sniffed, and that confirmed it. When she stopped for a moment, he went to lift her face, but she jerked her chin out of his grasp and finished, pushing a ring onto his finger.

His heart stopped then. For maybe an entire minute. "Mac . . ."

Now, slowly, nervously, she lifted her eyes to his. "We were going to do this once I graduated college, remember?" she asked, her voice hoarse. "We talked about it. Talked about seeing the world and having babies and doing crazy things. Then Mom and Dad died and it was like that great big world I saw suddenly got smaller and smaller."

He went to tug her in close, but she pulled back.

"I . . . um "—she held her hands up and backed away—"I was going to do this sooner, and then I told myself I didn't need to do it at all. But I have to."

Confused, baffled . . . well, everything—the ring on his finger and the nerves he could see bleeding out of her, Gideon just stood there when she began to pace.

"Do you remember that night? When my parents died?"

Gideon looked down at the ring. The gold glinted up at him and he rubbed the tip of his thumb over the delicate pattern inscribed into it. "Yeah. Pretty much every detail, Mac."

"I'd had a fight with my mom." The words came out soft and small and she sounded like the girl he'd held all those years ago, the one who'd begged him not to let go.

"I know, baby."

She stopped pacing finally and looked at him. "I blamed myself. For a long time. And . . ." She cleared her throat, the noise wet. Tears glinted in her eyes. "I blamed you. I hated . . . *everything.*"

Now, as she turned away and covered her face with her hands, Gideon just stood there. He started to say something, stopped himself. Tried again—stopped himself. It took three tries before he finally knew what he needed to say. "Do you think I wasn't mad at myself when my mom died?" he asked softly.

"It's not the same thing," she whispered.

"No. Because my mom wasn't in a hit and run."

Moira flinched. Resting his hands on her shoulders, he tugged her around and made her look at him. "And maybe I didn't have an argument with her right before she died . . . but I wasn't here, either. She died alone, Mac."

"No." Moira looked away. "She didn't. I was . . ."

Her words trailed off, but understanding dawned and Gideon cupped her cheek, guided her face back to his. "You were there with her, weren't you?"

"You couldn't be." She jerked up a shoulder in a shrug, but when he tried to bring her in close, she pulled away. "And the reason you *weren't* there was because of *me*. I pushed you away because I was too angry with myself, because I was too eaten up with guilt over how things went that day."

"Because you acted like a kid?"

She shot him a dark look. "I don't want you to be *understanding* about this."

Gideon shrugged and looked down. "I guess I could pretend to be pissed off, but . . . Moira, we spent the past twenty years apart." Lifting his gaze to the ceiling, he blew out a breath and realized that for some reason, he felt . . . lighter. Easier. "Actually, it's . . . better. Here I've spent so much time wondering what I did, what I could have done . . . and it wasn't anything I did—and maybe there's nothing I could have done."

She stared at him, her eyes looked tired and bruised. He went to her, cupped her face in his hands, and lifted her mouth to his. "There's nothing either of us could have done. The time wasn't right for us. I hate that and I think about all the years we could have been together, but lately, I've been thinking . . . if you and I were all content and happy, maybe it would have been even easier for him to get in."

There was no reason to name *him*. They both knew who Gideon meant.

"We were on edge when all of this went down and we needed to be. We survived it because of that. And now . . ." He kissed her, and when she slowly relaxed against him, Gideon tugged her closer, curled one arm around her waist. "The time is right—*now*. You, me . . . we're here. We're together. All those dreams, the world we wanted to see back in high school? The world is still there and my dream was always you, Moira. It hasn't changed."

She curled her arms around his neck and clung to him.

He hugged her tight, feeling everything in his world shift and settle into place.

Well, except for one little thing . . .

"So"—he nuzzled her neck—"about this ring . . ."

She pulled back and stared up at him. "What about it?"

He cocked a brow. "I think maybe you were in the middle of something. Then you got sidetracked."

"Sidetracked . . . yeah. That happens sometimes." Moira leaned in and pressed her lips to his, fast and quick, before she settled back flat on her feet and gazed up at him. A sweet, beautiful smile spread across her lips. "I just had to settle those things first."

"Consider them settled." He cleared his throat and backed away, crossing his arms over his chest before pinning her with an expectant look.

"Gideon, will you marry me?"

In response, he swept her up in his arms and swung her around. "Hell, yeah. I've only been waiting all my life."

A giddy laugh bubbled out of her as she clung to him.

He lowered her to the ground a moment later and kissed her. It turned to another kiss, then another. But when he would have urged her back up against the nearest surface— vertical or horizontal—she stopped him. "I want to show you something," she said, grabbing at his hands when he started to tug at buttons. "And then we're leaving. I was hoping you'd say yes, because we've got an appointment."

Gideon paused. "An appointment?"

"Yes. At the courthouse. I've got clothes in the other room and so do you."

"Clothes . . ." he said slowly.

"Yes. I'm not waiting any longer. I want to get married *today*."

Gideon blinked at her. "Mac, your brother and sister are getting married Sunday. Don't you want to . . . hell. Don't you want some big, fancy thing, too?"

"I don't need it." She kissed him again. "I need you. Just you. But . . . if you want to wait . . ."

"No." Slowly, he shook his head. "If you're certain . . . I think we've waited long enough. Considering we made our plans twenty years ago."

Her smile all but stopped his heart.

"Here," she said softly, lifting his hand and turning it upward. She brushed her fingertip over the ring.

He saw it then. The inscription.

It was the one inside her locket.

My Greatest Treasure

Slowly, he tugged the golden band off. Inside it, he could see the rest of the words.

Lies Here

The *i* was dotted with a small stone of green.

"I love it," he said quietly.

"I'm glad." She kissed him. But when he tried to deepen the kiss, she pulled back.

"Mac . . ." He groaned.

She laughed. "Pizza. Then courthouse. I actually bribed a judge, so don't dawdle."

"You . . ." Gideon closed his eyes. "I didn't hear that."

"Oh, hush. I just asked that he please make sure this stayed quiet until Sunday. He actually promised that the news wouldn't go anywhere, as long as he could be the one to break the news."

"Won't that kinda be upstaging Hannah and Neve?" He frowned.

"Since when is Neve ever upstaged?" Moira laughed. "Besides, it was Ella Sue's idea and I know my sister, I know Hannah. I'd be happy for them if the tables were turned. They'll be happy for me. It's family, Gideon."

"Yeah." He realized that he was smiling. "Family."

For the past twenty something years, he'd considered the McKays his unofficial family.

That was about to become very *official* very soon.

CHAPTER THIRTY-ONE

"I'd like to propose a toast . . ."

Neve couldn't even look away from Ian as the judge stood up, tapping his spoon against the silver flute. It seemed almost the entire town had turned out for the wedding.

Hannah sat in her chair with Brannon holding her hand and wished she could find a more comfortable position. Her back was killing her. She wanted to be enjoying her wedding and then she wanted to go and enjoy her husband—in bed.

But her back . . .

". . . now that the best man has offered his toast." Judge Steele spoke with a deep, kindly voice as he looked toward the McKays. They weren't blood cousins, but the connection between the Steeles and the McKays was a tight one, one that went just as deep as blood.

He winked at Gideon and then nodded to Ian and Neve before looking at Hannah and Brannon. "I hope to see yet another generation of McKays running wild through this town. It's been a pleasure knowing all of you, Hannah, Neve, Brannon . . . and Ian, I hope to get to know you better."

"As long as it's not in the courtroom, Your Honor!" Ian flashed him a broad grin and raised his glass.

Judge Steele grinned and then looked down the table. Neve hadn't gone with the traditional seating arrangement for the bridal table. Hannah had told her she was placing all the arrangements in her capable hands and Neve had run with it. Moira and Gideon sat side by side and now, with the judge looking at them, people in the crowd starting to call out. "You're next, guys!"

"Actually . . . they were first." Judge Steele grinned broadly as a gasp rippled through the room. "I had the honor of marrying Gideon Marshall and Moira McKay this Friday in my chambers. If I may present . . ."

The crowd erupted.

Neve gaped.

Ian and Brannon started to laugh.

But Hannah gasped. Then, as pain twisted through her, she made a low sound that really had no words to it.

It came during one of those odd pauses so everybody in the room heard.

As multiple eyes swung her way, Hannah looked down at her pretty wedding dress and closed her eyes. She could feel all reason and logic leaving her. Maybe it was to be expected, she supposed. She'd gotten married not even an hour ago.

And sometime very soon, she'd be having a baby.

"Well . . . this just takes the cake."

All the McKays—and the Campbells and Marshalls—swung their eyes to look at her. Moira looked a little uneasy as Hannah tried to smile. She was feeling a little put-out, though. She'd wanted her wedding night. Some cake. Dancing.

Some cake. She'd *really* wanted some cake.

Forcing a smile, she looked over at her new husband. "We're going to have to cut this short."

"She's in a hurry," somebody out in the crowd hooted. "Wants to get on to the fun stuff."

"Yeah." She eased back from the table. "Labor. These damn impatient McKays . . . I really wanted my wedding night."

Brannon reached over, rubbing a hand down her back even as a dull red flush crept up his neck. He was as bawdy as all get-out when it was them, but even *imply* sex in public . . .

And he'd missed the important part of her statement, too.

Men.

Easing upright, trying to maintain some dignity with her dress damp around her, she looked down at Moira and Gideon and smiled. "Congrats. You two should have done it ages ago." Then she looked at Brannon. The direct approach was the only way to go here. "Okay, Brannon. It's time."

"We haven't cut the cake," he said, crooking a grin at her.

"We can't."

A few others had caught on to what she'd said—she could tell by the buzz in the air.

Ian and Neve were the next two—and Gideon was already murmuring in Moira's ear—yep, they'd figured it out, too.

Brannon stood, frowning a little. "Is it your back?" he asked, leaning in.

"No." Huffing out a breath and tugging on her damp dress, she looked at him. "My water just broke."

Now whoops and cheers broke out for a different reason entirely

Brannon sank back into his chair, staring dumbly at his wife.

"What?" he said, looking dazed. "Oh, shit."

"Man up, mate!" Ian shouted, punching him on the arm. "You've got a wife to take care of!"

"Oh, shit."